MALEVOLENT INTENT

A LEE DANFORTH SUSPENSE NOVEL

R. S. HAMPTON

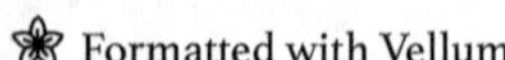 Formatted with Vellum

To my children

1

SHARPE

THURSDAY, 10:00 A.M.

Hurricane Umberto over Nassau, Bahamas

The woman sauntered down the Charleston sidewalk, her hair in a messy ponytail, half up, half down. Her cheap red dress, with big circles of sweat under her arms from August's thick morning humidity, clung so tightly that he could tell there was nothing underneath. The old man followed, easing his rusted Explorer over to the right side of the road until he came alongside her.

"Hey there!"

She stopped and turned, a bright smile plastered on her painted face. It wasn't Angela Matheson, the woman he was looking for, but this woman was the right size and age, although her hair was blonde, not strawberry. She would do.

"Sorry, thought you were someone I knew," he said.

He lifted his foot from the brake to drive on, then stopped, dropping the gear into park. He needed to slacken his anger a bit. Give him something to practice on before the real thing. In sniper school, he always encouraged his students to practice. It was time to take his own advice.

The woman ambled up to the window of his SUV as it rolled to a stop. "No, honey, but I can be anyone you want for an hour." The front of her dress gaped, her round breasts there for the squeeze. He suspected, given the wrinkles and a spot of something on the front, it was the dress she'd worn the night before.

Women should dress like this only in the bedroom.

The bile rose from his gut.

She leaned in the window, flirting as if he were some famous actor, not a worn-out ex-soldier who had run a hardware store for years before retiring.

"I can make it really good for you," she said as she winked, her fake eyelash starting to peel away at the outside corner.

"How much?" he asked, "and for what?"

"You a cop?" She backed away from his truck, her eyes wide.

"No, no, ma'am. I like to know what I'm paying for up front's all," he replied.

The woman relaxed and stepped back up to the truck, her black patent heels clunking on the sidewalk.

"Forty for a blow." Her face grew serious, as if she were negotiating some boardroom deal. "A hundred for more than that. Hour limit. No nasty stuff, you hear me?"

"Get in," he said.

Red Dress used the running board to climb in, leaning over to place her purse on the floorboard. He had to swallow the vomit that rose in his throat as he watched her breasts practically tumbling out of the top. It was all he could do to keep from stopping and dealing with her then.

While popping and smacking her chewing gum, she sang along with the radio as he drove, competing with the wind whipping through the window.

"Where are we going, honey?" she asked with another wink. The fake eyelash was barely holding on.

"Not far. Have some of my drink if you want."

He handed her the cold soft drink from the cup holder as he

watched the road ahead. She drained it in large gulps until he heard the bottle drop into the cup holder once again.

He continued along upper King Street toward North Charleston. It would not take long for the double dose of Rohypnol to take effect. He glanced over when she stopped singing. Slumped against the door, the woman's head rested on the open window frame, the wind whipping her hair. He pulled onto the freeway ramp and headed toward I-526, and hoped his buddies were ready.

As a child, his father had told him stories of the nasty things living in the marsh. There were long, thin fish in the deeper parts and giant snakes, he'd said. But the one thing even his father was afraid of was the alligators. According to him, they would make a quick snack of small dogs and kill people if they were close enough and unable to fight back.

He'd avoided the marsh his entire life.

Yet for the past year, he had carefully searched the Charleston area, his anger fueling his search. Nightly, he dreamed of what he would do to the woman who had disrespected him and his family, the myriad ways he would torture her in this very marsh.

He had finally found a small, brackish pond underneath one of the I-526 interchanges, the home of two old alligators. Rainwater kept it full, supplemented by the marsh water that ebbed and flowed from Charleston Harbor. He had already tested the gators with dead chickens, pigs' feet, and the occasional roadkill he found late at night. The animals weren't very selective about what he fed them. Then again, he had never fed them something this big. He glanced again at the woman slumped against the passenger door.

Exiting the freeway, he turned into the marsh. Pulling down a rutted track, he parked the truck, cut the engine, and listened to the quiet. Hearing only the sound of the cars bumping overhead on the freeway, he got out of the truck and walked around to the passenger side. Before he opened the door, he took in his surroundings. Even with the busy freeway overhead and traffic on Rhett Avenue, no one could see him. Satisfied, he opened the door and grabbed the sleeping woman as she fell into his arms.

Stepping gingerly from the high ground down to the edge of the marsh, he rolled the woman into the shallow water. Pushing her with his foot, she gently floated toward the center of the pond. Removing the cash from her wallet, he tossed her purse in after her.

Standing beside his truck, he waited, looking at his watch. He needed to know precisely how long the elimination would take. At the two-minute mark, the woman's body jerked violently and was pulled under as the alligator rolled, taking the woman with it. The water churned for thirty seconds until a second alligator appeared. The two beasts wrestled in the water as they fought over the woman. After several more minutes, the thrashing and fighting stopped, and the pinkish-tinted water calmed again.

His experiment had worked, but it had only increased his anger, not alleviated it. He had waited long enough. No more testing was needed. It was time for the main event.

Heading for the townhouse in Mt. Pleasant, he anticipated catching Angela long after she had taken the child to kindergarten. Parked two blocks behind the place the slut called home, he walked back, ducking in through the open patio gate.

Cars were lined up and down the street. What the...?

The party floored him when he stepped inside the house. He had underestimated what Angela would do for money, not realizing her habit had escalated to this point. A gray haze filled the room, and the overpowering smell of weed hung in the air. Lines of white powder ran in short lengths down the coffee table in front of dancing partiers. The heavy bass music caused the floor to vibrate under his feet. It was time he called her on it, stopped this.

For God's sake, woman, think of your child.

Climbing to the second floor, he had ducked behind the bathroom door when he heard voices.

"That isn't what you promised," Angela shouted over the blasting music.

"Take it or leave it." A woman's voice, deeper, older, replied. "It's all you'll get."

He peeked around the doorframe, but the main bedroom turned to the left, and the women were out of sight.

"Mommy," the child begged, "I don't waaaaannnnnna go with her. Just take me to Nana's. Puuullllleeeeeezzzeeee."

His hackles rose.

"Just give it..." Angela's voice was angry, bitter.

He ducked into the child's room, one eye at the crack in the door, as Angela stomped out of the bedroom and started down the stairs, a thick wad of dollars in her hand.

"Mooooooommmmmmmmmyyyyyy!"

The child's wail had triggered something inside him. He crashed into the master bedroom, catching the blonde off guard as he snatched the lamp from the bedside table and smashed it against her head. She was stronger than she looked, fighting him like a feral cat. They moved around the room, squared off against each other like light boxers in a ring. She finally made her mistake, and he hit her again, harder.

Straddling the woman, he beat her senseless. Once his anger was sated, he saw her blood on the floor and walls, spatters on the bed, the nightstand. Ripping his shirt off, he turned it inside out, and then, pulling it back over his head, he started down the hall. Glimpsing his blood-spattered face in the hallway mirror, he backtracked to the bathroom. It wouldn't do to scare the child.

Katie had escaped to her room. Her wails had broken his heart. He scooped her up then, pushing her small head against his freshly washed neck to quiet her, sprinting down the stairs. The thumping, smoke-filled living room gyrated with laughing bodies. A slippery eel, Angela was nowhere.

Scooting through the empty kitchen and out the side door, he had rounded the corner of the house and headed to the Explorer, walking casually, as if he were taking the child out for air. Her crying stopped as she snuggled against his chest. He had precisely the place to keep the child to protect her from that monster of a mother. He just needed to keep her quiet for a while. And until he could find something better to go with some lunch, a quarter of a dose of Rohypnol would have to do.

2

VERN

THURSDAY, 1:00 P.M.

Colonel Vernon Matheson's gut churned as he exited the jetway and headed for the baggage claim area. Standing six feet three inches without his boots, he cut an imposing figure even in his dirty Army uniform straight from Syria. Murmurs of "thank you for your service" floated by him. He nodded at each, never breaking stride. These people had no idea what he had done.

His taxi reached the three-mile-long Ravenel suspension bridge, where the Cooper and Wando Rivers merged. Matheson watched out the taxi window as Charleston's low profile reached from the bridge across the peninsula. Fort Sumter, squat and square in the white-capped ocean, was in contrast to the Morris Island lighthouse, a finger pointing skyward in the hazy distance of Folly Beach. The taxi dropped from the bridge onto Coleman Boulevard. He had not told his wife or grandparents he was on his way; he wanted to see their faces, especially his wife, Angela. He had to know the truth.

Jetlagged and hungry, he had the taxi drop him at his neighborhood, several blocks from his house. Matheson needed the walk home to clear his head. The taxi driver thanked Matheson for his tip and "for his service." For thirty-six hours, he'd reflected on that *service* while in a too-small plane seat, hopping from one hellhole to another. The military had made him what he was—a killer—then discarded him.

His stomach burned with the rejection.

He looked toward his townhouse. Was he wrong about his wife? He doubted it. For at least a year, she had avoided looking at him during every Skype call, answering off-screen, then handing the phone to five-year-old Katie instead. Matheson's fourth and final overseas tour complete, he longed for a hot shower and three days of uninterrupted sleep.

Comfortable for years in military clothing, his uniform was now a cloak of rejection. One of the first things he intended to do after a shower was to celebrate—and burn every bit of apparel he owned, except his boots. The brown Italian-made Kenetreks he had bought for himself were broken in to perfection.

Yet he could not make himself take the first step. This was not really home. It was the stronghold he would invade and conquer, a place where he would rescue his child. Did Katie need rescuing? His gut told him she did, even though he didn't know why. Stalling, he reached into his shirt pocket and, under the shade of an oak tree, pulled out the crumpled cigarette package saved to celebrate his freedom when leaving Al-Tanf. There were no smokes inside, just the reminder to quit cold turkey once he hit American soil.

Matheson re-enlisted the last time around without telling his wife. He felt compelled to continue with his team, relocated from Afghanistan to Syria to surveil the Islamic State. When Assad's regime collapsed, before shifting him to another pit where U.S. troops were not really wanted, the military decided that his flashbacks, along with his screw up, made it time for him to come home. The Army could call it a medical retirement all they wanted. He had been discharged against his will and sent home.

Although Angela had pretended his leaving again was a sore

point between them, he sensed she had stopped caring a long time ago. He thought back to the day he'd met her on the beach playing volleyball. She had been a redheaded menace, all freckles and laughter, an adult version of his daughter.

He pulled out his phone and stared at the photo of his five-year-old daughter. Curly red hair surrounded her cherubic face, tilted upward in laughter. That day, she had just turned her first pirouette in ballet class. Blameless in all this, Katie had spent more than a third of her life without her father. Matheson loved Katie, and he knew his daughter loved him, but he had relied on the hope that his elderly grandparents' love would be enough for his child. It would serve him right if Katie wanted nothing to do with him.

He had no idea what he would say to her.

Or her mother.

He crushed the empty package into a wad, stuffed it in his duffel along with the craving for a cigarette, and started walking. In his peripheral vision, he swore he saw Darrell. He stopped and looked across the street, but there was no one there. Four blocks down, parked cars lined both sides of the street in front of his townhouse. More were double-parked in his driveway.

He froze. Something was very wrong, and it was more than hallucinating his dead best friend.

A canary yellow Corvette convertible squatted diagonally across his front lawn, its top down in knee-high weeds. Heavy metal music blared out into the evening through the open front door. A broken shutter swung in the breeze. His entire house looked miserable and out of place in such a pleasant neighborhood, like a neglected child in an orphanage.

Laughter and loud voices peppered the break as one song melded into another. Anxiety filled his chest, and the back of his head felt as if someone had just slugged him. Even though it had only been eighteen months since he'd last been here, the place was a wreck.

He wondered if Angela had moved out and not told him. The party inside the house reminded him of the fraternity parties he had crashed with some of his high school buddies across town years ago. This didn't look like Angela. His gut twisted once more. He had to get Katie out of that house.

On the porch, he dropped his duffel behind a chair, then cautiously stepped inside. The living room was gray with the fog of cigarettes and the sickly stench of marijuana. Forgotten lit cigarettes left blackened circles on the coffee table. White powder formed neat lines on the dining table. People laughed and talked while waiting their turn with a rolled-up hundred-dollar bill. Others danced on a rug he had never seen, or lounged on furniture he had not purchased. There was no Angela in sight. The throb at the back of his head ramped up a notch.

Welcome home.

Overflowing garbage in the kitchen and crusty dishes caused his stomach to lurch at the stench. The back door was open, and another scruffy crowd filled the box-sized courtyard. Bugs made themselves at home around his kitchen light fixture. He checked the garage. The Volvo was spotless and in its place. The garage was cleaner than the kitchen, as if she had never been out there, never driven the car.

He couldn't think with the excruciatingly loud music slamming against his head. He walked up to a stereo he had never seen, traced the power cord to the outlet, and then jerked the cord from the wall. Blessed silence.

Then an uproar.

"Hey, what the hell, man, what do you think you're doing?" A man with dreadlocks turned to Matheson, his face screwed up in anger. He was surrounded by other irritated partiers shifting toward him, and still others with blank stares, too zoned out to care that the music had stopped.

"Where is Angela?" More blank faces.

"Who?" Sandy colored dreadlocks hung to the man's waist,

and tattooed sleeves extended from a T-shirt. He swayed as a joint burned between his fingers. Dreadlocks grinned, exposing his brown teeth as he shrugged his shoulders, looking around at the others as if he didn't have a care in the world.

Matheson tried again. "Where is the woman who invited you here?"

Dreadlocks shrugged. "We just came along for the ride."

"This is a private party." A ragged older blonde stood from where she straddled the arm of the couch, mascara smeared beneath glassy eyes, a red stiletto stabbing a hole in the fake leather seat.

Dreadlock's confidence grew with her support. "Yeah, man. You need to leave."

The finger headed for Matheson's chest missed, as Dreadlock drunkenly lurched to the left. With his right hand, Matheson grabbed the man's jacket and t-shirt into a wad and pulled the skinny man off his feet. His left hand locked onto Dreadlock's throat.

"This is my house, you asswipe. Home from the Middle East and haven't slept in about thirty-four hours. I'm tired, filthy, and hungry. Now you need to tell me where my wife is. And after that, if you and everyone else in this room aren't out of here in the next three seconds, I'll have the cops take you to the hospital after I get finished with every last one of you."

Dreadlock's face turned pink. Unable to stop himself, Matheson's fist closed tighter. Behind him, feet scrambled, keys jangled, then within seconds, cars cranked. The roar of the Corvette's engine and the squeal of tires in the grass signaled the death of his miserable front lawn.

Raising one eyebrow, Matheson made eye contact with Dreadlocks and lowered him back to the floor. The man gasped for air.

"Where is she?"

"She's upstairs."

Before he could ask another question, Dreadlocks scurried out the front door.

Angela!" Matheson's shout floated up the staircase in the now quiet house. He climbed three steps at a time. "Katie!"

Silence.

After the last three stairs, Matheson circled the railing and powered up his cell to punch 911, then hesitated. The police would hold him responsible for the drugs. The house was in his name. Working on the advance team for military police, he had learned that evidence could be conveniently attributed to anyone the officer wished, regardless of the truth.

The door to Katie's room was closed. He turned the handle and heaved a sigh of relief. Everything was in its place, the room was clean, and the bed was made, a far cry from its usual chaos of toys, the last time he was home. But no Katie.

"Katie! If you're here, say something to me. It's Daddy!"

Silence.

His mind darted in a hundred directions. As his chest compressed, he made himself stop to think. It was Thursday, and it was just past one in the afternoon. Katie should be in kindergarten at Mount Pleasant Academy. He let out the breath he'd been holding.

Would Angela have thrown a party like this in the middle of the day? No. It was entirely unrealistic for the woman he knew. So where was she? He shuddered suddenly, concerned that something had happened to his family. Something horrible.

Turning toward the master bedroom, he made an abrupt stop. A large red footprint pointed toward him on the carpet. "Angela. Are you in there?" He stepped around it, pushing the master bedroom door open with a sweaty palm, as he avoided the streak of blood down its front.

The smell hit him like a bludgeon. A woman's foot, motionless on the floor, extended just past the corner of the bed. Her bladder and intestines had obviously voided, and the odor combined with the musty iron smell of so much blood was unbearable.

But he had to know if this was his wife.

Blood spatters and a handprint smeared the short hallway wall on his right. He avoided the footprints and blood as he crept around to the side of the bed. The woman was face up, splayed on the floor, her blonde hair drenched in a pool of blood, her striped blouse ripped and off to the side.

He relaxed just a bit. His wife was a redhead. His heart rate jumped again. She could have recently dyed her hair.

A broken lamp lay on its side on the bed, blood on multiple ragged edges, a splintered hole in one wall above the bed. Blood spatter covered the jumbled bed and the walls. He looked down at his boots standing in blood. He should call the police first, but he had to know. The woman's face was so battered by the lamp that she was unrecognizable. The room spelled one word in Matheson's mind.

Rage.

But was she Angela? He forced himself to ignore the rest of the room and focus on the woman. Squatting, he reached out to check for a pulse on the woman's wrist. Nothing, despite the body still being warm.

Wrinkles spanned the woman's throat. Checking her hands, he saw several spots and realized the woman was at least fifteen or twenty years older. He let out the breath he had been holding and stood. Sweat trickled down the side of his head even though he could hear the air conditioner running full blast. Moving away from the woman, he searched the room. They weren't here.

Feeling the onset of a flashback triggered by the gore, he scrambled down the stairs three at a time. He was almost out the front door when he turned back toward the kitchen. Snatching the handset off the old kitchen wall phone, he cracked the sheetrock with his free fist as he punched 911 on the plastic buttons.

"911, please state your emergency."

"Help me. Hurry." Matheson was fading fast, and he knew he soon could not contain himself. Rivulets of sweat rolled down the sides of his face, soaking his collar. Rainbow-colored sparklers danced across his eyes, and would quickly turn black. He had to hurry before it made him collapse.

The female voice was calm and professional. "What is your location?"

Matheson inhaled to calm himself and get back on track. He had done this too many times. Just another mission. He gave her the address.

"What is your emergency, sir?"

Matheson thought he would scream if the woman did not move faster.

"Just get someone here. My wife is missing. I can't find my little girl." His breathing was shallow, and each breath increasingly difficult.

"Yes, sir, I will have the police meet you there to assist."

The blackness crept in. The woman's voice seemed to be in a distant tunnel. "Sir? Talk to me."

He remembered the part he had forgotten just before he dropped the phone on the floor.

"There's a dead woman in my bedroom."

3

LEE

THURSDAY, 2:00 P.M.

At low tide, the wide shell-covered beach on Sullivan's Island was exposed. I walked barefoot to the water, the soft waves lapping at my feet, helping me relax. At high tide, the water would crash within a few feet of my grandfather's house, *Isles End*, on the east side of the island.

Thirty years ago, according to my grandfather, there was a large, green, football-field-sized backyard on this property, with a row of crepe myrtles at the water's edge. Erosion and climate change had taken their toll, and I hated to think of the day when the storm-surge waters of a hurricane would carry the old house away.

In the distance, the sky was cloudless and a deep cerulean blue. That wouldn't last. Hurricane Umberto, now passing over the Bahamas, was projected to head this way, although it was still a bit early for NOAA to confirm. It still could turn and spin itself out into the Atlantic Ocean. If that didn't happen, I would be forced to close the shutters at my office, help the Judge get his big old barn of a beach house ready, and prepare for evacuation. Living here my entire life, I had hurricane prep down to a science.

I looked up from the beach to see my grandfather in his usual place on the porch. His Honor had been the most senior jurist in the Ninth Circuit, sitting on the bench in downtown Charleston. He had only retired because of the seventy-year-old age limitation on the county books.

My cell phone rang as I was about to call up to him and suggest dinner at The Obstinate Daughter or The Longboard in our little town, a mile down Middle Street.

"M.L. Danforth."

"Hey, Lee." MacCabe Lawrence's deep voice always made me smile. "Thank you for not making me wait too long for a decision. I know you don't like practicing real estate law, but I did think you'd take more time to consider my offer. This will be more civil and criminal cases and lots of lost people and things."

Mac was the owner of Lawrence Security Services, a company I'd hired for protective services and other types of security for my last case. As we worked the case, a significantly stressful one for me, he and I became good friends. He was intelligent, resourceful, and trustworthy. He'd felt the same way about me, he said two weeks ago, when he'd offered me a job.

After discussing it with my office manager and best friend, Clarice Richardson, the shift to working as an attorney with Mac on the investigative side of things, rather than on my own as a real estate lawyer, was the change I needed, especially since his clients were worldwide. But that wasn't all of it. Because of my past, which the entire community was now privy to, I needed to get the hell out of Charleston.

"Hey, Mac. The Judge will review the paperwork you sent back tonight and return it tomorrow morning. You know it's been time for me to stop practicing law. And the Timberline Farm case just kicked everything into high gear. Waiting would only delay the inevitable."

"Well," Mac huffed into the phone, "we'll have to wing this next case on a verbal agreement then."

"You're putting me to work already?" Unused to working for someone else, I was a little surprised. I expected things to move more slowly in the corporate world, not more quickly.

"Well, yes, and no. This is a personal favor to me, but we'll run your expenses and fees through the company to cover it. It needs immediate attention, and it will take me too long to get there from Atlanta."

"Ok, hold on a sec. I'm on the beach. Let me get my iPad."

I quickly tromped up the stairs, pausing at the top to wash my sandy feet. My grandfather's eyebrows raised in question. I motioned him to follow me inside as I grabbed my iPad to take notes, pulling the pen from its magnetic holder.

"Ok, Mac, tell me." I put the phone on speaker as my grandfather and I sat at the dining table. The Judge had signed a blanket confidentiality agreement years ago, as he was my legal sounding board for every case since his retirement.

"With my military background," Mac said, "many service people contact me asking for help. While I take on some cases, I pass others on depending on the nature of the problem and the location. My office just received a call from a recently retired Army friend, Colonel Vernon Matheson. He just got home from somewhere overseas, and he says that his house is a wreck from a massive party, his wife and daughter are missing, and there is a dead woman he doesn't know on his bedroom floor."

"Wait, I know this guy," I said. "He was one of my first clients when I hung out my shingle, and we still have occasional transactions, but it's by email. It's been ten years or more since I last spoke with him. Do you have a current number?" My heart ramped up significantly. Vernon Matheson was the most exhilarating man I had ever met—even more than Jack.

It all came back in a flurry. Handling a specialized real estate transaction for Matheson, the man had insisted on complete discretion to keep a family member from learning of his assets. I continue to handle the annual property tax payments and other minor corporate matters. When he insisted we only communicate by email, I thought I had offended him somehow, until we shook hands goodbye at the end of the first meeting. The electricity had zipped up my arm like I had been shocked as his gaze locked onto mine—*definitely the most electrifying.*

"I'll text it and the address over in a second. I'll call him back now and tell him that you'll get over there as quickly as you can. He has called the police, but he cut me off before I got the address." Mac hesitated. "You are authorized to hire criminal counsel if necessary. For this guy, basically, you have a blank check."

"He's that important to you?"

"You have no idea."

From real estate to murder, I was most definitely jumping out of a frying pan and into an inferno. I was not a criminal lawyer. The Judge and I would have to work together, just as we did in the Timberline Farm matter.

"Did he kill this woman?" I asked Mac.

"He says no, and I believe him."

"How well do you know this man?"

"Very. We went through the ranks together. He is one of the best soldiers I've ever known and a top-notch officer. He's saved my life twice. In my opinion, he should have retired when I did, and we could have worked together. But he refused. He got too attached to places with deserts and mountains to let go. He had a real fear of coming back Stateside, even to visit, and had difficulty considering civilian employment."

"So, you've told me your background. If you guys trained the same, then we're talking an officer trained—"

"Yes, he's a sharpshooter," Mac cut me off. "I have no idea what he did on his last tour. Something in Syria."

"Ok, I'll get those details later. What I hear you saying is that he can kill at the drop of a hat."

"Yes." Mac's response was grave, and we both knew this client might be in serious trouble.

"Send me his number, and get back to me the second you know more."

As I was getting dressed, Mac called again. "I called back several times, but he's not picking up," Mac said when I answered his call. "He didn't leave me an address, so I don't know where to send you. I'm concerned the police already have him locked up."

"So why is he back in the States now?"

"He was honorably discharged, but barely. I was unable to obtain a copy of any discharge orders, but I called a highly placed friend. One of Matheson's missions went sideways in Afghanistan. He lost two men, and another lost a leg and had to be flown out, first to Germany, then to the U.S. Then he had some other issues with flashbacks. The Army finally pulled the plug in Syria. I don't have his status, but I'll get it. The word is that Matheson disputed intelligence and took his team on a route that had not been cleared. In addition to what happened in Afghanistan, he has had other issues over the years, but my friend refused to elaborate. Matheson is held in such high esteem that no one wants to talk, even if there were problems."

"So he's angry because they kicked him out. And now there's a dead body."

"I know it doesn't look good, but give him a chance. He's a good man in a rough spot. I need you to be there and have his back."

"And I will, but I'm not leaving my common sense at the door."

"Wouldn't expect otherwise. I'll call you again when I have a confirmed status."

"Understood, and I'll see what the Judge and I can do from here." I was about to end the call when Mac spoke again, his voice filled with concern.

"Look, Lee, from what I could pull out of my friend, his discharge requires him to seek medical attention. That possibly means a psych eval from the VA, but I'm guessing. Once I get the orders, I'll send you a copy. I know you have some contacts there."

My stomach dropped hearing this.

"So he's a trained killer with a psych problem at a house with a dead woman he says he didn't kill and doesn't know."

Mac let out a long breath. "Consider all sides, Lee. Do your normal thing and see what is happening here."

"Will do. Send me his info."

We ended the call, and I shook my head at my grandfather. "I think this might be worse than actually having my own practice."

"Don't *fash, mo ghràidh*. Let's call the chief at Mt. Pleasant and see what he can tell us." This was another reason I kept my grandfather on retainer. His contacts are significantly better than mine. He punched a number into his cell phone and walked into the kitchen. I heard the coffee machine begin its obnoxious roar.

As he brought me a travel thermos, I knew he had obtained the location.

"158 East Broughton Street," the Judge repeated aloud to whomever he was talking with. I wrote it down. "I understand, yes. Certainly. Thank you, Chief. I owe you." The Judge laughed at something that was said on the other end. "Of course. No cheap stuff. I understand." He cut the call.

"I take it he wants a bottle of scotch for that information?"

"Yes, and nothing cheap. What a scoundrel. The town could do better than that snake." The Judge grabbed my arm as I was headed out the door. "Lee, as with your practice of law, you are simply dealing with people. Don't let your fear of being out of your element cause you to lose perspective and your common sense. You are a smart woman. You can handle this."

I looked into my grandfather's blue eyes, almost identical to mine, even though we weren't blood-related, then wrapped my arms around him in a hug.

"Not sure what I'd do without you, old man."

"Let's not find out," he replied softly. "Call me when you can and definitely if you need anything."

"Will do."

4

————

VERN

THURSDAY, 2:45 P.M.

Matheson fought to keep himself from going under as he crashed through the living room and out to the front porch. Mental flashes from years ago in Afghanistan wormed their way to the front of his mind, memories he did not want, particularly now. Triggered by smoke from the party, the dead woman's blood and gore were about to finish him off.

Collapsing on the porch's top step, he put his head between his knees, his hands gripping the top step. He counted aloud backwards from one hundred, forcing the picture of each number in his head to crowd out everything else, until finally, the world stopped spinning and the blackness receded.

A dark gray Audi pulled to the curb in front of his house. Attorney Lee Danforth got out and started up his sidewalk. It had been over ten years, but he still recognized her. What the...?

"Hello, Colonel." Danforth walked toward him, her face concerned. He knew he looked bad and needed a shower, but he could tell it was more than that. He focused on blue eyes that immediately trained on his, sharp with intelligence.

Wearing a suit and heels, her blonde hair in a professional

French twist, she gracefully moved up the sidewalk. Athletic and tan, she was tall enough in those heels to look him in the eye. A tweak of something started at the base of his spine and shot upward. She had changed—older, yet even more attractive than when they'd met. They had corresponded by email back and forth about once a year for the basic work he had needed. He had forgotten how sexy her voice sounded.

"Ms. Danforth. Didn't expect to see you here." He looked like crap and didn't understand why all of a sudden it mattered.

"Mac called me. He and I work together now. I'm to see what's happening here and call in other counsel if needed. He said you called the police."

Matheson sat up and tried to get his wits about him. He did not remember calling MacCabe Lawrence, a man he had known for most of his military career, and a former commander during Matheson's second tour of duty.

"I thought you handled only real estate," he said, stalling for time until he could pull himself together.

"You don't read your email, do you?" she replied with a soft smile. "Let's talk about that later. I think right now..."

Three black and whites screeched to a stop at an angle in front of the house, red and blue strobes flashing brightly in the neighborhood.

"We have to move fast now," she said. "Don't say one word to the officers until I say so. You and I haven't had a chance to talk." She pointed to the side of the yard. "Go wait over there until I ask you to come over. First, tell me quickly what is in that house."

He gave her a thirty-second rundown of the last half hour.

"You own this house?" she asked, not having been a part of that transaction. He had used the attorney suggested by the realtor for that closing.

"It is in my name, yes. My wife and child live here."

"Did you know about the drugs?"

"Hell no."

"I'll get the rest of the details later. If you have any travel information or paperwork to prove you weren't here until thirty minutes ago, get it for me."

"It's in my duffel."

"Please grab it then, and go stand over to the side next to the roses."

Some neighbors were beginning to filter out on porches while others were craning to look through their front windows. A uniformed officer about Matheson's age stopped at the foot of the porch steps in front of Danforth, and the others scattered out behind Matheson, two heading for the back, and two more next to him, all with hands resting on their sidearms. Too familiar with guns, Matheson kept his hands at his sides in clear sight, duffel at his feet.

"Ma'am, I am Officer Patrick Logan. Are you the owner of the house?" he asked Danforth, then looked over at Matheson.

"My name is M.L. Danforth. I'm Colonel Matheson's attorney." She pointed toward him. "Here is my card. I've instructed my client not to answer your questions at this point," Danforth said, "simply because I just got here and have not even had time to talk with him. I need at least ten minutes."

Matheson locked his eyes on Officer Logan, his shoulders automatically shifting backward to attention, his stance at command. He would give them no reason to suspect him. Body cues could be dangerous, particularly if unintended. He intended to keep his in line.

"I need his identification to be certain we are at the correct location."

"I can assure you, officer, that you are. My client gives you the right to access his home only to determine the identity of the woman in the upstairs bedroom and deal with her death. There are drugs in the home in plain sight that he discovered as he entered the home. He has nothing to do with those."

"See your license then?" the officer asked Danforth. Danforth pulled her wallet from her briefcase and handed the officer her business card, bar card, and driver's license. "Has anyone gone into the house other than your client?"

"You mean other than the fifty people who were here at a party? My client just returned home from active duty. Got out of a taxi at the corner a few minutes ago." Danforth turned and pointed toward him. "His wife and daughter are missing, and the little girl is only five."

"Where are all the people at the party?" Logan asked.

"Hit the road when they heard him call the police." Logan's reaction was to roll his upper lip into his lower one. Matheson could not tell if the officer was relieved at not having an additional fifty statements to complete, or disappointed, given he'd been told there was a dead body and the possible fifty witnesses were in the wind. Matheson tried to squelch his impatience. His wife and daughter could be in serious trouble while these guys were lollygagging.

"Dispatch has a recording of the details of his call," said Danforth. "Your investigators can enter the premises, but it's urgent that we find his family."

The officer didn't respond, but stepped back from the porch to talk with his dispatcher using his shoulder mic. Matheson knew the drill. The civilian police and military police were incestuous cousins. Only respond to what you are asked. Give no extraneous information. Do not volunteer. He was glad Danforth was here to handle it for him. Right now, there was no way he could get through this without help.

Logan waved over one of the other officers. "Ms. Danforth, after you talk to your client, we'll take his statement, and then we can have the detectives help you with the missing wife and daughter while we canvass the area. I've called in the crime scene crew, and there is a detective on the way."

"Thank you, officer." Danforth motioned to Matheson, and they walked to the car.

"Where are you going?" Logan called out to them.

"To sit in my car and talk where there's privacy. It's hot out here. We're sure not going in that house." Danforth pointed toward the townhouse.

In the car, the attorney began to rapidly quiz him, starting from the time he left Syria until the minute she arrived at the townhouse. She took detailed notes on an iPad, continuing until Logan rapped his knuckles on the passenger side window.

"We need to take his statement."

Matheson got out of the Audi, closed the passenger door, and leaned against the car as Danforth came around to stand beside him.

"What is your full name?" Logan asked him.

"Vernon Hartley Matheson." Matheson continued to fill in the factual details of his life, his assignments overseas, his family, and the specifics of his travel from Syria.

"Who is the woman in your bedroom?"

"I have no idea, but she is not my wife. Like I said, my wife and child are missing, and we need to find them." He looked at his watch. "It's been an hour now since I got here. Given the kind of party I walked in on and the woman upstairs, they could be in real trouble."

Logan scrutinized Matheson from head to toe and stepped closer. This intimidation tactic was silly, given that Matheson had eight inches and fifty pounds on the officer. Yet the pistol under Logan's right hand did count for something.

"You want to tell me again," Logan asked, "where you've been for the past forty-eight hours? I need to be certain I have it all down correctly. And you say all this can be verified?"

Matheson resisted the urge to show the officer his favorite right hook. Danforth touched his arm, and he felt a little electric zing pass between them. When he looked at her, she was shaking her head.

"Just give me the documents, Colonel," she said.

He pulled out his military orders and unfolded them. Danforth instinctively took charge, her words clipped, directed to the officer as if issuing orders to a subordinate. *Sir, yes, sir.* The instantaneous mental response bounced through his mind, and for a second, Matheson was glad he was no longer subjected to that crap.

As she directed, Logan stepped back from Matheson, then took a photo of the orders. Logan finally looked up, somewhat appeased by the details, but primarily because of Danforth's demeanor.

"You know this is one of our most frequent calls." He motioned with his head toward the house. "Sorry for the attitude, sir. Every time we get a call lately, it's for this residence. We got a call, in fact, just before yours, complaining about the noise."

"How frequent?" Matheson could easily guess, but wanted to hear it from Logan.

"Either the homeowner's association or the neighbors call every other day."

"For what?"

"The same thing you saw today. Your wife likes to party, man."

"Like this?"

"No, not quite like this. Today is different. People didn't end up dead before."

"Have you made arrests before?"

"A few, yes." The officer did not seem to want to elaborate. He glanced at Danforth, who was already making a note on her iPad.

"Look, Officer Logan," Matheson said, looking at his badge again to remember the man's name. I care about my daughter. I can deal with my wife later, but I need to find my child. She's only five."

The officer nodded but said nothing, his attention drawn to a line of arriving vehicles: a sedan and two unmarked white county cars. A uniform and a suit headed straight for Danforth and Matheson, the uniformed officer a higher rank than Logan. Halfway, the officer motioned to Logan. After he conferred with the lower-ranking officer, he approached.

"Ms. Danforth," the new uniform said, "I'm Captain Rick Norcross from the Mt. Pleasant Police Department. The Chief recently talked with Judge Rhineholdt, and wanted to be certain you had my personal assistance should you need it."

Matheson wondered who this judge was and why his attorney was being afforded special treatment. Norcross turned toward him before he could ask Danforth the details.

"Mr.—ah, Colonel Matheson," Norcross said, after glancing at his uniform insignia. The captain gestured to the man standing next to him. "This is the lead detective from my office, Dan Weaver. He will have questions for you."

Norcross was about fifty, a buzz cut on top, his uniform properly creased and spotless, former military, in Matheson's estimation. The local detective was the opposite. Dumpy with unkempt, greasy hair, he needed a shave, and his suit obviously had been slept in for more than a few days. Just from the way the man looked at him, Matheson expected the man to be similar to those he'd met in the military, jackasses without a clue who thought they knew everything.

The captain left the detective with Danforth and Matheson after Logan assured his superior he had what he needed for the moment. Weaver took Logan aside for only a few seconds, then returned to talk with Matheson.

"Look, Detective," Matheson began, "I know you have your process, but my daughter is missing. Can we start looking for her? I've been standing around here for more than an hour since I called, and your forensic team still hasn't appeared."

"Certainly," Weaver replied, intelligent eyes contradicting his physical condition, "but first I need to ask a few questions about the woman you found."

Even though exhausted, Matheson straightened to his full

height. Again, he felt the zing of Danforth's hand on his arm as she shifted to stand in front of him.

"Detective Weaver," Danforth said. "Please read the statement he gave to Officer Logan. He doesn't know who that woman is. I also gave his travel orders to Logan. You'll see that my client hasn't been here for over eighteen months. He just arrived here to find this mess." She pointed to the house's front door.

As Weaver waved for the policeman to rejoin them, Logan handed him the handwritten notes and the statement he had taken from Matheson. When Weaver began to read, Matheson dropped his duffel at his feet and clenched both hands in irritation.

"I need to get to my grandparents on Sullivan's Island," Matheson said quietly to Danforth, "so they don't hear about this before I can tell them."

"Uh, about that," Logan replied, his face chagrined. "I just sent a black-and-white to their house to look for your wife and daughter."

"Great." Matheson shook his head in frustration. "While I do appreciate your help, a shock like this from the police might kill them both at their age." His surprise return was already a disaster. "I'm assuming my vehicle in the garage is part of the crime scene?" He looked at Weaver, who nodded, then opened his mouth to speak. Danforth shook her head at the detective.

"We need to get to Sullivan's Island. My client can talk to you tomorrow, Detective. Please call my office." She handed Weaver her business card. "Let's go," she said to Matheson, motioning to her car.

"If you need me," Matheson said to Weaver while pointing to Danforth, "you can call her." He grabbed his duffel and headed toward the Audi, then pulled his spare deadbolt key from its ring and flipped it to Logan.

"Lock up this piece of shit when you're done."

5

VERN

THURSDAY, 5:00 P.M.

Hurricane Umberto makes landfall at Freeport, Grand Bahama Island

On the way to the island, Matheson gave Danforth as much information as he could. She had questions about the crime scene, his relationship with Angela, Katie, his grandparents, and what life was like eighteen months ago.

"Don't worry, there will be more," she said as they reached Sullivan's Island.

Turning right on Middle Street, they headed toward his grandparents' house. Matheson looked out the window as they passed the elementary school. Katie's laughter rang in his ears from their last Skype call. *Daddy, you're such a silly man.* Katie had collapsed in a fit of giggles, trying to teach him ballet, he on one side of the world, his daughter on the other. Just that one move accidentally in front of two others in the barracks had made him the butt of ballet jokes for the next week.

"Do you think Katie will be here?" she asked.

"Either here or in kindergarten. She should really be in school."

"Let's go ahead and call the school then." She slowed the car and pulled over to the curb to focus on the call. Matheson found the number for Mount Pleasant Academy and, after introducing himself, asked to speak with the principal. He put the call on speaker.

"Mr. Matheson, while we'd love for you to pick up your daughter, Katie didn't show up for school today." The principal responded, her voice warm yet professional. "We left a message for her mother on her cell phone this morning, but haven't heard back." Matheson looked at Danforth, then closed his eyes as he responded.

"I just got home from overseas, and haven't talked with my wife yet," he responded. "I thought I'd surprise them both. Once I get home, one of us will get back to you as to why Katie was out today. I appreciate your help." He cut the call and dropped his phone back in his pocket. Danforth put the car in drive and pulled away from the curb.

"Let's get to your grandparents, then," she said. "Maybe they will know more."

"I've been home for hours and I feel already like I'm spinning my wheels here." Matheson rubbed his face, feeling the two-day beard. What he wouldn't give for a shower and a shave, but there was no time.

"The cops have what they need to move forward," Lee said. "After we talk to your grandparents, then I'll get my team moving as well."

The garden gate slamming behind him broke the silence of the Sullivan's Island neighborhood. The barrier island was less than half an hour from downtown Charleston. It was home to residents who had been there since the 1970s, including his grandparents, interspersed with affluent newcomers from New York, Washington, D.C., and Chicago.

To Matheson, after his eighth birthday, the island was the place of a safe childhood, although a strict one. Once his grandparents took over from his parents, his life was filled with boogie boards on the beach, bicycles roaming the streets, and pickup basketball games at the town park. As they drove up in front of the house, he felt the comfort of his grandparents' town envelop him.

Coming through the front gate, he could hear Nana chiding him as a teenager for slamming it. Framed by the open front door, his Nana wore the blue flowered house dress she'd owned since he was twelve. Closer, he saw that she had significantly changed, her hair floating about her like a tornado in the breeze, the white ends twisted as if she had been pulling on it. Tears slid down her wrinkled face. His heart hurt at seeing his grandmother like this.

"Nana." She pushed open the screen door and wrapped her arms around his neck as he bent forward for a hug. Her whispers came out choked with sobs.

"Vernon, oh my God, you're home."

His grandmother was the only person he knew who could reduce a forty-eight-year-old man to a child in three seconds. She backed away to let them in the house, wiping her eyes on her apron.

His grandfather was waiting just inside. "Come on in, son. The police just left. They said you were at the townhouse with your lawyer, but wouldn't say much else. What's going on over there? Is this the lawyer?" Scowling, he pointed to Danforth. Matheson squinted at him. Even though Stanley Moore was usually stern, this rudeness toward her was unlike his grandfather.

"Yes." Matheson introduced Danforth to both grandparents, and tried to avoid the old man's eyes, unsure how he would be received. The last time he had been home on leave, the old cuss had threatened to beat the life out of him if he signed up for another tour. He thought Matheson should be home with his wife and child, not "playing soldier" as he called it, on the "other side of the world." As a young boy, he had always been afraid of his grandfather, worried that the man would beat him just as his father had beaten him. Yet it never happened. The old man had been strict, but fair, and had never laid a hand on him, even when he deserved it.

As usual, his grandmother began her usual fussing about, offering food and drink. Matheson looked for evidence of Katie while continuing to wallow in his guilt for not calling his grandmother days ago. He wondered if he could have prevented everything that had just happened if he had let his family know he was coming home. But then, if he had, Angela would have hidden everything he'd just seen.

And it was all his fault. He had ignored his family for so long; it shouldn't surprise him to find everything a mess upon returning. Since Katie had been about four, Matheson had called home for a few minutes each night before she went to bed. He had watched his child grow through those calls. He had not thought of it until now, but Angela had been on those calls less and less. At some point, with Angela insisting that Katie was busy with friends and sleepovers, the video calls had dwindled to once a week, then to once a month for the past six months.

Surrounded by the blessed smell of a baking casserole, Matheson wearily dropped his duffel next to the stairs. Standing behind Nana, his grandfather placed his hands on her shoulders. A single tear trickled down the man's face. Matheson had never seen his grandfather cry. He looked from one grandparent to the other. They both looked and acted so much older than they had eighteen months prior. There was something wrong with both of them.

"Da—where's Katie? Isn't she here?"

The old man stiffened at the words, and sudden confusion crossed his grandmother's face. "She's not here, son," his grandfather said. "I'm assuming she's at school. At least there she'll have been protected from whatever went on at that house of yours."

"She's not in school, Da. I called them. Where could she be?"

"Katie was just here…" his grandmother said, her eyes wide with concern. "I don't know where she's run off to."

"No, Althea, she isn't here," Moore said to his wife. He looked at Matheson. "I'm sure she'll turn up, son." His grandfather turned and headed toward the kitchen.

"Turn up!" Matheson said to his grandfather's back. "You have no idea what happened at my house."

"Oh, I've a good idea." The old man muttered under his breath.

"What in the hell does that mean, old man? What do you know that you aren't telling me?" Matheson took a step toward his grandfather, then stopped when Danforth grabbed his bicep and forced him to stop.

"Don't," Lee whispered to him. "You're upsetting your grandmother. Let's all go into the kitchen and sit where we can talk."

Matheson looked at his grandmother. Nana's confusion seemed to increase, and then the smell hit him. Instead of her usual citrus cologne, he was enveloped by body odor and a whiff of smoke that was more burned leaves than cigarette. His grandmother didn't drink or smoke. What had happened to his usually prim and proper grandmother? He backed away when the smoke odor threatened to trigger the Afghan movie reel in his head.

"Maybe Katie is at a friend's house somewhere." His grandfather's strained, gravelly voice floated out of the kitchen. "Maybe a neighbor has her, or she's at some dance lesson. I called Police Chief Stanton here on the island, and he said that the Mount Pleasant police are searching the neighborhoods around the school for her. I'm concerned about the hurricane rolling in, even though it's early. It could still turn." The old man's voice lowered as Matheson and Danforth stepped into the kitchen, followed by Nana. They all sat, with his grandmother's hands twisting the ties of her apron.

"They need to find that wife of yours," his grandfather said, the disgust evident in his voice.

Matheson couldn't bring himself to ask why his grandfather was so mad at his wife. He couldn't get past the fact that Katie wasn't here. His wife was in way over her head, and something was very wrong with his grandmother. He slid his chair back and bent forward to stop the vertigo. A keening started in his head, and Matheson slapped his hands over his ears. Katie could be anywhere. What had Angela done?

He heard the screech of dining chairs being pushed back from the table.

Da broke the keening with his raspy voice in a whisper next to his head, as Matheson felt his hand pat his back. "I'm sorry, Vernon. I know you're distraught over Katie and Angela. I'm sure they're okay, but maybe they'll be off on a short vacation somewhere. Angela doesn't tell us everything."

Vernon Matheson felt like he was in a bad dream from which he couldn't wake. He was anxious for his daughter, but for all he cared, if something had happened to Katie, Angela could go to hell.

6

LEE

THURSDAY, 6:00 P.M.

The doorbell rudely interrupted, the buzzer insistent. As I watched Matheson check his watch, I realized a half hour had passed.

"Let me get it," I said, heading to the living room. Mr. Moore was behind me, turning, then silently going upstairs to the bedrooms. At the front door, peering through the screen was Detective Weaver, his hand on the latch, ready to walk in without permission. I blocked him from entering the screen door.

"Had some more questions for your client that couldn't wait," Weaver said through the door, as he tried to scan the living room. He was searching for details that might be relevant to his investigation. It was clear that my client was a suspect. The husband usually was, even though this dead woman wasn't his wife.

Matheson's grandmother puttered up behind me and, in irritatingly proper Southern form, offered the detective something to drink.

"Thank you, ma'am. I'll take you up on that." Weaver pushed by me as she ushered him to a seat at the dining room table, where she poured him a glass of sweet tea. After setting a plate of cookies on the table, she began puttering in the kitchen.

I motioned to Matheson to follow me into the living room away from Weaver. "Let me run interference," I said quietly.

"I'll be honest with you," Matheson replied, "I'm running over forty hours without sleep."

"Not a problem." My demeanor automatically shifted into lawyer mode. "Let's see what he wants, and then you and I can talk with your grandparents for a few minutes more. We can regroup later after you've slept."

"I don't want to waste time that we could be using to find Katie," he said, "but I really have to get at least a few hours' sleep. I'm about to drop."

I put on my poker face to deal with Weaver instead of Vern, but it wasn't easy. For me, the man was like a magnet. Ten years ago, when Matheson came to my office to have me review the tax records for a property in Awendaw and to create the necessary paperwork to conceal his ownership, I was inexperienced and overwhelmed by the masculine energy he generated simply by standing in my office. I didn't ask him enough questions at the time. While the work he hired me for produced the result he wanted, my learning curve was significant, both in client relations and in the types of work I was competent to handle. I would not make that mistake again.

Today, his face was like steel, and even without sleep for days, he was clearly the Alpha in the room. Since we'd met, he'd climbed the ranks to Colonel, was apparently used to being shot at regularly, and had been discharged under dubious circumstances. Despite my attraction to him, I needed to focus on the problem at hand. Accidentally touching his arm as we headed toward the dining room, I felt the muscle flinch. It wasn't just me.

The Moores' beach house on Sullivan's was old, but well-maintained, and the furniture was a bit fussy. Walking back to the kitchen, I noticed evidence that a child had been here, with toys, board books, and a tiny pink sweater neatly folded over the arm of a chair. Even though the contents were all orderly and in place, I could tell that the house needed a thorough cleaning.

Once in the kitchen, I set the ground rules. "Detective, I understand you need information, but my client is exhausted, and I have not had a significant conversation with him yet. I can hear your questions now, but I cannot guarantee you will get answers until he and I have had a chance to talk."

"I know this is a difficult time for you," Weaver said to my client, ignoring me. "I need to interview you and your grandparents separately." He looked at me. "Do you also represent the Moores?"

"No. Only Colonel Matheson."

The detective's sympathetic face seemed contrived. "Then can I ask Mrs. Moore to wait in the living room?" He looked at Mrs. Moore. "But first, do you have a recent photo of Katie and Angela?"

Mrs. Moore left the kitchen, returned with a five-by-seven framed photograph, and handed it to me. The woman had strawberry blonde hair and appeared to be in her early thirties, while the child was about four or five years old. The grinning imp was a miniature version of her father, with a mop of curly red hair. I took a picture with my phone and smiled at Matheson as I handed him the photo. He took it and stared at the image. The look on his face told me he might crumble to pieces at any moment.

He handed the photo to Weaver, who also took a picture with his phone and began texting. "Thank you. I'm sending this photo to the department for distribution. May I have any cell number for your wife or daughter, and any social media accounts?"

Matheson told him the cell number, but had no idea if his wife even had social media accounts.

As Matheson's grandmother left the room, Weaver took out a small recorder. A crusty mustard drip ran down his tie. His hair was in an oily combover, and his suit was rumpled and dirty.

Then on top of it all, the man radiated indignation, as if *we* were wasting *his* time. Every inch of the detective radiated something foul beyond the physical, and given my last case involving cops on the take, I went on high alert.

Weaver clicked on the recorder and leaned forward. "This is Thursday, August 28, 2025, at 6:00 p.m. I am at the home of Stanley and Althea Moore. This is the interview of Vernon Matheson." He looked up at my client. "Colonel Matheson, I've read the statement that you gave to the officer at the scene. I'm finding it difficult to believe you have no idea who the deceased woman is, especially given that you discovered her in your bedroom. I need to clarify the timeline."

When Matheson started to answer, I placed my hand on his arm and felt a light shock as if I'd touched something electrical.

"You need to address your questions to me," I said calmly, even though I was beginning to get irritated. I was used to dealing with belligerent attorneys and bigoted judges, but it always involved money or property, never people's lives. Here, if I screwed up, it would affect my client and possibly his family directly.

I stared at Weaver until he finally made eye contact. "My client has stated clearly that he only arrived home minutes before, and does not know the woman. Is there a reason you're here rather than out searching for my client's wife and daughter?" I said.

Matheson's jaw worked back and forth as he clenched his teeth. I anticipated that at any moment, he would lunge across the table. That was precisely what the detective wanted. Weaver was baiting him, trying to get a reaction. An angry man might say things he would regret. I would have to remind Matheson that in Charleston, things trudged slowly, and that arrogance was a widely held virtue.

As Weaver looked down at his notes, I caught my client's eye and winked. Even if I was a bit nervous about all this, there was no way I would let my client see it. Matheson's shoulders relaxed slightly, and he unclenched his hands, shifting to hide them under the table.

"I need to clarify a few things," Weaver said. "Exactly what time did you arrive home? Matheson slid a receipt toward me. The top had the taxi company's name. The bottom had both a pickup and drop-off time.

"The taxi receipt," I said, "says he was picked up at the airport at 1:00 p.m., and that he paid for the ride at 1:45 p.m. You can contact the taxi company to verify this information." Weaver reached for the receipt. "My office will provide you with a copy." I dropped the receipt into my briefcase.

"Your call to 911 was logged at 1:59 p.m. Officer Logan arrived at 2:15 p.m."

"Is there a question here, Detective?" I asked.

"What were you doing from 1:45 to 1:59 p.m., Colonel Matheson?" Weaver asked.

"Trying to find my wife and daughter," Matheson replied calmly. "Fourteen minutes sounds correct. I walked from Coleman Boulevard to the house, then asked questions to one of the guys at the party, then rushed upstairs, but my family was not there."

"What about the woman?" Weaver asked.

"She was dead when I got there. I searched for Katie and Angela, then called 911."

"Why didn't you call 911 first?"

"Would you have called the police after discovering a ton of drugs in your house?" Matheson asked.

"What else, Detective? You were there for the rest." I asked.

"Your daughter's school principal confirmed she was not present today," Weaver replied. "Forensics told us that no other bodies have been found other than an adult female."

Matheson's impatience was raw as he leaned forward in his

chair. This man went from zero to sixty in less than two seconds. "Tell me something I don't know. Who was that woman?"

If I didn't do something quickly, he would choke the life out of the detective. Before I could think about whether it was appropriate, I placed my hand under the table and on his knee, giving it a soft double pat. Matheson leaned back in his chair and let out a breath, picking up on my nonverbal communication. If he could hold himself, we would get through this.

Weaver continued. "I have to withhold the victim's name until her relatives have been notified, especially given the nature of the body."

I patted Matheson on the knee again and slightly shook my head. "What do you mean by the nature of the body?" I asked Weaver.

"Ask the ME." The detective still refused to look at me. "Remind me again where you were last night between 5:30 and 9:30?" he asked Matheson.

The detective was trying to see if Matheson's story would hold. "You already know where my client was for the past three or more days," I responded.

Matheson pulled the military orders from his pocket and slid them to me. Weaver reached for the orders, and I pulled the papers away from him. The orders were clear enough for me to understand. Matheson had been on a C-17 from Syria to Camp Arifjan in Kuwait, then what appeared to be a private transport to Shannon, Ireland. The next hop was by a military plane to Pope Army Airfield, which I knew was part of Fort Bragg in North Carolina. There, he was formally discharged and then transferred to Joint Base Charleston on Delta.

"You and your officer," I said, "have a copy of the Colonel's orders, flight times, and arrival time."

I slid the military orders and receipt into my briefcase and prepared for him to leave. I'd already had enough of this. I would hash through the rights or wrongs of my behavior with the Judge later. This man was wasting everyone's time.

"Detective," I said, as I stood, "we're done here. You can arrange an interview at my office if you have additional questions. Advise me of any additional progress you make on this case."

Weaver kept prodding Matheson. "You left before our call to your CO."

"No," I said to my client, "do not answer him. You are exhausted, and I am directing you not to respond."

"You heard her," Matheson said calmly. "We're done here. Time for you to leave." He rose to his full six-foot-three height, glaring at the detective.

Weaver scraped his chair away from the table and headed into the living room. "I will set a time with your grandparents to interview them either here or at the station. I need you to stay in the area. Just in case."

The muscles in Matheson's neck bulged. "Seriously?" Matheson walked up behind the detective, looming over him. "You think I'd leave now? When my family is out there somewhere?"

Before I could react, Mrs. Moore's hand tugged the back of Matheson's shirt. "Vernon, let's have some manners, son," she said softly behind him.

He shrugged her off as he leaned over, his face close to Weaver's. "What are you not telling me?"

The detective glared at Matheson. "The woman found on the floor of your bedroom was part of a group under surveillance for the past few months."

"Surveillance for what?" I asked.

"For trafficking children in the area."

Mrs. Moore let out a *whoosh* of air like she had been punched. I pushed Matheson into the kitchen to comfort his grandmother, whose tears had begun in earnest. I needed this irritating detective out of the house. Now.

7

LEE

THURSDAY, 6:45 P.M.

Hurricane Umberto increases to Category 5

I moved the detective out onto the front porch and closed the door. "What an asshole thing to do. His grandmother is in tears."

Weaver shrugged. "Doing my job."

"Bullshit. If you had my client's home under surveillance, then you have a good idea where his wife and child are, or what Angela was involved in."

"Nope," Weaver replied. "No clue."

I stared into his eyes and got something more than a denial in response. A strange feeling swirled in the pit of my stomach, one I'd learned to trust over the years. He knew a lot more than he was telling me, I just didn't know why.

"Just tell me what's happening here."

With only a mental picture of the dead woman on my client's bedroom floor, I had no idea if what I imagined was correct—had Matheson's wife and child both been kidnapped? Had Angela killed the woman trying to escape from something? I didn't have enough information. Weaver's irritating voice interrupted my thoughts.

"I'm not saying anything about what the deceased was actually doing there," he said, "because I don't know. We were hoping your client could give us a little more information."

I shook my head. "My client has no idea what this woman was doing in his house, and you know that. He wasn't even in the country."

"Does he have any idea where his wife might be? It would help us find her and his daughter faster."

I might as well be talking to a wall. He was asking questions we had already answered. I needed to find out what he really wanted. "When will my client's house be released as a crime scene? There may be a hurricane, and he needs to get that house ready."

Weaver's response was expected, but not what I wanted to hear. "The Criminal Investigations Bureau will tackle the residence as soon as possible. The scene will be released whenever it is done, but I won't estimate when."

I turned to go back into the house. "Don't contact my client outside my presence." I gave him my card again because I was sure he had flipped the previous one I'd given him at the townhouse into the gutter. Watching him walk down the sidewalk, I made sure his car was headed down the street before I returned to the kitchen.

Matheson pulled out a chair for me and then sat across from me. Mrs. Moore placed a full glass of sweet tea in front of me. Mr. Moore had returned to the kitchen while I was outside with Weaver.

"You need sleep, Colonel," I said. "Maybe some food first."

He nodded, his face bereft.

"Of course he does." Mrs. Moore stood immediately and walked to the refrigerator. She began pulling out dishes and setting them on the counter, preparing to heat food for her grandson. Once she had everything the way she wanted it, she returned to the table.

"Just answer a few questions for me," I said to Matheson, "and then I'll have enough to go on while you hit the rack for a few hours."

"Okay. Fire away." He leaned back in the dining chair, and I watched his body relax.

"Why didn't you tell anyone you were coming home?" I asked him.

"I just got an early release and took it. Thought it would be a nice surprise." Matheson looked at his grandparents.

"I'm sure you haven't had time to think. But right now, can you guess where Angela or Katie might be?" I asked.

"No." Matheson tapped his fingers on the table until his grandmother silently placed her hand over his. His shoulders dropped, and he raked his hand through his short hair. Every inch of him radiated exhaustion. He finally looked up at me. "I know so little. And it's killing me. My child is out there somewhere, and I don't even have a clue where to look. I had no idea Angela used illegal narcotics, but then I haven't really had a conversation with her for over a year."

He stared across the living room and out the front window. I looked at Mrs. Moore, then Mr. Moore.

"What can you guys tell me about Angela's drug usage? With the level of drugs at her home, your grandson mentioned, I'm having to assume that Angela has a pretty significant problem. Did either of you see anything? What about you, Mr. Moore?" I asked. "Anything you want to tell me about your granddaughter-in-law?"

Stanley Moore looked at me as if I were something disgusting he had found on his shoe. I could feel anger rolling off him in waves. "I have nothing to tell you about that woman or any drugs.

And don't ask her," he shifted his eyes to his wife. "If you do, we'll have to listen to gossip from the entire island, and none of it will be true."

Matheson jerked as if his grandfather had hit him. He looked at the old man with astonishment. I watched Mrs. Moore's eyes flick away from her husband in embarrassment. The old man stood, turned away from me, and headed to the living room.

"I'm going out for a while," he said, the words tossed over his shoulder. "It's already been a day, and it's not even over yet."

"But Stanley, what about dinner?" Mrs. Moore rushed behind him.

"Get the boy some food," he tossed over his shoulder. "I'll pick up something later. I'm not hungry."

When the door closed behind the old man, I focused on Matheson's grandmother. "Mrs. Moore, any idea where Angela or Katie might be? What Angela's been up to lately?"

The woman shook her head, her eyes avoiding mine as she checked on the warming food. "No. I have no idea." She cleared her throat, twisting a dish towel with both hands so tightly that I waited for the stitches to pop.

I kept my focus on her. "Katie lived with you here on the island?"

"What makes you say that?" she asked, abruptly dropping the towel on the floor.

"There are lots of toys here, kid things. It looks more like Katie lived here than just visited."

"There are no toys here. I'm not sure what you are talking about." Mrs. Moore leaned over and swiped the towel from the floor, then stood and walked to the kitchen sink. She stared out the window, her back to me. I looked again through the door at the toys next to the living room couch and nodded at them to Matheson.

"Did she stay here with you a lot, Nana?" Matheson asked.

"Only to visit, son," she replied, "when Angela had a new job or somewhere she had to be. I was happy for Katie to be with us as much as she wanted."

Mrs. Moore began dishing up food and raised her eyebrows at me, but I shook my head. "Thank you. I have dinner planned with my grandfather."

"You know, lately, each time we had a Skype call," Matheson said wistfully, "Katie was here with my grandmother. Nana, you should have told me there was a problem."

Mrs. Moore released a heavy sigh, and Matheson laid the framed picture on the table and twisted in his seat to look at her. She pursed her lips as she stared out the kitchen window. He cut his eyes back at me. His grandmother knew more than she was telling. There was so much missing information, and trying to get Matheson's grandmother, much less his grandfather, to talk to me was like pulling teeth. He and I needed to speak alone.

"On those calls," I asked him, "did everything appear to be as it should?"

"Are you asking if Katie was happy and healthy? I didn't see anything unusual, but our Skype calls had dwindled over the past six months to one a month. Honestly, it was torture not being able to see and hear Katie regularly. Did they appear to be getting along? Was Katie clean and well cared for? I think so, but I don't know for sure." He cut his eyes toward his grandmother, hesitating for her to jump in. Mrs. Moore continued to stare out the window.

"Angela looked a little worn out," Matheson said, "but she always handed the phone immediately to Katie, so I can't tell you much."

I had to try one more time. "Mrs. Moore, is there anything we should know about Katie or her mother?" Refusing to look at either me or her grandson, Mrs. Moore continued to look out the window, only silently shaking her head.

I turned back to Matheson. "Are you aware of anyone who might want to do Mrs. Matheson harm?"

"No. As far as I know, everyone liked her. She had a lot of friends."

A spoon clanged into the kitchen counter behind him, and Mrs. Moore's muttered curse bounced around the room as a teacup shattered on the floor.

8

———

WEAVER

THURSDAY, 7:00 P.M.

Before leaving Sullivan's Island, Weaver punched in a number on a flip phone cell, the one he used only for his off-the-books transactions. This particular phone had been purchased at a box store in Mount Pleasant, and after a few more calls, it would end up at the bottom of the Intracoastal Waterway like the others. Changing burner phones frequently was the only way he could keep himself hidden from the ever-growing digital surveillance his police captain was addicted to.

The call was picked up by voicemail, forcing him to leave a message. There was nothing unusual about this. The man was difficult to reach most days. "We've got a problem, and you're not going to like it," he said. "Call me back as soon as you can."

Ending the call, he shifted focus, putting together a plan of what he would tell the head of Mount Pleasant's police department about the death investigation. He knew way more than he should in a typical investigation, and he had to be cautious not to overplay his hand when talking with his superior. And not do something stupid, like including information in his written report that he shouldn't have known at this early stage.

At the townhouse, Weaver had taken one look at the dead

woman and immediately recognized her as a buyer for Theron Fish, the trafficking king out of Savannah. Weaver's alarm grew further when he connected the dots at the old couple's house on Sullivan's Island after seeing a photo of Angela Matheson and realized she was a regular customer at the bar. Too bad she wasn't the one who had died. She had become a bit of an irritant to more than one of his guys.

They weren't really "his" guys. His boss, Clint Harbin, employed them. Weaver was just the organization's middle manager, the one who cracked the whip to keep everyone in line. Weaver came to know Harbin through Victoria Marshall, the lady who was currently on the run, wanted for murder. She had bribed him to destroy evidence against her son, Brad, when he was arrested for stealing in high school. Harbin had stepped in and directed him to threaten the only witness, ensuring that the case would be dropped. Later, Victoria hired Weaver again to investigate Brad's activities with a certain girl Victoria deemed inappropriate for her son to marry. Rich people's problems.

Pulling into a fast-food drive-thru for dinner, Weaver flipped open his wallet and pulled out his last ten-dollar bill. He was always short on cash, spending most of his paycheck online. He was a regular at three of the big sports betting sites and several smaller ones. His departmental paychecks never seemed to last very long, especially since Darla left him. She was good with the household money, but they always fought over what he spent on the gambling sites, and his twice-yearly trip to Las Vegas, where he really went all out.

She'd only been gone a week, and he felt like he was on a capsizing boat in the middle of the Atlantic. The flip phone buzzed on the passenger seat, and Weaver picked it up. "Yeah."

"What's this problem?" Harbin's southern accent boomed over the car's speaker, blaring out the window and into the face of the fast-food cashier who was handing him his order. She flinched at the loud voice and jerked the bag of food out of Weaver's hand.

"Give me just a second," he said into the phone. "I'm getting dinner."

"Sorry," Weaver pantomimed to the cashier, flipping her the ten-dollar bill as he turned down the volume on his car stereo. The girl released the food, and Weaver pulled his car around the building and into an empty spot.

"I've got a situation with a dead woman off Coleman Boulevard," he said, once the car was in park, window up, and his food unwrapped. "Sorry about making you listen to me eat. I've got to head back to the station, and tonight's going to be a long one."

"Who's the woman?" Harbin asked, his booming voice a habit given his continued appearances as the county's prosecutor.

"One of Theron Fish's buyers. She looks for the right circumstances, then pounces. Looks like she was trying to buy a kid from a lady who needed drug money."

From Harbin's long breath, Weaver understood that he was smoking one of his famous cigars. "Like I need to be any closer to that scumbag Fish," Harbin said. "They are on him after all that mess at Timberline Farm. Get yourself off that case."

Harbin may be the head prosecutor and used to ordering people around, but to Weaver's knowledge, he had no sway with Mount Pleasant's Chief of Police. And Weaver had no desire to get off the case. He needed to be up close and personal on this one, especially since he was implicated on both sides.

"The Chief already pulled me in. No way am I going to get out of this one."

"Why is Fish's dead lady my problem?"

Because I'm on Fish's payroll, you asshole. "The woman who was trying to sell her kid is one of our customers. The customer's name is Angela Matheson, the wife of some big-shot Colonel who just retired. But that's not the best part. Your favorite attorney represents Matheson."

"Danforth?" Harbin asked. "You've got to be kidding me. What did she get hired for?"

"Danforth is just searching for the missing family. She's letting the MPPD do the work for Fish's dead woman." Weaver took another bite of his sandwich and chewed in Harbin's silence, then took a slurp of his soft drink so he could speak. "I just finished talking with Matheson and his grandparents. With Danforth there, I had a hell of a time dancing around things. I know too much, and I'm not going to be good at hiding it."

"You'd better be. I barely got out of the last mess. If you pull me into this one, you'll regret it." Harbin didn't wait for a response but ended the call. Feeling a large cloud descend on his shoulders, Weaver raised his sandwich and took a bite.

Clint Harbin approached him a year ago with a proposition. The solicitor needed someone he could "trust" to watch over his drug suppliers. After recovering from the shock that Harbin, the head prosecutor for the three counties surrounding Charleston, was running a drug ring, Weaver listened to the solicitor and realized that this would solve his financial problems. So, before he could talk himself out of it, he said yes.

Harbin's operation was significantly compartmentalized, and Weaver had no idea where the drugs came from. Upon examining the packaging the drugs arrived in, he believed they were from a pharmaceutical company or a legitimate storage warehouse, rather than a homegrown producer, as they were all in pill form, in large bottles with generic labels affixed, as if intended for transportation to pharmacies.

Harbin had indicated his supplier was testing him with these drugs before they expanded into cigarettes and small consumer electronics, such as cell phones. Medications such as Cymbalta and Prozac were popular and would eventually re-enter the distribution chain at a significant markup. Harbin supplied small town pharmacies in the very rural areas, but Weaver didn't know how.

And he didn't want to know.

9

———

SHARPE

FRIDAY, 12:30 A.M.

Hurricane Umberto landfall projected for Melbourne, Florida

The breeze picked up for a few seconds, and he turned toward the swishing palm trees behind him. Just a breeze, common for Charleston, and no precursor to the storm this early. His family, having lived through Hugo, made him uneasy about this one. He could wait, and Hurricane Hugo's grandchild, Umberto, would solve his problem with Angela. He looked up, scanning the blue sky filled with fluffy clouds. The hurricane was still a considerable distance away and hundreds of miles off the coast of Florida. No, he would not use the hurricane as an excuse.

An alligator surfaced in the water, its eyes and the top of its body slithering through the murk, then disappearing into the marsh grass. Angela had disrespected him. Did she not care that a child was involved? She disrespected her husband and family as if it were an honor.

He'd known true honor when awarded the Army's sharp-shooter badge a lifetime ago. His accuracy earned him the moniker "Sharpe." Later, he earned the official title "Expert," but the name stuck. No one knew it here in South Carolina, but it was how he thought of himself, an expert sharpshooter. No longer in the military, he wanted this particular kill to be more personal. He wanted to see the fear in Angela's eyes before she died.

As he sat in his truck, his mind spun as to how to put this matter to rights. Red Dress had done little to abate the anger burning a hole in his gut. It was Angela's time now—no need to waste his rage on others.

Sharpe drove for hours, the sloppiness of his actions earlier still on his mind. He had no desire to spend the rest of his life behind bars, particularly not for scum that needed to be cleaned from the face of this earth. He drove by the townhouse for the fourth time. Even with no activity there, he could not be sure whether the crime scene had been fully processed. The patrolman assigned to watch the house was fast asleep, parked down the block rather than in the driveway, a second point of carelessness. Yet, if the evidence had been gathered, having the cop still watching would have been superfluous. He had to take the risk.

Parking two blocks away, he grabbed a full backpack and silently walked to the rear alley, stopping at the townhouse on the end. Quietly opening the wooden gate, he crossed the postage stamp of a backyard, pulled the crime scene tape from the back door, used his key to unlock it, and stepped into the kitchen, closing the exterior door behind him. So far, so good.

He had saved enough rubbing alcohol over the past few weeks for his experiment. Purchasing bottles of alcohol in different drug stores eliminated suspicion: two bottles here, one there, three across town, and so on. He had a dozen bottles—the best fire starter money could buy. Gasoline left a noticeable trail, an obvious accelerant. If you wanted to start something a little more anonymously, rubbing alcohol was your best bet. At least that was true, according to the local firemen. They enjoyed telling stories while drinking and playing cards. And he liked to listen.

He disabled the smoke alarms in each room to reduce unnecessary noise. He checked the windows and assessed the placement of each room's window to ensure sufficient air circulation. He needed the fire to burn fast and hot. All electrical panel switches were off downstairs, and he waited as the house wound down, preparing for its death.

Starting at the top, he checked the large bedroom at the end. The body was no longer sprawled next to the bed, yet nothing else told him forensics had been there. He poured the accelerant on the foam-based furniture first, then on the hardest-to-burn areas of the carpet. He hated burning the kid's room, but it couldn't be helped. Besides, she didn't need to remember anything about her old life. It had all been one form of abuse or another. No kid needed or deserved abuse. Discipline, yes. Abuse no.

Throwing an empty alcohol bottle under the dining table, he spun around the room, looking for anything he had missed. Possibly the garage, but the car's gas tank would resolve that problem. The main floor's hardwood was not real wood but laminate, a rapid-fire starter.

That should do it.

He started the fire with a generic set of matches commonly found in grocery and convenience stores. Beginning with the master bedroom, he soaked the spattered bed and blood-soaked carpet in alcohol. After the top floor was sufficiently ablaze, he used an entire bottle to splash a trail of alcohol down the steps to the living room.

Several ignition points would definitely lead the arson investigator to conclude that this fire wasn't an accident. Yet he didn't care whether they considered the fire arson or not; he simply wanted to eliminate his DNA.

Soaking the couch pillows, dining chairs, and all other polyurethane materials he could find first, he then hit the curtains for good measure. In thirty seconds, he felt the heat from the fire upstairs radiate through the ceiling. Tossing random lit matches throughout the main level, he finished and calmly left the same way he had entered, his breathing hard from the exertion. He was too old for this kind of thing.

In his estimation, from his research and the firemen's tales, he only needed five minutes. It took three.

The entire house was ablaze, a glorious sight. The whole neighborhood was asleep, blissfully unaware, but he decided it was time for him to bid farewell. At some point, one of the neighbors would catch a whiff of smoke. Or the car's gas tank would wake them all when it exploded.

He smiled. This was the most fun he'd had in years.

10

———

VERN

FRIDAY, 1:00 A.M., THEN 6:30 A.M.

His cell phone buzzed in a circle like an angry rodent. The clock next to his bed read one in the morning as he fought through his jet lag. Ignoring the phone, Matheson ripped himself from the skirmish in his head, making it to the bathroom to splash his face with cold water from the tap. He was exhausted and needed sleep, with no desire to talk to anyone, especially at this late hour. On the nightstand, one-fourth of the whiskey remained from what he used to knock himself out. He finished it and collapsed on the bed, hoping that he could escape his nightmares, if only for a little while.

The phone buzzing stopped, then started again. If he didn't answer, whoever it was would torture him the rest of the night. *What if it's Katie?* He sat up and snatched the phone. The letters "MPFD" lit up the screen.

"Matheson."

"Sir, this is Corporal Thompson with the Mt. Pleasant Fire Department. We have your townhouse in full blaze. I need to confirm that no individuals or animals are in the home."

"What?" He stood and began pacing, listening to the background noise on the call.

"Please, we are in a hurry here," the fireman responded. "Can you confirm there are no individuals or—"

"No one is in the home. I'm assuming the police department removed the body."

"Yes, sir. We are aware that this was a crime scene. I am just double-checking." A loud crashing noise came through the speaker.

"How did it start?" Matheson asked, but the fireman was gone. He collapsed back on the bed in a haze of alcohol and exhaustion. Let the damn thing burn.

At 6:30, when he rose again, he showered, the cold water clearing his head somewhat, and dressed in BDUs. The desert camouflage-patterned battle dress uniforms were only a little sandy, but he had nothing else to wear. He would head to the farm in Awendaw at some point for clean clothes, thankful all his things were there, rather than in the now charred townhouse. He had already planned to decorate and stuff Katie's new room with toys. It would just have to be faster.

Katie. Someone had his child, and he was powerless to find her. His life was in a downward, bottomless spiral. First, it was the mistake in Afghanistan where he'd called in the air strike to the wrong house, and that poor woman was blown to pink mist. Then the nightmares about his childhood increased, combining with more flashbacks from all his tours.

Then he'd really screwed up, taking the wrong route that led to the IED that blew up the Humvee and took his best friend Darrell's leg, causing his friend to take his life. He'd lost his job, and now he'd lost his family. His house had burned to the ground. What else could he possibly screw up? He wished he had been able to end it all before he'd come home.

No. Get that crap out of your head, man. You are stronger than this.

Katie needed him. She was out there somewhere, and he had to find her.

He grabbed his phone to check the weather report. Hurricane Umberto was just off the coast of Florida, about midway up the coast from Miami. There was still hope it would curve out into the Atlantic. It was strange how it followed Hugo's path with only a slight variation.

A picture of his five-year-old standing in the raging surf across the street from his grandparents' home flashed through his mind. No. He would find her. His daughter could not be left alone to go through a hurricane. He would not allow it.

Nana hadn't looked well the evening before, and it wasn't just because of the broken tea cups and mess on the kitchen floor that he had insisted on cleaning himself. Her skin was dry and pale, and he worried about her fainting at any moment. Now, when he entered the kitchen, both of his grandparents were seated at the table. Matheson's goal at the moment was caffeine, but he paused, watching the two people who, until he'd married Angela, had been his only family.

His grandparents stared down at their cups. Matheson rested his shoulder against the kitchen door frame, hands in his pockets, eyes cutting back and forth between them. Neither said a word, even when he crossed the room, grabbed his coffee, plated his breakfast, and sat at the table. Matheson chewed slowly, watching the standoff between the two. Just as he started to tell them about the fire, his grandmother quietly rose and began to clear the table. He didn't have the heart to tell them of this latest disaster and decided to wait.

Shuffling back and forth in front of the kitchen counter, Matheson swore Nana had shrunk. Even combed, her hair still had a rooster tail bouncing in the rear. He couldn't remember the last time he had seen her without her "proper hair." He looked at his grandfather. The old man's body language spoke volumes. The two were fighting, something Matheson had learned to monitor as a child with his warring parents, but he had never needed to with his grandparents. He took in a deep breath and let it out slowly.

"What's going on with you two?" His voice seemed to shock them both from wherever they had mentally traveled. Nana was the first to answer, even though she continued to face away from him.

"Nothing is going on with us. We're just upset about Angela."

He instantly picked up on the lack of reference to Katie. "I don't believe that for a minute. Nana, tell me what's happening here. When the lawyer asked questions about Angela and Katie, I heard curse words under your breath. I've never heard you say a bad word in my entire life."

She finally turned to face him. "Vernon, honey, you're just upset. The spoon was hot last night, that's all, and I dropped the teacup. There's nothing wrong here. And I talk to myself quite a bit nowadays. Don't worry about us right now. You should be concentrating on Angela and Katie."

Da hadn't moved from his position at the table and continued to stare out the window. The backyard was overgrown, the nose of his grandmother's Buick jutting out from the side of the house, the grass taller than the bumper. She used to keep it in the garage. The yard and flowers used to be beautiful, trimmed and pruned to perfection.

Matheson glanced at them. Both over eighty, their age didn't account for their behavior, particularly his grandfather's. The old man had always been the sharpest pencil he knew. Matheson pushed at them again.

"Da, what's happening here?"

His grandfather appeared as if he hadn't heard him. He was ramrod straight in the chair, his mind somewhere else as he stared out the window at a redbird that flitted from limb to limb. The old man appeared to be fascinated.

He tried again, a little louder. "Da?"

The old man startled and then shifted his gaze to lock on Matheson. His gray eyes were rheumy and unfocused. His body looked as exhausted as Matheson felt.

"What?" The old man stuttered. "What's wrong?"

"That's what I'm trying to find out from you."

"There's nothing wrong that your grandmother can't fix, even though I told her to stay out of it."

"Now what's that supposed to mean?" Matheson asked, looking at each of his grandparents.

The old man crossed his hands over his chest and puffed out his lower lip. He turned his face again toward the window. Matheson saw bruises on his arms, visible beneath his paper-thin skin. His hair was greasy, and he was in the same clothes he'd worn the day before that smelled faintly of smoke and bourbon.

Growing up with them, his grandmother took pride in ensuring they were properly clothed, groomed, and fed. His grandfather had never had to cook, clean, shop, or do any laundry in his life. If she was no longer able to do that, it partially explained their disheveled condition. Yet the old man had always taken pride in his looks, so much so that Matheson had a difficult time believing he would ever let himself get like this. A tall, stately man with white hair, Stanley Moore had always been a commanding fixture, a Vietnam War hero.

"Nana." He knew his sharp retort was too stern to address an elder, but Matheson had no time to waste. They were hiding something. "What is it that you are trying to fix? What is Da talking about?" Not responding, she tried to breeze by him, and he grabbed her arm.

"Vernon Matheson, you let go of my arm right this minute."

"Yes, ma'am, I will when you tell me what is wrong."

"We're just getting old, son. And for once, I will not let him push me around. Some things change as you get older. Some people," Matheson watched as she hatefully cut her eyes toward her husband, "just can't seem to understand what is happening around them."

Matheson's grandfather stood suddenly and strode around the dining table toward his wife. He stopped before her and leaned his six-foot frame forward until he towered over his five-foot-two wife. Matheson had been in that very position as a teenager until he finally outgrew his grandfather.

He shifted closer, ready to intervene. He had never seen his grandfather strike anyone, but there was always a first time. If he ever wondered why he loved war, he only had to look at the males in his family.

"I know full well what's going on." The old man's spittle hit his wife in the face as he shouted at her. "Don't make me look like a fool in front of Vernon. He's entitled to know what's been going on in his absence. You've kept your mouth shut now for over a year."

She backed away from her husband, only to wipe the spit from her face with her apron, then stepped forward again as she stabbed her index finger at his chest. Matheson couldn't resist a grin as he watched his grandmother poke such a surly bear this early.

"You waited until this happened just like I did. Why didn't you tell him?"

Da's shouts grew louder. "Because it wasn't my place. And I had no proof."

"Stop talking as if I weren't standing right here!" Matheson shouted at them. "Proof of what?" His grandparents went silent. He looked from one to the other. "Tell me right now, damn it, what has been going on. Right now—no more secrets."

Da opened his mouth to speak when Matheson's cell phone buzzed in his pocket. "What?" he yelled into the phone.

"Need you down at the morgue," Weaver said.

"Why?" Matheson retorted.

"You need to make an identification. Be here at eight-thirty when they open." The call was cut before Matheson could respond.

He clicked off the phone and strode to the front door, even as his heart hit the floor. "I need to leave. Do not think for one minute that this discussion is over."

"Where are you going?" his grandfather demanded. "You cannot yell at me and your grandmother like that, young man, and then walk away."

"They want me to identify a body at the morgue." Damn that detective and his cryptic demands. Which one would it be? Angela or Katie? The flashing started in his right eye with the slow creep of a migraine. If he didn't get this under control and fast, he would never make it to the morgue.

"At this time of morning?" his grandfather asked.

"I don't have a choice, Da," Matheson responded. "They want me to be there when they open. In traffic, it will take me almost an hour to get there." He had a sudden thought and felt the blood rush from his face as he turned to face his grandfather.

"Da, what if it's Katie?"

The old man looked as if he'd been slapped.

11

VERN

FRIDAY, 7:45 A.M.

Matheson slammed down the steps and rounded the side of the house at a run. The keys. He forgot the keys. As he turned back, a wad of keys hit him square in the chest. He swiped the keys from the ground as Nana's backside disappeared into the house. The front door slammed. He'd have to deal with their anger later.

The old Oldsmobile's engine was difficult to start. Faded leather seats matched a cracked dashboard, edges curling like a dried lake bed. A child's navy-blue sweater in the back seat caught his eye, and Matheson instantly wadded it to his face as the engine finally roared to life. Katie's sweet softness surrounded him. He folded it on the passenger seat beside him, determined to get through the next hour.

He called Danforth's cell and expected to leave a voicemail message this early, but she picked up immediately. He skipped the usual required small talk in South Carolina.

"Weaver wants me to identify a body."

"When?" she asked.

"At eight-thirty when the doors open. I'm on my way."

"I cannot believe that guy. I thought I made it clear he was to contact me, not you. See you at the morgue," she said. "I'm only a few minutes away at the office. Don't go inside without me."

"Understood." Matheson cut the call and dropped the phone in his shirt pocket. Just as he pulled onto Middle Street, he knew from experience that he shouldn't be driving. Pulling into the small parking lot at Breach Inlet, he faced the ocean and turned off the engine just as he collapsed across the front seat, his mind being pulled back to the war zone as he buried his face into Katie's sweater.

Looking up, he saw Darrell waving at him from the top of the path that led to the beach. Matheson closed his eyes and violently shook his head. When he opened them, the image of Darrell was gone. He tried to focus and be sure, yet the sound of the ocean waves faded.

The rifle-fire retorts told him they were significantly outnumbered; the enemy was scattered across the hills. Their sharpshooter was holed up in a half-collapsed barn on the nearest hillside, having the definite advantage with the high ground. His entire team was pinned down, with nowhere to move. He was trapped under an overturned wagon next to a well, with only a small crack on one side for his rifle. He kept the tip of his gun just inside the wagon in case the sharpshooter had a spotter, who would catch any movement.

Unless he called in a strike to the barn, they wouldn't make it. He would not be responsible for his entire team dying. These were his friends, his family. Sending the specific coordinates from his hiding spot, the response came quickly.

Two minutes out.

Returning fire to keep the other side engaged, he waited. Something moved, caught by the scope, a shadow in the open window from the direction of the rifle fire. He adjusted his rifle again on his shoulder, watching through his scope, and preparing to take the shot when the shadow moved again.

A young woman's face appeared, a teenager really, clearly defined in his scope. She was a football field away. Covered in a brightly patterned headscarf of red, green, and yellow, his scope was so intense that he could see the lashes that fringed her bright blue eyes. They searched for him out the window, and even though he knew she could not see him, her eyes seemed to stare right through him.

He shifted the rifle away from her. He refused to kill her or any other innocent without a reason. While many women here were as fierce as the men, others were non-combatants, caught in a war they didn't want and didn't fight. He adjusted his rifle scope again, finding her face once more.

Before he could register the sound of the helicopters, the woman's head disappeared into a cloud of pink mist. The force of the blast then hit him a second later, and the air sucked away from him was quickly followed by a cloud of dust that rolled over him, the wagon useless to protect him. The rations he'd had for breakfast threatened to come up.

Once the dust cleared, scattered pings from a single rifle shot blasted the stone wall somewhere behind him, the echoes rippling through the afternoon heat. He waited for additional gunfire, but for a few minutes, the village grew quiet. Goats next to his hiding place began to bleat. Someone was coming his way.

He tried to pinpoint the gunman's position through his scope, ignoring the bleating of the village goats, but saw no one from his limited angle. The barn hiding the sniper had been obliterated by the blast, as well as the houses below it where the girl lived. This was someone else—unless the sniper had escaped.

Hooves scattered frantically, the herd moving away from him. Something or someone approached. Underneath the wooden cart, he grasped the insides and ensured his feet were away from the open end. Footsteps approached, and the sweat dripped faster down his neck. He swallowed hard, his mouth unable to form spit because of the dust. He focused on the raw edge of a severed hand just beyond the end of the cart. A snuffle sounded from one of the village dogs as it inspected it, too close for his comfort. A paw stepped into his line of sight, then the toe of a dusty leather shoe...

12

LEE

FRIDAY, 7:45 A.M.

Hurricane Umberto stalled off the coast of Florida

My first coffee of the day surged through me to be quickly followed by a second in a travel mug. I had been going through my inbox, which Clarice dutifully filled to the brim each day, when Matheson's call interrupted my repetitive morning routine. I was a creature of habit, but with the Timberline Farm case still churning through the courts, all that routine was fast going out the window. I had thirty minutes before I needed to leave for the morgue, so I needed to get through as much of this pile as possible before then.

Every realtor and builder I represented seemed to need "one more" closing before I shifted to working for Mac full-time. New stacks of closing files were at my left elbow, containing title abstracts that had to be reviewed by an attorney, a requirement for every closing in South Carolina. Next to it were the final title policies for last month's closings and disbursement checks from those completed the day before. Old school, and somewhat paranoid, I signed everything, even those things I could—and should, I guess—delegate to Clarice.

I looked at the pile of paper, knowing I would have to work late tonight. Having declined Mac's offer of additional security was probably foolish. Working alone, especially since the Timberline Farm case, always made me nervous, since Victoria Marshall was out there somewhere. I punched the intercom button on my office phone.

"Hey Clarice, what's the news on Victoria?" I could hear my voice come through Clarice's speaker on the other side of the wall.

"The last I heard," Clarice replied, standing in my office doorway with a cup of coffee in her hand, "she was somewhere in South America, avoiding extradition."

"Good. I don't want to deal with her right now. Not with this next thing heating up."

Timberline Farm was my teenage workplace. As the assistant to its now-deceased owner, Jack Marshall, I was his secretary, then his friend, and later, in high school and college, his lover. Victoria was Jack's wife. She had killed Jack's estate attorney and then her own son. I knew that at some point, she would do everything possible to come after me.

"Well, you might as well get ready for her. You know she's going to make your life miserable if the Solicitor's office can ever get her back to the States," Clarice said.

"Yes, I know. Victoria will do anything to make herself look innocent, especially if she thinks it will make me look guilty of something. But I doubt Harbin's office is doing much. They are going to have to appoint a special prosecutor to get her extradited."

"You're probably right," Clarice said.

Jack and Victoria started the farm two decades prior, initially taking in homeless boys, then girls, and eventually expanding into two extensive facilities across Charleston and Berkeley counties in the Lowcountry of South Carolina. I was their guinea pig, experimented with and groomed by each into whatever they wanted to use me for. For Victoria, it was teasing older men with a very young girl to bring in more money. For Jack, I was his toy, his outlet for experimental behavior, religious, sexual, and otherwise, that as a Christian leader in the community, he had to keep hidden.

Used for years, and believing I was loved and in love, I was unceremoniously dumped by Jack when I was a senior in college and pregnant with his child. I had boxed that section of my life away, never wanting to think about it again.

Yet my past rose its ugly head when I was asked last year to investigate Jack and Victoria's son, Brad, his mismanagement of the farm, and his rape of one of the ranch girls. Against Clarice's advice and also against my better judgment, I forged ahead, eventually uncovering a trafficking ring exploiting the young children at the farm and throughout the community. Exposing the trauma experienced by the children at the farm, I also revealed my own, when my past with Jack came roaring into the present.

Throughout my entire life, including my relationships with others and my law practice, I suffered in ways I had never realized until now. I had been afraid of almost everything, harboring views of what "should" or "should not" be done based on the strict religious parameters Jack taught me as a teenager.

Only with the help of Dr. Zola DeLeon was I able to examine my relationship with Jack and understand how the PTSD from which I now still suffer affected me, making me extremely risk-averse, especially with my relationships with men. But it also made me recognize PTSD in others.

"What's happening?" Clarice asked. "What was that phone call about?"

"The Mt. Pleasant detective has insisted that Colonel Matheson meet him at the morgue at eight-thirty. I promise I'll clean out this inbox by the end of the day."

"Well, you need to get going then. There is nothing on the calendar today that's urgent. I'll fix you a to-go cup."

Military front-line experience or not, Matheson did not need the stress of seeing a dead body again, regardless of who. I could not imagine what wartime conditions had created in my client. Mac was already pushing me to get him to fulfill the order for medical treatment. Suspecting that the conditions in the military orders were not the norm, I reminded Mac on our last call that I was the man's attorney, not his nurse, doctor, or mother.

I grabbed my jacket. Luckily, I had my battle suit on, my favorite Alice + Olivia, which gave me an extra boost of confidence every time I had to go into the courtroom. I grabbed my purse and headed for the door. Regardless of the work piled on my desk, I knew that this case with Matheson would soon require every minute of my day. Something inside me said it also wasn't just the case. It was the man.

Accepting the thermos of perfectly prepared coffee from Clarice, I headed out the door to the parking lot on the side. Weaver knew better than to call my client directly. I'd have to call the Chief at Mount Pleasant on my way to the morgue in addition to giving the detective a few choice words once I arrived.

Driving toward the county morgue, I checked the weather. Hurricane Umberto was stalled off the coast of Florida, even with Orlando out in the Atlantic. The initial forecast had it making landfall at Melbourne, but it hadn't. This was not a good sign. I buzzed Matheson. The phone rang and clicked over to a full voicemail box. Undeterred, I tried again. Still no answer. Like a charm, the third time, he answered.

"Matheson." His voice sounded as if he were in a long, dark tunnel. Given what I knew from my own PTSD, that might be exactly where he was. Damn it, I needed to talk with Zola. If Matheson truly had PTSD or the more complex version, I was very much out of my comfort zone and needed her help.

"Hey, this is M.L. I don't know what that idiot told you, but don't rush."

"Why?" His voice was now alert. "I need to know whether it's Angela or Katie."

"It's neither," I replied. "I called the intake clerk at the morgue a few minutes ago. He's yanking your chain, and honestly, you're letting him. He wants you to take a look at the woman who was on your floor. Why? I have no idea. Do you?"

He let out a breath of air, and I waited for him to respond. "No, I don't. Why is this guy being such a prick?"

"Probably because he can. I'm going to visit with the Chief of Police after we finish. If he doesn't need you there to identify anyone, then there is something else he needs from you. I don't want him tying you up in knots while we determine his goal. Why don't you let me handle this? You're probably still jet-lagged."

"If it's related to my wife or child, you won't catch it. Besides, I'm almost there. And…"

"And what?"

"I need to be sure it's not her."

"You actually think the dead woman on your bedroom floor might be your wife?"

"I wasn't feeling too good when I found her, so…"

I thought about what my client was saying to me. Was there a possibility that he killed her, and he didn't remember? How could a man not know if a woman lying bloody on his floor was his wife or not? I decided to wait and see how this played out.

"Okay, it's your call. But if you get there first, wait for me to go in."

"Roger that."

I ended the call and quickly called my grandfather.

"Yes, my dear?" I loved hearing his Scottish brogue. My grandfather was my rock, and this was the time I needed him the most, out of my comfort zone, about to officially "step in it."

"I'm headed to the morgue. What can you tell me about the Medical Examiner?" I asked.

"She is thorough. Excellent on the witness stand."

"Ever heard of her being overly preferential to police?"

"Well, Lee," my grandfather's sarcastic Scottish brogue deepened, "the county does employ her."

"Yes, but is she fair?"

"I think so. Is there a situation to which I should be apprised?" he asked.

"Possibly," I replied. "The detective assigned to Matheson's case is being an asshole.

"Comes with the territory, my dear. Who is the detective assigned?"

"Guy named Weaver."

"Ah. The bottom of the barrel, then. I understand. He is untrustworthy, and I've heard rumors that he is dirty. I'll make several calls and see what specific details I can gather. I am sure Angus has run afoul of Weaver as well." The Judge hesitated. "Watch your back."

"Thanks," I said. "You know I will. And Judge,"

"Yes, my dear?"

"Thank you for always having mine."

"But of course. Call me if you need me."

13

VERN

FRIDAY, 8:30 A.M.

The morgue smelled of formaldehyde, dust, and strong disinfectant. The front receptionist area was vacant. Matheson popped the silver hotel reception bell on the counter so hard it bounced across the Formica counter several times. Even though Danforth had told him to wait for her, it was too hot to stay in the car. Still not seeing anyone in the office, he hit the bell again.

A large woman rounded the wall, approaching the thick glass as her flapping flats amplified through the tinny speaker.

"Hold your horses." Her southern accent oozed like honey. She set her mug of tea on her desk, perched bright green sequinned readers attached to a beaded neck chain on her nose, and then looked at him through thick lenses, an unspoken question on her face.

Matheson leaned over to talk through the speaker. "I'm here to meet Detective Weaver."

Her distorted voice responded. "And you are?"

"Vernon Matheson."

She checked what looked to be a logbook. "And the date of the incident?"

"Yesterday, I guess. I don't know. Weaver just told me to come here."

She pointed to one of the orange plastic chairs. "Have a seat."

The woman's bracelets jangled as she slowly pecked the keyboard with the brightly polished nails of her index fingers. Matheson stuffed his hands under his thighs to keep them from hitting anything within striking distance, but could not stop his knee from its rapid-fire bouncing.

The front door opened, and Matheson looked up. Danforth walked up to him in a different suit from the late night before, this one a deep, wine-red. Her long blonde hair was again up in a French braid. His first thought was what all that hair would look like unpinned. He squelched that thought, not wanting to get caught up in whatever he'd wrapped himself in when he'd met her ten years ago. He'd chalked it up to lust then and kept his distance. But the attraction was still here, though different. And stronger.

Danforth smiled, and Matheson wondered what the initials of her name stood for. She had always said "M.L. or Danforth" when he called. He would visit the bar association's website later and look it up.

She leaned over, her mouth close to his ear. "Did you not understand the words 'wait for me before you go in'?"

"Sorry," he whispered back. "It's been a rough week." The faint scent of her perfume lingered, taunting him.

Danforth sat with a huff, leaving an empty chair between them. He seemed to be pissing off everyone he knew just by simply living.

The receptionist's typing echoed loudly through the small metal window until they were interrupted by a short man in green scrubs. After introductions, Matheson and Danforth followed Assistant Coroner Bob Adger through double hospital swinging doors, down a claustrophobic hallway lit by buzzing incandescent tubes. At the end, Adger motioned for them to wait in the hall while he went inside the room. While they waited, Detective Weaver came through the double doors. He reached them but said nothing to either of them.

"Detective," Danforth said after thirty seconds of silence, "You can't continue to contact my client directly. Want to tell me why we're here?"

"I need him to confirm the identity in front of me." Weaver refused to look at her, and Matheson felt the anger start twisting in his gut. "This is my case, and I don't take others' words for things. But honestly, even with the photo you gave me, since I don't know how long ago it was taken, I think you should be the one to confirm that neither of these women is Angela. "

When Adger was ready, Matheson approached the window, took one look at the uncovered body on the table, and then frantically looked toward Danforth. He covered his mouth with one hand as nausea roiled in his stomach. Bolting down the hallway, he reached a lined garbage can in the corner with no time to spare. After the initial heave, his stomach refused to stop, and forced dry heaves continued.

The face of the Afghan woman, always present in his memory, hovered in front of his eyes. Smoke filled his nostrils as the memory of her exploding into pink mist rocked through his mind. She had not deserved to die so horribly. Collateral damage, she had been called, simply in the way of the air support he had called in to assist. He tried to breathe, forcing his mind to calm and stop the image.

Matheson felt a hand on his back, and a wet, white cloth appeared on his right. "This should never have happened." M.L.'s voice behind him was soft. "I knew I should have stopped it from the get-go. You are going to have to let me do my job, Colonel."

Matheson took the cloth from her, stood upright, and wiped his face. When finished, he tossed it in the garbage can. Weaver could dig out the vomit if he wanted DNA. Nervous about being too far from the garbage can, he lowered himself to the floor and stared from a distance at the window where the body waited, waiting for his stomach to settle. He focused on M.L.'s black pumps and muscled calves while willing his mind to clear.

The worn toes of two scuffed brown loafers appeared, with a tassel missing on the right shoe.

"Not now, Weaver." Danforth's voice was commanding enough that Matheson could see the man move two steps back. Standing, Matheson first looked at Weaver, then regretted it. It was all Matheson could do not to slap the extreme confidence off the detective's face. His body's reaction seemed to confirm his guilt to the detective.

He glanced at Danforth. "Reminded me too much of something that happened overseas." M.L. only nodded. He noticed that she kept her distance from him, as if he had leprosy. They walked back toward the viewing window. Did she also think he was guilty?

"Cover that body," M.L. ordered the detective. Weaver motioned to Adger inside the room. After covering the body and pushing it further away from the window, the assistant medical examiner returned.

"We need the bag," Weaver said. Adger retrieved a small child's backpack from a storage bin. As Matheson reached for it, Weaver shook his head. "Look at it. Don't touch." The detective requested Adger roll another table in front of the window as he pulled items from the backpack. Matheson recognized nothing until Adger reached the end, and Katie's hot pink rabbit's foot dangled from his finger. Vern had given it to her as part of her fifth birthday present.

"Where did you find that backpack?" Matheson asked casually, forcing himself not to react to the rabbit's foot. He took two steps toward the autopsy room. "I'm ok now. I can see that woman again."

Weaver moved to block the door. "I can't let you go in there.

This is still an active investigation. Only the ME, coroner, police, or the arson investigator can enter. You'll have to look from here."

Matheson drew himself upward as if in parade dress, not the sandy BDUs that now smelled of vomit. As if to issue an order, he turned to face Weaver. He felt Danforth's hand grasp his bicep. Her blue eyes locked onto his, and his anger began to recede.

"I need to see her up close. She has something specific that will let me identify her." He leaned over and whispered to her. "Trust me on this. I won't lose it again."

Danforth's eyes squinted as she nodded. She turned to Weaver. "Let him see her again."

"There are two of them." Weaver nodded to Adger and pointed to the bank of refrigerated doors. Adger wheeled a second body up to the window. "Just need to know if you recognize either of them," Weaver said.

"I can't be sure from here," Matheson said.

Danforth narrowed her eyes at Weaver and shifted to stand in front of Matheson, one leg thrust to the side, her arms crossed over her chest. "Let's get this over with. Let him in there. Now."

Weaver was shaking his head. "There are cameras..."

Matheson stepped so close to the detective that he could feel the man's coffee breath on his face. In return, knowing how badly his vomit breath smelled, he hissed in Weaver's face. "Then turn them off."

With Weaver's nod, Adger walked across the room and paused the camera over the door. He proffered each of them a cotton mask, a gown, and blue gloves. Matheson first walked to the table to examine the backpack's contents. He could not readily identify anything that belonged to Angela or Katie besides the rabbit's foot. He wondered again where it had been found.

Next, he moved to the second woman. Angela had a birthmark behind her right ear. Bending sideways, he saw nothing on this woman's head. Lying flat on the table, a sheet covered the woman's body except her legs and feet, which appeared to be missing. The distinct odor of pluff mud and cigarettes emanated from the body, as well as the normal odors of decomposition he was accustomed to from his tours. He watched as Danforth leaned over, inspecting the woman's ragged fingernails. The poor woman had put up a fight with something dangerous that didn't appear to be human.

"What happened to this woman?" she asked Adger as she stood. The examiner looked at Weaver, who gave a slight nod.

"Alligator," Adger said. "At least, that is the preliminary assumption. We'll know more later."

"Who is she?" Danforth asked Weaver.

"That's why you're here. We need her identified."

Matheson searched for anything familiar about this woman and came up empty. From a distance, she looked enough like Angela to be her sister. Yet up close, there were apparent differences from his wife. This woman had a mole on her collarbone, a small tattoo on the side of her hand, but no birthmark. And the hair was different. This woman was a bottle blonde, unlike Angela, who was a natural strawberry blonde.

He shifted to the body he'd seen initially and, along with the smoke, smelled a combination of cologne and the distinct smell of whisky. Matheson committed the scent to memory, wondering why the cologne was familiar. He had survived in Afghanistan by using all his senses. It appeared he would have to do the same in the States. He looked again for the birthmark behind the woman's ear, but there was nothing.

He looked at Danforth. "This woman is twenty years or more older than my wife. I don't know the other one either."

"Thank you, Colonel. Since they both matched the description we have for Angela, I wanted to be sure."

Danforth interrupted. "No, you wanted to screw with my client. You knew neither was Angela. I'll admit they look a little similar from a distance, but in the facial photo we gave you, even

I can tell neither is my client's wife. You didn't need him down here."

Weaver's lips twisted to one side, then back to the center. "I had to be sure."

"I need to know what you have on this woman, Weaver," Danforth said as she pointed to the woman found in Matheson's bedroom. "Stop the games."

"Human trafficking. Mainly children."

Matheson would never be able to hear those words in proximity to each other again without flinching. His imagination attempted to interject the possibility of what had happened to his daughter, and he turned to look at Danforth. Her eyes were wide, mouth set into a hard line. He focused on his attorney, and the disgusting image finally receded.

"We know that already," Danforth retorted. "What else?"

Their focus away from him, Matheson shifted behind Weaver and Adger. He slowly reached behind his back and felt the corner of the table with the backpack. Feeling the pink rabbit's foot touch his finger, he snatched it.

"From surveillance," Weaver replied, "we think she was there for a transaction."

"This woman tried to buy my client's child?" Danforth's voice was indignant. "You guys were watching and did nothing about it?"

"Ms. Danforth, I didn't say that we were there that day. I have no idea what was transpiring. That's what I need your client to tell me," Weaver responded. "I think he knows more than he's saying."

"Yeah, right. We're done here," Danforth said. "Go find my client's family."

14

LEE

FRIDAY, 9:30 A.M.

Matheson never said a word in the parking lot about the hot pink rabbit's foot he squeezed repeatedly in his left hand. I knew it was his lifeline to Katie, and with him on shaky footing, I said nothing. I was surprised that neither Weaver nor Adger caught that Matheson hadn't returned it to the backpack.

I was still shaken from the news that taking Timberline Farm out of the equation in Charleston had apparently done nothing to stop the trafficking problem. We needed to know who was behind it all, and I knew Victoria Marshall could easily reveal that. Perhaps Mac and I should discuss tracking her down ourselves, since Charleston County didn't seem to be doing much.

Matheson and I had paused underneath a giant live oak tree extending over the parking area of the morgue and waited to talk privately until after Weaver had driven away. Shaking my hand in the parking lot, Matheson refused to let go, his pale Caribbean-green eyes searching mine with a fierceness I'd not seen in a man since Jack.

There it is again. I was immediately rattled.

"I'm sorry I lost it in there." His gaze was still locked on me like a radar, or in his case, like a laser beam attached to a long-distance rifle.

"No reason to apologize. I toss my cookies regularly when I'm stressed." His heated focus on me scared me silly. My heart began to thump faster as my anxiety ramped up. I was one screwed up person when it came to relationships, and this man was pushing every possible boundary I had thrown up my entire life. To say I was attracted to him was an understatement.

Thanks to Clarice's long-suffering patience and the constant attention and treatment by Dr. Zola, my emotional life was finally beginning to emerge out of the tightly locked box I'd kept it in since college, when Jack dumped me and I'd given up our child for adoption. Being forced to be separated from two of the most important people in my life obliterated my trust in people, not just men.

Since I held everyone at arm's length, my love life was complicated. I never shared anything with anyone. I'd known Clarice for over fifteen years, yet I'd never confessed my relationship with Jack to her until this year. It was too painful. And embarrassing. And now this man seemed to be intent on blasting his way through my barricade.

We stood in the parking lot, no words passing between us as our hands were locked, yet a thousand unsaid things were transmitted back and forth. I could literally feel his pain, the trauma of whatever he had experienced overseas, undergirding the stress and concern he had for his missing daughter. He was teetering on the edge, and I could feel it.

It wouldn't be fair to any man wanting a relationship with me to have to unpack all my trauma, let alone for a man whose trauma far exceeded mine. Yet, did that make it more balanced? I tried to wipe these crazy thoughts from my mind and stay professional. This man was my client, nothing more.

Yes, I'd dated now and then, primarily for sex, sometimes for friendship, but never for love. Mac had made his attraction known, and I'd squelched it, immediately controlling the situation, just like I had to do with this one. And as I'd told Clarice, a relationship was out of the question. Besides, there was no way I'd ever let another man look at me or touch me without me being entirely in control, especially a client. I couldn't afford to get hurt at that level again. Yet this man looked at me as if I were his lifeline, his only reason for living.

Damn it, I could not look away. Nor could I deny the physical attraction between us. It first happened when I met him years ago with his off-the-wall real estate transaction. I'd done the work and had never seen him again. The attraction then frightened me a bit, and I was relieved when he told me that all future correspondence would be by email, given that he was perpetually overseas.

The attraction I felt for him frightened me even more now. It was stronger. I was also concerned that this might impact how I handled his case.

His dark, good looks were enhanced today by his constant five o'clock shadow and the outline of his well-developed muscles that strained in worn but neatly tucked BDUs. He had apparently spent most of his life outside in harsh sunlight from the crow's feet at the edge of his eyes. The added years and his life overseas had turned him into someone formidable.

His body naturally stood at attention. This man had none of the usual physical habits I'd experienced with men. He exhibited no wasted movement at all. Other than tapping his fingers on the table at his grandparents' house, he had no quirky habits. Since yesterday, however, there had been an intensely focused anger on his face. Alone just then, the anger dropped, and he looked at me with a painful, haunting expression, revealing his vulnerability.

I felt myself come unwrapped right there in that parking lot. But I couldn't do this. This man has issues—hell, I have my own problems—and he is my client. Just no. I tugged my hand again, but he didn't release it.

"We can't do this, Matheson," I said to him softly.

"I'm not sure we have the option of declining," he responded, his voice a whisper. "This seems to be bigger than both of us. I know I'm not in control here. Are you?"

I shook my head, unable to respond. The energy passing between us was something I'd never experienced. I let another minute pass, reluctant to let him go. He needed me now, I could feel it, but I had no idea what to do. Finally, I stepped back, our hands still locked.

"What can I do to help you? I think you're about to come apart." I asked softly.

"You know that only if you've been in the same type of situation."

"Not the same, no, but similar enough to know the desperation and hopelessness you're feeling." I slowly pulled my hand from his. If we didn't find his wife and daughter soon, this man would crack into tiny pieces.

"I'm headed to the police chief's office," I told him quietly. "It would be better if you went back to your grandparents. Your sheer size will cause a problem at the station."

Matheson broke his gaze, and I felt as if I'd been doused with a bucket of cold water. He reluctantly released my hand and bent to unlock the ancient Oldsmobile. I touched his arm. A jolt of familiar energy passed through my fingertips, and I jerked my arm outward, losing my balance. Matheson abruptly stood upright and turned, catching me with an arm around my waist before I fell. When I regained my balance, he suddenly released me.

"I'm sorry. I must smell terrible."

I stepped back, conscious of his heat radiating toward me with something else that was unidentifiable. "No, you don't smell, and I was just going to remind you—"

"No," he interrupted softly. "You wanted to see if it would happen again."

"What?" I asked.

Matheson looked at me, his eyes the color of the ocean, confirming he had felt the jolt of energy pass between us.

"You're scaring me a little," I said.

"No, this is scaring both of us a lot." He backed away from me and waited until I got into my car before getting into his. I had to get away from him. Now.

So, I fled.

As I drove off toward Charleston, my first thought was that I wasn't sure I could do this again, not just because of the man, but also because of the case. It was my first case with Mac, a serious criminal matter involving a small child. I needed to get a handle on my feelings and my actions before this man twisted my head so far around that I could no longer adequately represent him.

15

LEE

FRIDAY, 10:30 A.M.

Pulling the car into a Publix parking lot not far from the morgue, I looked up the number for the Family Psychology practice. My shoulders relaxed and stomach unclenched as I went through the process of booking an appointment with Zola's assistant. I took several minutes afterward to breathe, surrendering to the relaxation technique the doctor had taught me.

Back on track, my next call was to the Mount Pleasant police chief, where I requested an immediate appointment. While on hold, I thought through my various options. As expected, I could only have a quick phone call, as no appointment slots were available. Once the chief came on the line, I forced myself to use Clarice's honey approach to undermine Weaver, her saying that you "win more bees with honey than vinegar," or however it goes.

Voicing my concerns to the chief, I received only vague assurances and platitudes. No matter, I had plenty of other, less savory tactics I could try. And, of course, the Judge always had creative—and legal—ideas.

Pulling into the lot next to my office, I cut through the back garden, letting the smell of the confederate jasmine that covered the old brick walls wash over me. I had gutted and renovated the old building, converting it into my office below and an apartment above, which I rented to an English professor teaching at the College of Charleston when I moved out to Isles End with my grandfather.

"Honey, I'm home!" My shout got a laugh from Clarice in the kitchen, probably preparing her fifteenth cup of coffee of the day.

"How was Deadville?" She didn't look up as I walked into the kitchen. She was wearing a royal blue dress that seemed to float around her. Now that her children were grown and her husband had retired on full disability, I swore her entire paycheck went to her wardrobe. I needed to start taking notes. Mine consisted of suits for the office and worn-out T-shirts and shorts for the beach.

I grabbed a mug. "The victims can't help being there."

"I know," she smiled wistfully at me, "but the word morgue is so distasteful. Do you have a better word?" She took her first sip, testing the amount of half and half.

"I'll think of one, maybe. Do you have time to chat? I need to run a few things by you."

"Sure. Be there in a sec."

Dumping heated oat milk into my double espresso, I headed for my office. I collapsed into the leather desk chair that my grandfather had given me, which was so comfortable that I had slept in it on many occasions. It had been a graduation present, and even though it was almost two decades old, it was still in fine shape.

Clarice was more than her title of Practice Manager. She had been my best friend for fifteen years. We had been in and out of each other's houses with picnics and dinners, trips to the beach, track meets for her niece's friend, all the things that families did with each other. It did not matter our real heritage or color; we were family, a relationship that had been thoroughly tested with the Timberline Farm case. I did not relish the thought of all that racial discussion returning with Victoria's trial.

"What's up?" Clarice flounced onto the couch. When I didn't respond, she focused her attention on me, picking up on an unspoken vibe. I came from behind my desk and sat across from her in one of the comfortable chairs.

"There's that look," she said. "Did something happen today?"

"Yeah, you could say that." I didn't know what look I'd given her, but it wouldn't matter. Clarice, I swore, had a double dose of extra-sensory perception.

"Spill."

"Aside from this detective that gives me weird vibes, I have client issues."

"What kind of issues? Did he make a pass at you? Lie to you?" Her face was alarmed. "Oh no. Did he kill that woman?" Her eyes wide with concern, I knew she was mentally extrapolating about what might have happened to Angela and Katie.

"You're jumping to more conclusions than I am. Slow down, Speedy."

"Well, start at the beginning, then. You need to catch me up anyway." I brought her current, to the point where I walked out of the morgue. I hesitated to talk about what I'd felt with Matheson. Clarice had pushed me for a decade to do more than 'just hook-up,' as she called my quick liaisons. I wasn't sure Matheson needed to experience Clarice's match-making manipulations.

"What do you think happened to the wife and child?" she asked.

"At this point, I have no idea. Given the party he walked in on, I think the wife is into some serious shit. But the child? She should have appeared by now, either at the grandparents' house or a neighbor's. Weaver confirmed the dead woman was there for trafficking purposes, and that doesn't bode well for the child. If we don't find Katie soon, we never will. The first few days are the most important, and Weaver is futzing around like he has all the time in the world."

"What's your take on Weaver?"

"He's dirty—and the Judge confirmed that. For some reason, he's stalling. Is it related to the dead woman? To the drugs at the party? I have no idea, but he has something to do with whatever is going on."

"How do you feel about the Colonel?"

"That's what I wanted to talk about. I met him before you started working with me. You know our client, Island Transactional?

"Yes. One of the corporate retainer clients. You don't have a lot of business with them."

"'Them' is Vernon Matheson. I set up that offshore for him and several others." I listed off the company names that she would be familiar with from the accounting invoices.

"That's a long time ago," Clarice said. "He's not been to this office that I'm aware of. Why have you kept him under wraps all this time?"

"He hired me at the beginning of my practice to set up those offshore companies. He needed to hide his ownership of a large tract of land in Awendaw from his father and wanted the ultimate level of corporate shell game. I learned a great deal, especially about what is legal and what is not when moving money to the islands. I'm on retainer for small ministerial tasks related to those companies that are still on our books. Because my invoices are sent to one of the shell companies, I'd forgotten the connection until Mac called me to represent him."

"Why the recognition then?"

"You haven't met him. He's not someone you can easily forget." I could feel the blush start at the bottom of my neck and rush up my face. "I'll wait for your opinion the first time you meet him."

"Oh no you don't. You're not going to make me wait." I hesitated, and she scooted forward on the couch. "You are blushing! Spill."

"He looks at me the way Jack used to. Only more intense." I

let out a long breath. "His eyes talk to me without words, and I swear I can feel his energy the minute I walk into the room. When Weaver interviewed him at his grandparents' house, I made him understand what needed to happen with a simple touch." I hesitated, collecting my thoughts. "Yet now he's different. He is the angriest person I've seen in a long time. There's a lot hidden inside that man, even more than there was before."

Clarice was speechless for the first time in a very long time.

"I know. I'm unsure how to handle this. I've booked a session with Zola, but I'm already on a large roller coaster going very, very fast. I guess I'm making sure you are ok with the ride."

Indignant, she put her hands on her hips. "You know I have your back, just like the last time when you had mine with all that East End crap." The Timberline Farm matter had involved missing girls from her sister's North Charleston neighborhood and a realization on my part that I had ignored much of what the Black community had experienced in Charleston, both historically and currently.

"It's going to be more than that," I insisted. "I thought I had issues, what with my anxiety, the throwing up at the least provocation, and then Zola telling me I have PTSD. But this guy's is exponentially greater than mine, given his background and what happened to him yesterday. When I talked to Mac again this morning, he said even though Matheson left the military officially under a medical retirement, he has to have a psychological evaluation within five days of landing in the States. He's been here two already."

"Do you think he will talk to Zola?" she asked.

"I have no idea. I can already tell he's starting to crumble; I just haven't caught him when it happens. I'm going to try to talk to him about it today and see if he will meet with her."

"Why is his mental state your responsibility, Lee?" Her face now showed concern rather than alarm.

"You were there to shore me up, Clarice. This man has no one other than a drug-fueled wife and two very elderly grandparents. His daughter's disappearance is about to put him over the edge."

"I'll get with Zola as soon as possible and start putting together other resources just in case. But Lee," she reached out to take my hand, "please protect yourself. I don't want you to have to go through another fifteen years of grief."

"Neither do I." I squeezed her hand then let go as she sat back on the couch, her mouth twisted with curiosity.

"Why this man? Why now? I wanted you to have time after this mess with Jack's death. You need to be free, roam the world, have a love life for once with no strings, no baggage, and for goodness' sake, nothing like this." Clarice shifted forward on the couch. "What do you see in this man? Is he a bad boy with a good heart, maybe?"

"Honestly? I don't know, but my gut tells me to follow wherever this goes. I don't know why I'm attracted to him. I haven't had time to figure it out."

"Well, think about it now. How did you react to him when you met him the first time?"

"The same way. Almost an electrical zap." I rubbed my fingers together. "My heart rate jumps ridiculously, and I can't breathe." I forced myself to consider why I would even be attracted to this man. "But it's more than a physical thing. He and I are very similar in how we look at things. And I admire how he is trying to deal with all this himself. His character shows through, even when he's almost frantic over the disappearance of his child."

Clarice squinted at me carefully. "How did he react the first time, and then again now?"

"He feels it too. He confirmed it this morning." I could picture Matheson's eyes boring into mine back at the morgue parking lot. "I'm telling you, this man wants me and is moving hard and fast. And, as you know, he's married." I blurted out. "Just like the last time. This is becoming a trend."

"I need to meet him," she interrupts, "because you're not ready, and no, this isn't a trend."

"Yeah," I nodded. "I need your impression."

"Does Mac know any of this?"

"You are the only one I've told. Matheson can tell Mac if he wants; they are good friends after all. I will not tell anyone else, except my grandfather, of course, and I ask that you keep it to yourself. We have a child to find and a mess to wade through. I will not take any action until that is resolved. Then we will see. I need your help to focus. Make sure I'm representing him adequately and keeping my emotions under control."

Clarice stood, pulling me to my feet and enveloping me in a hug. "Like always, I'm here."

16

WEAVER

FRIDAY, 9:30 A.M.

Weaver left the Charleston County morgue knowing he had just pulled off one of the most stupid stunts in his career. His goal was to sidetrack Matheson and Danforth, get them to waste time trying to figure out what the death of the other woman that two street officers in Park Circle had pulled from the marsh this morning had to do with Matheson's wife.

The woman had been mauled by alligators, and to his knowledge, this was not something that routinely happened in Charleston. Frequent stories of alligator attacks came from Hilton Head and other parts of Florida, but most involved small dogs, with a few attacks on older people who were too slow to get out of the way. This woman, who was under forty, appeared healthy despite having lost the lower half of her body. Did it have anything to do with Matheson's missing wife and child? He had no idea. Yet.

Weaver doubted that either the man or his attorney knew anything about the attack on the woman, but if it threw them off base, even a little, it was worth his antics. And he had learned two things about Matheson and M.L. Danforth: Vernon Matheson had some serious mental issues, clearly exhibited by the way he reacted, and given Danforth's excessive reactions to most things involving her client, something personal was going on between them.

Pulling into a detective's parking slot, Weaver took his time before going into the office. He looked down at his wrinkled shirt, dirty tie, khakis, and scuffed loafers. He needed to get himself together. No one on the force knew that Darla had left him last week, and if he didn't clean up his act, it wouldn't take long before his direct supervisor, Captain Norcross, or even the Chief of Police would figure it out. The captain was all about the squeaky-clean image of the town's force, including his detectives.

At his desk, he flipped through the pink telephone slips handed to him by the officer at the front desk and stuffed them into his jacket pocket. There was nothing that couldn't wait.

"Weaver!" The captain's shout of his name echoed across the bullpen. A few of the other guys looked up, but with a glare from the detective, they went back to their business.

"Yes, sir." Weaver stood in the open doorway, waiting to be invited into the captain's office, where the chief of police sat in one of the guest chairs. This could only mean trouble.

"Got a call you should be aware of," the captain said, leaning back in his chair, an irritated look on his face as he gestured for Weaver to come inside and sit.

"Sir?" Weaver said, even though he knew exactly what was about to happen—Danforth.

"The chief here just got a call from an attorney, one you met with at the morgue this morning. She had quite a checklist of concerns, and every one of them was about you." Norcross shifted forward in his chair and flipped open a file folder on his desk.

"Sir, I didn't—" he began as he hitched his trousers up to sit.

"I have to tell you," Norcross said, interrupting Weaver as his index finger ran down a handwritten page in front of him, "that all of the things she told me sounded exactly like something you would do. I took you on here because I know you're a good detective, even though you were hung out to dry in Columbia."

Weaver had started in Columbia, South Carolina's capital. First, he began with the city police department, and later became a detective at the South Carolina Law Enforcement Division, also known as SLED. He had good arrest and conviction records, but there were several cases where he cut a few corners. While he wasn't prosecuted, the Internal Affairs investigation required him to resign or be terminated for his sloppiness. He resigned, telling his wife he wanted to be nearer the coast, to have a calmer work life, and be closer to the fishing.

What he really needed was to be several hours away from the bookie he owed money to. After his interview with the Charleston PD, they became uninterested following a conversation with the IA at SLED. Weaver was still unsure how Mount Pleasant had accepted him, but he knew better than to ask.

"Yes, sir. And I appreciate what you did for me, sir. But I—" Weaver looked for help toward the chief, but instead received the man's cold stare in return.

"So did he identify the woman?" asked Norcross.

"Looked at both but could identify neither," Weaver said. "He also looked through the backpack we found at the scene, but did not identify any of the contents. He took a pink rabbit's foot, and I let him."

"Why?"

"If we need a warrant later, it will make it easier since he's taken evidence."

Norcross looked at the Chief of Police, but neither man said a word. Weaver knew he had probably screwed up, but at the time with the rabbit's foot, he needed to take advantage of the situation, even if he never used it.

"And he might as well have told me to my face that he was guilty," Weaver added. "He threw up right in front of me."

The chief sat forward in his chair.

"Weaver," the chief began, "we need to tread lightly. This is a highly decorated officer who has been given a full medical discharge by the military for PTSD issues that occurred from all the operations he has been involved in. You might not have seen what you thought you saw."

Weaver remained silent, waiting to see what they would hit him with next. Had they figured out that he had deliberately had the autopsies of both women shoved down the line? Theron Fish's woman would most definitely be in the system, and his investigation would turn into a nightmare once her fingerprints were taken and she was identified.

It wasn't just Harbin's connection he was worried about, but his own connection to Fish. Weaver had been the one to tell the trafficker about Angela Matheson's need for money and the substantial value of her curly red-headed child on the open market—easy cash in little pink tennis shoes. For him, it had been a win-win situation until now.

He had to continue to slow down this investigation.

"What other woman did you have him attempt to identify?" Norcross asked. "The woman pulled out of the marsh this morning?"

"Yes, sir," Weaver said, directing his response to the chief. "It's a gut reaction, and she looks a lot like Matheson's missing wife. I still need time to connect the dots, but I think he's involved with both women, even though he says he doesn't know either of them. I mean, it's his house—"

The chief interrupted this time. "Where are we in locating his wife and child? They've been missing since yesterday."

"I have officers canvassing his neighborhood. Sullivan's Island is working on it because the grandparents are there, and we are getting as much information as possible."

"It's been almost twenty-four hours, detective. You know what that means with a missing child." The chief leaned back and crossed his arms over his chest.

"Yes, I know." Weaver tried not to show his exasperation. "I'm moving as fast as I can. This Danforth woman is just not helpful. She's constantly in the way."

"You don't know who this woman is, do you?" Norcross asked.

"Danforth?" Weaver asked, his face twisted in confusion. "She's just a local lawyer."

"She's Judge Rhineholdt's granddaughter," said the chief. "His heir apparent. That man can make your life, and mine, absolutely miserable if he wants to."

Weaver sat back in his chair. He had heard of Judge Rhineholdt mostly from Harbin. The retired judge had been partially responsible for pulling Harbin into the actual arrest of traffickers out at Timberline Farm. The solicitor was afraid of the old man, but Weaver had never asked why. Just one more thing he didn't want to know.

The chief uncrossed his arms and pointed an index finger at the door. "Ok, Weaver. Keep going, but try to stay on the good side of that attorney. Your priority is finding the wife and child. Once the ME has finished, then we can meet again to discuss what evidence you have concerning the dead woman."

17

ANGELA

FRIDAY, 9:45 A.M.

The house was a charred mess, still smoking as the firemen combed through the ashes, putting out hot spots. Angela stood on the sidewalk, a block down from her nearest neighbor, her body tense with shock. She stepped behind a hedge that ran along the sidewalk in front of a section of townhouses and continued to watch through a gap in the leaves, hiding from her neighbors.

She hated them all. They had called the police on her every week, even though all she wanted was a little fun, an escape from the drag of being a wife and mother. She hated her life, even though she was responsible for it. She thought being married to someone like Vern would be better than her life as a waitress. He'd never known who she really was, where she came from, and how fast she was headed downhill with the booze and the parties.

When she got pregnant, she leaned on his grandfather for help, begging and pleading for him to make Vern understand there was no way she could get an abortion. She was religious, and the baby was a precious thing, yada, yada, yada. All of it was a lie. She just wanted a new source of funds.

And she got it. And Katie.

She'd fallen in love with her daughter in the first minute after she popped into the world, and for the first three years, she had been the perfect mother, clean and sober. Then Katie started pre-school, and there were too many empty hours on hand. With no prior experience or higher education, she found no job that would take her other than waitressing or cleaning houses.

She looked down at the dirty jeans and T-shirt she was wearing, immediately craving the feel of a warm shower she had anticipated all morning. Waking at the apartment where she usually crashed when she was too messed up to go home, she'd gathered her things and flipped Merle off as she'd left. He was part of the reason she was in this mess.

Yet most of the responsibility was hers. Sean had made it too easy after she'd injured her ankle, with his pills and pillow talk, but he'd also given her a legitimate way out, even pushing her hard one night to let him take her to the rehab center himself and check her in. She'd declined. She wanted to ride the roller coaster just a little longer before Vern came home and reality came crashing in.

Her husband would never understand, Mr. Big Military Man. Vern had chased his dreams for years, and in his world, Angela knew she was an afterthought. Her dreams did not count. Only Katie was important to him. She could tell from the calls he made that he really didn't want to talk with her, only with her daughter.

Katie. She loved her daughter, but sometimes, especially lately, she wished she had never been born.

Now with Vern's grandmother, her precious child would be in school. Angela would have to pick her up this afternoon via car share, given that the Volvo in the destroyed garage in front of her was just a smoking metal shell. She closed her eyes and tried to remember what day she had dropped Katie off with Althea. Angela grabbed her phone and looked at the date.

No. No, no, no, no, no. NO!

Her heart sank as the memory of what she had done the day

before came rushing back. She pawed through her purse, locating what was left of the cash the woman had given her, solid evidence of her actions. Angela collapsed on the grass behind the hedge, tears streaming down her face.

Surely she had not done this.

But she had. With no fix for days, Angela had been desperate for money. All of Vernon's credit cards were maxed out, and the autopay wouldn't clear them for the next month of purchases until Monday. There was no money in their joint account except for one dollar, to keep it open so Vern wouldn't get a notice. Stupid Ellison wouldn't give her anything anymore, and her other sources had dried up. Only Merle would give her just enough to tide her over.

She hadn't been thinking yesterday. High on coke and having fun at the party, she needed more—and different. She'd called the number Eddie had given her. The woman had arrived in less than half an hour, and Angela had been free then. She had grabbed one of the guys at the party who sold her the H-bomb for the release she needed.

And now that she was out of the drug-fueled haze and insanity of the night before, the reality of what she had done hit her square in the chest like a sledgehammer.

She had sold Katie.

18

VERN

FRIDAY, 10:00 A.M.

Hurricane Umberto's intensity builds as it slowly spins north off the coast of Florida

Matheson jerked awake, confused for a second until he remembered he was in the morgue parking lot. Nana's old clunker was hot, old, and dusty, but his nose was filled with the stench of the familiar mix of smoke, whisky, and cheap cologne.

He cracked the car windows to let out the hot air. Trained to awake on command, he had mentally scheduled himself for thirty minutes. Although exhausted, he had no time to sleep longer. He had to find his daughter. His clothes were soaked from the sweat of his nightmare, the continuing segments involving his parents and the fights that never ended. They weren't exactly like his flashbacks, but just as vivid, just as real.

Leaving the morgue, he headed toward Mount Pleasant, pushing the Oldsmobile past the speed limit. Reaching his neighborhood, he parked the car as close as possible to what was left of the townhouse. To say it was a total loss was not even close. It was flat. And black. The heat of the fire must have been tremendous.

Only lumps of melted appliances, the frame of the car, the steps out back, and the concrete pad were left. Not even the fireplace remained standing.

Tendrils of smoke twisted slowly in circles toward the cloudless sky. Several firemen were still at the scene, combing through embers, one with a fire hose in the crook of his arm, scavenging for hot spots. The house on either side was charred as well, and his neighbor's roof was burned on one side. He stood alone on the sidewalk, not daring to talk to anyone, lest he be lashed with the anger of his neighbors. Returning to the car, he called his grandparents, where he unfortunately had to leave a message, then his insurance agent, and finally a rental car company.

He was starting to spiral. This time might be bad, and he needed to be somewhere out of the chaos. What he really wanted was to talk to Danforth. He felt she would understand, but he couldn't force himself to call her. It was moving too fast, and he was going to scare her away if he didn't slow it down. He needed to be home. It was the only place he could be himself and let loose. Quickly, he started the Olds and headed toward Awendaw.

As he slowed to turn left, he could swear he was watching Angela get into the back of a small white car, yet when he blinked, both Angela and the vehicle were gone. His hallucinations were getting worse.

The farm looked exactly the way he'd left it. The front porch was covered with eighteen months' worth of leaves, and the yard desperately needed attention. Wisteria vines had overtaken the oak next to the house, and purple flowers draped gracefully from its branches. Built of weathered gray cedar siding, the house had not seen a coat of paint in thirty years. A shutter flapped against the house softly in the breeze, crooked from a broken hinge, but otherwise, the hurricane shutters were still closed and locked as he had left them. A sudden gust lifted leaves in the front yard to form a tight funnel. Fascinated, he watched as it disappeared around the side of the house, reminding him that he would need to double-check this house and his grandparents' house in preparation for a possible hurricane.

No one knew of his ownership except for Danforth. Down on its heels twenty years ago, he had come across it when hunting during his first break between tours. The farm was forty minutes from Charleston, a peaceful place near the monastery at Mepkin Abbey, with the Francis Marion National Forest adjacent on three sides. Asking around at Seawee Outpost, the neighborhood country store, the locals told him it was one section of a large plantation that had been divided among the heirs. No one could remember seeing any family members after the old man who had lived there died a few years prior.

Curious more than anything, he had gone to the courthouse in Charleston and talked with the property clerk. When shown how to read the record books, he learned that the entire 200-acre tract was up for auction at a tax sale for a paltry few hundred dollars due to unpaid agricultural back taxes. Unable to resist, he consulted a lawyer friend to determine the best way to make it difficult for anyone to determine ownership.

Intensely private, he did not want others to know about his affairs. But mostly, he needed to hide his ownership of the farm from his father. Even though he'd not seen the man since he was eight, he'd received letters recently from him at his military APO address. The man was destitute, brazenly asking for money even though he had given up any parental rights over forty years ago, which, in Vern's opinion, was ludicrous. The man had told the world Vern was not his son and had no rights to give. Yet, now, if the scoundrel learned he owned property, he would show up with his hand out. Uncomfortable using his friend for the purchase, someone who could easily be connected to him, he looked for a new attorney.

That was when he had met M.L. Danforth. He hired her to establish the various levels of shell corporations required to purchase the property. He waited patiently through his next tour overseas for the necessary year and the family's right to reclaim it. They didn't. To ensure he did not repeat their mistake, the small agricultural taxes were automatically paid each year from an account in the Cayman Islands, and Danforth had been on a small retainer for one of the companies to ensure there were no issues.

He thought about her now. Hiding his surprise on the first day home, it was immediately clear that she had changed and was no longer the young, inexperienced attorney just starting on her own. The lines on her face and her abrupt manner from last night at his grandparents' house revealed that she had been through things just as he had, having experienced and toughened to the world's hardness.

And today, he confirmed that she felt the same irresistible draw, a strange yet exhilarating sensation.

He focused on his farm. The old house, once restored, would be magnificent. Usually, he would begin removing the shutters, but with a hurricane possibly heading in this direction, he would leave them for the time being. The last time he'd looked, Umberto was churning in the Atlantic with an expected landfall into Florida soon. Yet, if it followed Hugo's path, South Carolina would be its target.

On each thirty-day annual leave, he would bring Katie here, first as a baby, then later as a toddler, watching over her as he worked. He had thought of bringing Angela only once, but changed his mind. He hadn't trusted her then to keep the property's existence a secret, and didn't trust her now.

After Katie grew and could no longer keep the farm secret, whenever he came, he would tell Angela he was going hunting. Given the plethora of game in the National Forest, he had no trouble bringing home results. On the long flight home with nothing else to do, he had ruminated on a growing desire to move his family to Awendaw and officially make it home, even though it was forty-five minutes from Katie's first-grade school on Sullivan's Island. Yet something continued to nag at him to keep the place under wraps. His gut had saved him repeatedly, and he was not about to ignore it now.

His home had remained hidden in the woods for years, protected by locals from hunters. As he crossed the threshold, the front door creaked with its need for oil. All his efforts through the years had been spent on the inside, hoping that while he was overseas, the poor condition of the outside would deter any break-ins.

Over the years, he had made one internal change, then another. As a result, the kitchen had been completely overhauled, the electrical and plumbing redone, and the roof repaired. A fresh coat of interior paint was completed on his last break, and the wood floors were refinished the time before.

He removed dust covers from the comfortable leather furniture and breathed in the unique smell of something he had unknowingly but desperately missed. Home. His place of silence and peace was now his place of refuge.

He checked his phone for cell coverage. Two bars were enough to get by. The electricity and internet cable were in place. Bills were also paid from different accounts in the Caymans. The internet location was temporarily hidden using a VPN, although he would add security layers now that he was permanent.

At the kitchen table, his computer connected, he logged on to the Weather Channel to check the status. Umberto had increased in size and speed, now a Category 5. It had followed the eastern coast of Florida, causing havoc along the beaches and coastal cities. It was too soon to tell, but heading toward Georgia was not a good thing. Especially considering how fast it was moving.

He closed his computer and turned on the sink faucet. No water. He'd forgotten to turn on the pump and the propane for the tankless water heater. The pump, which was out back in the shed, looked good. He turned on the power and was rewarded with its quiet hum.

After a long, hot shower, clean clothes, and shuffling in groceries from the Outpost, he gave himself ten minutes of silence, a form of meditation he had tried overseas. It was the only thing that partially held back the nightmares. When finished, he began thinking through his hurricane preparation. His gut told him it was coming here, just as Hugo had almost forty years prior.

He was familiar with the details of that hurricane. Parts of Sullivan's Island had been wiped completely flat in 1989 when it made landfall at Breach Inlet, and the forest behind where his house sat now had been devastated, timber flattened for miles, tree tops mangled. Blue tarps were the standard roofing material for the next year or so. He had no idea how this small house had managed to survive, but it had. That storm had been a category four when it hit, killing sixty before it was done.

Hurricane Umberto was now out there, already larger than Hugo. But the storm was days out, and they had plenty of time—unless this was the first one that showed them all how foolish they were for ignoring climate change. He would buy plywood tomorrow to board up the shed. Right now, he had to get going.

He slowly closed the front door and locked it back, wistfully wishing that he could stay. Even getting ready for a hurricane was better than what he was going through now.

19

VERN

FRIDAY, 12:30 P.M.

Matheson turned on Highway 17, heading toward Charleston, with his brain churning. He was tired of the nightly battle of his parents, reliving the dream where they threw plates and even furniture at each other, before his father set the house on fire. He'd had the dream all his life, but over the last six months, it had ramped up in frequency and intensity. Just the thought of that dream, with the neighbors standing on the sidewalk watching as their home burned, and his father taunting his mother about burning their life down, made him wonder if his father was psychically torturing him. He had not seen the man since he was eight, when he had been deposited with his grandparents, and if his dreams were correct, the man was not even his father. In his dream, his father accused his mother of having an affair with his best friend, resulting in a pregnancy. As a presumed bastard, his father had regularly taken out his anger on him. Matheson's brain recognized the scenario as a recurring dream, but his heart knew it had really happened.

His grandparents refused to talk about it, so he was constantly left with this nightly diatribe of his warring parents. Yet Matheson swore to himself that he would not allow an abusive childhood like his to impact his daughter. Never had he thought he would have children of his own. But he'd instantly fallen in love with his curly-headed daughter, and as she grew, he loved her more than he ever thought possible.

He thought that when he found Katie, he would stay away from her if it would make her life better, even though it would kill him. But what was he thinking? He knew he could never leave his child. Katie had taught him what real love meant. He would not give that up.

He pulled into the Seewee Outpost for gas and something with caffeine in it to help clear his head. When he finished pumping the gas, he went inside. Grabbing an energy drink, he headed for the cashier.

"Hey, you're that guy who lives over at the place where we hunt."

"Yeah," Matheson said slowly, and wondered if he'd kidded himself about his home being secure. He looked closely at the kid in front of him, probably just out of high school.

"It's ok, man." The kid held up his hands in surrender. "My daddy told me to keep my mouth shut. Only a few of us know the deal, and we've kept it that way. Kept tabs on the place for you."

Matheson pulled out his credit card and handed it to the boy. "Appreciate it. Pump four."

"I'll tell my dad you're home." The boy punched a handheld machine next to the register for the gas amount. "Want to give me your number? He'll want to talk to you about continuing to hunt there, I'm sure."

He slid a scrap of paper and a pen toward Matheson, who hesitated. He wasn't sure how much he wanted to get involved in the surrounding community, yet if his land was to continue to be used for hunting, he needed to be sure who he was dealing with. He did not want to get shot on his own land. Writing his number on the paper, he slid it back to the boy.

"I'm just getting settled. Please ask him to call me next week. We can all get together and have a beer, maybe."

"Yeah, that sounds good. Staying for a while?"

"Yes. I'm in the States permanently now." He didn't know if it would be in South Carolina, however. That would be up to Angela and Katie.

"Well, good luck to you. We all sure appreciate your service." The boy grinned and gave a two-finger salute goodbye as Matheson started for the door.

Starting the car, he headed for Mount Pleasant. There was that service again.

He had been called before General McNight, his commanding officer on the day his duty in Syria was to end. Matheson knew there was no way his last disastrous mission could be shoved under the proverbial prayer rug. He could offer no excuse for the IED missed by his security detail, the one that blew his best friend Darell's Humvee skyward like an oil geyser, leaving pieces of men and machinery scattered around him—including Darrell's leg, ripped off above the knee.

"Colonel," General McNight began as Matheson entered his office, "you have been an outstanding officer. You have led some of the finest soldiers in this Army to do exceptional things, particularly under the arduous circumstances of this sand pit. But you know as well as I do, it is past time for you to call it a day."

"Permission to speak freely, sir."

McNight cocked his head at an angle, something he did when concerned. "Go on."

"I accept responsibility for the mission. It should have been me in that vehicle, not Jenkins. While I would like to blame the intel, even with the best intelligence possible, there's always a risk. But we shouldn't have missed that IED."

"Matheson. You were on the wrong road. Your men say you've been out of it for some time. I had to pry it out of them. They tried their best to cover for you, so don't blame them."

Matheson felt as if he'd been slugged. "Is this on the record, sir?"

The General's reluctant expression showed Matheson his CO had made his decision. "Sit down, soldier."

Matheson reluctantly lowered himself into the leather chair opposite the general's desk. A two-star, McNight had been like a father to him for years. But Matheson knew the man's hands were tied. He'd screwed up, again, and now he'd suffer the consequences.

"Your actions as commander were a complete failure, but I think you know this. With Jenkins having such a serious injury, combined with the deaths of Wilson and Davis, the JAGs are looking at charges. Especially if Jenkins dies."

Matheson had spent time in the brig throughout his twenty-four-year career, but only for minor infractions. Fear rippled through his gut more with the thought of his best friend's death than with the serious prison time. He'd not known his best friend was that close to the edge. No one would tell him a thing.

But the General was not wrong. He had crossed the mental line of stability a long time ago. Daily, he saw the woman from the village explode over and over in his head. His flashbacks, new ones, were out of control, impacting more than his ability to command. Most days, he had barely enough reality to make it through. Confined to solitary confinement in a military jail, he would never survive. His mind would kill him.

The general shoved a stack of documents toward him. "I have paperwork you need to sign. There are special requirements. You will receive an honorable discharge, actually a medical retirement, but the stipulations require you to seek medical attention stateside."

"Stipulations?" Matheson asked. "What medical attention? Is there any way that I can get out of that?"

"Son, cut the shit. We are way beyond a negotiation here. I've never done this before, and probably never will again. If you know what's good for you, sign." McKnight pointed to the signature line on the first page. "I'm sticking my neck out here for you."

Matheson picked up the pen. He had no choice, and he knew it.

WHEN MATHESON WAS close enough to Mt. Pleasant to have five bars, he dialed her number.

"M.L. Danforth." Her voice was curt and to the point. He tried to maintain the same coolness, but found he couldn't. He was drawn to her without knowing why, even though women, especially after this disaster with Angela, were not in his future.

"Good afternoon."

"Feeling better, Colonel?" Her voice immediately lost its harshness, and he hoped she had forgotten about the humiliating event that had occurred this morning at the morgue.

"Have you received an update on my daughter?"

"No. I checked after we left the morgue, but the police haven't been very forthcoming. Do you want to stop by my office? We need to make a plan. Waiting on the police seems like it might be a torturous waiting game. We should also discuss your corporate situation and see if any changes are needed."

"You aren't going to ask..."

Danforth cut him off. "Let's talk in my office. After my last case, I don't trust cell phones."

"I have a better idea. Meet me on the island at Dunleavy's. I have a friend who might be able to help us. It will save time as I'm across town, and we can meet halfway. We can talk there."

"Alright. I'll wrap up what I'm doing here and meet you in less than an hour."

He was glad she agreed to meet him outside her office. He did not want to be alone with her at the moment. His immediate attraction to her years ago, he'd tried to pass off as insignificant, even though it floored him. Single and alone at that point, he'd seriously considered asking her out. But he couldn't, not with his transient soldier's life. She had just begun her career and needed to be left alone, so he set up email communication to avoid her.

Now that it had occurred again, with the attraction even stronger, he wasn't sure how to proceed. She appeared to be as afraid of loving and trusting as he was, probably because he was married. But he had not imagined the attraction—it was real; she'd confirmed it at the morgue. He didn't believe in storybook romances like this. His head wasn't screwed on right, and his attraction to her at this very moment was wrong. Just plain wrong.

20

VERN

FRIDAY, 1:30 P.M.

Hurricane Umberto's possible landfall from Jacksonville, FL, to the Outer Banks of NC

Matheson waited at one end of the bar at Dunleavy's, as far away as possible from the other patrons. It was early afternoon, and the popular restaurant was busy. Located on the main intersection in Sullivan's Island, the tourists routinely made it their first stop. Even after a shower and clean clothes, the smell of the cologne at the morgue was still trapped in his nose, badgering him about where he had smelled it before. He had dropped off his grandmother's Olds and walked the mile back to the bar. The rental car company was scheduled to bring him a car, as his family's Volvo was a burned-out frame.

Sitting at the bar, he craved a drink, but ignored it. He was here to talk with Cherie. He thought it might be easier to speak with her if he ordered food, but with no appetite, it would be a waste. With a look, she signaled a silent apology that she would be moving toward his end of the bar soon. As the local hangout's bartender for the past fifteen years, Cherie was the information baroness of this side of the Cooper River. She would know best what Angela had been up to while he was overseas, and maybe where he could find Katie.

He had worked at Dunleavey's in high school, bussed tables, and helped the owners, when they were slammed, rarely caring if they paid him or not—anything to keep him from having to return home to his grandfather and the old man's rules. He looked around the bar at the decor that hadn't changed in twenty years. Finally, when the staff changeover for the lunchtime shift was complete, the familiar raspy female voice caught his attention. He turned to see outstretched arms from Cherie, a cigarette hanging from her lips, black hair in a low ponytail halfway down her back, now heavily streaked with gray.

"How is my boy? Come here and hug me, will ya?" Cherie didn't wait for an answer. Her wiry arms wrapped around his shoulders, and Matheson was instantly enveloped in a cloud of cigarette smoke. Something released inside, and he returned her squeeze before leaning back to study her face. Crow's feet now radiated from her laughing eyes—but she was the same Cherie.

"How are you?" Matheson tried to smile but couldn't make his face do the job. At least here he didn't have to pretend.

"Doing much better than you with everything that's going on. You look pretty rough. Have you eaten? I could use something before the next kangaroo dance."

"I'm here to regroup, about to meet someone while I wait on a rental car, get some caffeine, and then search for Katie. I can't even think about food. It's been hours since she disappeared, and no one—not even the police—has any trace of her. They told me to go home and wait for them to get in touch. Seriously? The townhouse was torched. And no one has seen hide nor hair of her since yesterday. I'm terrified, Cherie. She's only five."

She patted his arm as she let go, her dark eyes full of sorrow. With a sigh, Cherie stepped back and checked him from head to foot.

"You're going to be okay. You made it out of that hellhole over there in one piece. They'll find Angela and Katie. You probably need to take their advice and stay put. Let them do their job. Besides, from what I've heard, you just got off a long flight when you got here. When's the last time you slept?"

"Some last night. I had a catnap in the parking lot at the morgue." Alarm crossed Cherie's face when he mentioned the morgue. He held up his hand as if to stop her concern.

"Wasn't her." He let out a long breath. "I'm not going to let them 'do their job' because they aren't doing anything. The guy in charge wasted an hour this morning with a stunt that makes no sense. I need to find Katie."

Cherie moved behind the bar. He watched as she wrote up an order, dinged the bell in the cook's window, and then turned around to face him.

"If that's for me, you'd better double it. I'm waiting on someone."

Cherie grabbed the order, made the change, dinged the bell again, and lit another cigarette from the one she had just finished. "What've they told you about Angela?" she asked.

Matheson replied. "The cops won't tell me a thing. There was a party going full blast when I arrived last night, and a woman was dead on my bedroom floor. Now, even though I was a half a world away, I'm pretty sure I'm a 'person of interest,'" his fingers made air quotes, "in Angela's disappearance and, who the hell knows, possibly even this other woman's death."

Cherie's face blanched. She hesitated before she spoke again, and Matheson could tell she was measuring her words. He wished she would blurt it out.

"Look, whatever you're going to say, just say it. Or better yet..." He felt a hand on his shoulder. Danforth sat on the stool next to him.

"Are we going to talk here?" She looked around at the busy bar.

"We're here to meet my friend Cherie." He motioned to the

bartender. "She's known me and my wife most of our lives. You got here just as she was about to tell me what's been happening while I was overseas."

Cherie nodded to M.L. "You're that lawyer involved in that mess out at Timberline Farm." Not waiting for an answer, she looked back at Matheson. "You've seriously lawyered up."

"Just getting help from a friend." Matheson was getting irritated. "Stop stalling. What do you know?"

"You've been gone a long time, you know," Cherie replied, "with only short visits home. The last time, what was it—over a year?"

"Eighteen months."

Cherie took another drag on her cigarette. "How much do you know about your wife while you were gone? What did she tell you?"

Matheson forced himself to sit calmly and not shake the information out of her. Cherie was his oldest and most trusted friend, someone he had known his entire life, or at least since his grandparents had taken him in. He had met her on his bicycle one day when he had ridden out in front of her car. The accident totaled his bike and damaged her Subaru. Instead of getting mad at him, once she learned his story and why he was in such a hurry, she introduced him to the bar owner, and they promptly put him to work to pay off the repair costs. He had never forgotten how kind she had been to him.

He leaned toward the bar and lowered his voice, looking to see who was nearby. No one else sat at the bar, and the closest patron was in the second booth, thirty feet away. Matheson spoke quietly, almost afraid to hear the answer.

"Just spit it out, Cherie. It can't get any worse than this."

"Well, actually...it can." Her face flushed with embarrassment. "We gave her a job, well, I did, as a waitress while you were gone. She said you told her to talk to me when the bills got too much for her to handle. I could guess at your pay and knew it was a lie. But she's your wife, you know? She worked here for about six months before I let her go."

His paycheck covered much more than Angela's expenses. She had plenty of spending money. And Cherie was the easiest boss in the area. "You fired her?"

"Had to. She was high on the job and screwing up right and left. Couldn't keep it together enough to write the customer's orders correctly. She took the wrong food to the wrong people, basic things." Cherie's face was sadder than he'd ever seen. "I'm sorry, man, but your wife has a serious problem."

He hadn't wanted Angela to be this irresponsible, at least for Katie's sake. The tiny glimmer of hope to have his family on his utopian farm was instantly snuffed out. A heavy weight settled on his shoulders.

He looked at Danforth. "That's not the Angela I knew. But that's not realistic. I've been gone a long time. If I'm honest, I can't remember the last time I've had a serious conversation with my wife." He saw her watching his hand as he shifted the rabbit's foot from one to the other, but she said nothing.

Cherie leaned across the bar and slowly rubbed his upper arm in sympathy. "I'm sure it isn't. She hid it well for the first few months. But after that, she must have started doing something different, stronger maybe, because I saw a definite change in her personality. She began to hit me up for more hours and said she had more bills to pay. From what I could see, everything she made went into her habit. Honestly, Matheson, I hate to see what your credit will look like. I hope you had it locked up tight. The gossip was that she took out a second and then a third mortgage on your house."

Danforth leaned toward him. "I'll check on that. To do that, she'd have to commit forgery, and that's a serious felony."

He had paid no attention to the house, checked no payment status, and done nothing else. He and Angela agreed that she would take care of things here so he wouldn't have to worry about her or Katie while he was away. Home was his farm, and as soon as he completed the exterior renovations, he'd planned to move his family to Awendaw and sell the townhouse, regardless of what Angela wanted.

If Angela's habit was this bad, what condition would his daughter be in? He refused to think of his daughter with strangers doing who knew what. His head began to pound.

"What do you know about Katie?" M.L. asked Cherie.

Cherie shrugged, her face a mask of sadness. "She was always a happy little girl whenever she was here, but that wasn't often. This isn't a place for a child, even though some come here, especially with a flock of tourists. Many days, Angela would drop her off at the Moores' house and pick her up after her shift. Ask Vernon's grandparents, especially his grandmother. I know Katie was with her a lot."

Matheson shook his head. "They've been trying to hide something from me since I got home, especially when the detective came by."

"Well, honestly, your grandmother may not remember a whole lot. She has been a bit forgetful."

Matheson sat back and looked at his friend. Another surprise. "For how long?"

"A while now. I've rushed food to her several times because she forgot Katie was with her, and she needed to feed her. "

His daughter had been living with no fully functioning adult, and no one felt they could tell him. He could not decide whether that said more about him or his friends.

21

LEE

FRIDAY, 2:00 P.M.

Cherie turned from the bar and retrieved platters with two loaded hamburgers and piles of fries from the window, setting one down in front of Matheson and the other in front of me. She grabbed a ketchup bottle and shoved it toward us.

"Eat," she said to Matheson. "We both have a lot to talk about. And you're hangry." Cherie gave me a wink. While eating something was good for him, my client and I needed to talk, but not in a crowded bar.

"Thanks for the food," Matheson said as he ate one-third of his hamburger in the first bite. "But I'm not hangry, Cherie. I have the right to be as angry as I want."

"Can we move to a booth?" I looked at Matheson, then at the bartender. "We have a lot to talk about, and I'm uncomfortable with us up here. I feel like we're in a fish bowl." As the words came out, I noticed a scruffy-looking man perched at the other end of the bar, listening to everything I was saying. I looked around the bar and pointed to the only open booth that was in the far corner. "How about there?"

After Cherie got someone to cover her at the bar and we

moved, Matheson grabbed his burger and took another huge bite. One more bite, and it would be gone. He took a pull from the straw in his soft drink as I pulled out my iPad for notes, picking at the fries on my plate.

"Who else knows about Angela's drug problem besides you?" I looked at the bartender.

"The whole island." Cherie was shamefaced. "And most of Mount Pleasant and Charleston. She got around quite a bit."

"Got around?" I needed to be sure I understood her meaning.

"Don't make me spell it out in front of him." Her voice was confrontational. "This is hard enough as it is."

I felt and then saw a movement to my right. The man from the bar was standing next to me. In a leather vest and oil-stained jeans, he shifted toward Matheson with his right hand extended.

"Name is Eddie. Sorry to eavesdrop, but I couldn't help but hear your talk about Angela."

Matheson accepted his hand, but I could tell he didn't appreciate the man's butting in. Where had he come from? "We're having a private conversation here," I said.

The biker held up both hands and silently stepped back from Matheson, his expression a smug little smile.

"I don't mean to butt in. I just *knew* her, that's all." His stressing of the word 'knew' started to have Matheson out of his seat like a rocket, but then he checked himself. "Whoa, man," Eddie said, "I didn't touch her. Others did, but I wasn't one of them."

Matheson's eyes focused on me. Our gaze locked for seconds, but it felt like minutes. When I thought he could hear me, I spoke softly. "Let's hear what he has to say. It may be a step in finding Katie."

After formal introductions, Eddie Cantrell told us he lived at the end of Sullivan's Island nearest Charleston, making a living doing odd jobs and whatever painting he could scrounge. Angela would talk to him when the pub was slow, but that had been "a while ago."

"Do you know anything about what Angela was taking?" I asked.

"I don't know for sure, she never said. When I met her, she was wrapped up in it pretty good, though." Nothing indicated that he was lying, but I still did not trust one word out of this man's mouth.

"I know that part," Cherie interrupted. "She broke her ankle playing volleyball at the beach. It was a stress fracture. At least that's the story she told me. I don't know the doctor's name, but I think that's the first time she started taking pain pills. But I think there was more than one doctor, honestly."

Matheson looked at me then. "I didn't know anything about this."

Eddie responded then. "Weren't no doc involved that I know."

I nodded to Matheson and turned back to Eddie. "How did she get the drugs then?"

"When she talked to me about it, she used Craigslist. She bragged to me that she met this guy who called himself "Blue-Mickey420" or something like that online." Eddie snickered. "No self-respectin' man would call himself something like that even online."

"What was her name?" I asked. From the corner of my eye, I saw Matheson finish his hamburger and then reach for mine.

"CrispyChick," he said. "She used it for everything she said. Was proud of it for some reason."

I wrote down the names and a few variations after questioning Eddie further. "How often did she meet this guy?"

"A lot, I think. She'd get whatever he would give her, as much as she could pay for. She sort'a bragged about it, don'cha know." He looked directly at Matheson. "And don't make me go there, man, I don't know how she paid him, if you get my drift. I know what she offered me if I'd pay her in cash. Like I said, I declined."

He rose from the booth after finishing his beer. "I wish I could help you more, but that's all I know. I just thought you ought to know, she being your wife and all."

"My daughter is also missing. Know anything about that?"

Eddie looked away, suddenly embarrassed. "No man, didn't know she even had a daughter. I hope you find her."

The look on Matheson's face almost did me in. Angela cared so little about her daughter that no one knew the child existed. From his face, I could tell that Matheson was absorbing that guilt as his own.

I watched Cantrell shuffle out the door. I didn't like coincidences, and the man's convenient offer of information made me uncomfortable. Was any of it real? Why did learning about Katie make Cantrell uncomfortable? Two witnesses told us that Angela had a real problem, but neither knew anything about Katie.

"What else do you know?" I looked back at Cherie. Something wasn't adding up with her either, but I couldn't pinpoint what it was. "Or rather, what have I not asked that I should have?"

She let out a long breath of smoke and set the lit cigarette on the edge of Matheson's empty plate as she stared at his uneaten fries. Finally, she looked up at Matheson, her forehead wrinkled in concern, the look of a worried parent for a child, their ages the appropriate number of years apart. The connection between them was so strong, I might as well not have been in the room. Matheson trusted this woman, even if I couldn't.

"Your wife screwed half the county, man." She held up both hands, apparently because of his temper. "Don't shoot the messenger. You asked."

"What would she do with Katie when she was out?" Matheson's voice was so quiet I could barely hear him over the noise of the restaurant.

"I don't know. I guess she was with your grandmother, but honestly, I don't know."

He looked at me. "This is a mess."

"Yes, it is." I nodded. We were silent as Cherie stood to take our empty plates to the back. She returned but didn't sit, winding the strings of her bar apron around her waist before tying it in a bow as she got ready to return to work.

She looked at Matheson. "I'm sorry about Darrell. You guys had been friends for a long time. We all thought he would get better, not worse. And I know I could have told you about Angela myself. It's not like you didn't have Skype or email."

"It isn't your fault, Cherie." Matheson was quiet for a moment, and I wondered at the comment about Darrell. "So you think Angela would take Katie to Nana's when she had things to do?"

"Most of the time, I think. But I heard her make arrangements several times for Katie to stay with a friend."

"Do you have the name of that friend?" I asked.

Cherie sorrowfully shook her head.

"Do you know which doctor prescribed the pills?" I tried once more.

"No, I don't," she replied, "other than it being a 'him' and he was located in Mt. Pleasant." She shifted to look back at the bar. "Look, I've got to get back to it. Call me once you find Katie. She's got to be someplace safe. Angela may have her issues, but Vernon, from what I saw, she might not have been a good mother, but she loved Katie."

Matheson stood, hugging Cherie. "I appreciate the information. I know it was hard for you to tell me."

"Just be careful. After what that Eddie guy told us, I don't know who or what you're dealing with."

After Cherie left, he sat across from me. "So what do you think?"

"Everyone's avoiding any mention of Katie," I replied. "Either they don't know, they act like they don't know, or, like Eddie, they got uncomfortable and embarrassed when her name came up.

Doesn't give me the warm fuzzies. I don't know if it's just because I got off a trafficking case, or there's something there."

"Yeah. I got the same vibe. What do you suggest we do next?"

"We need to get organized and not go into this haphazardly. I have a team, and I do better with them in play. We, meaning my office, will need constant contact with Weaver. I understand why you wanted me to meet here with Cherie, but from now on, we don't need to be on public display. I don't trust that guy, Eddie, and I can't figure out how or why he suddenly appeared. I don't trust Weaver. He's stalling, and I have no idea if he is having you followed."

"Understood. So, where is your office now?"

"On Archdale Street downtown. We can meet at my grandfather's if we need to be on this side of town. Both places are swept regularly, secure, and private. I'll introduce you to Clarice, my practice manager, and you'll have the opportunity to meet my local investigators, who have also worked with Mac before. We will do this together. I know you're stressed about your wife and child, but we do this as a team, or we don't do this at all."

He stood and helped me out of the booth.

"I'm heading for my grandfather's and then my office. Please drop by later today."

"Yeah. I need to check in with my grandparents, then make one more stop. I'll meet you at your office in an hour or two, if that works."

Outside, as Matheson drove away in a rented black Tahoe, I dialed Weaver's number. He answered on the second ring.

"I need a status on Colonel Matheson's family, please. Have you located the wife and child?" I clicked the phone to speaker.

"No, we haven't. Volunteers are gathering behind the Sullivan's Island PD office to search the island."

"Please keep me advised."

Weaver's voice, while curt, was professional. "Will do."

My appointment with the police chief must have made the rounds, but Weaver's voice still made my skin crawl with apprehension. At least there was a search. I punched the number for Matheson. He needed the news.

22

VERN

FRIDAY, 3:00 P.M.

After receiving Danforth's call, Matheson shifted into battle mode, the autopilot movements he had used for years to get himself through challenging situations. His mind began to formulate lists of possible people to contact for more information and places to search. He started at the Sullivan's Island Town Hall on Middle Street, where he quickly learned that the search was in its early stages, and no one had any information about either Angela or Katie.

Checking in at the police station next, he ended up answering Chief Stanton's questions, his fourth time in twenty-four hours after Logan, Weaver, and, of course, his attorney, and got very few of his questions answered. What he did learn was that they had piss-poor organization and needed a lesson in operational design and control. Everything moved so slowly that he felt like pulling his hair from his head by the roots. His child had been missing for almost an entire day, and still no one knew anything.

Then he got the idea to contact his friend Darrell's cousin, known for crossing many lines, especially when drugs were involved. Getting no answer, he left a message.

At his grandparents, he found no one home, even though the

front door was unlocked. The dining table held a note from Nana —she and his grandfather had walked over to meet the monsignor at Stella Maris to pray for Angela and Katie. He was sure his grandmother had gone, but doubted about his grandfather. The note requested that he meet them there if he got home before five p.m. Shaking his head, he left the keys to Nana's Olds and a note of his own, locking their front door. Sullivan's Island was safe, but they shouldn't push it.

In Charleston, he pulled up to M.L.'s office on Archdale Street. The last time he worked with her, she was in rented offices in a shared space, a one-room affair with a centralized receptionist for a half dozen other solo attorneys. Now she was in a coveted area of Charleston in an office of her own. Grabbing his laptop case, he was greeted at the front door by a tall, attractive Black woman in a fuchsia jumpsuit, her hair in wild curls around her face.

"Clarice Richardson." She offered her hand, and he shook it. "Welcome, Colonel Matheson. I am Lee's practice manager. I'll take you to her office. Later, you will meet the others in the war room." She pointed to the double French doors, which had a punch code lock over the doorknob. "Follow me." She led him into an office on the left behind a receptionist's desk. "Go on in. I'll bring you coffee."

"Thanks, I take it black."

"Wouldn't have expected it any other way." Her smile was warm and comforting, just like his favorite actress. He had hidden his fascination with the character Olivia Pope from the guys overseas, watching the series he'd saved on his iPad in bits and pieces only when alone.

Matheson walked into a large office, one end of which was lined with books. To his left was a modern glass-topped desk on free-form steel legs. Behind the desk was a tricked-out leather office chair framed by rows of law books next to a modern computer station with an iMac. In the middle of the room, two overstuffed chairs flanked a comfortable couch in a muted yellow and pink plaid. A small bar was built into one corner.

The entire wall opposite the desk was a large window of four-inch panes that overlooked the rear garden. The flowers surrounded an old, massive oak, and the garden was enclosed within a brick wall that appeared to be hundreds of years old.

The door opened, and M.L., with two cups of coffee, motioned for him to sit on the couch. She handed him a cup and collapsed into a chair. He had never been around a woman as confident as this one and made a note never to bullshit her. The fallout would not be worth it. After a sip from her coffee, she set it on the side table.

"I need some background to plan the next steps appropriately. Everything you say to me in this room is confidential. If there is something specific that you wish only between us, I will not tell my team unless necessary, and only after I clear it with you."

"Understood," he said. "I need to be honest here. Aside from our obvious chemistry issues, I feel that I can discuss anything with you. I've been overseas for so long that I'd forgotten what it's like to really talk with someone. So, I guess this is a warning. There's been a lot going on with me, and you might be in for more than you bargained for."

"I doubt that. But whether you want me to or not, we need ground rules after what happened this morning."

"Ground rules?" He couldn't blame her. They had to get a handle on whatever this was before it buried both of them.

"You are my client. I'm not pushing away whatever is physically attracting us to each other. I'm not sure that I could even if I wanted to. I'm just putting it on hold. Can you do that also? The stakes are too high here to do otherwise."

"Agreed. I want my daughter back." However, it went without saying that they would have to remain physically apart. He wasn't sure he could accomplish that.

"Then tell me about your relationship with Angela." His

attorney was now all business. "I'm not looking to pry into your world, but I need information based on what Cherie told us. We have a lot of ground to cover with friends, relationships..." She hesitated. "I also need your gut reaction to what is happening here."

He looked at the floor, studying his worn Italian boots on her expensive rug.

"We met on the beach. She was big into beach volleyball and played in local tournaments. She was tan, a natural redhead with freckles everywhere, always in shape. I watched her play some nights over at Santi's, and then we would have a beer and eat tamales. Just hung out, had a good time." He finally looked up. "I thought I'd finally found someone. She didn't seem concerned that I would come and go a lot. She was interested in the military life, and I thought maybe..."

He looked up at her.

"I wasn't here long, just a month. We saw each other for most of that time, but I thought we should take some time to think about it. She was fun and interesting. I wanted us to see how it would work long-distance before I committed. Then my next tour began, and I headed overseas."

He wiped his hand over his face. "I received an email about six or seven weeks later, insisting she had to talk to me. I Skyped her. And of course, she was pregnant and didn't want to have an abortion. Da insisted I do the honorable thing," he looked away, embarrassed, "so I did."

"Was Angela a party girl then?"

"Yeah. But so was I."

"Think she's still one now?"

"I talked with Angela and Katie fairly regularly up until about six months ago. Angela never said anything about parties. But you know? Now that I'm thinking about it, over the last six months, I never saw Angela on camera. She would answer the Skype call off-screen, and it would be Katie that I saw every other week. Never Angela. I could hear her talk, but she never showed her face."

"It didn't strike you as unusual then?"

"I was so caught up with what was happening to me overseas that nothing would have struck me as unusual."

23

VERN

FRIDAY, 3:30 P.M.

Matheson was having a difficult time with everything that was being said about his wife. Even though they'd had to get married, it wasn't a chore to marry or live with Angela. But as the years dragged on and he was longer and longer overseas, he could see how Angela might have grown resentful. He had to admit that his family was not his priority during that time.

His sanity was.

"Does what Cherie told you ring true?" M.L. asked him, causing him to focus on his attorney.

"I can see Angela having a good time; she always did, but that party I walked in on? It's too far over the top. Drugs at that level were never her thing. My wife was a young, attractive woman and, from what I knew, a good mother to Katie. A glass of wine or a beer with dinner, maybe another afterward? Sure. Maybe a joint every six months. Possibly. But I don't see her in any of this."

He set his coffee next to hers and leaned forward, his forearms on his knees. "You want my gut reaction? I want to obliterate someone or something, but I'm just unsure where to start.

After what I learned today, if it is true—and that is a big if to me—divorce is a given, and Katie's custody will not be shared."

"We can talk about finding you counsel for your divorce later. We have to find Angela first, praying she leads us to Katie." She continued. "You understand this may get much worse before it gets better," she leaned toward him, "especially since Weaver is talking about trafficking, kidnapping."

He searched her stricken face, wondering how a lawyer could be so concerned about his child and his problems. How could he consistently shove his fears about Katie away when this woman was more concerned than he was? How fucked up was he?

Pretty damn well fucked up.

He stood and walked toward the wall of windows facing the garden. This was the first time he had forced himself to think about his life, his wife and child, and how he felt, not just the standard lip service he gave others because they were his family. Abruptly, M.L. walked to the bar and opened a crystal decanter, pouring them both one finger, handing him a glass as she returned. How could she read him so well?

"The good stuff. My grandfather got me started. I'm not advocating alcohol to solve a problem, but now and then it helps. I think you're teetering on the edge here."

"Sounds like I need to meet your grandfather." He ignored her comment about how close he was to losing it, even though she was right on target.

"Hang around long enough and you will. He's a force to be reckoned with and part of my team. Even at his age, his mind is sharp." She took a sip of scotch, then continued. "I need to know if you will cave on me when things get rough. I can tell you've been through a lot overseas, and Mac filled me in on a few things. I understand you're required to get medical treatment."

He stiffened automatically and turned toward her. "Caving is not in my vocabulary. And what exactly did Mac tell you about the medical requirement?"

"Colonel Matheson, I'm not trying to offend or pry into your affairs. I'm trying to get to know you as a person so that I can best represent you. I've had issues myself with anxiety and PTSD. It hits you at the most inappropriate times. The last case I worked on involved children who were taken and trafficked. It changed me.

"Several times, Mac held me back from blasting into the houses where they were kept and stealing them back. Either I was falling apart, or I wanted to be Rambo. Now I'm prepared. We have a team, and we'll have a plan. According to Mac, you're the type who consistently goes off plan, goes rogue. I can't have that."

"You can call me Vern. I'm no longer military, so Colonel Matheson is unnecessary, and no one calls me Vernon except my grandmother. My mother named me after a poet, Vernon Watkins, but never told me why." He shifted uncomfortably. "And yes, I've been known to go out of the box a bit."

"My friends call me Lee. I think we've firmly crossed into that territory," she said.

"Friends. Is that what this is?" He couldn't keep from smiling. It was a hell of a lot more than that, and he hoped she knew it.

"Talking to somebody helps," she said, still focused on his mental state. "I know. Like I said, I've been through it."

Matheson took a sip of the best scotch he'd had in years and forced himself to concentrate on the problem at hand. He had to make it through whatever they would find concerning Katie. Could he? It was evident that his attorney didn't think he could hold up, and if he was honest, neither did he. He needed to find out what Mac had told her.

She took another sip of her drink. "You thinking out of the box isn't an issue, Vern. Not telling me what's happening with you is a big issue, and acting dangerously would also be a problem. I can't jeopardize my team."

"Understood." Mentally, he did understand her concerns. Yet he wasn't sure he could actually control himself. He'd been a loose cannon for several years, and he knew it. It was how he'd gotten himself to this state. He made himself comfortable again on the sofa, and once again, she sat across from him.

"So, what are your triggers?" she asked. "Apparently, smoke from what I saw at the morgue."

Matheson studied the woman across from him. She couldn't possibly want to hear what he went through with his crap. He was not about to tell her about the flashbacks and the other weird things that had been happening for months. She would run so far from him he'd never see her again.

She continued. "I have an appointment tomorrow with my doctor. Go with me. Or if you don't want to go there, I'll have her come here."

"No ma'am." He got to his feet and walked back to the window. "I have no desire for any psych guru to mess with my head," he threw over his shoulder. "I don't need drugs." He turned to face her, squeezing the glass in his hand so hard he thought he might shatter it.

"I don't take drugs," she said. "We talk. She helps me work through things. Do you want your medical retirement to be honored? Your clock is ticking. You have to get started." She grinned at him. "I don't want to lose a client before I can send him a bill."

She was right, damn her, even though he knew never to trust a lawyer. They were always way ahead of you. "She. How am I supposed to talk to a woman?"

"You're talking to me."

"Yeah, but that's different. I don't know her well enough to be having a conversation like this."

"And you know me that well? She's ex-military, just like you. Has some of the same tours, just with different responsibilities."

"You're my lawyer. You're required to keep it confidential."

"So is she. You're over-thinking this, Vern."

"I'll think about it." If he had to talk to someone, a military background would help. "Why are you pushing me to do this?"

"We have to get to the bottom of these things now. I hope for the best, but prepare for a disaster. I have to know what you will do when things go south, especially when dealing with the nasty world your wife is possibly drowning in." She stood. "Drink your scotch and let's get the team going on finding your wife and daughter. I'll text Zola that you'll be coming with me."

Matheson wiped his hands down his face. Of all the things he had promised himself he would never do, she had talked him into going to a shrink.

24

———

WEAVER

FRIDAY, 4:00 P.M.

Hurricane Umberto increasing speed

Harbin was pushing at him, hard. The man was getting nervous, and Weaver knew that wasn't what was needed. He was sitting outside the police precinct, about to go inside when the solicitor's number appeared on his cell.

"Yes, sir," Weaver answered.

"They want me to take more," Harbin told him. "I need a versatile warehouse solution other than storage units. I've rented one, I swear, in every location across Charleston. I need other options. There are too many cameras, and having our dealers come and go is causing some friction. You need to start coordinating all of this. I can't do it."

"I can try a few things, but I'm not taking responsibility," Weaver replied, "and there has to be something in it for me. I agree that the storage units need to be eliminated. The police can get into them pretty easily, sometimes even without a warrant, depending on who is managing them. Your guys should be required to store what they sell, not just pick it up."

"Still risky. There are family members, children."

"Some of them, maybe, but not most of them. Why did you get into this business if you're so risk-averse? You forget that I talk with these guys every week. They're not going to care if it means more money for them." Weaver let out an exasperated sigh. "Just an idea. It's your call." Weaver waited for the lawyer to think about his solution.

"Let's test it with one or two," said Harbin, "but only those who don't have family. See how it goes. If it works out, we can discuss a bonus."

"I'll get back to you." Weaver pulled the phone away from his ear and was about to end the call when Harbin's voice continued.

"I'm hearing things through the trafficking task force I was assigned to after the arrests at Timberline Farm. Know anything about that?"

"No." Weaver closed his eyes. *Shit shit shit.* "What are you hearing?"

"HSI through SLED will probably take over your murder case. They know the dead woman's a trafficker." Weaver could hear Harbin's wooden desk chair creak.

"How do they know that? The autopsy hasn't been done yet," Weaver replied, his stomach ulcer beginning to burn. "I didn't tell them. There's no need for them to stick their nose in this."

"They got a call from a certain attorney's office requesting information on local trafficking. Got them all riled up, I hear."

"Danforth?" *Damn it.* Weaver would have to place the dreaded call to Fish that he had avoided until now. His loose mouth was catching up with him.

"Well, either her or her new employer, but yes."

"What do you mean by her new employer?" Weaver pulled out his leather notebook and flipped it open, pulling out the attorney's business card. He hadn't looked at it when she handed it to him, but stuffed it in his notebook. "Yeah, I see it on her business card. Lawrence Security Services out of Atlanta. Who is that?"

"Ex-military guy who regularly contracts with Homeland Security," Harbin said. "He and Danforth's client are tight. You know she's just a real estate lawyer. Has no idea what she's doing when it comes to criminal law." Weaver didn't bother to tell the solicitor that she could hold her own pretty well. "But this guy," Harbin continued, "Mac Lawrence, he knows his stuff."

"What about the old man, her grandfather?"

"He knows exactly what he's doing. Was on the bench for over thirty years. He's a sly old dog. Still has my secretary wrapped around his finger. Don't let him fool you."

Weaver had to get ahead of her and wondered if there was someone at her office who could spy on her, until he remembered something about the Timberline Farms guys trying that and getting caught.

"What are you going to do about Fish?" Harbin asked.

"Why don't you give him a call?" Weaver asked. "Let him know you're on his side."

"I don't think so." Harbin chuckled. "Not someone's phone number I want cozied up next to mine, demanded by a telephone company subpoena. Besides, isn't it time to let HSI take him down? Maybe step in his shoes?"

Says the prosecutor, who is scared of having his drugs kept in the garage of any man who has a wife or child.

"Let's see how it goes when I call Fish. I'll keep you posted."

Weaver ended the call before Harbin could play the trafficking kingpin guessing game, then made another call. At the end of that conversation, he snapped his flip phone closed and let loose a string of profanity that would have embarrassed even the guys in the bullpen. His informant, a part of Homeland Security's team inside SLED, confirmed that traffickers were implicated in the possible abduction of a five-year-old child from Mount Pleasant.

Weaver knew the source had to be Danforth because he sure hadn't told them. She was the only part of his investigation who had the contacts to initiate something like that. Just giving a call to HSI wasn't enough. You had to have connections and the details to back up whatever you alleged. The department didn't have the time or resources to run down every anonymous call. He knew. He was once part of that department before they had effectively kicked him out.

His next call was to a confidential informant on Sullivan's Island. He had tagged the guy several times for small-time drug offenses and made him a deal on the last one to keep him from being a three-time loser. Yesterday, he had made sure the part-time painter would keep his eyes and ears open about anything related to Angela.

"Hey, Eddie," Weaver said when the man answered his call. "Got anything for me?"

"Yeah, actually. Met that military guy and his lawyer today at Dunleavy's. Primed him up a bit for you."

"What did you tell him?" Weaver asked.

"Anything he wanted to know about his wife." Eddie chuckled. "And a few things he didn't."

"Where did you send him?"

"Where you told me to. I made up some shit about Keith, but with a bit of time, they'll figure it out, but they should run in circles for a while."

"Thanks, man. I owe you when I see you."

Weaver needed to get ahead of Danforth and find the Colonel's wife before she spilled her guts. He punched in the number for Keith Ellison, the wiry ex-con who took care of the North King Street area for Harbin.

"Yo," Ellison answered, his voice clearly irritated. "This had better be good. I'm not supposed to be up for two more hours."

"Trying to run down that redheaded chick. The one who kept

calling you at all hours of the day and night. Where can I find her?" Weaver asked.

"She'll show up. She always does, strung out and trying to trade sex for a hit of anything she can get. Why do you want her?"

"Got people looking for her, and I need to find her first." *Or before they find you.*

"Why?" Ellison stifled a yawn.

"That's not your concern, now, is it, Keith? Just text me the minute you have her in your sights. I need to talk to her."

"What's in it for me?"

Weaver shook his head. Sometimes, he wondered why he had even moved to Charleston. There had to be other places where the people were not so absolutely stupid. "Your job, dipwad. Just text me when she gets to the bar."

Weaver was striking out here. He needed to find Angela Matheson faster than this. Even if she just gave Danforth a few names, that would be enough to unravel the entire spool of yarn, implicating him in both Harbin's and Fish's networks. He scrolled until he found the doctor's number, needing to protect his friend, and left a message.

"Hey Sean, how are you?" Weaver asked when the physician returned his call. The busiest orthopedist in the Lowcountry, Weaver had involved Dr. Sean Carlton in Harbin's system against his better judgment. It had proved lucrative. The doctor got people significantly hooked on something for pain, usually OxyContin. At their final appointment, the doctor provided three things to the patient: a final prescription, a referral to several local clinics to help them get off the drugs, and a telephone number for when they got desperate. To date, 85% of Carlton's patients have used that phone number. He received a bonus for every one of them.

"Thought I'd better give you a heads up that your redhead is about to give you an even bigger case of heartburn."

"Oh man," Carlton laughed, "I thought once she met Ellison, my troubles would be over."

"She's gone missing along with her kid. I need to find her before either the cops or her husband does."

"Don't know anything about that." Carlton's voice was subdued. "Can't help you. But because of her, we need to discuss my percentage. I think it's time I got a little bump for all the trouble she caused me."

"We can talk about that after you find her for me. The trouble she causes will be nothing compared to what will happen if we don't find her."

25

LEE

FRIDAY, 4:30 P.M.

Grabbing more coffee, we headed to the conference room. I introduced Matheson to my investigators, Angus and Nikki Garrett, and to my grandfather. After we brought everyone in the room up to speed, Matheson sat down and took out the pink rabbit's foot and set it on the table. He powered up his laptop and then flipped it around to show me a full inbox of spam. Both Hawkeye Clarice and my grandfather were observing us. I would definitely get an earful later.

"I'm looking at anything Angela did online," Matheson said to the group. "If we can locate Angela, maybe we can find Katie. My wife is a ditz when it comes to computers. I had to set everything up for her. I know her password, and I used the same one for everything."

Angus snorted a laugh.

"Yeah, I know," Matheson continued, giving a tired smile to Angus, "a hacker's dream, but making her use a different password for everything would have been a nightmare with me being overseas all the time. And because I was always away, she agreed to keep everything important in the cloud rather than on her computer. I feel stupid because I could have accessed anything I wanted that way, but I didn't. I thought it important she have her privacy."

"Once you take a first look," Nikki said, "if you want to give me the information, I can run down all the rabbit trails."

"Why don't I give you the login and password," Matheson responded, "and let you take the lead. I don't want to miss something."

"Lee, dear," the Judge interrupted. "I believe we should begin now, looking at the trafficking angle. MacCabe's contacts should be involved early to be beneficial."

"You're right, Judge," I replied. "We need to get everything going at once. I've kept Mac up to speed, and he's probably already called HSI, but I'll call him once we're done."

"What do you mean by 'the trafficking angle'?" Matheson asked my grandfather.

"If a dirty detective stupidly volunteers that trafficking is part of the equation, it probably is. We have a big problem in this city, and I'm sure Lee has caught you up with her most recent foray into that quagmire."

"She mentioned it." Matheson looked at me, his face twisted in pain at the mention of his child possibly being abducted, before turning back to the Judge.

"Colonel," my grandfather continued, "I do not want to increase your distress, but there are not enough of us to search every nook and cranny for your daughter. We need as many boots on the ground, so to speak, as we can get."

"I understand that. Both Mount Pleasant and Sullivan's Island are looking."

"Yes. However, Homeland Security has a statewide team headquartered in Myrtle Beach and a coordinating desk within SLED. Either may have already heard something about the transaction at your townhome. If your daughter has been spirited away, we must consider that possibility. If you have concerns, it would be prudent for you to discuss this with Mac."

Matheson nodded and turned back to plow through the emails on his computer.

"I have something," Nikki said after a few minutes, looking up from her computer. "Angela spent a great deal of time searching for narcotics in the past thirty days. She primarily uses Facebook for most of her connections, but Tinder seems to be her main dating outlet, although she also uses other dating sites almost as regularly. Facebook reveals a pristine life, complete with photos of perfectly styled clothes and hair. The rest, not so much."

"This is the first I've heard about social media," Matheson said. "The more I learn, though, the more stupid I feel. I mean, Tinder?"

"I would have expected this level of perfection on Instagram," Nikki said, "but I can't find an Insta account for her. Do you know if she has one?" she said to Matheson.

"Unfortunately, no."

"At least there are no photos of Katie," I said, scrolling through Angela's Facebook page. "That's a real problem when parents indiscriminately put their kids' photos up for the world."

"She didn't want anyone to know she had baggage," Matheson said, his voice laced with disgust. Clarice looked at me, her face scrunched in concern.

"What was that look?" Matheson looked first at Clarice, then at me.

"From our last case, we're just a bit sensitive to children and pretty happy Katie isn't anywhere online. Maybe it was for a different reason, but it's a good thing, Colonel." Nikki said, gently smiling at him.

Traffickers were notorious for using photos of children online, tracking them, then kidnapping them. With older children, elaborate ruses were created to entice them away from home. I'd had several long conversations with Mac about his work as a contractor for Homeland Security and several of their past trafficking operations.

Nikki found no other social media. Spam was downloaded as they searched her inbox to help reveal places she had tried to find a supplier. Apparently, Angela had contacted anyone she knew, seeking references to doctors or any other place where she might find narcotics for cash, no questions asked.

"Ok," said Nikki, "so buying on a per-pill basis at the rates she was spending, I'm calculating Angela needed $200 a day to continue her habit."

"Oh man, that's a lot," Matheson replied. "She'd been talking the last six months on WhatsApp about how hard it was to pay the bills, but I never imagined this." He dropped his head forward, his hands running through his hair, causing it to stand on end like a hedgehog.

Angus had been working on Craigslist, searching the names Eddie had given us at Dunleavy's: "CrispyChick" and "BlueMickey420." Matheson went behind him to watch as he pulled up several threads from Angela, each more desperate than the last, but nothing under BlueMickey420.

"I've hit a roadblock with BlueMickey," said Angus. "I think the guy's info is bad." He looked at me. "Intentional?"

"Possibly," I replied.

He looked up at Matheson. "But, here, look at this." I stood beside him as we watched Angus scroll. We read the entire thread between BlueMercury420 and CrispyChick. Angus looked up at me. "We need tae respond like we're Angela. Try to get him to meet." Now and then, his Scottish brogue came out when he was stressed or angry. "If we can get a lead from the dealer who supplied her, maybe we can locate her quickly."

Matheson nodded to Angus. "Do whatever you think you need to do. I want to be a part of whatever action you take. Sitting around waiting will kill me."

Angus created his own CrispyChick message and hit "Send," then looked at Nikki. "Want to trace this IP address?"

"Sure. Give me a second."

Angus next began searching through the calls from Angela's cell phone number. With Matheson still the owner of the T-Mobile account, every call she made for the past five years was listed. After downloading the list, Angus searched each month's bill for repeating numbers, tediously reverse-searching online. To Matheson's surprise, his wife kept a detailed contact list on a cloud-based spreadsheet.

"You know, this isn't like her." He turned his computer toward me. "She isn't organized at all. This contact information from the cloud is crazy. I don't see anything else unusual, but this is the first time I've looked at it in a year and a half."

"Maybe she was subconsciously hoping you would look." I pointed to the computer screen. "Anyway, just look through all the contacts and see if you recognize anything or anyone that looks suspicious to you. Angus will continue to check all her calls. We'll first contact the people she talked to the most, then divide and conquer with the rest."

"Do you think the police have checked this account yet?" he asked.

"As the forensics team most likely arrived after the house burned, they are behind and may not have subpoenaed T-Mobile. Even if the department is moving quickly, depending on their contacts, going through the usual route to get the list of calls could take some time, weeks even."

Angus looked at Clarice. "Did you ever discover why forensics was delayed at the scene?"

Clarice looked up from her computer. "No. No one can give me a reason. They all act like it's commonplace for them to arrive the next morning, but that's not normally the case, you well know." Angus had been an investigator for years with Charleston County before he and Nikki set up shop. He would have to call in a favor or two to get to the bottom of this screw up.

Meanwhile, Matheson noted Angela had five physicians listed in her cloud contacts. He called each office in alphabetical order.

The first three offices, because of doctor-patient privilege and the HIPAA rules, refused to talk with him, requiring written authorization from Angela or her death certificate. He was not allowed to have her information, as none of them had Matheson listed as her next of kin or emergency contact. And at the moment, he had no death certificate.

The fourth call yielded results. A young receptionist had heard about his missing child and the torched house close to their office. She was more than happy to talk with Matheson about Angela's chart. He put her on speaker phone, and we all listened to their conversation.

The doctor had prescribed painkillers for a broken ankle Angela had had almost a year ago. When it was clear she was addicted, the physician referred Angela to several detox centers, one at the Medical University of South Carolina and the other at what appeared to be a private hospital. The receptionist had no information on whether Angela had gone to either of these centers.

As Matheson thanked the receptionist for her help, the Craigslist message dinged on Angus's computer, a message from "Kevin."

"Heard about your house party and the dead woman. You ok?"

Angus began typing.

"Yeah, I'm good. Little screwed up. Need something to keep me going."

Two minutes passed before a reply was posted, making me a bit nervous that Angus might have unknowingly made a mistake —until the computer pinged.

"ER bar. Tonight after midnight. Let's say 1:00. You know the drill."
Angus grinned at me as he lifted his fingers from the keyboard.

"Well, we don't know the drill." I looked at my watch. "But we have several hours to figure it out. What do you think the ER is for?"

"It has to be the Emergency Room, that bar underneath the

Connector, not too far from the three hospitals," Nikki replied. "I can't imagine a real doctor selling drugs like this outside any hospital emergency room."

Matheson spoke as he typed. "I'm going to put Angela's contacts into mine, then contact all of them at once, asking for help. There are too many to do one by one."

"Can't hurt at this point," I replied, then shifted toward my grandfather. "Judge, do you see anything wrong with him sending out a mass email? Some strategy I'm ignoring?"

"The man is simply looking for his wife. I see no issue with this, Lee," the Judge said.

Nikki looked up. "The IP address for this Kevin guy pings too many places. It's like a spider web on a map, all the locations it has routed through so far, and it's still going. This is going to be a dead end. And I'm wondering if this is a setup. It was too easy."

I looked at my grandfather, who shrugged. "There is always a risk with an investigation," he said. "You all should go to this meet, not just you or Angus."

As Nikki and Angus began calling the most frequently used numbers, Matheson copied and pasted every contact from Angela's Gmail account into his own, then added those from the spreadsheet. In a global email to nearly 2,000 contacts, Matheson asked for help with information on Angela's or Katie's current whereabouts.

"I'm not finding anyone in her contacts named Kevin. I guess he's just on Craigslist." Matheson said.

"Let us know when you start getting responses to your emails," Nikki said. "Clarice and I will organize all that information in our system." Clarice nodded.

Immediately, he received twenty-three incorrect address notifications and another dozen out-of-office replies. Then he did the same thing on her Facebook Messenger, sending the same message copied and pasted to all her Friends. If the Charleston rumor mill could not find his wife, she would never be found.

Email responses began rolling in, and it didn't take long before we had reconstructed Angela and Katie's schedule for the past two days. One of the neighbors emailed that Katie was last seen the morning he arrived, just after breakfast, at a playdate with another neighbor.

Matheson turned his computer around and showed me the email. "Weaver had to know this if they had canvassed the neighborhood. This neighbor lives across the street from my house. They're not going to tell us anything, are they?"

"Don't assume they are moving as fast as we are," I said. "They have other cases, and I think they believe Angela may have Katie stashed somewhere while she's off having fun."

After the play date, the neighbor believed Angela walked Katie back to the townhouse for lunch at 11:30. Then what? In a follow-up email, the neighbor stated that they didn't know. Not one other person knew where Angela had taken Katie just before noon or where either of them had gone beyond that. It was a dead end.

I checked the doctor's office hours for the one Matheson had previously spoken with, then grabbed my iPad and stuffed it into my leather bag. We were lucky, as the doctor had late office hours today. I motioned Matheson toward the door.

"Where are we going?" He asked.

"To visit a doctor."

26

———————

LEE
FRIDAY, 7:00 P.M.

Hurricane Umberto makes landfall on Puerto Rico

Matheson and I walked into the doctor's office. The blonde receptionist smiled and looked Matheson over appreciatively, then frowned when she saw me enter the door behind him. The waiting room was decorated with floral wallpaper and prints of hunting dogs. Uncomfortable chairs were in rows, with a few people waiting in various forms of boredom.

"Hi, Mary," Matheson said. "I talked with you about my wife, Angela Matheson." He rested his hands on the counter, a polite smile on his face. She smiled suggestively at him in return while ignoring me. It was all I could do to keep my eyes from rolling skyward. I would love to have the effect Matheson had on people.

"Oh, sure, I remember. Did you want to make an appointment for Mrs. Matheson?"

"Well, I'm in a hurry today for the necessary information. When is Dr. Carlton's next break?"

"He has a full day today, I'm sorry. Maybe next month,

Thursday the twelfth at 11:00?" The girl double-checked her computer screen. "That is his first opening."

"That's just not going to work for me. I need to talk to him today. Right now, in fact." Matheson wiped the smile from his face to make sure she understood.

The blonde tried her prettiest smile at him, almost a flirt. "Mr. Matheson, he is slammed. Dr. Carlton is one of the busiest orthopedists in Charleston. Like I said, he won't be able to see you until next month. Can I leave him a message? If this is urgent, I'm sure he will call you tonight when he is finished with his patients."

"Why don't you just call him and have him come out. I'm sure he'll be happy to see me." Matheson's response to the receptionist, even though pleasantly phrased, was a command. He leaned over the counter as if he might jerk the poor receptionist up by her hair. I interjected before this could get out of hand.

I handed the girl my card. "Mary, we are investigating the abduction of Mrs. Matheson and the Colonel's daughter. This is a true emergency, and we won't take more than five minutes of the doctor's time. We need to see him urgently. Now."

The receptionist sat nonplussed. Her hesitancy gave Matheson the needed compulsion to start down the hallway. Before I could react, Mary had jumped from her chair and caught his arm, slowing him down. She was so frantic that Matheson took pity on her and stopped. I shook my head and waited to see what she would do.

She was almost apoplectic. "Mr. Matheson—sir—let me tell him you're here, and find out how long it will be before you can speak with him."

Matheson nodded his thanks and retraced his steps to the sitting area. When she was out of sight, he smiled broadly at me and winked. I stood beside him as I whispered, not wanting to disrupt the half-full waiting room.

"Look, dude, you need to let me handle this. You're back in the States, remember?"

He walked away from me, reached for a magazine, looked at the cover, then dropped it back on the table. Apparently, Good Housekeeping was not his favorite. He sauntered back to me, a deception, as I could see he was as tense as a cheetah.

"Yeah, well, Mac said you were that kind of girl." He whispered as we sat together, waiting.

"What kind of girl?" I asked."

"One who isn't afraid of violence." He winked at me. "And I have a feeling that's what it's going to take to get the good doctor out here."

"What else did Mac tell you?"

"Nope. You'll have to get that from him."

I would make that call once we are done here. If we were to work together, I needed to know precisely what Mac was telling the clients about me, especially to this one.

I would give the doctor fifteen minutes to appear. Otherwise, I knew my client would force his way in. The person closest to us in the waiting room was a lumpy-looking middle-aged woman sitting on the overstuffed couch in an ankle boot. She stared at Matheson as if he were crazy. He wasn't nuts, but he was definitely a pressure cooker waiting to blow. The longer it took him to find Katie, the more uncontrollable I knew he would get. Right now, however, I had to admire his control. He stood, paced, silently checking his watch as the minutes passed, then sat again, tossing the pink rabbit's foot from one hand to the other.

Exactly fifteen minutes later, as I expected, Matheson stopped flipping through magazines. His patience had evaporated. At the counter, he waited politely, trying a smile once again. I remained seated, trying to come up with an alternative plan to get the doctor out here faster.

"Mary, we're still here. And my wife and daughter are still missing. I need to talk to Dr. Carlton. We're not going to wait here all day."

"Look. I told you before," Her voice took a sarcastic tone. "He has back-to-back patients all day. I told you I would do what I could. He won't be able to see you for a while."

"A while won't do it, Mary." Matheson let his voice increase several notches. "And I don't think he wants his other patients to hear what I have to say." Four more people had joined the party by then. Several put down their reading material, anxious for the reality television show to begin.

"Mr. Matheson, please. Keep your voice down."

Cocking his head to one side, Matheson tried again. "I'm just being honest with you." He turned to face the other patients in the waiting room. "Would you nice people like to hear an interesting story about Dr. Carlton while you wait?"

I held back a smile when that got Mary's attention. "Sir, please. There is no call for this. If you follow me, I can let you wait on Dr. Carlton in his private office."

Matheson tipped an imaginary hat to the people in the waiting area. "Sorry, folks, maybe another time."

The doctor's office was lavish. His wall of glory held a diploma from the Medical University of South Carolina and another in orthopedics courtesy of Duke, a well-regarded regional medical school. Photos established him as the doctor for several area sports teams.

After a minute, the door opened and a flustered man in a white coat entered the room. "Dr. Sean Carlton" was sewn in blue script on his chest. He was holding a file that I hoped was Angela's. The doctor moved impatiently around us and sat behind his desk, placing the file before him and straightening his tie.

Dr. Carlton cleared his throat, flipped open the file, and looked over his frameless readers. "I presume you are Mr. Matheson." He looked at me. "And you are…?" His voice was impatient and resentful.

I placed my hand on Matheson's leg as he shifted to stand. His leg flinched under my hand, but he remained seated. I extended my hand with my card. "Attorney M.L. Danforth. I represent Colonel Matheson as we search for his missing wife, Angela, whom I understand you know, and their daughter, Katie."

The doctor's face blanched, and his irritable behavior suddenly disappeared. "They're missing?"

I nodded. "Yes."

He leaned forward in his chair, and his eyes locked onto mine. "How can I help you?"

"You can tell me everything you know about my wife," Matheson said, "so I can find her—and my daughter."

The doctor squinted at Matheson, concerned. "I'm not quite sure what you mean. I treated her for a fractured ankle. I put it in a cast and it healed nicely. I haven't seen her in weeks."

When he looked at me, I let Matheson continue. This could give him some control and keep his anger in check.

"I came home from being deployed overseas yesterday. There was a raging party at my house, and neither Angela nor Katie was there. My house has now been burned to the ground, destroying any evidence there might have been, another delay in the search for my family."

"I am very sorry. Your story is unfortunate. What does that have to do with me?" He looked from my client to me.

Matheson scooted forward in the too-small guest chairs in front of the desk. "Well, the police can't find either of them. My family and friends tell me that you were her doctor, and that it's because of you that Angela has a narcotics problem."

Carlton immediately closed the file folder and shoved it in the top drawer of his desk. "Now see here—" He placed his hands on his desk as if he was rising to leave.

"No, Dr. Carlton, stop right there." Matheson blocked the door. "I need to know everything, and I mean everything, about how you got Angela hooked on what I suspect is OxyContin." He pointed to the man's chair. "Now sit down and start talking."

27

LEE

FRIDAY, 7:00 P.M.

Carlton shook his head, a look of extreme irritation on his face. "I'm not responsible for the patient's inability to follow my directions. Besides, you are not listed as a next of kin or listed as a person I may inform under HIPAA. I was doing this as a courtesy. You forced your way in without an appointment, and I have other patients to attend to. This meeting will have to end. You have interrupted my day long enough."

That did it. Matheson locked the door. He then strode back to the doctor. He turned the man's chair to face him and leaned over him, his face inches from the doctor's as he placed his hands on the armrests.

"I'm not leaving here without the information I need." Matheson's voice was soft, but controlled. "Now you'll tell me how we got here. Fast."

The doctor nodded his acquiescence, his eyes wide, the bluster gone. His hands were jittery. "Sure, please have a seat. I'll tell you what you want to know." I could feel Carlton's nervousness.

Matheson returned to sit in the guest chair beside me.

"She broke her ankle playing beach volleyball, and I put her in a cast for 6 weeks. She kept telling me she was in a lot of pain. Initially, that's normal, but weeks later, she shouldn't have needed any meds. However, everyone experiences pain differently. I try not to judge the real pain level of my patients."

Matheson crossed his arms over his chest. "Gets you off the hook that way, doesn't it?"

The doctor looked away. "I stopped writing her prescriptions after four months, but for her, it was too late. Some people have a much lower addiction level than others. I referred her to a program at MUSC and another independent clinic across the river. To my knowledge, she never went to either."

Carlton hesitated and looked down at his fingers. His nails were bitten to the quick. Angela might not be his only problem patient.

I spoke up. "Was that the last you saw of her?"

"Well, no."

I looked at Matheson. He nodded. We were about to hear about how social Angela was, and I suspected that was Matheson's real fear.

"She was creative about how she asked for the prescriptions," the doctor said, his voice almost a whisper. He continued inspecting his fingers, refusing to look at the man before him.

"Do I want to know how creative?" asked Matheson.

"Probably not. Let's just say that I took advantage of that creativity, and..."

Neither of us said a word. It was enough just watching the doctor wallow in his misery.

"She took it a little hard when I told her my wife would disapprove of our relationship. She began to interrupt my practice, making hang-up calls at my home almost every night. I was desperate to get her off my back, so I connected her to a guy I know."

I interrupted the doctor. "A guy? I need a name."

He shrugged. "I don't have a name, only a phone number. I

told her she could meet him at the bar downtown under the freeway. That place on King Street." The doctor looked away from me.

What a creep. He had referred Angela to a drug dealer rather than try to get her the help she needed. I kept going. "Did you ever see her again?"

"No."

"What else can you tell us about Angela. Anything about her child?"

"There was a babysitter once. An old woman."

"What old woman?" Matheson enunciated every word.

"Don't know. Your wife handed the kid over to her once when I picked her up for a date. Called her the babysitter." The doctor started fiddling with things on his desk, picking them up and putting them down, anxious for us to leave.

"Describe her."

"White hair, dumpy, about seventy. Typical Charleston matron. She drove an old green Oldsmobile. The kid knew her."

If either of us had doubted anything about the doctor's story about Angela, at least this part rang true. Matheson's body turned rigid. The energy in the room elevated several notches.

I continued. "When did you see this old woman?"

"Two days ago."

"You mean you've been carrying on with my wife until now?" Matheson leaned forward, and I touched his knee, hoping to stop him from attacking the doctor. His hands gripped the seat so hard his knuckles were white.

"I had to cut her off after her antics this past weekend. I couldn't take any more."

"What day exactly?" I made him keep talking to me as the throbbing vein in Matheson's temple looked about to explode.

"Wednesday. She said some guy she met wouldn't give her anything, and her other sources had also dried up. She was desperate."

"Was Katie with Angela on Wednesday when you saw her?" I asked.

"Yeah. That was the day she gave the kid to the old woman. But I only saw Angela for about an hour, if that long." The doctor suddenly looked toward the wall. "It's one pill for thirty minutes of...for a blow... That's all I would give her." He turned back toward me. "She said she had to find another hit before she was due to pick up the kid again. The old woman wouldn't keep her long. Something about a fight, but I wasn't paying attention. When I arrived, I saw them going at it in the parking lot, but I was too far away to hear."

"Did Angela take Katie with her to see the guy at the bar?" I asked.

The doctor's face turned red. "How the hell would I know?"

Matheson lunged across the desk, his hand grabbing the doctor's tie and jerking the man toward him. "You said you were only with her for an hour, and she needed a fix pretty bad. Where would she go? Where did you send her?"

"I have no idea." He pushed at Matheson's chest. "Enough, please. I don't know anything else. Leave me alone."

We went out the back rather than deal with Mary.

I grabbed his arm as he stormed toward my car. "Matheson, just hold on. Don't go flying off to accuse your grandmother of anything. A lot of what this guy said was a lie."

He pushed my hand away. "But the car was right. An old green Olds. She knows something. I knew it when she wouldn't tell me last night, and then again this morning."

As we rounded the front corner of the doctor's office, heading to my Audi, a tan SUV at the opposite end of the parking lot turned the corner of the office building and went out of sight. Matheson stopped and stared.

"What's wrong?"

"I heard someone call my name. Did you hear anything?" He scanned the area around us.

I shook my head. "No."

"And that's the second time I've seen that SUV today. I think somebody's following me."

"Do you know who it is?"

"They've always been too far away, but my gut says it's somebody I know."

28

VERN

FRIDAY, 8:30 P.M.

Matheson's head felt as big as Nebraska. After retrieving his rental car from the lawyer's office, he beat it to his grandparents' house. Arriving just after the late summer sunset, no one was home, so he resigned himself to wait. Collapsing on the living room couch, the jet lag finally won. Kicking off his shoes and sliding off his jeans, he lay down for a quick combat nap.

Buzzing started to torment him. He slammed his hand repeatedly on his phone, but could not stop the incessant buzzing. Realizing that his cell phone was not the source of the racket, he headed toward the noise, desperate to stop it. The pounding grew louder.

"Alright already. Just stop." Oblivious to his navy avocado-printed boxers, he wrenched open the door. Weaver tried to push past him, but Matheson blocked and shoved him backwards.

"Where's your warrant? I didn't invite you in."

Weaver hissed at him. "I can get a warrant if I need to."

Matheson laughed. "We're at that stage of the game, are we? A judge won't give you one? Don't have enough evidence to charge me, do you?" Matheson's sarcastic tone turned dark. "Get off my damn porch."

Weaver sneered at him. "You don't own this house."

"And you are sloppy, dude. It's obvious you don't know shit." Matheson closed the screen door, locked it, and spoke through it. "Contacting my attorney now. Get off the porch."

As he texted Danforth, Weaver spoke to him through the door.

"I need to talk to you about a list of things. We've had a problem at your townhouse. I need to discuss that with you. Additionally, some neighbors mentioned that you were sending emails. Lots of them."

Matheson shrugged. "Yeah. My townhouse burned to the ground. I've already been there today. And I can email anyone I want. They're my neighbors."

Weaver's voice became more insistent. "You need to let us do this and stay out of it. It is screwing up our investigation. Some of the people on the street now refuse to talk to anyone but you. It's not helping."

Matheson had no time for this. He whirled around to face the man after firing off his text to Lee.

"Have you found my daughter?"

"We're working on it as hard as we can."

Matheson shook his head. "I've seen how you work. That's not anywhere close to hard enough." He slammed the wooden door in the detective's face and watched through the living room window. The detective walked back to his car, making himself comfortable in the driver's side, slapping a pack of cigarettes against the opposite palm for a smoke.

Matheson could hear angry waves of the Atlantic crashing on the other side of Fort Moultrie for the first time since he arrived home, even with the door closed. The impending storm had been forgotten in the frenzy to find his family, but he knew the storm couldn't possibly be this close yet. After pulling on a pair of jeans, he alternated between looking at his watch and out the window to confirm that Weaver was still waiting at the car. Finally, Lee's gray Audi parked behind the detective's sedan.

In jeans, a T-shirt, and sandals, his attorney walked past Weaver's car without a word. He could tell she was unhappy, coming through the gate, bounding up the steps, and coming through the door as he let her in. As she crossed the threshold, he realized she was more than unhappy. She was livid.

She looked at Matheson, her blue eyes blazing with anger. "You let him in?"

"No, and I haven't said anything. Weaver thought he would shock me with the townhouse being burned, but…"

"Enough." Lee threw up her palm. "Stop speaking." She looked at him like he'd grown antlers. "You did talk to him, admit it. With this guy, one word is too much, Vern."

Her hair was pulled back into a ponytail, and her t-shirt splayed a vintage Marshall Tucker Band logo across her entire chest. A woman who loved southern rock and roll. If he wasn't already attracted to her, that right there would have sealed the deal.

But right now, she was an angry warrior fighting for him, although at the moment, it was *with* him. He loved it. Yet he had the presence of mind to back away a few steps. Given their physical history, if he accidentally touched her now, he might go up in flames.

Weaver got out of his car and began walking up the sidewalk. Matheson almost felt sorry for the guy. He had never seen a woman this angry in his life. Her shoulders were thrown back like a linebacker's, her eyes fierce, and her hands clenched as if she were ready to punch something.

"You understand what a warrant is?" she shouted at Weaver through the screen door. "I told you, politely if you'll remember, that you were to contact me," she pointed to her chest, "and not him." She stepped outside on the porch and slammed the wooden door. As Matheson watched through the front window, the woman landed on the detective like a hawk on a rat.

Her words were loud and harsh. "Do you have information for my client?"

Weaver reached for the screen door handle. She shook her head and stepped squarely in front of the door. "Nope. You are not allowed in this house."

"The Moores—"

"His grandparents don't own this house. He does. I am his attorney, and I actually handled that transaction. You may not enter." She stepped toward Weaver, almost nose to nose, and he took a step backward. Then another, and another, until Weaver was off the porch and standing in the front yard.

Matheson heard the floor creak on the staircase. His grandfather came downstairs and stood with him by the window.

"What is all this about? I heard your attorney loud and clear upstairs, boy," Moore said.

"Yeah, she's not happy. I didn't know you guys were here."

"We came home and saw you on the couch. Didn't have the heart to wake you. Althea is upstairs asleep, and I was reading."

The two men listened as Danforth drilled Weaver.

"Tell me what you came here for," she said, her voice dropping several notches, "and let's get this over with. My expensive dinner at The Longboard is getting cold, and I'm sure my grandfather, Judge Rhineholdt, is getting antsy. You know him, don't you? He sure knows you."

At the mention of the Judge, the detective again stepped backwards, this time several steps until he found the sidewalk. His demeanor lost its aggressiveness. He ripped out his small notebook and flipped through several pages.

"First, Captain Norcross has received a complaint from Dr. Sean Carlton. Apparently, both of you visited the doctor yesterday and interrupted him while he was seeing patients. Is this true?"

"I interviewed Dr. Carlton yesterday, yes," Danforth replied.

"He came to us to file a complaint, but Norcross talked him out of it, even when what he described fit the textbook definition of assault by your client."

"Witnesses?"

Weaver shook his head. "He didn't have any."

"Then thank you to your Captain, but that doesn't absolve you from barging in on my client this time of night."

Weaver looked at his notebook. "Second, your client stole evidence at the morgue."

"What proof do you have of this?" she asked.

Weaver's face was indignant. "I can get you the evidence list and show you that a pink rabbit's foot is missing."

"That doesn't prove that my client took it, only that it is missing. Your chain-of-custody issues are not my problem. Next?"

Matheson grinned. He almost felt sorry for Weaver.

"We have had follow-up interviews with the teacher and the principal of the daughter's school," Weaver said. "They were very concerned that Katie was missing. Both had interesting things to say about Angela, you might want to hear." He looked at the picture window toward Matheson.

She stepped sideways to block his view. "Detective," she said, her voice exasperated, "you talk only to me."

Weaver's expression was resigned. "Look, Ms. Danforth, it would help us all if we could work together."

Lee's expression was incredulous. "Tell me what else you know," she said. "I'm losing what little patience I have left."

"We canvased the neighbors, talked with others connected with the school, and have started on a list of Katie's friends. From all indications, Katie rarely lived at home. She lived here or stayed with her friends on the weekends. Angela had a routine of forgetting to pick Katie up from school. According to the principal, the child never participated in after-school events, as Angela continually forgot to pick her up."

"So, when is the last time your information says Katie was seen?"

"We don't know at this point."

Danforth shifted back and crossed her arms over her chest. "You've not talked to the neighbor across the street?"

He opened his notepad, flipping several pages in. "Bertrice Simmons?"

"You tell me."

"Not been able to catch her. She's not been home each time we've tried." Weaver looked at Danforth. "But that could be because your client has emailed the entire world. It would help if he would stop doing this so we could move forward with our investigation."

"And his emails hamper your investigation, how?" Danforth asked him.

Matheson shook his head. As usual, Weaver was holding out on them. Bertrice was easy to find by email and even easier on Facebook. The woman had talked freely, and her love for his child came through even on FaceTime. Katie had been with her the previous morning for a summer playdate with her daughter. The woman was distraught over Katie's disappearance.

Lee was tapping her right foot, her arms still crossed over her chest. "What else?"

Weaver looked back at his notebook, then flipped it shut. "I don't have anything else to tell you."

"That's my cue to get back upstairs. That's one angry woman." Moore chuckled and headed for the stairs.

Matheson could tell Danforth had reached her limit. "You know what? You need to find that child. There will be no cooperation from me or my client until you do. And stop accusing my client of ridiculous things." She twirled her finger and pointed to the detective's car. "Don't come back here ever, without a warrant. You're just wasting my time."

Entering the house, after she closed and locked the door, Lee turned to him, her face flushed and sweaty.

"You knew you were probably a person of interest in the disappearance of your wife and child," she began. "All spouses are. I don't care that you were on a plane. They can twist things hard when they have someone they want to tag for something. What part of "don't talk to them," her fingers made quotation marks in front of his face, "without me, did you not understand?"

Matheson looked at his lawyer. Her anger was an amazing sight. Her eyes blazed, and she transformed into something he had never seen in a woman, even the ones he worked with overseas. This woman was invincible. He bet she would be hell on the battlefield. She stood in the living room, her mouth twisting in anger as her arms came up and crossed over her chest. He liked her spunk. Most women, including his wife, had been intimidated by him, but not this one.

She snapped her fingers before his face and forced him to focus on her eyes. "Vern, Do. You. Understand?"

"Got it. Won't do it again, even though I didn't do it this time." Matheson made a mental note to do whatever it was whenever he could, if he could see this warrior woman again.

"Be at my office tonight at 10:30."

Matheson immediately drew himself to attention and sarcastically saluted. "Yes, ma'am." He thought she might actually slap him, so he instantly dropped his arm back to his side.

"Until then, stay out of trouble at least until I can finish my dinner. You think you can do that?"

"Yes, ma'am. I'll certainly try, ma'am," he answered in his best military voice, as one hand flipped the pink rabbit's foot around and around on its chain.

She rolled her eyes and slammed the door on her way out. Hands on his hips, he watched her go to the Audi and screech off toward the town. Wrong or not, this woman was something else. For the first time in weeks, Vernon laughed.

29

LEE

FRIDAY, 9:30 P.M.

"I'm never going to have a moment's peace during this case, am I, Judge?" Having lost my parking space close to the restaurant when leaving to get rid of Weaver, I'd had to walk a significant distance. I was tired, sweaty, and aggravated, and still furious at Weaver, at Matheson, and most of all, at myself. I needed stability and organization, and ever since Matheson came into my life, it had been a chaotic mess. Even this dinner reservation had to be delayed

"Why is it that Weaver gives me absolutely no respect until I mention your name?" I said, building up to a serious rant. "I feel like I'm hiding behind your coattails."

The Judge picked up his wine glass and took a sip, watching me calmly over the rim.

"You're not going to respond?" I asked.

"Not until you're back to yourself, my dear. Finish your dinner. I'll order another unopened bottle of this wine to go home with us."

"I don't think wine will solve my problem."

"It might pair well with a long walk on the beach. You are

going through something that I have not seen you experience since you were in college. It might help if you talk about it."

"I've already talked about it with Clarice. And Zola."

"It has not helped, apparently. Why?"

"I don't know. And I've lost my appetite."

"Then we'll take all this to go and get home where we can have a conversation about this. I cannot bear to see you in such pain."

ON THE BEACH with an illegal glass of wine in a red party cup, my feet were bare, my jeans were rolled up to just below my knees, and I was beginning, finally, to unwind. My grandfather was beside me, and we were walking from one end of the island to the other, a two-mile journey each way.

"I think I need to start running with you every day," I said. "The end of the island is a long way." My knees were already feeling the strain, and I considered myself healthy. My grandfather said nothing, but even in the dark, I knew he was laughing at how out of shape I was.

The wine bottle was safely encased in his backpack, hidden from the beach patrol, although I doubt if one of the locals had the balls to give a ticket to the Judge. Years ago, the small community had come to the beach every evening with a glass of their favorite cocktail to watch the sunset and generally enjoy each other's company. However, once the town grew significantly and college students began to use the beach as party central, the Town Council was forced to pass a law banning all alcohol on the beach.

"Start from the beginning, Lee," my grandfather said, "and tell me what is happening to you."

I did. I began on the first day I met Vernon Matheson, and finished with the confrontation with Weaver that had occurred an hour earlier. I left out nothing, not one angry thought, or erratic emotion. And sure enough, spelling it out in chronological order in front of my grandfather while walking on the almost empty beach released me from whatever hold the situation had on me.

"Do you feel better now?" My grandfather stopped in the soft, low-tide surf, a smile on his face.

"Yes. You were right, as usual." I tapped the rim of my cup to his. "I just needed to get it out of my system, I guess."

"That is part of it, true," he replied, "but the way your mind works is why it is helpful. What is most important for you is to lay it all out verbally so that you can see how all the pieces fit. This is why we talk through all of the legal theories aloud together for your cases."

"And also why I use Clarice as the sounding board for all the facts." I grinned at him. "This is so interesting."

"Exactly. Did you not realize that you do this?"

"Not to this extent, no."

"You always have, my dear. You are a verbal learner. Yes, you can read it and understand, but your mind, for whatever reason, needs verbal confirmation before you can organize it into your mental filing cabinet."

"I still don't know what to do, Judge."

"About what? This man?"

"Yes."

"There is nothing to do. You have already taken the correct steps. Your internal compass is guiding you on the right path. The circumstances of his life must be taken care of before you can attempt any relationship."

"You're not worried about his past, or the things he's done?" I asked him. "Or the possibility that he might be guilty of something horrendous?"

"Do you believe he could have done such a thing?"

"Factually, it's possible given the timeline of the past two days."

"That is not what I am asking. Put away your lawyer hat and put on your personal one. I'll even allow you to use that ratty Boston Red Sox hat if you must." He grinned.

"No." My answer was immediate. "I feel his energy the moment he comes into the room. He is conflicted, stressed, angry, and confused, but he is not a vicious killer, despite his employment."

"Then let life do as it will, Lee. Whatever happens will happen. If you attempt to force something, you know what will happen."

"Yes, it always blows up in my face."

"Exactly." He took my free hand with his. "Your emotional life is not a courtroom, Lee, that can be strategically planned the way that you think it should go. And given your history and the trauma your prior paramour put you through, attempting to block yourself further from someone loving you will only make it worse, not better. If someone hurts you, then so be it. You have a strong support team, and I am always here for you. But you cannot grow if you continue to try to control every tiny thing around you."

I continued walking, taking another sip of wine. "Other than the physical, I don't know why I'm attracted to him."

"Because there has not been enough time for you to figure that out, Lee. Don't rush this. If it takes years for you to be comfortable, so be it. Simply because he appears to be in a rush does not mean you have to be."

I nodded, then realized he couldn't see me now that it was dark. "You're right. I'll chill a bit and let it unfold however it will." I walked a little further, listening to the sound of the waves. "We need to get a handle on Weaver."

"Yes, I've made a few more calls. It appears the man is up to his eyebrows in drugs and extortion."

"How did you learn this?"

"I have my sources."

"I need a copy of your little black book of snitches, Judge."

He laughed. "No, I think that shall go with me to the grave. You should develop your own network, Lee, especially now that you will be working with Mac."

"Understood. So that is definitely why everything has been moving at a snail's pace."

"Most likely."

"So how do we catch him?"

"At some point along the way, we will need to set him up. However, the circumstances must be right. As in the Timberline case, the dominoes must fall at exactly the right time."

"Then you need to get more involved in this case, Judge. You may see the specific piece to jerk from the Jenga pile before I do."

"I will be excited to assist, my dear. There is nothing I love better than to twist a dirty cop in the wind."

30

VERN

FRIDAY, 9:30 P.M.

After having his butt verbally handed to him again by Danforth, Matheson needed a beer. He headed for the bar Angus had identified, hoping the detective had not decided to tail him. If the cops appeared, he would swear to Lee that he was doing what she had asked: get a beer and stay out of the way.

Since he was neither a downtown rich kid nor part of the med student crowd growing up, he had no prior experience with this place. On its website, the ramshackle building snuggled up to the underside of the cross-town freeway. This expressway cut through the middle of the city, and divided a thriving black community in half. Several blocks from the massive three-hospital and medical university complex, the bar's claim to fame was its number one status in national sales of a certain cheap beer. He wasn't sure when med students had become the working class.

On the truck's radio, the newscaster was detailing the devastation in Puerto Rico. The Category 5 hurricane, which had blasted over the island and had glanced off the end of the Dominican Republic, was heading north, northwest, at a rapid clip and was building strength, if that was possible on the Saffir-Simpson wind scale. The winds were reported to be over 150 miles per hour, and after the last Hurricane Hunter aircraft flew through, they noted that the speed was climbing toward 160 mph and moving forward at 35 mph. The wind scale didn't go that high, and the announcer's words conveyed the NOAA forecaster's concern over the speed.

Matheson felt his stomach drop. He had no clue how to find his daughter, and the thought of her being alone in the storm frightened him more than anything he had ever experienced. His only option was to find this dealer, track down his wife, and find his child.

Driving by the bar, parking was best several blocks toward the nicer end of the street. The freeway was the current dividing line between the more upscale and seedy establishments, with the bar on the seedy side. Matheson took his time and cased several blocks on either side, venturing down several alleys before parking. Gentrification was taking hold on the seedier side, and before long, he knew the peninsula of Charleston would only be for the well-to-do.

Angela must have been desperate, because the woman he knew would never have set foot inside a bar like this in the daytime, much less the garbage-strewn weeds under the crosstown freeway at night. He had trouble reconciling the things people were telling him with the woman he had been married to for five years. He had to face the fact that he didn't know his wife even one little bit.

He thought back to when they had met. That summer had been carefree. They'd spent many days on the beach or playing volleyball on the public court. Matheson couldn't remember a time when he had been so relaxed. Besides being attractive, Angela was interesting, someone he wanted to get to know better. Yet with only thirty days leave, he had little time to get to know her in depth. Even after they were married, he felt they were close, especially after Katie had been born. After talking with the doctor, he understood lately why his wife had been so distant.

He looked around at the bar and shook his head. This was not his wife.

Beer in hand, Matheson sauntered by a pool game in progress and sat on a stool to watch. The crowd was thicker than he expected for a weekday. Two guys caught his attention. In the corner, deep in conversation, the first man was tall with a basketball-shaped beer gut in a dirty red ball cap. The other was rangy with facial scruff and tattooed sleeves, wearing a straw cowboy hat with a chunk missing from the brim. When a group of students in faded green scrubs piled through the door, laughing and talking, ready for a party, Matheson shifted to a different part of the room.

Ball Cap motioned for Cowboy to follow him outside. Matheson watched them leave as he casually finished his beer and then moved to the outside porch. The two men walked across the street and into the shadows. They exchanged something, with their hands immediately going into their front jeans pockets. Ball Cap nodded when they were done and walked north on King; Cowboy headed back to the bar.

"Hey, Blue honey." The voice was accompanied by the click of heels down the steps as a woman strutted by Matheson. Cowboy grinned, and the two met in the middle of the street. When he reached out to put his arm around the woman and give her a side hug, Cowboy's T-shirt sleeve slid up his arm, revealing a swirling design in blue ink with the number 420 in the center.

Even in a town this small, it was too easy. He carefully pulled out his phone and took a photo, then called Junior, Darrell's cousin. Once he had more information, he would pass it all on to Lee and her team.

"Hey, Junior. Did you find out anything?" Matheson tried to keep the impatience from his voice.

Darrell's cousin's whisper told him to wait one minute. A

screen door slammed. Matheson knew he'd fled to the backyard to talk.

"Yeah, I did. Sorry, man, my wife had me trapped after dinner." Junior paused to catch his breath. "You don't want to mess with these guys."

"Who are they?" he asked Junior.

"DJ says this 420 guy is some scrawny white dude who has been dealing most anything for the past few years. Says he likes the ladies and gives them freebies to get them hooked."

"What does he look like?"

"My cousin says he's thin, about five ten, and wears a ratty old cowboy hat and boots. Has stringy hair in a scruffy ponytail." Matheson watched as Cowboy, with the same description, strolled in front of the bar, making scores and telling jokes. He'd never seen drugs sold out in the open like this in Middle America, USA.

"And I'm supposed to be afraid of that?"

"He has backup, some gang. Some of them are supposed to be real heavyweights, and all of them carry."

"What's the deal with this Emergency Room bar?"

"What do you mean?" Junior asked.

"You think he'd have somewhere a little less public to do his deals. Like a dead house somewhere, or a back room, not front and center on one of the busiest streets in Charleston."

"What the—?" Junior asked. "You're there now, aren't you? I can hear the noise in the background. Have you lost your mind?"

"Don't worry about me. What else?"

"Well, DJ says the uniforms that patrol that area are on the take. And there's a deal about 'protection' with the bar."

"You mean like wise guy protection? In Charleston?"

"It's all over, not just in the big cities. You know that. Supposed to be some big shot detective over in Mount Pleasant. He moonlights there when he's off duty."

"What else?"

"Detective Dude carries a blade, and my cousin says he knows how to use it. He may look fat and slow, but he's not. DJ says not to underestimate him for one second."

The man Darrell described had to be a different detective. It made sense, though, why the investigation was so slow. If Weaver was a part of the drug network, he probably already knew where Angela was and didn't want to disclose his involvement. Yet Matheson could not visualize Weaver being fast with a blade; a big Desert Eagle pistol was more his style.

"After all the nasty people Darrell and I dealt with in Iraq, and you're worried about one blade? Have any more details of what this guy looks like?"

"No, that's all the info I got. You need to stay away from these guys, Vern."

"Well, whatever. Don't you worry about me. I will do whatever it takes to find Katie."

"Where do you want me to meet you? You need a wingman."

"Look, Junior, I appreciate your loyalty. I know you're offering this because of Darrell, but don't worry about me. I appreciate the information. Really. But I don't want you involved in this."

"Don't do this alone. Let me—"

"No man. I'm not going to risk it. You don't have nine lives like a cat."

31

WEAVER

FRIDAY, 10:00 P.M.

Dumping the last of the boxes onto the floor of the trailer, Weaver stepped back and took a look at its inhabitant. Rato wasn't the smartest, but he would be the least suspected. Weaver had rearranged the way Harbin had set up the business to be more efficient and capitalize on each dealer's strong points. Rato had tried to deal, but failed miserably. Even though he was willing, he just wasn't cut out for it. The two of them had shifted the boxes at night in a windowless panel van Weaver had rented for the job to avoid inquisitive neighbors. The Mexican's new job was to guard the drugs.

"*Nadie entra ni sale, Rato,*" Weaver said to the man as he was leaving, reminding him of his job. "*Te llamaré cada vez que un concesionario llegue para realizar una recogida.*" Each time a dealer needed additional product, they were to call Weaver with the amount needed and the detective would arrange a drop off.

"*Entiendo,*" Rato responded, nodding his head in understanding.

This storage trailer in North Charleston was one of three. There was another on the eastern side of the county in Awendaw, and a third at the very western part of Charleston, in Ravenel.

The other two "sitters," as Weaver mentally referred to them, kept to themselves in their rural neighborhoods. The other two mobile homes were in uninhabited areas and were easier to access without neighbors nearby. But it was the trailer in Dorchester Village that did the most business.

Setting up the distribution this way allowed Weaver to control the pills warehoused, the amount given to the dealers, and he would know to the minute how much money that dealer owed. There was no question when the nightly count came in, whether a dealer was short either on pills or funds. It only took one example, made six months prior, for the dealers to understand that Harbin had given him full authority and that he meant business.

Now that he had this chore accomplished, Weaver had to deal with his day job. He didn't appreciate getting his ass handed to him by Danforth, but guessed he should have expected it. He wasn't on top of his game lately, that's for sure. Given that the Colonel had PTSD, Weaver thought it might be easy to get the man sidetracked, and maybe even detained in jail or in the hospital, anything to get both Matheson and Danforth out of his way so that he could find Angela Matheson first.

His flip phone buzzed with a call. Sean Carlton. "Hey Sean," he answered. "What's up?"

"I need you to give this man whatever he wants." Sean's voice was terrified.

"What man?" Weaver asked. "What are you talking about? What's happening?"

"He thinks I have something to do with some woman. I've told him I don't know what he's talking about. You gotta help me." Weaver heard a loud slap followed by a "uuumph," and then something heavy hitting a wooden floor.

"What woman?" There was only silence in response. "Sean, talk to me. You're not making sense."

"Where is Angela Matheson?" The whispered voice that responded was not Sean's.

"I don't know who that is." Weaver felt a jolt of pain slam through his chest. Was this Matheson? Would Danforth even allow her client to do something like this? Or was the man a loose cannon, having come back from overseas with half a brain?

He heard a chuckle on the other end of the phone. "You are as stupid as you look, aren't you, Detective?" the whispered voice said. "Tell me where she is and I'll let your friend go."

"I'll have police there in less than three minutes," Weaver said.

"You don't even know where I am," the voice said. "Give me her location. Now."

"I don't have it. Even if I did, I wouldn't tell you, Matheson."

Another chuckle floated over the phone. "Boy, you are way off base," replied the whispered voice. "Either give me her location, or you'll be next."

"Who is this?" Weaver asked. "The only person I know who wants the location of Angela Matheson is her husband. If you aren't him, then who are you?"

"Say goodbye to your friend."

"Wait!" Weaver shouted, but heard only labored breathing. "Sean?"

"Help me." Sean's voice whispered.

32

SHARPE

FRIDAY, 11:00 P.M.

Hurricane Umberto offshore at Jacksonville, Florida

Leaning on the hood of the SUV, Sharpe raised the air rifle and looked through the sight from the third level of the commercial parking deck. The darkness covered his presence. He focused on the front left corner of the doctor's office, the first of three cameras. The *whump* of the first muffled shot was covered by the traffic on Coleman Boulevard. Looking through his sight, he was rewarded by broken glass. His second shot cleanly hit the next camera.

Taking his time, he disassembled the rifle, returning each piece to its black, tablet-sized case. Stowing the weapon, he donned a new baseball cap, making sure the bill blocked his face from the remaining camera or any others at businesses he might have overlooked. But he doubted there were any. People here were too trusting. And his training made him too careful. The parking deck was camera-free, although he was sure they would be installed after this.

Tracking the soldier and his attorney had been too easy, especially when the detective got involved. None of them watched their back. He had been delighted when he'd learned Matheson had returned home. Together with his lawyer, they were piecing together the trail of his trashy wife, relieving Sharpe of the need to conduct any investigation. Once they found Angela, he would snatch her up himself.

Moving the battered SUV several blocks away, he cut through the alley to the medical center. The rear parking lot was empty. Sliding along the back of the building, he stopped directly under the camera. He wished there had been no streetlight, but taking it out would have been overkill. Standing in the truck bed, he looped a rope over the old camera unit and used his full body weight to dislodge it. When it dropped into his arms, he took a better look at it—absolute garbage from China.

The naive receptionist had not blinked that afternoon when he pretended to be a state inspector checking their system. He had hours and took his time "inspecting the building," noting anything especially flammable. The polypropylene stuffing of the couch and waiting room chairs was precisely what he needed. The alcohol he used as an accelerant was already in the supply room, saving valuable time and leaving no trace. Once the match was lit, the furniture would melt in less than a minute.

Office procedures here were outdated. Everything was on paper rather than a computer, making it easier than expected. His own physician used a tablet, notes typed immediately during the visit by a flunky who followed the doctor around like a dog. Not this guy. The doctor had been generous with his money when it came to his office decoration, but frugal with the things that mattered, which explained the caliber of the receptionist.

The doctor's house had been the same way. He smiled at the silliness. There was no alarm system, cheap door locks, and the good doctor was mystified when the car keys were plucked out of his hand just inside the house. Carlton had assumed he could buy his way out of the problem, but it was the worst thing he could have tried. Just the offer of money sealed his fate.

The man's phone contacts provided Sharpe with surprising information. Calling the number the doctor had sworn was his supplier had been eye-opening when Detective Weaver answered. He kept his own voice to a whisper and instantly had another target.

Hog-tied in his trunk, it wasn't easy to transfer Carlton from the Lexus to the truck bed, especially when Carlton realized he was being kidnapped. He begged and cried, but it made no difference. The doctor's house quickly went up in flames.

"Asshole." Checking on the doctor in his truck bed, Sharpe slapped another layer of duct tape across the doctor's mouth and covered him again with a tarp. He'd dumped the doctor's car in West Ashley and left the keys in the front seat. He was sure it had been stolen by now.

Moving to the back door of the office, he looked at the dead-bolt and, without hesitation, gave it a swift kick with his steel-toed boot. The door only cracked open, not bouncing against the interior wall, it would have done if he were younger and stronger. The alarm was still dead, just as he had left it earlier that afternoon.

The doctor's office yielded stacks of bank-wrapped hundred-dollar bills in the locked credenza behind the desk that only took a letter opener to pop. He stuffed the money into the small back-pack he was wearing. Drugs were stashed in a locked square metal fishing tackle box, each brightly colored group in its section. That tiny lock snapped easily, forced by a pair of scissors. Those, he tossed about on the floor.

When finished, he headed directly for the examination room. The glass-paned cabinet he had seen earlier in the day shattered with a kick, the small lock useless against the force. With gloved hands, he reached in for the bottles of isopropyl alcohol. With one in each hand, he took his time, splashing the alcohol throughout the building, returning to the supply cabinet until all two dozen bottles were empty. He took a rest, grabbing a water from their break room refrigerator, as he let the alcohol soak in.

Sharpe pulled books of matches from his pocket. The reception area and each office quickly ablaze, he reserved the final three books for the end. He tossed them into the doctor's office, the blaze immediately burning a hole in the antique carpet, a finger of fire licking the hand-embroidered silk curtains. With a *whoosh*, the fire was up to the ceiling in seconds.

The office, converted from an old house built at the turn of the century, burned quickly and intensely, fed by alcohol and inexpensive furniture. Outside and away from the toxic fumes, he took one full minute to enjoy the smell and feel the intensity of the fire before he turned away, ready to rid the world of one completely useless physician.

Driving away from Mount Pleasant, Sharpe turned up the radio, waiting for the weather report at the top of the hour. The storm was off the coast of Jacksonville, Florida. NOAA predicted the hurricane to head steadily north, curving with the land until it made landfall somewhere between Jacksonville and the Outer Banks of North Carolina.

He had no time for this hurricane.

At the marsh, Sharpe hoisted himself into the long bed and threw back the tarp after catching his breath. He ignored the muffled screams as he reached for the hog-tied doctor. The man's squirms were useless with the amount of tape around his hands, legs, and head. He wrestled the man to the edge of the truck bed and pushed him over. The *whoompf* from the slam of the doctor's body onto the muddy ground was followed instantly by a *whoosh* as air escaped the doctor's lungs.

Sharpe stopped and looked around. There was no one. He continued, hurrying to have the job finished by his friends in the marsh. Eyes bulging, the sharp tang of fear emanating from the doctor was stronger than the stink of the pluff mud nearby. Sharpe leaned over, upside down to the man on the ground, resting his hands on his knees to give himself a breather. He spoke to Carlton in a conversational tone.

"I just want to be certain you know why you're in this position."

He did not expect a response, of course, given the man's taped mouth, but felt it his moral duty to be certain the good doctor understood why he was about to die. He stared into the man's eyes, only receiving a blink in response. He continued.

"You have quite the reputation, hooking people on drugs. For what? Money? Sex? What will your children think when all this comes out? Or your wife?" That got a reaction. He wondered if it was his wife, but thought it was likely his children. Carlton tried to beg, his voice a whine. Sharpe shook his head. "Nope. Nothing you can say can turn this around." He stood erect then, his voice taking on a more threatening tone. "There are others you hooked, you know it, I know it. And then there are the other scumbags you dealt with. I'm cleaning up every last one, hear me? Every last one. I made my decision, and that's final. You'll have to deal with it."

Snatching the man's feet, Sharpe began the march to the water's edge. The trip was slow, given the doctor's squirming and begging, and Sharpe's exhaustion. Halfway to the pool, he dropped Carlton's feet.

"I can't go any further. They'll have to come get you when they're hungry." The smell of the doctor's bowels fouled the muggy air, and his eyes blinked rapidly.

Sharpe used his feet to roll the man into the grass. The alligators would play with their food a bit before dragging it into the water. Besides, the doctor needed to feel the pain and comprehend the extent of the pain he had caused others. Sharpe would wait a bit, but then he had to drive by the lawyer's office before going home.

Safely inside the cab, Sharpe rolled down the driver's side window and waited patiently for the alligators to find their meal. It took ten minutes, instead of two. But he was rewarded when a loud snap and a splash broke the night air.

Then all went silent.

33

LEE

FRIDAY, 11:00 P.M.

In my office, I called my client, and Matheson picked up on the first ring.

"Where are you?" I asked, unable to hide the irritation in my voice. "You were to be here at 10:30." I'd purposefully told him to arrive early, even though I was certain that he would drag in late. However, I didn't expect him to ignore me completely.

"You told me to chill and get a beer," he replied.

"Where are you?" I asked again. "I have a serious suspicion you're at a bar where you shouldn't be."

"Now you're my babysitter?" he retorted.

I waited silently until he finally gave in and told me what he'd been doing and the information he'd obtained from his friend Darrell's cousin. I couldn't decide whether to scream at him or fire him. First, his behavior at the doctor's office, then talking to Weaver. Now Matheson had beelined himself to the bar on North King Street to watch the drug dealer. Irritated, I cut to the chase, trying to keep my voice calm and professional.

"Vern, while I appreciate your vigilance, I need you to let my team do their job. You've given me gossip from some friend's cousin. I can't use that in court. I need hard proof, and we don't need you screwing things up before we get there."

"You're not moving fast enough." Matheson's voice was matter-of-fact. "My wife and child have been missing for over thirty hours. And there's a hurricane headed this way."

I'd already heard the forecast for the storm. The National Hurricane Center had it making landfall somewhere between Florida and North Carolina. My pulse increased several notches just at the thought of the word "hurricane."

"Look, if you want to do this alone, I'll let Mac know. My team has been working non-stop, chasing down all the responses generated from your emails and social media calls."

"Now wait, I didn't mean--" His voice contained an edge of annoyance. I would have preferred contrition.

"You know you are a loose cannon. You've admitted to me as much. I don't know how you conducted your operations overseas, but that's not how we do business here. If you want us to continue working with you, I'll need you to get here now. We need to be in place well before midnight, and you're the one slowing us down."

My thumb was on its way to stop the call when he responded. "I'll be there as soon as I can." Finally, his voice carried a hint of remorse. I let out a frustrated sigh and paced back and forth, then punched in Mac's number.

"This client of yours is a handful," I said before Mac could say hello. While I didn't want to dramatize Matheson's actions, the case was already spiraling out of control, and I'd only been involved for a little more than a day. My team was working way beyond office hours, and I wasn't sure when any of us would get sleep. And now there was the hurricane. While my discussion with my grandfather helped me sort things out, it did nothing to resolve the issue with my client and his renegade behavior. I needed Mac to step in. After all, it was his friend.

"He can be a bit forceful, yes."

"Forceful. Is that what this is?"

Clarice stuck her head in the door. "We have a problem." Her concerned expression told me it had to be serious, so I punched the call to speaker.

"Mac, you're on speaker." I looked back up. "What's up, Clarice?"

"The doctor you visited earlier today? His office has been torched, just like the Colonel's townhome. The doctor's house was also ransacked, partially burned, and he's currently listed as missing. The police are looking for Colonel Matheson. They're on their way."

"Mac, you hear that? Does your client have an affinity for fire? This is the second time that something related to him has burned."

Mac didn't hesitate. "Lee, this man saved my life more than once. He doesn't play games and is one of the best leaders I've ever seen in the field. Yes, he's a bit unorthodox, but so are you. If all this is going on, his wife and kid are in serious trouble. Don't bail on him now. He needs you, but I'm sure he won't admit it."

I blew out an exasperated breath as Clarice stepped into the room when Mac's call ended. "Lovely," I said. "I thought the Timberline Farm case was nuts. This is getting worse by the minute. We're all here working late, waiting on him, and he's over at the bar already." I looked at her. "What's your take on him?"

"Well, even though Matheson is all over the place, I guess I would be too if my wife and child were missing and someone was torching every place I came in contact with. He's jet-lagged, has orders with a time limit, and I'm quite sure, just from the vibes I'm getting, that he does need Zola's help." She looked out the window toward the back garden even though it was dark. "And it is absolutely amazing the way he looks at you."

"The personal thing is off the table until this is done. You know that."

"I don't think he got the memo," she retorted. "What do you think's happening?"

"The same as you. My gut says his wife has seriously pissed off someone in high places and now she, and unfortunately the kid, are paying for it."

"Can the police provide any help at all? Someone other than Weaver, I'm saying."

"No," I said, "and the Judge has pulled all the strings he has. They are just slow." Sometimes Charleston could be slow, but when the forensics team didn't immediately arrive at the townhouse after Matheson called Mac, I knew there was a problem.

"Who is coming to talk to Vern now? Weaver?" I asked. Clarice shrugged. "Whoever it is, please put him in the vacant office down the hall. Call Matheson now and tell him to come through the back. He'll be here any minute."

"Got it."

I turned to go to the conference room, then shifted back. "You know you don't have to stay for our planning session tonight," I said to her.

"This is the first case from Mac," Clarice said. "It's important, and I'm not sitting this one out. I'll keep an eye on that detective when he gets here. I don't trust him for a minute."

"Neither do I."

I LET Weaver stew a bit before I went to the vacant office.

"We have another problem," was the first thing out of his mouth, as if *we* were a team. The man was sweating heavily even in my air-conditioned office.

"And what is that?" I sat, not bothering to get him another coffee. He could drink the dregs of his cold one, given to him by Clarice.

"The doctor you interviewed yesterday is missing. His house

and office were torched, the office still burning. I need to find him."

I feigned indifference. "And this has to do with my client, how?"

He was insistent, his demeanor desperate. "Carlton didn't come home from work," he said, "or at least his car isn't there. His house has been ransacked. The fire department does not believe he's in the burning office, but they can't confirm that because the fire was so hot."

Someone was cleaning up behind Matheson. Or had my client reached his breaking point, and instead of being at a bar on King Street, had been torching Carlton's office? I remembered the roaming SUV, the person Matheson said he could not recognize. Was that a ruse? Several possibilities arose, one a little more likely than the others, but I couldn't be sure. I'd told my grandfather that I didn't think Vern could kill. But his constant rogue behavior was beginning to cause me more than heartburn. I needed him to get out of his own way so that we could find his family.

"Is the fire arson?" I asked Weaver.

"Like I said, suspected, but not confirmed. But the fire is the least of my worries. I need to find Sean."

"You know him personally?"

"I need to see your client," Weaver said, ignoring my question. "Where is he?"

"He isn't here, and given the late hour, he won't be. You just talked to him a few hours ago when you interrupted my dinner."

"I need to talk to him again now. If he has an alibi, I need it. Otherwise, I don't mind telling you, he's my primary suspect for Carlton's disappearance."

I held out my hand, and he squinted in confusion. "What?"

"Warrant? I need to see it."

He shook his head. "I just need to know where he's been for

the last two hours. He's not on Sullivan's Island still, I checked. His grandmother doesn't know where he is."

"Either give me the warrant for his arrest or get out of my office." Weaver stood and flipped his empty coffee cup into the trash can as he walked out the door. "This is harassment, detective. Do I need to call the Chief again?"

34

LEE

FRIDAY, 11:20 P.M.

Hurricane Umberto churns off the Florida-Georgia state line, slowing to a crawl.

All six-foot-whatever of him strode into my office, without one ounce of contrition. I pointed to a seat on the couch. The four of us were to go to the bar downtown, and I needed him to be focused on the task at hand before we entered the conference room with the others.

Matheson sprawled in the small chair, all arms and legs like an octopus, more relaxed than I'd seen him in the past two days. I wondered how many beers he'd had.

"We need to account for every minute of your whereabouts since you left Syria down to the minute you sat at this table," I told him, "particularly the last few hours."

"You know where I've been." He squinted at me as if wondering what I was up to.

"Not exactly. I know where you've told me you've been. We need a firsthand witness who can confirm where you've been at all times."

"There are times I've been alone. Are my grandparents

supposed to sleep with me? What about when I'm in the car alone? You're not being realistic, Lee."

"Look, first your townhouse burned, then the doctor's office we visited."

"Seriously? Carlton's office?" Matheson's face showed genuine surprise.

"Yes, and he's missing." I retorted. "Every building you walk into ends up on fire. Weaver was all over me about where you've been. We need to be prepared."

"I don't burn things down. You know I had nothing to do with any of this."

"Honestly, I don't," I replied. "You left here with exactly enough time to torch Carlton's office, and were in the middle of something when I called you. Were you really at the bar? Do I need to get Clarice to check on our fire insurance for this building and up the coverage?"

Matheson shifted forward in his seat, his anger building, shown by the throbbing vein at his temple, until he caught my smirk. "Yes, I was at the bar." His voice was low and controlled. Even though my last comment had diffused him, I'd definitely hit a nerve. "They have video, and you can check it tonight when we get there."

He knew I wouldn't blow our cover and do that tonight, but if he pushed me, I'd return tomorrow.

"Vern," I said softly, "can you see how your actions can be twisted and why clear alibis are necessary for every minute of every day? Sit with Clarice and tell her exactly where you were and who you have been with since you arrived. I need to know where the holes are so we can figure out how to plug them. We have a few minutes before we need to get moving. We cannot allow the police to have even a millimeter to squeeze through with an accusation."

"You don't trust me." His voice was cold.

"Give me a break, Vern." I could not keep the exasperation out of my voice. "I'm trying to protect you. That's my job. Mac is available on video in the conference room if you'd like to discuss hiring a new lawyer. Talk to him. Seriously, though, with your temper and how your world is crashing down around you, I think you should be able to see it from my point of view."

He nodded his understanding, but I could see from the flexing muscles on the side of his face that he was still angry.

"You gave Clarice a copy of my orders?" he asked.

"Of course. That part is covered. Give her the complete timeline after that, and when you guys are done, join us in the conference room." I stood to leave, then remembered I had another question. "Where did you get the information that you gave me on the phone? About the drugs and Weaver's involvement?"

"From Junior, my best friend Darrell's cousin who lives in Goose Creek." Matheson's fingers on one hand began tapping on his leg.

"How well do you know Junior?" I asked, feeling uncomfortable that another person I didn't know might be privy to our plans tonight.

"I've seen him once or twice when Darrell and I were home on leave."

"Did he meet you at the bar?"

"No, I just called him. Junior, I guess you can say, is connected to the dirty underside of Charleston."

"You trust this cousin not to spread what we're doing?" My alarm was growing.

"Yeah, I do." Matheson was way too relaxed about Junior. "He knows what I'm capable of."

I did not *even* want to analyze that response. "After you finish with Clarice," I said, heading to the door, "we'll quickly plan what we're doing at the bar tonight about that dealer."

Angus and Nikki were working in the conference room. The Judge was on his MacBook, and Mac was present in the background via video. Lawrence Security Service's main office was in

Alpharetta, Georgia, north of Atlanta. I wasn't sure how well this long-distance employment situation would work, and tonight would be a good test.

"What did you find out about this guy we're meeting tonight?" I asked Angus.

"His real name is Keith Ellison," Angus said. "We are dealing with a small-time hustler who has been in and out of the state system for the past fifteen years. The bad part?" Angus slid several sheets of paper toward me. "This guy likes his weapons. He is always considered armed and dangerous."

"I'm sure Vern will be able to find out whatever we need." Mac's voice came through the speaker. "He's had experience with questioning suspects in difficult places overseas. Weapons won't bother him for a minute."

"Mac, you haven't been around him lately," I replied. "He's not reliable at the moment, so much so that I'm thinking of getting him to sit out tonight."

"He'll never go for that." As I was about to continue, the conference door opened, and Vern and Clarice joined us. As they found seats at the table, I spoke to the conference receiver. "Mac, before I forget, I'll call you once we're done here, and we can review a few things."

Matheson gave me the side-eye from across the table.

"The plan," Angus began, "is to be at the bar at midnight on North King Street, and honestly," he looked at Matheson, "we're cutting it close." There will be four of us. We'll need to spread out to watch for the dealer and for Weaver."

"I think I should handle this alone. It's part of what I did overseas—" Matheson began.

"No, absolutely not," I interrupted him. "You aren't a singleton, Colonel. This is an investigation, not an enemy encampment where you're looking for combatants to kill through a rifle scope."

Matheson looked like I'd slapped him, and I realized then

that I'd crossed a line, but it was too late. I nodded for Angus to continue.

"We'll park approximately here," Angus said, pointing to the map he had on a large monitor set up for the group to observe, "and will go in here and here." He pointed to two points on King Street. "We need to surveil the neighborhood as best we can, staying out of sight. This Ellison guy could have partners, guys helping him, who knows."

"I'll have the audio equipment that will capture whatever he says from a significant distance," said Nikki. "Remember that whatever you say," she looked at Matheson, "will also be captured."

"Copy," was Matheson's quiet response.

He looked away from Nikki, and I could see his frustration from the squinting of his eyes and the way he was gritting his teeth. Yet, I could not let him run roughshod over Charleston, and he had to know it. However, with so much of his past possibly a trigger, I needed to know the details if I was going to avoid those landmines. Something about my 'rifle scope' comment was clearly one of those.

After discussing a few more details, we all broke to get food and to pack up to go. That gave me enough time to call Mac back privately from my office.

"Hey," I said when he answered.

"Before I forget," Mac replied, "tell the Judge that I checked with Homeland Security in MB. They are to get back with me with anything they find about the child."

"Got it. I hope they know something. I'm getting a bad feeling. That little girl has been missing too long."

Mac was silent.

"What?" I asked.

"Maybe you need to cut the guy some slack, Lee."

"You're kidding me. Detective Weaver is all over me. Every time Matheson talks with someone other than me, someone dies or something gets torched. And that's not all. Something's going on with this guy mentally. You knew he needed help, but I think it's more urgent than either of us expected."

"How so?" Mac's voice told me that he was holding something back.

"Just a gut feeling. He can't hold in his temper. He wants to do his thing his way, mostly on his own, and yes, I know his child is missing, but it's more than that. It's like he wants revenge for something. And there's this energy thing I don't know what to do with."

Mac hesitated, and I waited him out until he finally spoke. "He's already called me about that energy thing. I feel like I'm in middle school here."

Yes, Matheson had a right to talk with his friend, but I wish he hadn't. "What did he say?"

"He has feelings for you. I know, to a small extent, anyway, what he's feeling, even though we've sorted that out, I guess."

I had no idea how to respond to any of this. So, I didn't.

"Look," Mac said, "let him think he's running the show with the dealer. I know you won't let him go too far. He needs to feel like he's in control of something in his life."

"Mac," I tried to keep the exasperation from my voice. "He's already referred tonight to 'what he's capable of.'"

"And if you want to know the truth," Mac's temper was ramping up, "if he told you details, which I seriously doubt, he gave you only one-tenth of the facts. The man is a walking death squad."

"You're making my point, Mac. And you want to let him loose on Charleston?"

"Lee, if you trap this man into a corner, we both are going to regret it. Let him have a little breathing room."

I took in the inference he was trying to force me to see. I had no idea where this man's line was drawn to figure out where this "breathing room" might be.

"Can you at least work on him a bit to talk either with Zola or go to the VA for help? I've asked him to go with me to Zola, but I'm pretty sure he'll back out. I know the clock is ticking on his orders. What happens if he doesn't comply with the order?"

"Most likely, it will result in a 'dismissal,' a separation from the military, equivalent to a dishonorable discharge, due to the prior events in Afghanistan and then the recent one involving his team. Matheson himself alluded to his negligence when we talked, and that it rose to the level of manslaughter. He'd lose his retirement, any unemployment he could claim, and he'd be out of luck for other government benefits, such as student loans, that sort of thing. He's fortunate he got out with a medical retirement. Someone had to throw some hefty weight around for that to happen."

"So, if he doesn't get evaluated, he'd lose any VA benefits at the time when he needs them the most?" I asked.

"Yes, absolutely. I'll have to talk with him and get him to make an appointment. I'll let you know when that is."

"Can I get a complete copy of Matheson's file? I'd like to know exactly what happened over there. If I'm supposed to be his support system, then I need to know what I'm up against. He's not going to tell me."

"I'll see what I can do, but you know that's pretty confidential. You might want to be a little patient and let him tell you. There's a lot that needs context, not some heavily redacted governmental file. And honestly, Lee, there's a lot that he won't be able to tell you. Ever."

The realization that there would be a massive block of Vern's life that I'd never see or hear about caused me to blink. I was silent as I thought through what that meant. There might be no way that Vern could ever be back to normal. And actually, Vern may not have ever been what I considered "normal."

"And Lee," Mac paused again. I waited. "He's not one to enter into things lightly. He never has been. He has serious feelings for you, and this isn't any jealousy talking on my part. He said he felt this way the first time he met you years ago, but felt like he shouldn't pursue it then. He doesn't feel that way now. He's all in."

Part of me was exhilarated, and the other part of me wanted to choke the life out of Vern for talking with Mac. And after this conversation, if I was honest with myself, there was a significant amount of trepidation on my part.

"I'll take care of this Mac. It won't be a problem."

"I just don't want this to get out of hand. There's too much at stake for him. And for you."

"Understood." I didn't know how to tell him it had already gone way past out of hand, but I wasn't going to have a detailed discussion about this with my employer, regardless of their friendship.

What a mess.

35

LEE

SATURDAY, 12:00 A.M.

The bar was in full swing by midnight. Angus had Matheson move the rental car closer to the bar on a side street, its nose facing the bridge entrance in case we had to slam out. Watching from the car, it didn't take us long to spot Cowboy, as Matheson had named him. Even though we all knew his 420 Craigslist nickname and his real name, Ellison was still Cowboy to us, especially after we all saw the hat.

After seeing his face, "Weasel" would have been a much more fitting description.

There was no sign of Detective Weaver, but we waited to be certain he was not around before we headed toward the bar to meet with Cowboy. Because of Angus's reminder of Ellison's priors and his affinity for weapons, I had no desire to send Angus and Nikki alone to talk with this dealer, but did not want to risk being seen by Weaver.

"Weaver should be here somewhere," I said. "If the detective truly protects the dealer or the bar, he should have shown his face by now."

Matheson shrugged. "I think we'll be hidden well enough across the street, so that even if he's here, it won't matter."

"You three," Nikki said to the rest of us, "head out across the side of the parking lot so you will be hidden in the dark. I have Weaver's photo, and will look inside the bar. If I come outside with a beer, that's my signal that he's inside. I'll think of something to keep him occupied while you guys talk with Cowboy." She handed the recording equipment to Angus. "Don't forget to use this," she told him.

Angus switched off the overhead light and eased open the passenger side car door. We were reasonably sure Cowboy and the guy from Angela's email, Kevin, were the same, even though Nikki could not trace the Craigslist message specifically back to Ellison. We would be in a predicament if they were two different people and showed up simultaneously. According to Matheson's friend, however, the man he described was the same one Matheson had seen. And it was doubtful a second guy would poach on Cowboy's territory.

We waited in the shadows beneath the freeway, watching Nikki go inside the bar. A few minutes after midnight, Cowboy appeared, stepping outside the bar and heading across the street toward us, right on schedule. When he stepped into the edge of the shadows, Matheson angled to cut him off on one side, Angus the other. Nikki appeared outside the bar, sans beer, and took a different route to cross the street, down half the block, and into the parking lot from the opposite side. I followed her route.

The flame of a Zippo lighter broke the darkness as Cowboy lit a cigarette. Matheson backed against one of the concrete posts in the darkness. After finishing his cigarette, Cowboy looked around. Seeing no one, he turned back toward the bar. Matheson materialized from the shadows and blocked his path. Nikki clicked on the recording gadget she held in one hand, keeping a safe distance while hidden behind a support column.

Cowboy blurted out his confusion. "You ain't her."

Matheson stayed away from the circle created by the street light. "No, you're right. I'm not female."

The man stubbed his cigarette butt with his boot while spitting out a loose piece of tobacco.

"Looking for Angela, perhaps?" Angus stepped out, cutting Cowboy off in the other direction. Nikki and I advanced toward them but stayed back fifty feet, still blending into the darkness. Angus had supplied me with a tiny camera set up for night photography, and I focused it on the dealer.

Cowboy responded. "Don't know no names."

The man was a foot shorter than Matheson and a hundred pounds lighter. Matheson hooked his thumbs in his jeans pockets and cocked his elbows to either side to appear open and friendly. *Yeah, this man was as pleasant as a cobra.* Anger rolled off him in waves.

"About your height, blonde, pretty, probably jean shorts and flip flops?"

"Man, that describes about half the bitches in that bar over there." Cowboy pointed at the bar.

"Look at this photo." Matheson held up his phone with a photo of Angela.

The man's grin in the dim street light made him look like a ferret. "Don't know her. I'll see you 'round." Cowboy stepped toward the bar.

"I don't think so." Matheson's voice was low and cold. Angus shifted again to cut him off, keeping him away from the circle of light.

"I dunna believe you want to go without telling us what we need to know." Angus's Scottish-accented words floated toward Nikki and me as Matheson stepped closer. "Tell me about the woman. When did you meet her and what did she want?"

"You've got the wrong guy. Don't know her." As Cowboy started to turn, Matheson grabbed the man's neck and pulled him even further into the darkness. Cowboy struggled, and Matheson lifted him several inches in the air with one hand.

"Her name is Angela Matheson. She's gone missing along

with my five-year-old daughter. And I think you, my friend, had something to do with it."

The man's head thrashed as he struggled to speak, desperate for air. "Don't know her. And I ain't your friend."

I waited for the man to yell for help, even though it would be a problem for him if he did. No 'King of the Hill' in this man's world ever begged for help, not if he wanted to keep his kingdom. Dropping him back to his feet, Matheson kneed the man hard in the groin, sending him to the ground. Cowboy curled in a ball while trying to pull something from his pocket. Angus snatched the phone as the display activated and flipped it to me. The cheap flip phone was open. I scrolled to the contacts, but there were too many for me to check. I'd do it later. I modified the settings to remove the password.

Shoving one arm away with his boot, Matheson stood on it, his other boot resting firmly on Cowboy's chest. "Nope. One more time. Tell me about my wife."

"I'll tell you what you want to know if you'll let me get back to my business. I'm losing money out here pissin' with you."

"Toss everything over there." Matheson pointed to a dirt spot ten feet away, then stepped back and let Cowboy sit with his back against the piling. The dealer rummaged through his clothing, then stopped and reached for his hat. Matheson spat out another order. "Forget the hat. Guns and knives in the dirt. And anything else you're carrying."

Cowboy tossed out two knives retrieved from his boots, a Smith and Wesson from the back of his pants, and a set of brass knuckles. While I doubted that was everything, Matheson appeared reasonably satisfied.

"My wife?" Matheson asked the dealer.

"That woman would do anything," Cowboy said, "I mean absolutely anything, for another hit."

I stepped forward. "What did you sell her?" I asked.

"Whatever I had that would feed the beast." He let out a snort. "She didn't really care."

"How often did you see her?" Matheson asked him.

"'Bout once a week at first. When it got up to every day, it was just too much, ya know? She was starting to cause me problems with my other clients, and definitely startin' to attract attention around here. No money is worth that. And now this. She is a world of trouble, man."

Matheson lowered himself to the man's eye level. "From what I hear, the attention shouldn't bother you. You seem to have everything wrapped up tight."

"Man, I don't need that kind of attention. She was spending a lot of money every day. When she started running out of cash, she promised to find more. Said something about a sugar daddy, but that never came through. Then came the offers of things I didn't want."

"Like what?" I asked.

"I don't do drugs for sex." The dealer said flatly to me. "Catch a disease that way."

Matheson hauled Cowboy up. With his hand twisting Ellison's collar, he pulled the dealer to his feet. Their faces were a few inches apart. "How did you contact her?" Matheson spoke through his clenched teeth.

"She called me."

"What about the first time?" I asked, shifting toward the men.

"She came into the bar. Asked around for me until she found me. Said some doctor gave her my name."

Damn Carlton.

"Was my daughter with her?" Matheson asked.

"In there?" The dealer pointed toward the bar and laughed. "Didn't know there was one. Honestly, I didn't care. This is a business, man." He scratched his left ear, his eyes shifting to the ground.

I caught the lie. "When did you see the child?" I asked,

lighting up his face with my cell phone so the camera would get better video.

Cowboy kept his gaze locked on mine. "Don't like kids, lady, don't want 'em around."

"When was she here last?" Matheson asked.

"Haven't seen her for months now. She moved on to somebody else who would let her trade."

An obvious lie. Matheson looked at me and slightly shook his head. Carlton told us he had seen her just two days ago, and the Craigslist conversation definitely wasn't months ago.

"And who would that other dealer be?"

"Man, if you think I'm giving up names for you—"

Matheson lunged for Cowboy's throat. Angus grabbed him by the arm and pulled him away from the dealer.

I could barely hear Angus's whisper. "You need to let me talk to him. If you keep on with this, you're going to get us all thrown in jail."

Matheson wrenched his arm from Angus's grasp and punched Cowboy in the stomach. Cowboy let out a strangled yelp as he frantically searched for something at his waist. Matheson snatched the switchblade wedged in the man's belt next to his stomach. The noise drew several looks at us from the bar. Matheson casually stood and turned as if he were talking to Angus. He waited until the lookers returned to their conversations before standing over the man.

"Give me names." I watched Matheson's face as he fought to control himself.

The dealer shook his head violently. Matheson shifted, and Angus intervened again, murmuring as if he were calming an angry horse. "Whoa, man. We're at the limit here. Keep it in check." He turned to the man on the ground. "Dude, just tell him what he wants. He's gonna get the names one way or the other. You really want to see the inside of an emergency room tonight?"

Cowboy scrambled backward on his hands and knees, his

eyes on the glint of the switchblade in Matheson's hand that flipped continually open and shut. Backed up to the concrete post, he stopped. "I can't." His voice was a whine. "They'll kill me."

I shoved my body in front of Matheson, my hands pushing against his chest. Forcing him to look at me, I said nothing, only shook my head. "You want me to let him go?" I looked over my shoulder down at the dealer. Thankfully, the dealer realized I was the only thing keeping him from getting killed.

"Wait!" Cowboy begged. Breathing hard, he started talking. "Dorchester Village. It's a trailer park. A guy named Rat. Uses the Spanish version, uh, Rato. Just ask around there, everybody knows him."

I turned to face the dealer, resting my back against Matheson's chest, where I could feel if he moved. His heart pounded violently in his chest.

"Where else?" I asked.

Cowboy hesitated, and I took one step to the left, as if I was letting the monster loose again.

"Wait! Wait, wait." Cowboy tried to catch his breath. "Place in North Charleston, up near Wannamaker Park. Fair something or other. A double name. Biker dude named Merle used to be up there. Should still be, if he's not dead. He's kinda the end of the line."

I leaned over him. "You're making this shit up. Just tell me where the woman and her kid are. Then we'll leave you alone."

"No. I swear, go check those guys out. Maybe they know where his wife is. I don't. Don't want to. Never want to see her again. And I promise I never saw a kid. Swear to God."

The names he had given me were too low on the totem pole. "Who's running this show?"

He shook his head. "Ain't no way I'm going to tell you that."

"Seriously?" I pointed over my shoulder to Matheson. "You want him to beat it out of you?"

"No." Cowboy frantically shook his head. This was taking way too long. I could see people at the bar craning their necks to figure out what was happening on this side of the road. Even in the gloom, I could see the dealer trying to figure out who would kill him first, Matheson or whoever he worked for. I clicked my phone light back on Cowboy's face.

"Then tell me." He squinted and held up his left hand to block the light.

"A fat man named Weaver runs the show. A cop. Don't know the money man."

While I expected to hear Weaver's name, I was dismayed to hear there was another person over him. The Judge was right. We were going to have to set Weaver up somehow.

"If you're smart," I replied, "you'll get out of here and forget this happened." I turned to head to the street.

Ellison piped up. "Wait, my phone."

I shook my head and kept walking. "Nope. Insurance."

"You don't need insurance," he whined, "I'm straight up, I promise."

I laughed. "Yeah, right." This weasel was too funny. I felt a hand grab my shoulder from behind. I turned just in time to see Matheson's foot hit the side of the man's head with a roundhouse kick. It sent the skinny dealer flying back to the concrete piling. As he slid unconscious to the ground, I hurried over, feeling the man's neck for a pulse. It was weak, but steady.

"We need him to testify against Weaver, Vern," I said softly. "Were you trying to kill him?"

Matheson was silent, but I could see from his gaze that killing the dealer was exactly what he wanted to do.

36

SHARPE

SATURDAY, 12:45 A.M.

Hurricane Umberto drops to a Category 3 and turns north into the Atlantic

Sharpe watched the struggle through the windshield of his pickup, a birds-eye view of the soldier taking out his anger on some skinny guy, a third one holding him back. At least there was finally some action. After dumping the doctor, his hunch to circle back to the lawyer's office had paid off. He got there just as the four of them piled into a four-wheel drive vehicle.

His butt was sore, and the need to go had made him use an empty Coke bottle. He had cased the place—and others—repeatedly in the old battered SUV, but he preferred the old pickup for his dirty work. The SUV was parked just down King Street, and the license plates had already been switched to those of a car down the street. He would leave it there until he needed it again.

Backed into a weedy parking spot under the bridge, he cracked his window, hearing enough to understand that this was another place Angela had looked for drugs. He scanned the underside of the bridge, seeing poorly hidden cameras in strategic locations.

He waited patiently in the shadows as the group casually strolled from under the bridge and disappeared down the block. When it was clear they were not coming back, he snapped on thin surgical gloves and made certain the overhead light was out before he cracked the door. He stepped out, his eyes alternating between the crowd at the bar and the lump in the shadows. Just before he started toward the drug dealer, he stopped and slid back into the shadows.

An unmistakable cop in plain clothes stood on the crowd's edge in the middle of King Street, talking to an older, dumpy bouncer at the familiar bar. Now what was Weaver doing here? The young cop had a gun and a radio on one hip. Both men were pointing toward the very spot he needed to go.

The younger man started toward the slumped figure under the bridge. As the cop approached, Sharpe heard the radio squawking in the night air. The cop put his hand on the dealer's neck, checking for a pulse, then spoke into his radio.

"Across from the bar underneath the overpass. He's alive. He'll need a little patching up."

The radio screeched with a woman's garbled words. The cop answered. "Will do. I'll wait across the street until they get here." More erratic words, with only "10-4" as his response. The cop looked at the crumpled dealer for several seconds and rechecked the man's pulse. Satisfied, he slowly strolled across the street. He slid onto a barstool at the outside bar, where a bartender slid him a beer. Sharpe watched as the cop popped the top and turned the can upwards.

Weaver talked with several of the bouncers, then disappeared inside. The bar had to be a distribution point. He looked at the cameras again and swapped his baseball cap for the bucket hat he used when fishing, which would better hide his face.

It was time, and he needed to be quick about it.

Sharpe made sure the driver's side door of his truck was not latched and slowly shuffled toward the shadows, a tactic he had picked up from his surveillance of the homeless. The music and loud conversation from the bar seemed a mile away, as his focus shifted from the cop to the man at his feet.

With a hand on each ankle, he pulled the man further into the shadows, reaching where he had parked. The lift gate would make too much noise, so he had to heft the man into the truck bed. With the dealer's head hanging off the end of the tailgate, Sharpe fondled the old army knife in his pocket as he caught his breath. Using duct tape, he strung up the man like a ranch calf for slaughter.

Closing the truck's tailgate caused a *clunk* sound, and he waited a few seconds to be certain no one had heard the noise. Still unseen, Sharpe started the truck and snaked away from the bridge, crossing through an adjoining parking lot to the freeway entrance, but not before sticking his hand out the driver's side window and giving one of the cameras a wave. Laughing, he buzzed up the window and headed away from the bar.

Taking his time, he took the I-526 exit for Rhett Avenue, curling around the swamp in a complete circle. With the dead gas station the only business structure off the exit ramp, traffic breezed by. Drivers barely slowed for the train tracks. He sat and watched for a time, waiting to be the sole vehicle in sight.

He turned into the old gas station that stood at the edge of the Park Circle neighborhood, railroad tracks running within twenty feet of the left side. A white concrete-block building, it was trimmed in forest green with a thick white stripe just below its center. The nearest neighbor was a psychic, and beyond that, a hair salon. Little houses converted into businesses had parking slots out front.

Vacant for several years, the gas pumps had finally been removed, and not even a 'For Sale' sign remained. The property was located in an area with poor traffic flow. While the surrounding properties shifted and changed over the years, this one remained unchanged. He had no idea why and did not care. Real estate wasn't his business.

The building was shaped like an L. The empty corner was fenced off for garbage cans and propane gas tanks, neither of which was there now. He opened the rotten gate to the fence and tried the back door, giving it a quick kick to gauge its weight, unsurprised when it popped open. The small windowless back room was exactly what he needed. Even if someone peered in through the dirty windows in the front of the store, they could not see into the rear.

Tailgate open, he pulled the drug dealer out, letting his head hang off the end. His nose was broken, his face a mess, and he struggled to breathe. Again, the thought of using his knife to end the man's life made him pause, but that was too easy. If this had been war and the beaten man a combatant, it might be fair to end his suffering, rules of war or no. The point here was to prolong the distress as much as possible and repay the suffering of others.

The injured man hit the ground with a *whump*, his forced exhale of breath was followed by a moan. Sharpe smiled as he leaned over the dealer. He watched and waited until the scumbag was breathing somewhat regularly again.

Gathering one blue-jeaned leg and a cowboy boot, Sharpe took his time, the skinny dealer's head bouncing along as he dragged the man into the back of the gas station. After adding another layer of duct tape across the man's mouth and checking that his arms and legs were secure, he left the man prone on the dirty concrete floor.

37

WEAVER

SATURDAY, 12:30 A.M.

Weaver stood in the closet-turned-office of the Emergency Room bar and watched the dozen security cameras that were splayed across the back wall. He had been working at the bar as the security head and backup bouncer for the past two years, even before Darla had left. It was one of her bones of contention that he worked a full-time job as a detective, then worked half the night at this run-down bar. It was the most lucrative part of the deal he had made with Harbin.

Casually watching the cameras as his other bouncers took care of the bar, about midnight, he saw Danforth across the street under the freeway. The bar's cameras were strategically placed not only inside and outside the bar, but under the concrete overpass of the I-26 exits that fed onto the Septima P. Clark Parkway, otherwise known in Charleston as the "Connector." Weaver never had to step a foot outside the bar to see exactly what was happening over the entire block.

Two others accompanied Danforth and her client. They apparently had scheduled the meet, as the scrawny dealer appeared unconcerned, sauntering out to the parking lot while lighting up a cigarette. Ellison had not been there long before

Matheson stepped out from a concrete pillar to block the dealer's way back to the bar. Yet from the beginning, with no sound, Weaver could only guess that the crew was hunting Matheson's wife, and Ellison didn't want to cooperate.

With four to one odds, Ellison was not only outnumbered but outsmarted at every turn. Weaver watched Ellison's last-ditch effort to retrieve his phone from Danforth, then Matheson's martial arts kick that threw him against the concrete, knocking him out. Weaver wished he could have heard what they had discussed, but even without sound, he knew Matheson was serious about obtaining information about his wife. And if Ellison gave up his or Harbin's name, things would escalate, and quickly.

Once Danforth and her crew were gone, he called one of the moonlighting officers from Charleston PD on the bar's patio outside to call 911 and check on Ellison. Weaver thought about being a witness to what he'd seen, but his daytime employer wasn't aware of his nighttime gig, and he needed to keep it that way. His job as a detective didn't allow moonlighting.

The officer checked Ellison's pulse as he called for an ambulance, then went back to the patio to wait. The night's fun and games over, Weaver started to turn from the monitors when he saw a blurred figure in one corner of the monitor for the outermost camera. He adjusted the light to infrared, and although he could not see the face, he had a clearer picture. Weaver watched as the figure on the camera picked up Ellison, hefted him into the back of a pickup truck, and proceeded to hog-tie him. Another monitor showed the officer with his back turned toward what was happening, engaged in a conversation at the bar.

First Sean, now Ellison. Someone was killing everyone Angela Matheson had been in contact with. This was his chance to find out who it was. He watched the truck begin to move, then, to his surprise, a hand jutted out the driver's side window and waved at the very camera he was watching. This had to be the man who had taunted him on the phone. This was his chance to get Sean's killer.

Grabbing his keys, he called the officer. "I need to leave for a few minutes. Keep things locked down while I'm gone." He didn't wait for a response.

Following the truck, Weaver slalomed through other traffic, sparse given the late hour, even on a weekend night, he guessed, because of everyone's worry over the hurricane. At one point, he was close enough to see the license plate, but it had been smeared with mud that kept him from reading the numbers and letters. On I-526, he thought he had tailed the truck too closely when the brake lights lit suddenly and the truck swerved, taking the Rhett Avenue exit.

Weaver took the exit, watching in the distance as the truck's taillights turned right. To Weaver's surprise, the truck turned neither left nor right, but headed across the street to the abandoned gas station. Turning right off the circling off-ramp, Weaver watched as the truck pulled to the rear of the building. A block away, Weaver got out of his car and walked back to the gas station along the privacy fence separating the neighborhood from the street.

From fifty yards away, hidden behind a bush, Weaver could see the truck's outline cast by the freeway lights at the intersection with Rhett Avenue. The person, a man, he thought, roughly pulled Ellison from the truck bed to the ground and dragged him into the back of the building. The man was about the same height as Matheson, but thinner, yet from this distance, he couldn't be sure.

As the man turned to head back to his vehicle, Weaver moved deeper into the bushes, ready with his cell phone. The driver got inside, and as the old pickup turned back onto Rhett Avenue, Weaver took rapid photos, capturing both the truck and the driver. With a bit of enhancement, he would soon know who killed Ellison.

38

VERN

SATURDAY, 6:30 A.M.

*Hurricane Umberto three hundred miles off the coast of the Florida-
Georgia line.*

Matheson's autopilot woke him up long before sunrise. He had slept for four hours. He would much rather be in Awendaw, but this was the best way to trap his grandparents into a confession and secure himself the alibi Lee required. His grandmother knew something about where Katie was, and he was going to find out exactly what it was. Last night, he'd returned home to find his grandmother's Oldsmobile in its spot, but his grandfather's truck was gone, and their bedroom light was off. He'd have to question the old man as to where he was slinking off to.

Dragging himself out of bed this morning, he took a cold shower and dressed. He packed his duffel and gathered everything else to move himself to Awendaw. He spent half an hour on the phone, making sure neither Angela nor Katie was listed at any of the local hospitals as he waited for Nana to wake up. He was about to see who had not responded to his email and forward those to Nikki for follow-up when he caught a whiff of his grandmother's cologne.

"Vernon Hartley Matheson."

Matheson was twelve all over again when his grandmother used his full name. He heard her walking down the hall toward his bedroom, her house shoes slowly slapping the hardwood floor.

"There's no good reason for you to do all this calling. Let the police do their job. You aren't eating, and I don't think you slept much last night. Why isn't that lawyer doing this?"

She picked up the empty whiskey bottle from his bedroom nightstand. Without a word, she dropped it with a loud clang into the garbage can and stomped away. He waited. Knowing her habits, he knew it was safe to come out once he smelled coffee. In the kitchen, she had started breakfast. He didn't have the heart to tell her he had no appetite, but if she was distracted, it might be easier to get her to talk.

With a whiff of something burning, Matheson went to the stove, lowering the heat under the bacon. Nana's concerned eyes were locked onto something near the garage. She was a thousand miles away, just like the first night. He stepped next to her at the window and gave her a one-armed squeeze, trying to see where she was looking. He could see nothing unusual—just the old two-car garage they used for storage and a corner of the roof of the little shed built fifty feet away for gardening tools, hidden behind some bushes.

He looked at his grandmother. Two deep wrinkles vertically sliced her forehead just over her nose, her eyes glaring at the garage. A sudden gust of wind thrashed the branches of the big oak in the backyard, breaking her concentration. She looked up at him and smiled, then shifted to the stove to check the bacon.

"I guess you heard about the hurricane."

"Heard what?"

"You're back in South Carolina now, son. Need to put your

hurricane app on your phone and check it regularly until at least November," Nana said, unruffled, as if telling him she was leaving soon for church. "Coming here now, and soon."

Matheson felt his heart rate jump. Katie had been missing for two days, and he would be damned if she rode out a hurricane this way. He took out his phone and pulled up the weather forecast. Umberto was now a Category 3 as it moved up the coast, currently just off the coast of Georgia. Charleston was at the dead center of what the weather guys called the 'cone of uncertainty' that extended between Savannah, Georgia, and the Outer Banks of North Carolina.

He needed to know their routine for boarding or shuttering the house. His grandfather had made him help when he was a kid, but that had been too long ago for him to remember where things were kept and which board went where. With two houses to get ready, he needed to get organized.

She was staring at the garage again, and his worry increased. "Nana, what's wrong?"

She jumped, touching her hair as if she had been caught doing something she should not have been. "Why—what do you mean?" Her voice shook.

"Nana, I know you aren't giving me the whole story, and I don't know why. If you think I don't know anything about what Angela's been up to, you're wrong. I've learned all about her drug problem and how crappy a mother she was. You won't hurt my feelings by telling me what you know. So, please sit down and tell me your part in all this. I won't be angry. I need to know what has been happening to Katie this past year. Catch me up."

She refused to look at him, instead shaking her head and pressing her lips into a thin, tight line. Removing herself from his grasp, she opened the refrigerator, retrieved a carton of eggs, and set them on the counter next to the stove. Vern's concern grew as her hands shook while she removed the burned bacon onto a plate covered by a paper towel.

"Nana, please look at me."

She continued with breakfast. "Katie's fine. I'm sure of it. There's no need to worry."

"Do you know where she is?" He grabbed her shoulders again and turned her to face him. He tried to keep the desperation from his voice.

Her face blanched, and her eyes were wide with fear. Matheson realized he had been way too rough with her. This was his grandmother, not a drug dealer. Backing away, she wrenched open one of the kitchen drawers and grabbed a carving knife. Hands shaking, her eyes blazed with terror. Her fear was palpable.

Vern held up his hands in surrender and took a step toward her. "Nana? What's wrong?"

She backed herself into the corner of the countertop, raising the knife overhead with both hands, preparing to strike him. Her entire body shook as if Parkinson's had instantly taken control. Shocked, Matheson tried to reach out for her once more.

"Young man, just who are you? And what are you doing in my kitchen?" Her shrill voice was almost a scream.

He felt hands pat his shoulders from behind. His grandfather leaned in with a whisper at the side of Matheson's face. "She's just confused. Happens now and then. Go on now and come back in a while. She'll be better then."

Reeling from his grandmother's confusion, Matheson backed out of the house, grabbing his duffel and the garbage bag with his uniforms. Following him, completely ignoring her husband, his grandmother wielded the knife out to the front porch. Her face was twisted in anger as he sped off, gravel slinging from the edge of the road as he watched her shaking the knife at him in his rear-view mirror.

As he pulled to the intersection at Middle Street, he looked to his right to check for traffic. Darrell was sitting in the passenger seat next to him. Shaking, Matheson immediately pulled the car to the curb after he turned and looked at his friend. Darrell was no longer there. Grasping the steering wheel, Matheson closed his eyes and began counting backwards from one hundred. When he finished, he put the car in gear and headed toward the town.

It wasn't until he was two blocks from the town that he realized that the cologne that his grandfather had been wearing was the same odor that clung to one of the dead women in the morgue.

39

LEE

SATURDAY, 7:30 A.M.

The Judge and I were ensconced in the conference room, having had an early breakfast before heading into the office at seven. He was set to make another round of calls at eight to learn what SLED and HSI had found out about Katie, if anything. We spent the hour until SLED opened going through every piece of information we had to see if there was anything we had skipped. The Judge began his calls promptly at eight, leaving me to listen on speaker as he went through his list of a half dozen contacts.

"This isn't looking good, is it, Judge?" I asked. We'd just finished the call with Mac's contact in Myrtle Beach for HSI, who provided us with very little information beyond the basics of their surveillance. Because it was an ongoing investigation, and because a child matching Katie's description wasn't specifically determined to be involved, the information we received was practically useless. The Judge was compiling all this in a report for the file. I had already added the recording of the conversation. I felt a rising sense of dread at the possibility that we may never find Vern's child, and what that would do to him.

"It will be difficult going forward," the Judge replied, "when, like he said, most of the officers normally involved in trafficking investigations have been temporarily shifted to other states for the president's ongoing immigration enforcement actions."

Politics. One of the things I hated most about this country was how politicians seemed to interfere when they shouldn't, and not get involved when they should. I could tell by my grandfather's frown that he was as frustrated as I was.

"At least we confirmed that the woman Vern found in his bedroom definitely was involved with a trafficking group out of the Midlands. I wonder why they branched south into Charleston," I said.

The Judge glanced at me, his eyebrows raised in surprise. "You're not going to acknowledge your part in wiping out the trafficking group in Charleston? Of course, they will branch into our area. There is no one here now."

"Fish is still out there. You would think that with Brad's death and the arrest of Breaker, Morris, and those guys in Savannah working for Fish, that one of them would turn on him."

"And maybe they will. It's early days, yet. Do not forget the implications that more than one police department was also involved."

"It's a wonder I don't have a target on my back."

My grandfather quickly turned toward me, his fingers frozen over the keyboard. "Have you had any indication that anyone is planning to harm you?"

"No. Just a comment."

"I will talk with Mac about your personal security."

"It's not necessary, Judge."

"I think it is."

Several weeks ago, the apex of our investigation of Timberline Farm resulted in the death of the local trafficker, Brad Marshall, the arrest of his employee, criminal charges against the farm manager for being an accessory, and the complete shutdown of trafficking in most of the Low Country. It had, however, not stopped the leader, Theron Fish, located in Savannah.

I shook my head in frustration. "It's like a hydra. Or playing whack-a-mole."

"Yes, my dear, it is. However, if we, along with other government agencies, remain diligent, we might actually make a little more progress. We know they are out there. And knowing that Weaver is a significant connection to them, we may be able to make yet another inroad, fighting trafficking and drug distribution in one fell swoop."

"And HSI is working on that in conjunction with SLED," he continued. "Fish cannot instantly set up a group in Charleston, now can he?" He rose and stretched, heading for the small refrigerator where he plucked two small bottles of water and tossed one to me.

"You cannot be impatient with things like this, Lee. Trafficking cases do not come neatly tied to the state solicitor or the DOJ with a bow. You wish for everything to be black-and-white, as in your real estate practice. Criminal matters do not work that way."

"I feel like I'm back in the year I graduated from law school."

"Yes, law school teaches you the 'why' of things, but not the 'how.' But everyone who either shifts careers or positions within a company feels the same. Unless you get out of your comfort zone, Lee, you will never grow."

"As you've reminded me for the past fifteen years, at least."

As he sat, he closed his computer and turned to face me. "It should make you feel better to remember that you are involved in Colonel Matheson's case only as support and investigation. There will be no need for you to file any action. Mac has authorized you to hire criminal counsel, and I believe, as I am sure you do as well, that is wise."

I took a long drink of the water. "Of course. I'm just frustrated because our investigation is taking too long. Katie could be in another country by now, and I'm running out of places to search."

"And the wife?"

"She is involved with Weaver somehow. I can feel it. I don't see her leaving Charleston, not when she has suppliers here."

"That isn't what I mean, Lee. Are you still searching for Matheson's wife, or have you lost focus due to your feelings? You did ask me to monitor your behavior."

I could feel the blush travel up my neck. I hated having everyone know my personal business, even though I was the one who came to him for advice. And to Clarice.

"I did. And from both of you watching us like a hawk last night in the meeting, I can assure you that you're doing a good job." I needed to get the conversation back on track and away from my personal life.

"For any of us to find Katie," I continued, "yes, we have to find Angela, whether to confirm she actually, God forbid, sold the child, or left her somewhere."

"These matters take a lot of footwork, phone calls, and searching." My grandfather began filling his briefcase and packing up his laptop. "The drug dealer's phone was helpful. Angus and Nikki are pulling the information for your "Cowboy" and running down every contact on his phone. They have requested SLED assistance, and I believe they will get it.

"I'm not going to be able to get away from this, am I?" I asked the Judge.

"You mean child trafficking?" he asked. He shook his head, letting his shoulders relax as he let out a frustrated sigh, snapping the latch on his briefcase and shoving it aside.

"Katie may just be lost," I replied, "but if there is any possibility that she was taken, I need to help move heaven and earth to find her. I can't live with myself otherwise."

The Judge looked at me with evident tenderness as he reached over and took my hand. I leaned over and gave him a quick hug, then turned off my iPad and gathered my own things to go back to my office.

"So, how are we going to trap Weaver in all this? And if he's not the leader, you can be sure he's not going to give up whoever that is. Do you think Fish is the one supplying the funds?"

"There could be anyone at the top of this food chain, Lee, and how we catch Weaver depends on the circumstances. If the potential incarceration period is significant enough, and the possibility of parole is low enough, it should provide a sufficient amount of leverage for him to talk."

"And on top of that, no cop wants to be incarcerated. They'll have to keep him in solitary, won't they?"

"Most likely, but that would be up to the warden. All of this provides a suitable consequence for us to get him to squirm."

"Or maybe..." I hesitated, tapping my fingers on the conference table.

"Or?" he asked.

"I could just get him locked in a room for fifteen minutes with Matheson and get the information a hell of a lot faster."

My grandfather stared at me as if I'd lost my mind. "Certainly you jest, Lee."

I smiled at him. "Of course." However, after what I witnessed last night, it seemed like the easiest option.

40

VERN

SATURDAY, 7:30 A.M.

Matheson knew he was in over his head. Even if either of his grandparents knew things about Katie, he might never get it out of them. Sand, bombs, and bad guys he knew. Old people's mental health issues, he did not. He picked up his telephone to call 911, realized it might do more harm than good, and dropped it back into his shirt pocket.

Shaking as severely as his grandmother, he drove north two miles to the end of the island before he pulled for a second time into the parking area reserved for Breach Inlet, the water passage separating Sullivan's Island from the Isle of Palms. Several fishermen lined the bridge, and he could see a pod of dolphins slipping through the calm surface of the slack tide.

He closed his eyes and tilted his head back. Between his hangover and his grandmother's threats, his breaking point was threateningly close to the surface. Matheson listened to the heat ticking off the vehicle as he fought hard to get his rapidly beating heart to settle.

He had hit his limit, and this morning was more than he could handle. Overseas, he boxed off his emotions, partitioned every type of event under its mental filing tab, and moved forward, one step at a time. His buddies were killed, injured, or mentally screwed up, but it was all part of the job. They knew it. He knew it. It was just the way it was.

However, here the problems were emotional, and he had no idea how to address them. He tried to push them away by simply telling himself his grandparents were old. Yet he couldn't just pass this off so simply. Nana had been terrified of *him*. The woman who loved him all his life and had cared for him since middle school was flat-out petrified. Something had happened for her to be this way, but what?

He knew in his gut that Angela was involved with whatever was wrong with his grandmother. And what had Angela done to his grandfather to make him so incensed?

His most pressing problem was not his grandparents or his wife, but his child, who was still only God knew where. The daughter he had not planned, but the one he loved from the moment she made her first cry. Yet the one he barely knew. There were so many things he had missed, things he now wanted desperately more than anything. And she was gone.

Tears began, a first in his life. Even with the beatings from the man who said he was not his father, then later from the stern tongue lashings from his grandfather, Matheson had always suffered in silence. Crying in front of either man meant you needed another beating or lecture. Crying in middle and high school meant you were a pussy and were subjected to bullying. Crying in the military meant you were weak and could get you killed, even by your own kind. He had never risked it. Never.

Yet with no one around, he let himself go. Sobs filled the car until he was exhausted. Closing his eyes, he tried to rest. He would head to the farm in a few minutes and get himself together. He listened as the sound of soft waves of Breach Inlet filled the car until *every muscle tensed at the burst of rocket fire breaking the silence. Curling into an ungainly ball, he slammed himself into the passenger-side floorboard of the Humvee and covered his helmet with his arms. He waited for the next one to hit the vehicle and blow him to pink mist.*

Feeling around for his rifle, he grew alarmed when he could not find it, but did not dare open his eyes. He needed to play dead, not knowing how many were outside. He could smell the sand, dust, and explosives through the open windows of the military vehicle. He held his breath and counted, waiting, not daring to look.

At the count of one minute fifty seconds, he opened his eyes. Crammed into the floorboard of the rental car, his neck was twisted at an odd angle. He waited, unsure of his location, then realized another flashback had gripped him. Pulling himself into the driver's seat, he saw that nothing outside had changed. He was still at Breach Inlet, the soft breeze coming through the two-inch crack in the window. The fishermen had finished for the morning and were heading back from the bridge with their poles, one with a bucket and the other with a string of fish.

The only difference was an old motorcycle with high handlebars and flames drawn on its gas tank idling in the parking space next to him. The helmetless driver was surveying the area, appearing simply to take a break before heading on, much like Matheson himself. The man threw up his hand in a greeting when he spied Matheson watching him. He backed the motorcycle, left the parking area, and turned the corner toward the Isle of Palms. Just as the Harley flew over the Breach Inlet bridge, a loud pop caused Matheson to lurch again for cover, even though he understood it was the backfire from the motorcycle.

Enough. He needed help. Otherwise, he might never find his daughter.

Matheson dialed the number, and Lee answered immediately, even though it was early in the morning.

"Hey," he said. "Everything ok with you this morning? Or are you still pissed at me from last night?"

"You could have killed him, Vern."

He smiled at her use of his first name, wrapped in her southern accent.

"I need to talk to you. There have been some things that have happened this morning that we need to talk about."

"Not a problem," Lee said. "I'm at the office. The Judge just learned that SLED needs to meet with you. They are taking over the death investigation from Weaver. The Judge is talking with them now to see what they will tell him. He's also followed up on Homeland Security."

"You're kidding." He started the car. "That's good news, right? I'll head to your office now."

"Can you check in with the search team at Sullivan's Island first? Nikki is to brief me this morning, and I understand it's pretty rough stuff about Katie that you don't need to hear right now."

"Oh, hell no, I'm not sitting this out. I'll meet you there after I run by the SI Fire Department. Don't start without me." He waited for a response. "Lee?" Abruptly, she was gone. Someone needed to teach that woman phone etiquette.

Clarice escorted him into the conference room after he'd grabbed a coffee. Stepping through the door, he had obviously caught Nikki and Lee in a serious discussion. Both women wore tense expressions as they huddled over a stack of papers on the table. They turned and looked up as he came in.

"Don't mind me," he said, as he looked from one woman to the other.

"I was updating Lee on what Angus and I learned," said Nikki. The lines across her forehead and a crooked smile conveyed concern. "You sure you want to hear this?"

"If it involves my daughter, of course I do." Matheson unsuccessfully tried to squelch his indignant tone.

"First, tell me what the SIFD told you," Lee said.

"They have covered the entire island and knocked on every door."

"And they didn't find her."

"Nope. My grandfather was there. He said he had checked all the houses and garages within a three-block area around their home. He looked a bit ragged, like he's run a marathon." Matheson shifted in his seat. "Maybe he's not sleeping well. I don't know. I've never seen either of them like this. It's throwing me for a loop." He ran his hands through his hair. "Okay, now you guys."

"I don't think you need to hear this, Vern," Lee said.

"Well, I'm not leaving, so you might as well start talking."

She nodded to Nikki. "Let's get started then."

"According to some of the mothers of Katie's friends," Nikki began, "when Katie was allowed to come for sleepovers, her clothes were generally dirty, her hair was always unkempt, she was sometimes bruised, and she was ravenously hungry. It was almost, they said, like Katie, in the eyes of her mother, was a stray dog. I'll be honest with you. I've seen a lot of abuse, but their descriptions..."

The bloat of guilt in his gut was large enough to choke him. He wondered if Lee had children of her own. He knew she would never allow them to be in this condition. He wished he were somewhere he could beat his head against the wall.

"To their credit," Nikki continued, "your entire 'village' has taken care of your child. The teacher ensured Katie had a double portion of food at lunch. The principal would often clean her up in the mornings and let her change into the extra clothes she kept on hand for emergencies. The consensus is that Katie's a very bright girl. Her teacher even thinks she should jump into the second grade after pre-K rather than start at first."

Matheson knew his daughter was precocious, but he had no idea she was also a brain. A pain shot through his heart as regret instantly replaced his pride. He had no right to be proud, given that he had ignored most of her life. He'd had nothing to do with this. She might as well have been an orphan. And for what had he given up his only child? A career of killing people? A job that in the end shot him out like a cannon with no skills he could use on the outside? He would do better once he found her. He had to. He had a lot to make up for.

Damn it, where was she? He leaned forward, his head in his hands, as Nikki continued.

"Several parents discussed whether to get the Department of Social Services involved, but they were afraid the state would take Katie, and none of them wanted that, especially for your grandparents, who the entire community supports. Several people said they knew your grandparents were in their later years and were concerned about what would eventually happen to Katie. You have no idea how much better they feel knowing you are home."

"Except that she's missing," Lee whispered.

"Yes, except that." Nikki nodded as she took another sip of coffee.

Matheson almost crushed the coffee cup in his hand. Red heat of embarrassment crept up his neck. The entire town knew about his wife and her problems. And no one—not Darrell, his best friend in the military, who had to have known all this through his wife, nor Cherie, his best friend in Charleston, told him how bad his family situation had become. Not even his grandparents. After this was over, he and Katie would never be able to live anywhere in the town again. And part of him would never trust his friends or his grandparents again.

He took a big breath. His dirty laundry was not Nikki's problem. He turned to Lee. "What's our next step?"

"I was hoping you would tell me. Angus and Nikki have exhausted Katie's friends, the neighborhoods, and the hospitals. Their next attempt would be to talk with your grandparents."

"About that." Matheson felt as if his body and mind were slowly coming apart. "My grandmother did not recognize me this morning at breakfast. Well, she did, then when I brought up Katie, she turned on me. Grabbed a carving knife and came after me."

"Seriously?" Concerned, she reached for him, grabbing his forearm tightly. His heart rate increased at her touch.

"My grandfather said it has been happening 'now and then,'" he replied, "whatever that means. So what she knows about Katie will stay in her head. I am not the person to talk to her about it."

Lee looked at Nikki, then punched a button on the black conference telephone in the middle of the table. "Clarice, can you step in? We have a problem."

Clarice was there immediately. "What's up?"

"I need to see if Dr. DeLeon can move us up in her schedule. Can you delay the SLED meeting until later this afternoon?"

"They didn't give me a time yesterday before I left; they just said they wanted to make the Colonel available. They were supposed to confirm this morning with a time, but it's Saturday. I don't know what effect that will have, and everyone's off kilter because of the hurricane. I'll give their office a call."

"We need to find the child," Lee said, "and their help could make the difference."

The thought of his child alone in a hurricane made him cringe. "We definitely need to find her."

41

VERN

SATURDAY, 9:00 A.M.

Clarice ushered Matheson into Lee's office, where Dr. Zola DeLeon was waiting. The doctor was a tiny woman who looked to be about fifty-five. She was barely over five feet, with cocoa skin and deep brown expressive eyes surrounded by laugh lines. Lee had told him the doctor was Bahamian, but had grown up in Florida. He had asked Lee to come with him. After the introductions, where the doctor insisted he call her by her first name, they began.

"Thank you for coming," he said. "Every day has been a challenge, especially with my daughter missing and my grandmother losing it this morning. Now with this hurricane coming, I have to admit I need help."

"It's good we could work this in before we all have to evacuate. Can you first tell me a bit about what happened to your grandmother?"

"My grandmother didn't know who I was this morning. At first, she did, then she flipped, and then I was some intruder. She wielded a meat carving knife at me as if I were a thief breaking into her house. It was unbelievable. One second, she knew me like always, chastising me with my full name no less, the next—

poof." He snapped his fingers in the air. "I was a thug breaking into her house."

Concern crossed Zola's face. "Do you have someone, a home health aide, perhaps, you use regularly to assist your grandparents?"

Matheson snorted. "Assist? You've never met my Da." He couldn't stop the sarcastic tone in his voice." They don't have anyone helping them as far as I can tell, unless you count the monsignor praying with them."

Lee placed a hand on his arm, and he forced himself to relax.

"I'm sorry," he said, looking at her. It's just been too much. I snapped a bit this morning."

Zola's smile was comforting. "Angela never told you they were having issues?"

"Never said one word," he shook his head, "apparently way too busy with her drug issues to notice." If his wife were here right now, she might not fare well in his current state. He took a calming breath and counted to ten, even though he knew it was useless. His anger continued to rise.

"But you know, neither did my best friends say anything. One of them filled me in yesterday, but I had no idea it was this bad. While everyone in the world knows about Angela, I don't think anyone knew the extent of my grandmother's condition. I'm at the point where I have no idea what to do."

"I do." Zola pulled her cell phone from her jacket pocket. "I have medical practitioners who might be able to help. I never hesitate to recommend either of them when I can. Let's get Kris there to run interference. She'll be in a better position to tell me what your grandmother needs."

Matheson looked at Lee. He had asked her to stay with him when he talked with Zola. It had been a long time since he had been this close to a woman who made him feel this way, and he was grateful. He found her hand and wrapped his around it.

She looked up at him, confusion passing across her face. "What?"

"Nothing. Just thank you." He spoke to Zola. "You might be wasting your time. If you're trying to get them into a facility, they will never move from that house."

"Let's just see if they will have someone come in daily. Kris is a miracle worker, I promise."

Matheson was hesitant. "You trust her?"

Zola didn't hesitate. "Of course. She's my best friend."

Matheson felt himself relax for the first time in a week. Something about Zola made him believe she was genuinely interested in helping him with his grandparents. He had never felt this vulnerable, even in a mission where he was the lone ranger, surrounded by a dozen enemies. He looked down at Lee's hand still resting inside his. He placed his other hand on top, and his eyes met hers.

"I appreciate the help from you both. I can't remember the last time someone was this nice to me when I've been such a jerk."

Lee grinned. "Oh, I'll repay you in spades, bucko. You wait."

"You're welcome," Zola responded, then she grew solemn. "Having Kris involved will also be important for you, not just your grandparents. Something you do or say might trigger them. We need to know what that is, and quickly, I'd think."

He had to agree with her. "That was apparent this morning, even though I have no idea what I said that could have been the problem."

Zola nodded her head in agreement. "I just sent you Kris's information. Give her a call for your grandparents. Let me call her now, and then you and I can chat."

Matheson felt the buzz in his pocket with the contact information. He had no desire to talk about himself—his problems were just that—his. Yet with a pointed look and another squeeze of his hand, Lee left him alone. Terrified.

. . .

WHEN ZOLA FINISHED her call with Kris, she sat down on the comfortable couch and chairs, facing each other.

"Vern, can you tell me what issues you've been having?" she asked.

Matheson hesitated. "I'm not sure I can." He replied softly. He had told no one about what he lived through and wasn't sure he wanted to do so now.

"Everything is confidential, I promise you." She folded her hands in her lap, waiting for him to talk. "I can't help you if I don't know what's bothering you."

Her leather bag was on the floor, and there was no pen, paper, or recorder to take notes on what he said. He wondered if she had an eidetic memory. After a minute of silence, realizing she would wait on him all day, he began. First, he gave her a brief overview of his previous military assignments and the types of missions he had been involved in.

Describing the nightmares about his parents, everything began to tumble out, as fast as he could talk about his childhood. He unloaded all the sights, sounds, and smells that he could remember of the day his father burned down their house. But when it came to the combat scenes, those that made him black out during stressful periods, he had a difficult time describing them. He explained about the final explosion that cost Darrell his leg, then his life, how he had barely lived through the IED himself, then everything that had happened since he got home— the dead woman on his bedroom floor, his missing wife and child, Angela's drug problem, and the harassment by Weaver.

He explained how he had immediately gone back to Afghanistan when he had smelled smoke at the morgue.

"When you smelled the smoke, did it feel like you were truly back there?"

Matheson could only shake his head in the affirmative. "I

wanted to leave all this behind me," he said quietly, "but I couldn't. It followed me home, and now everywhere I turn, there's something else. It's all piling on right now, and I'm not sure I can take it much longer."

"Are you familiar with the aspects of complex PTSD?" she asked him.

"Only what I've lived through." He gripped his thighs tightly as he spoke. "And what I was forced to talk about to the shrink provided by the military. He wasn't helpful. And I didn't tell him everything. It would have seriously impacted my career, and both he and my superior officer were aware of it. I was going through the motions so that the military could," he used his fingers as quotation marks, "say they did something."

Zola nodded her head in understanding. "People who have experienced as much trauma as you have," she said, "will continue to experience fight, flight, or freeze responses long after the events. When did these nightmares and blackouts begin?"

"I've always had nightmares about my parents," Matheson replied. "I can't remember ever sleeping completely through the night. The blackouts? About two years ago. I was able to handle living with them—until I wasn't."

"Have you had any experience that might be categorized as hallucinations?"

He immediately thought of Darrell and how he saw him at random times and places. "You mean seeing things that aren't there?"

"While technically not part of the DSM-5 criteria, the manual we use to diagnose disorders, for PTSD or even the Complex PTSD, I have found that many of my clients experience true hallucinations, whether they see things, hear voices, or talk with people who are not physically present. Their brains are unable to distinguish between what is real and what is not, and they experience all types of sensory hallucinations, even taste, touch, and smell."

He looked at her and blinked. "I don't think so," he said, "but would I know?" He could feel his heart slamming in his chest. Darrell had been sitting in the passenger seat of his car the day before.

"Please don't stress about my questions," Zola said, giving him a knowing smile. "I'm not telling you that you should have these things. Let's just be aware of the possibilities. For goodness' sake, let's not prepare for all the symptoms to occur at once."

"Understood," he replied, even though her response did not make him feel better. It made him feel crazy.

"Was there a particular event that elevated these experiences?" she asked. "I believe that your level of traumatic exposure correlates to the level of your symptoms."

"I can't go into detail, but years ago we had an op into an area close to Pakistan. Too many of my team members were killed. It was a bloodbath. It was during that operation that I realized I only cared for my team, not America, not the military. Those men had saved me from death multiple times. And what did I do? Let them die."

"Were you injured?"

"Surprisingly, no, well, not seriously. A bullet through my calf, some cuts and scrapes," he replied, "and I think that was part of it."

"It could be. I'm sure you experienced survivor's guilt because you were not injured when everyone else, I'm assuming, was either injured or killed."

Matheson dropped his head into his hands, hiding the tears he could no longer hold back. "Every last damn one of them was killed. And it was all my fault."

42

VERN

SATURDAY, 10:00 A.M.

Hurricane Umberto 400 miles east of Miami at a Category 4

Matheson walked toward the back window of Lee's office after he finished with Zola. He was mentally exhausted, but hopeful that one of the half dozen treatments she outlined to him might work to stop what was happening in his head. He had scheduled his next appointment with her for the following Monday at her office, refusing to go to the VA hospital. He had too many horrible memories of military hospitals and had no desire to set foot in one ever again.

The garden flowers were in full bloom, the explosions of color almost artificial, especially after he had lived in such dry, arid countries for so long. The room and the garden revealed a great deal about the woman. What could she do with the farm? He'd been around her for just over two days and was shocked at its effect on him. Imagining her in the flower garden at his home in Awendaw, a feeling of warmth flooded him.

His farm needed a woman. He needed a woman, no, he needed this woman.

He shook his head violently to get himself back to reality. His child was missing, and his wife was most likely responsible. There was no time for warm and fuzzy feelings. He continued staring out the window even when she stepped into the room. Her cologne and energy reached across the room, enveloping him in a soft, warm hug. Damn it, he needed her, wanted her right now more than anything, to have her wrap her arms around him.

Though it hurt his heart, he forced himself to think about Katie. He couldn't get the picture of his daughter being trafficked out of his head. He felt guilty for constantly pushing her face out of his mind, but he could not bear to see the things that his imagination was creating. Scenario after scenario floated through his mind like a horrible video clip.

"What happened with SLED?" he asked as Lee moved to stand beside him.

"The hurricane has messed with everyone's schedule," she said. "It's picking up speed, though, and everyone here is talking about Hugo." She blew out a frustrated breath. "I gave them what information we have. Still don't know when they will be here."

"Did they tell you anything more about the dead woman and what they think about where Katie is?"

Lee turned and settled into one of the overstuffed chairs. "Just that the woman was part of the trafficking ring that the department has been surveilling for the past few months. The main trafficking group is in Myrtle Beach, but they have infiltrated here significantly. I learned that the hard way a few months ago."

He gave her a look he knew showed his skepticism. "I'm having a difficult time believing there is that much trafficking here."

Her response was matter-of-fact. "Human trafficking is a large problem here in South Carolina. I became heavily involved in my last case when they operated out of a childcare facility up north of Awendaw. It's not too far from your property, actually."

Matheson felt his heart leap at the thought of his child being involved, and something like this so close to his home. If that location was close to his farm, would they be able to live there? He was jumping to conclusions, just like his imagination.

"I honestly thought it was part of Weaver's bullshit. Do you think she was trying to take Katie?"

Lee shrugged. "It appears so, but she was stopped from doing so. That's another pressing question I have for you right now. Did you know anyone at that party? Any of your friends there?"

"No. Not one person. And I had no idea how long the party had been going on, possibly for an hour, maybe longer. Angela left the door wide open, and this bunch moved in to use the house for whatever they wanted. The few I questioned didn't even know who she was. But I'm guessing. I don't know anything other than what I told you before." The party felt like it was a year ago, rather than Thursday.

Matheson relaxed into the couch across from her, stretching his arms up and resting them on the back as he continued. So tired, he wished he could lie down and take a long nap. This room—this woman—made him feel safe. Comfortable. Emotional. Too bad she was his damn lawyer. Did she have this effect on all her clients? He was married, damn it. Yet he had never felt free to talk with anyone like this. Not Dr. Zola. Not even Darrell.

"I wish you'd been with me when I walked into that party at the townhouse. Looking back, every type of person was at that party, from rich to poor, every color, every personality. And I didn't know one of them. It was strange, like a movie set." He stared out at the garden, then continued. "All I could think about was Katie. She shouldn't be in that type of situation. How many other parties did she have to deal with? How has it changed her? What have I done by leaving her with a mother like that?"

He couldn't look at Lee, but he had to let it all out. "I don't love Angela, and I think I never have. My attraction was physical. When I left after that month's leave, I'll admit that I wanted to see her more, but I also wanted to take it slow and learn to get to know her long-distance. But there was never enough time for my emotions to get involved. I married her when she got pregnant because Da insisted, and I stupidly agreed."

He picked at the cuticle around his thumb, embarrassed. "I love Katie more than I love myself. But I've been gone so long that I don't even remember what she looks like, smells, or sounds like. Don't get me wrong, I have snippets in my head from time to time, but the calls were so infrequent over the past year…" He swore he would not get emotional in front of her. He focused on his fingernails. "It's like she's not real. I know she is, but it's been so long…"

He had never been this emotional in his life, and it was making him crazy. It was as if his mind and body were about to collapse. She moved to sit beside him.

"Could someone have come in from a different direction and gone upstairs without you knowing?" He let her get him back on track.

"Absolutely. Every door in the house was open, leading to the garage, the front porch, and the backyard. Anyone could have come in at any time, killed the woman, and then left without anyone taking notice, even before I arrived." He thought back to all the people in the house. "Or, honestly, even after I arrived. The music was so loud that even using the lamp to kill her, no one noticed. There must have been fifty people there, and honestly, the AC/DC was so loud from working overtime with the open doors that the windows shook."

Lee's pen softly tapped her opposite wrist, her gaze intense as she stared at him. Matheson could see the wheels turning in her head. She shifted the conversation. "You know…at the morgue…"

He side-stepped her question before she could get to his flashback. "Do you know why Weaver thought he had to put me through that?"

"The SLED officer told me it's how he operates," she responded. "He puts witnesses under surprise duress to see how they respond. According to Zola, the problem is that while reactions under extreme stress are usually accurate and reasonable, they can also be attributed to other factors. Your reaction to seeing that body, in her opinion, was normal." She thought for a moment. "However, to Weaver, according to my grandfather, your actions would imply absolute guilt."

Matheson shook his head. He cared little what Weaver thought. But he did care what Lee thought. He needed to tell her at least the basics of the truth. "Look, I need to tell you a few things. I've had a few issues during my last two tours. Nothing big, just things I can't seem to shake. Something happens every time I smell smoke."

"Like what?"

"Weird things. I see things I know aren't there. Seeing that woman at the morgue caught me during one of those."

"What weird things?"

"I can't talk about this to your face."

"Did you tell Zola this?"

"I tried, but with this part, I couldn't get the words out."

She stood, and instead of walking to the other side of the room as he expected, she pulled him up, wrapped her arms around him, and pressed herself against him so he could talk without looking at her face. "Try with me."

He wrapped his arms around her, his chin resting on her head. In flat shoes, she fit against him perfectly.

"It's usually a sound or a smell. The smell of smoke can make me black out in an instant. I live every day with the sound of gunfire in my head, usually triggered by a sound or sometimes stress. I have repeated nightmares about my hellacious family. Then two incidents happened in Afghanistan..." He hesitated, not knowing what would happen if she wanted more details.

"Just tell me what you are comfortable with, Vern. I promise you this isn't a race. It's a method of trust. I'll listen to whatever you want to tell me."

"But I don't want you to know these things about me. You won't look at me the same way you do now."

She stepped back and looked up at him. "What makes you say that?"

"Because the things I've done and seen are horrific. You'll think I'm a monster."

"Vern, you've been trained by the military to do horrible things to people. Unless you did them outside your orders, why would I be concerned about you doing your job?" Having no answer, he shook his head and pulled her into him again. "How often have you been triggered since you've been Stateside?" she asked. Her arms were now wrapped tightly around him, her voice muffled against his chest.

He counted in his head. "Four or five, including the nightmares. I have them every night when I try to sleep. A bottle of something usually solves that, but with my parents' history, it's not good for me to go there." He was glad she was not looking directly at him. "But lately, I have." He pulled away and started for the door before he completely lost it. "Look, I need to go. I appreciate the help for my grandparents."

She refused to let go of his arm. Her tight grasp stopped him from leaving and forced him to turn back to face her. "Vern—"

He stared at her hand on his bicep, then at the deep blue eyes staring at him. Just the warmth of her hand caused an electrical shiver to run up his arm into his shoulder. Every inch of him suddenly softened. Was it a ploy? His gut told him no. It was real.

"I understand how your deployments and now this have affected you. It doesn't matter. But I will warn you—what you want from me won't happen quickly. I have things in my own past that need to be resolved in my head."

He shifted his gaze back out the window. "Yes, what I've done does matter. You might not think so now, but it will be a problem."

She gave him a smirk. "Given all the crap you've put me

through, I don't think there's any way I can think less of you. We're already at rock bottom." Her attempt at sarcasm made him smile.

"Yeah, Mac called and gave me hell about you." He moved to take her in his arms again. "I know I'm out of control right now. Katie's being missing has me twisted up pretty badly."

"Not Angela?" She stepped back, one eyebrow cocked skyward, then she went serious. "I'm sorry. That had no place in this conversation," she hesitated. "We're pretty far out of bounds, ethics-wise, today. I've even violated my no-touch rule."

He couldn't hide the disappointment in his voice. "I needed that touch."

She held his face with her hands. "I know you did, but Vern, one of us has to have their head on straight, and right now, I think we both can agree, that's not you."

He stepped away from her grasp and took in a big breath, then blew it out. "You're right." He stared at her, soaking in everything he could about her, the way she looked, smelled, and how she'd just felt wrapped around him. After what he would do to every one of Angela's drug dealers, and then Angela, she would never look at him again.

43

VERN

SATURDAY, 11:30 A.M.

Matheson found Dorchester Village near the Ashley River, and eventually located Rato's trailer on Norden Street after a bit of persuasion from the park manager. The man gave him a little more resistance than he had anticipated, and when parking his car, he wondered if Rat had received a heads-up that he was coming.

He stood in the street and looked at the clumps of gray clouds moving quickly overhead. The hurricane was on its way. Too close for comfort, given he had no idea where Katie could be. Up and down the street, people were loading their cars, preparing to evacuate. Umberto was almost a Category 4 as it crawled north, sucking up the warm water from the Gulf Stream. At the end of the street, he saw the familiar brown SUV head toward him, then turn.

It had to be Weaver following him.

Going through the chain-link gate, Matheson walked up to the fifty-year-old trailer, wondering how it was still in one piece. While most of the neighborhood tried their best to make the area livable, this one was not. A rusted grill sat on its side in the overgrown yard, and bags of garbage slouched next to the house.

Knocking on the door, Matheson heard the old trailer creak with the weight of the occupant's steps. Impatient, he pounded a second time, then a third, and the door finally opened. An eyeball stared at him through the crack. Stale air wafted out.

"What d'ya want?" The crack in the door opened a little further.

"I just need information." Matheson smelled the odor of unwashed skin, bad breath, and leftover sausage, with a smattering of marijuana and cigarettes. The man let the door open a bit further, revealing baggy gym shorts and a dirty T-shirt. Greasy black hair flopped over the man's pockmarked face, which needed a shave. Rat's beady eyes and sharp nose explained his nickname. As Matheson reached for his wallet, the dealer shifted away from the door. Matheson held up his hands to show they were empty.

"Whoa, man. Just getting a photo out of my wallet. No reason to get antsy on me, now. Just trying to find someone." He showed the man the photo of Katie and Angela on the beach.

"Don't know peoples. Go away." The man went to shut the door, and Matheson blocked it with his foot. The man did not look afraid; he just didn't want to be bothered.

"I'm looking for my wife and child. Take another look."

The man's focus was on the oversized brown boot blocking his door. Matheson shoved the door, causing Rato to fall backwards into the room. A sawed-off shotgun sat on the kitchen counter, and Matheson snatched it, the man still huffing to pull his bulk from the floor. Confirming the gun was loaded, Matheson hoped he didn't have to use it. There was enough killing in his head.

Two rusted chairs shoved underneath the kitchen counter were the only furniture. The counter itself was cluttered with empty pizza boxes and dirty dishes. Matheson saw a large cockroach scurry by, but it was the containers behind the man that caught his eye. Boxes—heavy-duty plastic with locking flaps

—were stacked around the walls and down the hall—dozens of them. The trailer was simply a flimsy warehouse hiding in plain sight. Given the volume of whatever was in the boxes, he couldn't decide whether that was smart or the most stupid thing he had ever seen. Rato was likely just a caretaker, and not a dealer.

Holding the shotgun on the man, Matheson looked inside one of the open boxes. Large white pharmaceutical bottles of OxyContin were neatly stacked in the box, the kind the local pharmacy used to fill prescriptions. In a separate box, the bottles were blue, unlabeled. Either the man had an inside supplier, or they had stolen a truckload designated for the entire state. Matheson bet on the inside source, but that was another can of worms he had no time to open. This would be SLED's problem, not his.

No wonder Angela came here. And how stupid Cowboy was to give her this location. He must have thought she was too messed up or stupid to give away the supply house. Or maybe he didn't care. If she told anyone, she would have been eliminated. A ripple of fear ran down his back at the possibility of how this had affected Katie.

Finally getting to his feet, the man was indignant. "Away from boxes! None of your business! Who are you and what do you want?" A string of Spanish followed, most of it curse words. The man moved toward Matheson, but a wave of the shotgun made him back off.

"Take another look," Matheson held up the photo once again. "The woman came to see you. Maybe with the kid." He shoved the photo under the man's nose. A flicker of recognition flashed over the man's face before he closed down again.

"No see. No kid." His black eyes bore into Matheson, daring him to contradict him. "You leave before they come."

"Who's they?"

"No. No talk. Go. Fat man will be angry."

"You saw one of them, I can tell. The woman or the kid?" Matheson shoved the end of the shotgun toward the man's chest, just out of his reach. "My bet is it's the woman. Pretty, huh?" The recognition flashed again.

Damn you, Angela.

Matheson's patience was running thin. He had been here too long already. Whoever the man's boss was, he needed a better keeper of the merchandise. Probably this guy was somebody's cousin, a return favor that the boss would quickly regret. Matheson would bet his entire savings account that the boss—the "fat man"— was Weaver.

"Look, man, I just need the information, and if you give it to me, I'll act like I never saw all these boxes." When there was no response, Matheson switched to Spanish.

"*Si quieres vivir, solo dime lo que quieres saber.*" His Spanish was a bit rusty, but he was certain he had gotten his message across. Tell and live. He shoved the gun in the man's face, resting the double barrels on the man's cheek hard enough to make an imprint.

"*Solo vi a la mujer. Ella vino una vez. Le vendí diez pastillas.*" Angela had been here. Matheson wondered what she had used to pay the man for the ten pills he had sold her.

His question about payment was out of his mouth before he could stop it. "*¿Con qué te pagó ella?*" The man looked away and blushed slightly, giving Matheson his response. For a second, Matheson thought about killing the man just for the retribution of having sex with his wife. Yet, in this case, Angela had been the one who had suffered. "*¿Qué pasa con la niña?*"

"No niña. No child. See no kid." The man was holding his hands up, waiting for the gunshot that would end his life.

"I'm taking your gun," Matheson told him as he lowered the shotgun. "You'd best leave before the cops get here."

As SOON AS he got to his car, he called Lee, the shotgun on the seat beside him. "I found her next stop, but there's something you should know."

"What's happened?" Lee's anxious voice could not hide her concern. "I'm putting you on speaker. The Judge is here with me."

"Nothing happened. I just asked him questions, that's all. Chill, for God's sake. You need to bring that warrior woman back, Lee. I need to talk to her, not the whiny, scared lawyer version who's afraid of her own shadow." Hearing only her grandfather chuckle, he could tell he had shocked her, so while she regrouped, he kept talking. "North Charleston has a real problem. We need to let SLED in on this pretty quickly." He gave her the details of Rato and the trailer, especially mentioning the "fat man."

"I know," she began, her voice now strong and her irritation up front and evident, "that warning you not to interfere isn't doing any good. You're not worried about whoever comes after you? From what you tell me, the man at the trailer can identify you. We know Cowboy can identify you. You could be poking a mighty big bear here."

Matheson replied. "If I don't find Katie, I won't care who finds me."

"Is everything in that trailer in plain sight?" the Judge asked.

"Yes, sir," he replied. "The boxes are sitting in the living room instead of furniture. You can see the stacks of them through the living room window. The trailer is clearly something other than a place to live."

"I'll let SLED deal with that," Lee said. "Give me the address." Vern recited the address, then she continued with her questions. "What did you learn about Angela? Or Katie?"

He tried to hold in his anger. "That my wife will do anything for drugs."

"I think you knew that already." Lee's voice was sympathetic.

"Yes, but not to this extreme." He hesitated before saying what he felt. "I cannot tell you just how disgusting this place was, Lee."

"What about Katie?" Lee asked.

"Nothing. She's fallen off the face of the earth." Matheson's gut twisted even further. He looked at the shotgun on the seat beside him. He needed to get rid of it before he was found with it or before he used it when he shouldn't. "I took the man's gun."

"Why would you do that?"

"To stop him from using it on me. It has the guy's fingerprints. You should be able to identify him if he's in the system."

"Bring it to me now. Vern, you're running too close to the edge here. Damn it, I knew this would happen."

She wasn't telling him anything he didn't already know. "I'm on my way to the next guy."

"Then you need to hold off a few minutes until I can get Angus to you. Don't go to the next place without him."

"I don't want you or your office involved."

"It is in your best interest for us to be with you. Mac thinks so. I think so. Please don't argue with me about this. Where do you want Angus to meet you?"

"At the Waffle House on Long Point Road."

A HALF HOUR LATER, after removing his fingerprints as best he could, Matheson handed the shotgun to Angus through the rental car's window. Nikki was in the driver's seat of their Toyota Land Cruiser, the engine running. Wearing blue rubber gloves, Angus took a second to look at the gun carefully, then placed it in the trunk of his car.

"Which guy had this?" he asked Vern.

"Rato. The first guy Cowboy told us about."

"Ok, so we're going to the next one? What was his name?"

"We?"

"Wouldna push back at me if I were you, lad. The woman's got a fierce bite to go with her bark, and she's all teeth just about now."

Matheson let out an exasperated breath. "Merle is next. I swear my life is a country music song."

Angus laughed.

Matheson nodded his head toward the gun in the trunk as he spoke to Nikki. "There's only fingerprints. The guy was too pitiful for me to draw blood." Nikki nodded at the information and left, heading toward Mount Pleasant.

"She'll take the gun to a private lab we use," Angus said.

As they left the parking lot in the opposite direction, Matheson knew he was avoiding the truth. He didn't want the gun in his possession to kill someone, and at this rate, he might use it, especially if he found Angela. With Angus's careful look, Matheson could tell the man knew exactly what he was thinking.

44

WEAVER

SATURDAY, 11:30 A.M.

With Keith Ellison probably now in the stomach of an alligator, Weaver had a problem, particularly since he had no idea what information had been given to Danforth and Matheson. And he still had no idea who had killed his dealer or his friend Sean, only suspicions that Matheson was involved. Enlarging the photos from the gas station showed only the truck's make and model. The license number was unidentifiable, and the driver was always in shadow.

The MPPD also had nothing on the potential arsonist of Sean's office, and no leads on his friend's whereabouts. Weaver was sure Sean was in the exact location as Ellison, but there was no way he could disclose this information without implicating himself further in this quagmire. All video cameras within a reasonable distance of Sean's office had been removed, either the lens destroyed by a gunshot or physically torn from the building. The planning involved screamed "military operations." He needed to get to his office and figure out how to obtain Matheson's file from his captain's office. He would bet money that the Colonel knew how to handle serious weapons.

Making his usual rounds of the three monitored "storage facilities," as Harbin referred to them, Weaver stopped abruptly three trailers down from Rato's location in Dorchester Village. Vernon Matheson's rental vehicle, or one identical to it, was parked in Rato's driveway. Weaver backed around the corner and parked, winding through the back yards of the trailers on foot until he reached the back door of Rato's trailer. Even with the trailer's walls so thin, he only caught the end of the conversation.

The door slammed, and Matheson stepped out of the trailer and headed to his car, a shotgun in his hand. Now would be the opportune time to arrest the man. He was in a trailer full of narcotics and other drugs, and his prints would be on the shotgun he was carrying. If Rato were dead inside, Matheson would never get out of jail. Weaver shifted, readying himself to make the arrest, until he heard Matheson speak.

"Nothing happened. I just asked him questions, that's all. Chill, for God's sake. You need to bring that warrior woman back, Lee. I need to talk to her, not the whiny, scared lawyer version who's afraid of her own shadow." Matheson listened for a few seconds, then continued. "North Charleston has a real problem. We need to let SLED in on this pretty quickly." He gave her the details of Rato and the trailer, especially mentioning the "fat man."

Danforth would call SLED in the next minute. Stupid Rato had practically identified him as running the show, and Harbin would never implicate himself, but let Weaver twist in the wind. He slid back around the corner of Rato's trailer, making sure Matheson could not see him. Scrambling for anything to save himself, Weaver took out his phone and began taking photos of Matheson, with the address of the trailer across the street in clear sight, as well as the gun in the man's hand.

"If I don't find Katie, I won't care who finds me." Matheson was still talking, and Weaver could feel the handcuffs that would be around his wrists tighten with every word. "The boxes are sitting in the living room instead of furniture. You can see the stacks of them through the living room window. The trailer is clearly something other than a place to live." He recited the address and complained that he could not find his wife or daughter.

Yeah, well, get in line, buddy.

"I took the man's gun," Matheson said. "It has the guy's fingerprints." Then, "I'm on my way to the next guy."

As Matheson drove away, Weaver's mind ran scenarios. Other than skipping town, there was not much he could do to insulate himself, particularly if Rato talked. There was no time to move the pills, and he needed to call Harbin to let him know everything was about to blow. Or did he? If he got Rato out of the way, they would lose only a warehouse. Harbin could quickly make up for that loss. There would be nothing here to implicate Weaver.

Right now, Matheson was heading to the "next guy," whoever that was. Weaver had to eliminate Rato, who had most definitely identified him, then Matheson. Without her client, Danforth would have no reason to look for the redhead or her kid.

He turned back toward Rato's trailer to get rid of that problem, then find out where Matheson was headed next. He had a few guesses, and Weaver would make the rounds, doing his everyday detective work, while checking all the regular two-bit dealers. According to Sean, that was all Angela could afford at this point. *Stupid redhead. This is all because of you.*

Weaver opened the door to the trailer and took a good look at the man sitting on the floor. Looking behind him to be sure the neighbors weren't watching, he quietly closed the door, seeing a brown SUV slowly cruise in front of the trailer. He waited to see if the vehicle would stop, watching out the living room window as it turned the far curve and never returned.

"What did you tell him? Weaver asked Rato, who was on his feet, fear etched across his face.

"Nada!" the man replied, starting for the door.

Weaver reached for his service pistol, then changed his mind. He needed the man alive, if only to teach the others a lesson. But just barely.

45

LEE

SATURDAY, NOON

"Our circumstances have arrived, I see," said the Judge, as I completed the call with Vern and dispatched Angus to be Matheson's partner, insisting that the investigator not let the man out of his sight.

"How is the best way to handle this?" I asked him, thinking aloud as I continued, "We have directly connected Weaver to Cowboy."

"Yes. Weaver's number was one of those in Ellison's phone, and we have Nikki's recording of him clearly identifying Weaver as the person in charge of a drug operation."

I pulled over a legal pad and began making notes. "And we just learned," I said, "that most likely Weaver is connected to this pill stockpile through Rato's 'fat man' comment."

"Yes," the Judge replied, "but that is only a guess, and that is something that came through your client, not firsthand. The person from SLED handling the follow-up questioning him will need to get that information."

I added that note to the list, then looked up. My grandfather was watching me closely, a smirk on his face. I could tell that he was entirely at ease and fully in his element in assisting me with this call. The court system lost a serious jurist when putting this man out to pasture. Their loss, my definite gain.

"Do we go local? Or call SLED back?" I asked.

"Ha! After what you experienced with your last matter, you wish to talk with the police chief in North Charleston? Or our illustrious solicitor, Mr. Harbin?"

I laughed. "No, Clint Harbin is not going to get any phone call from me. SLED it is. You make the call."

"Chicken."

"No, Judge. I am wisely using my resources. This entire town stands at attention when you walk by. I'd be a fool not to utilize that."

The Judge picked up the receiver to the desk phone on the conference table. His face grew serious. "I will refer to your client only as a confidential informant, Lee. He does not need to be identified at this point, especially given that we do not know what physical damage occurred at that mobile home, nor whether this Rato person has been more seriously injured than the alleged bloody nose."

"Agreed."

He punched in the number of the man he had talked to only an hour ago. While the call was being routed through the switchboard operator, I ensured I had the correct address, pulling it up on the online map and locating it using Street View. It was as Matheson had described.

"Wallace." The curt voice answering the call sounded like someone I never wanted to be arrested by. I went to the SLED website and clicked on the man's photo.

"Bob, it is Augustus Rhineholdt again, but on a different matter."

"Judge, I thought you were retired. You're keeping me busy. What do you have? Do I need to get the HSI guy back on the line?"

"Not yet," the Judge said. "Let me give you what I have, and then you can disseminate as needed." The Judge proceeded to give him the specifics, going down our checklist with his index finger to make sure he did not skip any point. As he described the drugs, he, offhandedly, estimated the number and the value.

"Have this address?" I could tell the sheer volume of OxyContin made Wallace very interested.

"Of course." The Judge recited the address I'd written on the page. "The only missing piece to the puzzle is who originally set up this operation and gave the initial funding. I have a difficult time believing it was Detective Weaver."

"Where did you get this information?"

"We have a CI, Bob. I am not at liberty to give out the name."

"Someone connected to your missing woman and girl?"

"Bob..." My grandfather's body stiffened, letting me know that he was not about to involve Matheson in this, even though Wallace was quickly connecting all the dots.

"I understand. But you need to warn your CI that they may have to testify if this turns out to be something big."

"Of course, but I don't believe you will need this informant. The information I was given made it very clear that the evidence you will seize is in plain sight through the living room window."

"I guess this amount would have to be if packed into a mobile home."

"That volume is a guess, based on the conversation with the informant, but I do agree with you."

"How long ago did your CI see all this?"

"Less than half an hour ago. But Bob," the Judge said, "you should get someone to that location now. With the local detective involved, there may be a way that the drugs or their minder can suddenly disappear that we have not anticipated. Is there someone in Narcotics who can get there quickly?"

"If I had gotten this call from anyone other than you, I'd take my time. But if you tell me all this is there, then yes, I can have an officer there pretty quickly."

My grandfather looked at me, and I winked back at him—definitely a proper use of resources on our end.

"Then do it, please. And you might want to get the ball rolling to look for Weaver. Once he hears about this raid, I believe that he will be challenging to find."

46

VERN

SATURDAY, 1:00 P.M.

"We need to do a few things first," Matheson said to Angus. "I need to ditch this rental car. It sticks out in these neighborhoods. Besides, I need my own wheels."

Angus nodded. "No problem. Get on I-526 and head toward Savannah. I have a friend who works on a car lot on Savannah Highway. Let me call him."

"Nothing fancy. A truck of some sort, preferably with four-wheel drive." During the twenty-minute trip, Matheson continued to think aloud as he looked out the windshield at the darkening sky. The fringes of the hurricane's clouds, even though infrequent, were definitely moving toward Charleston. Since it was somewhere off the coast of Florida, the storm had to be huge. He hoped it would travel on up the coast and stay offshore for several hundred miles. Yet that wasn't currently his level of luck.

"Check the weather, Angus. My place needs to be ready, as does my grandparents. Then I need to consider whether there will be any repercussions from the raid on Rato's mobile home."

"SLED will take time to get set up," Angus said. "I think that's probably a worry for tomorrow, or maybe no' a worry you should have."

Matheson glanced at him. "Still. Something I have to consider."

"Agreed," Angus said as he pulled up a weather app on his phone.

Matheson was concerned that someone would come for him now that the word was out. Even with the layers Lee had created on paper, a tract of land as large as his was still too easily found. He continued bouncing his thoughts off Angus.

"This makes no sense to me. The woman who could have taken Katie was dead on my bedroom floor. Then someone burned down my house. To hide the evidence of who killed her? Most likely. Did her competition kill her and take Katie? And who in the hell would that be?

Angus replied. "We would hope the woman was killed by someone trying to protect Katie. But that doesn't quite make sense either. Of course, Katie is of the age where she could iden-tify anyone who took her." He looked down at his phone. "Umberto's moving toward us. I think the only decision now is whether it will stay off the coast as it goes north or turn inland at some point."

"Where is it now?" Matheson asked.

"Still off the coast. Looks like it stalled, but it's soaking south Georgia. I think it will hit Charleston or maybe just north of us, Georgetown."

"What damage will that do if it stays that far off the coast? I haven't lived here in twenty years and don't remember living through a hurricane even before then."

"A lot of beach erosion, some damage to the houses along the beach, but it depends on how large it is and what category. That far off as a Category 3, you don't even need to board up the houses. However, it is currently just under a Category 4. The ocean is too warm, and if it stays offshore and moves slowly, it will only get stronger."

"The faster we find this guy, the faster I can get my grandparents' house ready. And mine."

"I thought yours burned," Angus said.

"That was the townhouse in Mount Pleasant I bought for Katie to be in the best school district for kindergarten. I own a farm out in Awendaw. That's where I first met Lee. She was the attorney I hired to help me buy it."

"I didn't realize you knew her."

"Yeah." He changed the subject. "I think my grandparents know more than they are saying. For some reason, they don't want to tell me, or maybe they can't."

"Clarice said Zola had talked in detail with Kris about your grandmother. You might want to check in with her. I think she's scheduled an appointment for your grandparents to meet with her.

Matheson let out an exasperated breath. "Yeah, I was supposed to have set that up." He looked over to Angus. "But I keep thinking. Has my grandmother taken Katie? Then forgot where she put her? It seems such a ridiculous thought, yet her actions this morning make it seem possible. How much do you think this Kris person might be able to help?"

"Clarice says she's a miracle worker, but I've only met her once. Lee's assistant is pretty grounded, not prone to exaggeration. Talk to her about it and then make up your mind."

Following Angus's directions, he turned into a used car lot on the outskirts of town. After some discussion and a thorough negotiation between Angus and his friend, Matheson paid cash for an oversized 2015 Ford F-150 Offroad, its faded blue paint having been through hell. Yet the engine had been recently replaced, and the truck sported new all-weather tires. He wondered where the vehicle had originated, given that Charleston rarely needed heavy-duty tires. Still, he appreciated that it was on the used car lot, patiently waiting for him.

The engine had been upgraded for serious speed. Inside, the seats had been re-covered with soft, royal blue leather; a new sound system had been installed, along with the necessary air conditioning for the Charleston climate. With the paperwork from the dealer, Angus followed him in the truck as they dropped the rental car at the airport.

He immediately named the truck Blue. No imagination, of course, but for him, it fit. Matheson called Lee's cell number. She answered as if waiting with her thumb hovering over the phone.

"Vernon. Give me an update." He could hear the stress in her voice. "Did you find the other dealer?"

"On the way." He clicked the phone to speaker mode so Angus could listen. "I just bought wheels so I wouldn't stick out. Debating with Angus over protection."

"I'm sure you mean the metal kind that uses bullets. Not a good idea at the moment. But you're a grown man, and you're used to having it on you. Just keep it locked up."

"We decided we didn't need any firepower, Lee," Angus interjected. "Unless you have additional information that says we should stop and get some."

She didn't respond. "Angus says I need to check in about my grandparents."

"You never called Kris. Or your grandparents. Clarice just got off the phone with them."

"Yeah, I've been a little busy. Anything accomplished? Or were they their usual stubborn selves?"

"Your grandmother agreed to talk to Zola and Kris, but your grandfather was a hard no, as you expected. They plan to meet with her soon. Any problem with that?"

"As long as Nana is fine with it, there shouldn't be a problem. Not surprised Da refused. He's not big on revealing his feelings."

"Like someone else I know."

"Yeah, well..." Matheson replied. "Thank you again for your help. I've never had to rely on anyone for help before. It's a new thing for me."

"Not a problem." She was all business now, and he couldn't blame her.

"We're moving toward the end of day three of my five-year-old out there alone. While I don't want to push her, but..." Matheson couldn't say it aloud. He would never hurt his grandmother, but he had to know what she knew about Katie. "I hope Dr. Zola can find out whatever Nana knows. And fast."

"These things take time, Vern. Anyway, I thought you might be interested in a call I received. SLED reports that a "confidential informant" gave them a tip this morning. They look like real heroes now, thanks to you."

He laughed. At least something was going right. "Yeah? What happened with that?"

"You haven't been listening to the news, I see."

He laughed. "No. Not something I'm used to. We don't have twenty-four/seven news in the sandbox."

"They're saying it was the largest drug bust in the history of not only Charleston County, but the entire State of South Carolina. You should be proud of yourself for that part at least."

Matheson wished that he could see her face. "What does that mean?" He was ready to find Katie and get back to his life. Their life.

"Rato was in no condition to talk with SLED. What did you do to him?" Her voice was just above a whisper.

Matheson looked at Angus, then back to the road. "Like I told you, I didn't do anything. Just asked questions."

"Well, he was thoroughly beaten to a pulp by the time SLED arrived. I think they got to him in time. If we hadn't called SLED quickly, the guy would probably be dead."

"I didn't do that, Lee. I promise." He gripped the steering wheel so hard his knuckles turned white.

The interesting part of this entire day has been Weaver," she said.

"What about him?" Matheson had no desire to discuss the detective.

"According to SLED, he's been suspiciously absent after the bust. No one can find him."

"Out on the street covering his own CIs, I bet. Making sure everybody's in line."

"That, or covering his butt," Lee said.

"That too. Or maybe he's in this so deep someone eliminated him."

Matheson suddenly longed for a conversation with Lee that did not revolve around drugs, his wife, his missing child, or a dirty cop. He longed to sit all night and talk to her. Just talk. He put the thought away in his mental box to pull out later when alone.

"Listen," he told her. "My phone will be off. You'll have to wait until I call if you need something from me. I don't want it to ring at the wrong time."

"Don't make me have to call in a manhunt for you and Angus."

He laughed. "Yeah, I know you're a badass, you and your cavalry. Trust me. We'll be fine."

"Just text me, Lee," Angus replied. "I'll keep mine on silent, but I'll check it frequently. Keep it to emergencies, though." He looked at Matheson and grinned. "I'll keep this guy in line."

47

VERN

SATURDAY, 3:00 P.M.

Retracing his path on I-526, Matheson and Angus headed for a different part of North Charleston.

"We may be walking into a problem here," Matheson said.

Angus's forehead furrowed with concern. "And how is that?"

"The drug bust was successful. If Merle is set up as significantly as Rat, a protection party might be waiting for us."

Angus looked thoughtful as he stared out the passenger window. "I remember that dealer telling us Merle was the end of the line. The other guy's problems may not affect this one, particularly if they aren't part of the same system."

"From what Darrell's cousin tells me, the entire town is under one point of control."

Angus replied. "I have been in this town most of my life. To an extent, I'm still an outsider, but I've never heard even a whiff of something this big. Too much to risk in such a small town."

Matheson nodded. "Maybe so. I guess we'll find out."

"So, who is Darrell?" Angus asked.

"My best friend. We were in the army together. Met at boot camp and discovered we had played against each other in high school football. He went to Summerville, and I went to Wando."

"Does he live here now?"

"Well, he used to, up above Joint Base Charleston in Goose Creek. He's dead now. Killed after an IED hit his Humvee." This wasn't exactly true, but he refused to get into the details.

"Man, I'm sorry." Angus's voice was concerned.

"Yeah, me too." Matheson tried not to think about the last call he'd had with Darrell. He thought of his best friend every day, carrying the guilt of causing his friend's injuries daily as well.

"He has a cousin connected to Cowboy's world here?"

"Junior has been in and out of trouble his entire life. I've only seen him once or twice at barbecues at Darrell and Brenda's house."

"Think his information is good?" Angus looked skeptical.

"Has been so far." Matheson shrugged.

The war-zone look and feel of the apartment complex was what Matheson expected. The double-named complex that Cowboy had identified, Fairfield-Dunham, was easy to find. The entire complex required significant maintenance, and oil stains on the pavement had worn through the asphalt layers. The owner had given up, likely due to a lack of funds or fear. Some apartments had boarded-up windows, others had broken glass, and only half appeared occupied. The shotgun now being tested for fingerprints could have provided a little comfort, but he needed information, not blood.

That didn't mean he didn't want it.

Suddenly, Matheson heard a loud burst of Katie's laughter in his head. It caused him to jerk the steering wheel as they wound their way through the complex. He glanced at Angus, but the investigator was squinting at two women ahead on the sidewalk. One was a fuzzy blonde in tight shorts and a tube top; the other was an older woman in a flowered house dress, leaning on a baby stroller. They stopped talking as Matheson pulled up and buzzed down the passenger side window. All his cool air floated out the window, replaced by the stinky, hot outside air.

"You ladies know where I might find Merle?" He used his most charming smile, the one that usually helped him get what he wanted. Neither woman said a word, but pointed across the parking lot to a row of townhouse-styled apartments, one with an open door and a man sitting on the stoop.

Matheson looked back at the women, tilting his head down to see out the passenger window. "Is that Merle?"

The blonde nodded her head. "Don't tell him we said nothin'. Enough problems around here."

He nodded at her request, his smile still intact. Buzzing up the window, he rolled forward. Angus looked to the man seated on the front step, then to Matheson.

"Drive around the loop once and let me out down the block. You see if you can get anything from him. I will check around and see what we're dealing with. Maybe I can see inside his apartment. We might get lucky, and she's here, but we need to be sure no one inside can blindside us."

Nosing his truck around the loop, he let Angus out after the man sitting on the stoop was out of view. Returning to an empty parking slot, the two women in his rearview mirror were still watching him. He had seen it all before, just not in the States.

As he got out of his truck and walked toward Merle, the disposable needles that littered the side yard caught his eye. He approached the seated man carefully, catching a glimpse of Angus as he crossed between the buildings at the back of the property. Where he had been assigned, he'd seen too many users who had gone violently off the rails.

"Merle?" The man acted like he hadn't heard, picking at the cuticle around his right thumb. Matheson shouted the man's name.

"What?" Merle's irritated voice shouted at him as he looked up, squinting into the sun. The afternoon heat from the late summer sun bore down, and a bead of sweat trickled down Matheson's spine. He took the photo from his wallet and held it out, blocking the man's view of the sun with his shadow.

"You see this woman? The child?" The man swayed as he leaned forward to look at the photo. He tried to grab it, but Matheson moved it out of his reach. "Just tell me when you saw the woman, and I'll be on my way."

"Ain't seen the kid. I'd remember. Cute. She'un yours? Given the man's slurred words and mountain speech, Matheson could barely understand him.

He nodded to the man, straining to understand. "Yes, she's mine. What about the woman?"

The man swayed once more, staring at the photo. "Yeah."

"When?"

Merle looked toward the sun once more. "Yesterday. She stays here sometimes. She was angrier than a mama bear. Almost bit my head off'n me 'cause I didn't have enough. Well, that ain't true. I wouldn't give her more'n one. She didn't have enough money."

"What time does she usually show up?"

"Comes at night. Always the last one before I call it quits. Need me to tell her you're lookin' for her?" Merle turned his head to look over his shoulder. "That guy behind me packin'?"

The man wasn't as strung out as he looked. Angus, now standing behind the man, cocked his head and grinned at Matheson, mild surprise on his face.

"No guns," Matheson said. "We're just looking to find my wife and daughter. Don't want any trouble."

"Yeah, well. She's the trouble. Another guy's already been here today looking for your wife. You tell her it's time she moved on outta here."

"Yeah? What did the other guy look like?" Angus asked, walking around to face Merle.

"Greasy-headed old fat man thinks he's a badass. Whipped out his badge like I didn't know who he was."

Weaver. Matheson asked a few more questions to be sure.

"Thinks he's sumpin' special, that man," said Merle, "but everybody knows he's trash."

"Trash how?" Angus asked him.

"He's the big man's enforcer. Just got tagged for a load, though. Heard the cops took one of his places."

"Who's the big man?" Matheson asked. Cowboy had acted like Merle was the bottom of the barrel for dealers. And maybe he was, but he wasn't afraid to talk to them. Matheson wondered why.

"The big dog at the four corners of law. Don't know his name. But that's the rumor."

"Why are you telling me all this?" Matheson asked.

"'Cause my times a comin'. Need to leave here with a clean slate."

Angus walked around to stand beside Matheson. He held out his hand toward Merle, a folded bill between his fingers. "We weren't here."

Merle reached up and snatched the money. "Done. Zipped." He swiped his index finger and thumb across his lips, then stood, swaying as he walked inside the townhouse.

"Did you see anything inside? Matheson asked as he and Angus headed back to Blue.

"From what I could see," Angus replied, "either Merle's a hoarder, or he's using this place as a recycling sorting station. Never seen so many cans, all crushed, a mountain in a corner. I guess that's his side gig."

"At least we have a good lead this time for Angela," Matheson said. "I'll come back tonight and wait until she shows. Still not sure why he decided to tell us all that."

"I'm coming with you," Angus said quietly, "just in case the guy was lying. Or if it's a setup."

"You may be right." He stopped and faced the investigator. "I'll need you to help me keep my anger in check once I find her. I know she's chasing her own demons, and I know this technically isn't her fault. But if Katie isn't with her, and if she can't assure me my child is safe, I'm not sure what I might do." Matheson looked to the other man, hoping he understood.

"I have your back, man," Angus said, slapping him on the back as they walked to the truck.

"You know, Rato could have been lying to me about what Angela did to get drugs from him. But if he isn't..." Matheson opened the driver's side door. "I'm telling you, man, I felt my stomach start to heave thinking about it."

"He might be lying just to jack you up. We aren't dealing with the most reputable sort here." Angus shifted in his seat toward Matheson. "We need to eat now while we have time."

"Yeah, I know," Matheson replied, "Eat during downtime because you're never sure when you'll get to eat again." He pointed to the ignition. "Let's go. If Merle is right, we have hours before she arrives. We can plan contingencies as we eat. Check in with your boss so she doesn't send out a search party."

Using aerial views of the entire complex emailed to them by Nikki, they spent lunch at a steakhouse planning possibilities, intending to reconnect well before the time they thought Angela might arrive. With hours until midnight, Matheson headed to Sullivan's Island. He needed to search the garage for supplies for boarding up his grandparents' house, and the physical labor would help him work off some steam. He could easily get the entire house boarded in the time he had if everything was there and ready.

As usual, no one was home on Sullivan's Island. Matheson checked the garage for the boards required to prepare his grandparents' house for the hurricane. The large sheets of plywood leaned against the wall on one side of the ramshackle garage, each with a black, hand-painted number corresponding to a particular door or window. The front door was "zero." From his memory, the first window to the right was "one;" the rest continued to the right around the house. He slowly flipped through the boards. All the numbers were in order. On the shelf in the back of the garage were the bolts to attach them to the house, and although rusty, they were in the same place they'd always been.

He checked that his grandfather had the correct tools for the job, then headed toward the house with the first sheet of plywood. Suddenly, he stopped and looked back toward the house. A tiny corner of the roof of the garden shed, hidden by overgrown shrubbery, was in a clear line of sight from the kitchen window of the elevated house. He'd forgotten it was there.

Was this what his grandmother had been looking at? He leaned the plywood against a tree and walked over to the shed, pushing back the wild rhododendron and privet. The structure had recently been repaired, the roof reinforced, although the windows were too dirty for him to see inside. On the small door, there was a new lock. He would have to ask his grandparents for the key and how they wanted him to get the little room and the garage ready for the hurricane.

Until then, he had work to do.

48

LEE

SATURDAY, 5:00 P.M.

*Hurricane Umberto gaining strength off the coast of Brunswick,
Georgia*

I finished my last real estate closing for the day. It was also the last on the office calendar until we knew where Umberto would make landfall and the destruction it would cause. It had been years since I'd worked like this on a weekend, but the entire town was horrified that a repeat of Hugo was on its way.

"I will let the driver, Tim, know that you are coming along with us." The Judge said to me as I walked into the conference room where he had been working. He pulled out his cell phone and began to call a number. I placed my hand on his and shook my head.

"I can't go with you. Not this early."

"Why not?" he asked. "I thought you completed all your closings and everything else had been transferred or shifted to next week."

"Judge, I can't leave Charleston yet, and possibly not at all. I'll stay holed up in my office and ride it out."

"Not if it is a Category 4 or higher." The Judge's anxious expression shifted to exasperation. "It is too dangerous, Lee."

Tired from the stress of working closings in and around Matheson's case, and to get them out the door before the hurricane, I sat at the conference table wishing for a large, thick-crust pepperoni pizza and a giant soda. Not a fight about evacuation with my grandfather.

"This old building is brick and concrete block," I replied, "with steel supports. It has survived many hurricanes and floods. And you know the storm surge never gets this far inland. If it does for the first time in history, the professor upstairs has already left town, and I'll camp up there if the flood waters get close."

"I know you are a workaholic, Lee, but surely you don't intend to work through this storm. Certainly, Clarice will not be here with you."

"Of course not. She is leaving in about an hour to start packing their car after she gets all the wires out from the closing. Just as you are going to the island and packing up your car. I'm assuming Tim is outside, ready to take you?"

"I'm not leaving if you're not, Lee," Clarice shouted from her desk out in the reception area.

"We talked about this, Clarice." I retorted.

"Ladies, if this oak tree in the back garden falls, the entire building will be crushed." His voice was louder to make sure Clarice heard, too.

I put my hands on my grandfather's shoulders. "I will be fine. I will accompany you today and ensure that Isles End is completely boarded up and that everything is tied down and ready for the storm. It is still in the Atlantic Ocean, not even to Georgia yet. We have at least a full day before it gets close, possibly two. There is nothing for you to worry about."

"It is following Hugo's path, Lee," the Judge insisted. "I am convinced this storm will be at least that large, if not larger. The water is much warmer now than it was thirty-five years ago, and this storm could speed up quickly."

"It is still way offshore and not near Charleston yet. Don't borrow trouble, Judge." This was my grandmother's favorite phrase when someone was overly worried. "It could stay offshore and continue heading north."

"Please don't use my wife's words against me. You know I only care for your well-being." I stood, walked over, and hugged him. His arms came around me then, holding me tightly.

"You're not leaving because of him," he said quietly, his soft beard pressed against my face. "That is the real issue here."

"And you are correct. I have talked at length with Angus, who is still with him. He has the possibility tonight of finding his wife, and then, hopefully, his child. Once that happens, then yes, absolutely, I will get out of town and go to at least Orangeburg. An hour inland should be far enough."

"Do you have a reservation at a hotel?"

"Yes. Made it last night."

"Knock, knock." I turned to see Clarice standing at the conference room door. "Judge, she won't listen to you any more than she will listen to me. She's like one of those old-time fishermen on Sullivan's who refuse to leave the island even when they know better."

I unwrapped myself from my grandfather and then went over to Clarice, giving her the same hug.

"I love having a family that cares about me," I told them. "But I'm not leaving. So, Clarice, gather your belongings and get on the road. The freeway will soon be converted to a one-way system, so it should be faster for you to get up north to see your kids. I don't envy that drive, though. Judge, I'll grab my purse and help you pack on the island."

49

VERN

SUNDAY, 2:00 A.M.

Traffic in the apartment complex was sparse until just before midnight. A rusted ten-year-old Mazda pulled into a parking space two down from Merle's front door. Matheson slithered down in his seat to hide as much bulk as possible, and Angus did the same. The passenger-side door opened, and a frail, older woman pulled herself from the car—a false alarm. Then two men in an expensive BMW 7 Series, the wheel rims alone costing more than two weeks of Matheson's military pay.

More time passed, and Matheson grew fidgety. Another car. This time, to his shock, he was rewarded by his wife emerging from a beat-up taxi. Sweat broke out across his forehead. He must have made a noise, as Angus quickly looked toward him.

"It's her," he whispered to Angus, then to himself as he watched her pay the cab driver. "Please have Katie with you," he whispered, but she was alone. Matheson's heart slammed into the floorboard of his truck. "Angus, what has this woman done with my daughter?" The slap of fear hit him broadly in the chest. Katie was clearly in the wind.

Slumped in Blue's cab, Matheson used the bill of his baseball cap to hide his face. At least his ratty old truck didn't stand out in this neighborhood. As Angela walked to Merle's front door, Matheson was shocked at how much his wife resembled a scarecrow. A sleeveless t-shirt revealed arms with little muscle, giving them an almost skeletal appearance. Oily hair hung limp on either side of her face. When she turned toward his truck while scanning the complex, he could have sworn she knew he was watching her. He could tell she had the jitters even from across the street. He could feel his smoldering anger begin to rise.

I need to hear her side of the story.

"Angus, this is bad. She looks awful."

"We'll get her the help she needs." Both men watched as Angela slowly walked to the townhouse.

"She's not going to go voluntarily," Matheson said. "I've seen this overseas. She's going to fight us every step of the way."

"There are two of us, one of her," said Angus, "and we can call in reinforcements at any time. Just keep your cool. We're good."

Angela shuffled through the front door, going in without a knock, as if she were a resident, just like Merle had said. Bile rose from his stomach, thinking Angela might be shacked up with Merle permanently and not just for the night. Each time he learned something new about her, it was emphatically worse than he had expected. Matheson didn't want to discover anything else about his wife. He wouldn't be able to take it.

The dome light was off; the only sounds were the soft click and thump when they closed the truck doors and headed for the townhouse. Resisting the urge to barge in through Merle's front door, he knew Angela would be focused on a fix. Waiting between the buildings, shouting began, then silence. After ten minutes, Matheson and Angus headed for the apartment.

The door unlocked, Matheson used his elbow to shove it open, the smell like a goat shed. As they stepped inside, Matheson motioned for Angus to wait, giving themselves the full three minutes necessary to stop any gag reflex. Flies buzzed from half-eaten food on the kitchen counter, and garbage was heaped in the corner. The sink was a cesspool, clogged with something, the water dark and rank, mosquitoes breeding on its surface.

Matheson slowly crept down the hall. One bedroom was set up for recycling, with stacks of newspapers and piles of cans, bottles, and plastic. A sordid bare mattress occupied the floor's center, its corner torn as if retrieved from a dumpster. Merle was spread across the mattress, unconscious. Matheson kicked a worn biker boot, but the man only snorted and rolled to one side.

Odds and ends of drug paraphernalia were scattered about the floor next to the bed. Used to the endless havoc drugs had caused to his friends and enemies across the world, he knew enough to know what he was seeing. Pulling on cheap gloves he'd found underneath his grandmother's sink, Matheson picked up a box of white powder and, with a sniff, tossed it aside. Talcum powder to cut the drugs. Another tiny bottle of yellow liquid had a label from a local veterinarian—horse tranquilizer.

They found Angela in one of the bedrooms, tied to a chair. His wife was physically unresponsive, with only a light, thready pulse. Her purse was on the floor, her phone inside, and her wallet empty. Drugs and supplies were scattered on the floor around her.

"Call 911," said Angus.

"They will be too slow," Matheson replied, "and honestly, may not even come into this complex. Where is the closest hospital? Back in Charleston?" Slitting the duct tape binding her to the chair with his pocket knife, Matheson hefted his wife into his arms and headed toward the door.

"No, Trident is not far, right at I-26 and Hwy 78."

"I'll drive, and you call ahead. Tell them it's an overdose."

Weaver was blocking the front door. "Well, well. If it isn't the lovely couple." He reached for Angela's throat, and Matheson jerked her body out of the way.

"If I don't get her to a hospital soon, she'll die. Move."

"I don't think so. You're planning to ditch her just like you did the others."

"I have no idea what you're talking about. Get out of my damn way." Matheson shifted Angela and turned sideways to shove Weaver backwards out the front door.

A handcuff was suddenly snapped around Matheson's left wrist. As Weaver pulled his arm behind his back, Angela's feet dropped to the floor. "Grab her, Angus." Using his right hand, he tossed his truck's keys to Angus. Get her to the hospital while I deal with this jerk."

Angus hefted Angela over his shoulder, and as Matheson pulled Weaver out of the way using his handcuffed wrist, Angus headed for Vern's truck.

"He'll be on a seventy-two-hour hold in Mount Pleasant," Weaver yelled after Angus. "You can tell your lawyer not to try to get him out. I'm just trying to protect him."

"Keep your mouth shut, Matheson. She'll be there." Angus shouted as he placed Angela carefully in the truck.

"This isn't necessary, damn it," Matheson growled at Weaver. "My wife's seriously ill. I need to talk to her. You're taking valuable time away from finding my daughter."

"It's for your own good," Weaver sneered. "Unless you want me to charge you now with kidnapping and murder."

"What? Of my wife?" Matheson yelled at Weaver, then remembered what Angus had just yelled at him and clamped his mouth closed.

"Everyone you come close to disappears, and I'm pretty sure I know why. We'll talk about that when we get to the station. I just saved your wife's life," Weaver said, "and possibly yours."

50

VERN

SUNDAY, 2:30 A.M.

A trickle ran down the side of his right cheek in the silence, his eyes watering from the sudden blast of sand ripped across his face, as if he'd walked in front of a sand twister spiraling on the beach at his grandmother's. Only he wasn't on Sullivan's Island. He was still here in this deathtrap of a country, deaf from the blast that had come too close to killing him. A woman was crumpled in the doorway of a mud house, her eyes wide as if she were alive. Her colorful clothing was dust-covered, and one leg was twisted at an awkward angle. He knelt before her and placed two fingers on her neck to check for a possible thread of life, a cultural and religious violation that could have had him killed—had she been alive.

The cold seeped through Matheson's clothing in the cell. He shook himself from the memory, desperate for sleep but knowing he couldn't. He had faked it throughout the hours, head and shoulders down, his arms circling his knees, to keep the others in the cell away. But it hadn't stopped their clanging on the bars, the yelling and singing the entire night. Years ago, he'd had his share of visits in the military brig for the same drunk and disorderly type thing until he grew up and got hold of himself.

He lay on the cold bench, staring at the ceiling. He was being set up to take the fall for murder. Multiple murders, actually. Someone was following behind him, cleaning up each of the filth he had talked with, implicating him along the way. Who was doing this?

It had to be Weaver. His popping up suddenly at Merle's apartment just at the 'right' time, more than willing to take Matheson to jail, had been too convenient. The detective had tried to make Matheson a suspect from the first minute, wanting to tag him with the trafficking woman's death even though it was not possible, most likely to cover his own handiwork. But why would he kill his own dealers? To protect himself and cover up whoever was behind all this? Too many possibilities ran through his mind, none of which he could absolutely say was reasonable, although all were possible.

Matheson had to get released. He knew Lee was fighting for him. Yet Katie was still out there.

Alone.

"Matheson!" The voice shouted down the walkway between the holding cells.

"Here." Matheson stood and stuck his hand through the bars, a useless move given the jailor knew who was in which cell. Matheson shook his head at his silly response. His reaction time was slow, and his rationality was fading. At least in jail, he'd had only one flashback. That alone was a triumph.

Weaver was probably going to interrogate him.

"You're out." The jailor's words caught him off guard.

Matheson tried to keep his voice calm and not cause an additional problem for himself. "What do you mean?"

The jailor rattled the keys to the antiquated door and shooed Matheson out of his cell. "I don't make the rules, dipwad. Just get out of my cell. Somebody's here to get you. Let's go."

Matheson wondered how long Lee had been sitting in the waiting room. And why had Weaver kept him here when he had no intention of questioning him? He signed for his personal articles and waited as the electronic doors shifted. The first one opened, letting him step into the box, then closed behind him. The next one in front opened, letting him out into a hall, another door, and into the waiting area of the department. The claustrophobia made him desperate to leave.

Lee stood as he walked out the door and motioned with her index finger to her lips for him to stay quiet. He didn't say a word until they were both inside her Audi and on the way to the hospital.

"Angus filled me in on everything that happened today. I think you're lucky you found Angela."

"You're right. Have you had a chance to talk to her?"

"No." Lee shook her head. "She's been out of it the entire time. Nikki is sitting with her now. I sent Angus home to get some sleep."

"I think Weaver may be behind the disappearances." Matheson realized he needed a shower. "He's going after every person I've made contact with, and now he wants me out of the way. The only reason he would be doing this is to protect his involvement, whether it's with the drugs or with the trafficking. He may even have Katie."

"Let's see what Angela has to say before we start throwing out possibilities. Weaver insists he was trying to protect you. He refuses to give his superiors the details, making up a story that he won't share until he has more evidence. The police chief was livid when the Judge talked with him. Weaver has been officially put on desk duty, for whatever good that will do. He was pretty desperate to get you out of the way, though."

"I've been making the rounds of his dealers. Of course, he wants me out of the way."

"Clarice had an alibi down for the exact time and location of each fire or abduction." Lee glanced at him, her eyebrows raised. "Seems that little exercise came in handy."

"I'm sorry I was so difficult about that," Matheson replied. "Guess it saved me."

"Weaver's captain was also pretty pissed at him for his poor handling of all this. If my grandfather has his way, the man may lose his job."

At the hospital, Angela was still comatose. After talking with the doctor, Matheson pulled himself together with fortification from two coffees from the hospital cafeteria vending machines. Lee had insisted that Nikki go home, then, after talking with the floor nurse, suggested they quickly hit an all-night diner or a fast-food place. Matheson had no desire to eat, but his exhaustion would lead to a mistake if he weren't careful, and food and caffeine helped keep him moving forward.

"How was Angela when you found her?" Lee asked. "Angus didn't give me those details."

"It had to have been Merle who tied her to a chair, then left her by herself. I don't know if she gave herself the drugs or he did, but the doctor said just now that the amount was enough to cause an overdose."

"Does the doctor think she'll live?" Lee asked.

"Yes, but she's so thin he's concerned about organ failure. If she comes out of this, she'll be in the hospital for a while. She has a difficult time ahead of her." He looked at her sadly. "He wasn't very hopeful."

"Not good."

"No. I was hoping that when she wakes up, you could talk some sense into her."

"Nikki said at one point she regained consciousness and mumbled that she left Katie with Nana, but I doubt she knows what day it is, much less where she left your daughter."

When they returned to the hospital, Matheson collapsed into a chair in the empty waiting room. "You should go home. But I don't want you to..." He hesitated. "I just need you here." He didn't know what to tell her. He needed her here, someone to shore him up, to keep him moving forward. Not just anyone—her.

"What's happening?" Lee asked.

"I'm running on empty and I..."

"You're on the edge of losing control."

"Yeah." Matheson heaved a sigh. "Thank you for under-standing."

"No need to thank me. Now lie down across those chairs and sleep. I'll wake you if I need you."

51

SHARPE

SUNDAY, 3:30 A.M.

Hurricane Umberto increasing in speed off the coast of Savannah.

The truck followed some distance behind, slowly matching the Mexican's pace as he trudged along the sidewalk, heading home from a very early breakfast at the neighborhood all-night taqueria. Once the Mexican was released from the hospital, where they patched him up from a severe beating, and released on bail, Sharpe had no trouble finding him. Everyone had habits. The Mexican ate his food while perched on a stool at the counter. Sharpe had a clear view through the brightly lit front window.

The clumps of storm clouds in the night sky were oppressive as the outer rings of the storm began to spin several hundred miles away from the center of the storm. The hurricane was significantly offshore, but the weather report had changed. Umberto was intensifying, and Sharpe could feel his nerves on edge. Charleston had not had a significant hurricane since Hugo, and the weather nerds were beside themselves with their predictions.

Sharpe waited several blocks down the street, his truck nosed out of sight from the restaurant. The old green tarpaulin was ready. He was getting restless. Dawn would be here soon. The Mexican finally finished his food and plodded down the sidewalk in obvious pain. Sharpe wondered why they had released him from the hospital. The man didn't look well. He drove slowly beside the man, calling out in Spanish from the open window.

"Need a ride?"

The Mexican shook his head. "Gracias. Home not far." He pointed with his flapping hand ahead of him, but in no specific direction.

Sharpe pushed harder. "Oh, come on. It's too late to be out here walking. I'll be glad to give you a ride. You live in my trailer park." The Mexican stopped on the sidewalk and squinted at Sharpe. Comforted that he was talking to a neighbor, the man nodded and reached for the door handle.

Sharpe gave the man a ride home, dropping him off, then pulling around the circle as if he were going to his own house. He allowed the Mexican to enter the mobile home, giving him time to settle in. He could be patient. But in the end, he wasn't.

Snapping on rubber gloves, he waited only thirty minutes before returning to the mobile home park and backing his SUV into the Mexican's driveway. He turned the knob and found it unlocked. Before stepping inside, he looked around the neighborhood. There was no movement among the other trailers. Many appeared to have already been evacuated. A television from one trailer down the street was the only noise.

He opened the door and stepped inside. Empty boxes lined the living room walls, and the kitchen counter was covered with dirty dishes and takeout containers. Sharpe crept down the carpeted hallway until he reached the room at the end of the mobile home. Surprising the sleeping Rato, he covered his mouth with a pillow. It took an interminable five minutes before the man stopped breathing. He rolled the body in a ratty comforter from the bed, and after checking to be sure the neighborhood was still clear, dragged the body outside and dropped it into the bed of his truck, covering it with the tarp.

The man was too heavy. Sharpe could feel the pain begin in his back from lifting him. This had to be over soon before his body gave out on him.

On his way to the derelict gas station, he heard a call on the police scanner he kept in his truck. The details of an emergency call to the hospital were transmitted to the police. A woman who matched Angela's description was *en route* to Trident Hospital. Pulling a U-turn in the middle of the road, he headed for the apartment complex where he'd heard Angela had been found.

I was too slow, damn it. I should have gotten to her first.

At the apartment, he had to wait. One police car was parked with its engine idling in front of a six-unit townhouse building with an officer in the driver's seat. Another officer exited the building's front door. It provided Sharpe with the apartment's location. The policeman closed the door behind him, climbed into the vehicle's passenger side, and the two officers left. Sharpe waited another ten minutes before circling to the rear of the building and parking his truck.

The smell inside the apartment was unbearable, worse than anything he had ever known. He could not believe that Angela would come here, regardless of her desperate need for drugs. He needed to find her dealer, yet it was impossible to imagine anyone living in such filth. He carefully crossed the threshold in the dark, still hot from the August heat. The buzz of flies was loud. Leading right-handed with his old gun, he turned each corner softly, careful not to make the slightest sound.

He found the man he was looking for in the back bedroom, out cold, the distance through the empty cans and rotted remnants of food only twenty-five feet from the front door. The odor was so strong that he had to breathe through his mouth until his sense of smell could adjust. The man was unconscious, on the dirty mattress. Sharpe leaned down to search for a pulse and found one so thready he knew the man was close to death. Sharpe stood there, wondering why the police had left him here. If he were dead, it was a crime scene. If alive, the man needed medical help. Either way, walking off wasn't the proper procedure, but Sharpe appreciated the officers' assistance.

Hefting him upward while trying not to gag, the man was barely warm even in this heat, weighing less than a hundred pounds. He considered leaving the man where he was and adding a syringe to finish the job. Yet that would not serve his purpose. This scumbag had to disappear just like the others. He had to pay. And so did she. Eventually.

Using the duct tape he'd brought to be sure the man couldn't make enough sound to cause a problem, he held his breath from the stench and flipped the man over his shoulder like a sack of rice. He would have to burn his clothes; the smell would never come out.

Stepping into the humid night, his truck was parked a hundred yards behind the complex. Years earlier, the old hospital had been razed after repeated flooding; the land was too swampy in winter. A gust of wind whipped against his back, shoving him suddenly forward. Looking up, he could see from the glow of Charleston in the distance that a line of heavy clouds was headed his way. He needed to get moving.

Another gust in the thirty-mile-per-hour range whipped across the abandoned property between the apartment complex and his truck. He could no longer ignore the vast reach as the hurricane got closer. At a Category 4, Umberto was massive, and he knew from experience that short blasting gusts that were even further extended from the center were always the first sign. The forecasters expected it to increase soon to a Category 5. If that happened, most of Charleston would quickly resemble a war zone.

He picked up his pace. Memories of Hurricane Hugo caused outright fear in many people in the area, including himself. He had seen firsthand what Mother Nature's raw strength would do when angry. If Umberto hit them dead-on as it was forecasted, that idiotic governor would call for a mandatory evacuation. Then where would he be? Tossing the man in the truck bed, he hog-tied him, anticipating a struggle of some sort, but getting none. Quietly waiting, he made sure no light appeared in any of the apartments from his noise.

He needed one more night, but with the gusts being thrown off Umberto, he knew he didn't have it. He cranked the truck, leaving his headlights off from the parking lot to the street. Within seconds of hitting the main road, he was blocks away heading toward Rhett Avenue.

One more to go.

52

VERN

SUNDAY, 8:00 A.M.

Lee woke him later and insisted that he go home or to his grandparents. He needed a break after being at the hospital for hours. She would sit with Angela and wait for her to wake up, and would call him immediately if she learned where Katie was. He had almost reached his grandparents' house when his cell phone rang.

"Angela's not talking," Lee said abruptly. "She woke fifteen minutes ago, but I couldn't get her to talk to me. In my opinion, she knows something, but she's out again."

"I'm almost to Sullivan's. Want me to turn around?"

"No. I'm waiting on the doctor. He may not talk with me, but I can try." He could hear the impatience in Lee's voice.

"Just keep me posted. After I get through here, I'll head back there. Maybe just seeing me and how angry I am will jolt her memory." He parked Blue in the driveway behind the Olds at his grandparents' house, and his grandmother met him at the front door.

"You got yourself a truck." His grandmother said as he reached her at the front door. "And you boarded up the house. Thank you, son."

"I did," he replied, looking at his truck. "She looks a little rough, but she'll do. And I had some extra time yesterday."

They sat at the kitchen table, always the center of Nana's house. Only one window was unboarded to let in natural light. He would cover it just before the storm when he covered the front door. But before he could tell them about Angela, the old man shifted to face Matheson, his face indignant. "Where were you last night? You look, and smell, I might add, like you need a shower."

"In jail, then the hospital."

The old man's eyes turned to steel. "What fool thing did you do this time? Are you injured?" Here was the man Matheson grew up with—forceful, negative, downright mean. He could ask his grandfather the same question, but Matheson was not sure he wanted to know the answer.

The old man shifted forward in his chair. "You know, a man should control his wife way better than you have. Your grand-mother has been beside herself."

This wasn't about him. It was about whatever Angela had done to—or God forbid *with*—his grandfather. "What did she do to you?"

"Nothing that's any of your business." The old man crossed his arms across his chest and glared at him.

"If it involves my wife and my child, it is my business."

"Your child is fine." Moore looked down at the table.

"How do you know that?" Matheson kept his voice calm as he tried to rein in his anger.

"I just know."

Matheson stood and leaned over the table to get in the old man's face. "Tell me what you know, old man! Last night I found Angela. She doesn't know what happened to Katie. Whatever is going on with you and Nana, I need your help. She's my daughter, and for God's sake, your granddaughter."

The old man stood, his index finger flailing in the air. "A fine father you've turned out to be."

"Look, I just need—"

His grandmother stood then, interrupting the fruitless argument with each arm extended, shoving the men apart like a football referee. "Enough, you two. Now sit and behave." Moore stomped out of the room, and Matheson could hear him pounding up the stairs, then the shower running.

"That lady lawyer you hired called some medical person," his grandmother said. "Someone named Kris will be here soon. What did you tell her?"

Matheson's grandmother was her usual self again, her makeup intact, complemented by a recent visit to the beauty shop. It was a stark transition from their last interaction. Matheson decided the best way to tackle this problem was to hit it head-on. "You weren't yourself the last time I saw you. Got me worried." He could see the hackles rise on her neck like a primped poodle. His grandmother, at this point, was most definitely back to her typical self.

"Whatever do you mean?"

Matheson couldn't squelch a grin at hearing that phrase, one she had responded with his entire life when she was accused of something. He reached for her hand, his thumb caressing her paper-thin skin.

"Nana, you didn't know who I was. Standing here in this kitchen, dirty, your hair all wild, you threatened me with a butcher knife. Please tell me what is wrong. You know I'll help."

His grandmother's eyes grew wide with disbelief. "I never did that!"

Matheson stood his ground. He squeezed her hand. "Oh yes, you did. The lawyer just happened to catch me right after you had threatened me. If you want to know the truth, I was pretty torn up about it. I come home, and Angela's gone. Katie's gone.

You and Da are out of your minds. She offered help, and I took it."

"Well, I'm not talking to anyone about a mental condition I don't have. They'll put me in the crazy house."

"Nana, no one is going to put you anywhere. Just get an evaluation and tell them the truth, for God's sake. You know something about Katie that you're not telling me, and you spend the afternoon praying at Stella Maris?"

"Vernon Hartley Matheson, I'm as torn up about your family as you are. Don't try to make me the bad guy here. And I haven't been to Stella since Sunday mass. That wife of yours..." His grandmother suddenly looked away.

"What?"

"I think you know what. She was hooked on drugs. I found them in her medicine cabinet at your house while I babysat Katie one night. That night, Angela never came home. I took Katie to school the next morning and made plans to pick her up that afternoon, but Angela called and said everything was fine. I almost took Katie away from her that day, but your grandfather refused to get involved. He said you would take care of it when you got home."

Matheson sat back in the dining chair, wondering why his ever-demanding Grandfather had kept far away from this situation. It was not like him at all—the man never relinquished control of anything. Why would he give up control of his own grandchild?

He remembered the note and got up to retrieve it. "If you didn't go to Stella, what is this?" He thrust the note toward her. She took it carefully and read the words written in her handwriting.

"I don't know what this is about."

"Give me the Monsignor's telephone number, please."

"It's on the bulletin board where it's always been. What are you doing?"

Matheson called the priest's office in the Catholic church two blocks over. The priest answered promptly and, after Matheson explained the situation, agreed that, since mass had been cancelled due to the evacuation, he could visit with them immediately before he did the same.

"Why are you making him come over like this?" Her expression showed both alarm and dismay.

"Because maybe you'll believe him. You don't believe me."

His grandmother sat in a huff until she realized her priest was on his way. In her flurry of tea-making and cookie-plate preparation, Matheson focused on his grandfather.

"What did Angela do to Da that made him not want to get involved?"

His grandmother threw up her hands. "Why did you invite the monsignor over like that? I'm not ready!"

Matheson continued to push. "What is going on with him? And where was he last night?"

As if on cue, his grandfather came down the staircase, freshly showered, his wet hair precisely combed. Mr. Moore spoke, his face questioning. "Where was who?"

"You, you old coot." Matheson hoped that his attempt at levity wouldn't backfire, and they ended up in another fight.

Da sat and looked expectantly at Matheson. "What do you need to know?" The old man's face was happy for once, unconcerned. Matheson would have whiplash from the rapid changes in his grandparents' behavior before this was over with. It was like the man's shower had wiped the slate clean.

"I'm trying to find out why you're so angry with my wife."

"Well," his grandfather began, "your wife is a slut and your child has disappeared. What else do you want to know?"

Matheson had to hold himself back. "What did she do to you?"

"She made a pass at me, if you want to know. I'm her grandfather-in-law, almost three times her age, and she wants me to have sex with her for money. You would not believe the things she wanted to do to me for that money. Not me, young man. It would have been better six years ago if you had taken the child and left that woman where she belongs—in the gutter."

Matheson clamped down his retort. His wife might do a lot of things, he'd learned, but propositioning this old man would not be one of them. His mind flipped back to the apartment where he had retrieved her and reminded himself that the Angela he knew no longer existed. But that wasn't what caused his blood to rise, causing a throbbing in his right temple. He married Angela only at his grandfather's absolute insistence. The words of rage thrown at him all those years ago still echoed in his ears.

"You will NOT embarrass your grandmother, do you hear? Marry that woman and move on."

Matheson clenched his fists and looked at his grandmother. Her face did not seem the least surprised at this revelation. "Nana, did you know about this?"

"Yes, of course, but I don't believe it. Why would a woman like Angela proposition a man who can't even get it up?" Before he could react to his grandmother and the loud harrumph in reply from his grandfather, the doorbell chimed.

Letting the priest in, Matheson gave the man a polite hug and cut to the chase. "Monsignor, were my grandparents at Stella yesterday?"

The sympathetic smile on the portly priest's face was genuine. "They certainly were. Given the circumstances, I clarified that they could come at any time for assistance. They were with me for over an hour, distraught over the news of the possible death of Angela and the fact that Katie has yet to be found."

Matheson looked calmly at his grandmother. "Well?"

Mrs. Moore shook her head in defiance at the priest in front of her. "Father, you are making this up. We did not do such a thing. Now sit down here and let's have a tea."

The Monsignor's eyes grew wide, his hand going to his chest. "Althea, are you alright?"

"Of course."

Matheson shook his head at the priest and raised his hands in surrender. Kris, the nurse, needed to be a miracle worker because his grandmother required one. "Monsignor, if you can talk with my grandmother for a few minutes, I need some air. We're waiting on a nurse I've asked to help.

53

VERN

SUNDAY, 9:00 A.M.

Category 5 Umberto is off the coast of Savannah, Georgia

Instead of walking around the block like he'd intended, he'd walked to town and back on the beach at low tide, then dove into the water and swam as far as he could before returning, which was foolish. The rip tides had already begun, along with powerful waves. He'd most likely inconvenienced the priest, but he'd needed the break to clear his head and get rid of the smell of the jail.

He had called Lee to get an update. Angela had awakened and, according to Lee, had insisted she be transferred to Roper Hospital in North Mount Pleasant. She refused to talk to anyone but Vern, so Lee headed back to her office.

Bounding up the steps, he burst through the door ready to apologize. With the Monsignor's help, he might get to the bottom of what was happening with his grandparents.

"Nana?" Grabbing a towel from the downstairs bathroom, he strode into an empty kitchen. Three plates of food sat half-eaten, dinner in pots still warm on the stove. The grandmother he knew would have never left her kitchen in this state. Flitting visions of the men he had questioned scrolled through his mind, with thoughts as to what they had possibly done to his grandparents. He felt the adrenaline rush as it spiked. Where were they?

"Nana!" His voice echoed as he reached the top step to the second story. "Da!"

He checked each of the three bedrooms. Nothing. He turned to head downstairs to the phone list to call the priest. Hearing a noise at the front door, he jumped down the stairs three at a time. At the landing, he paused.

Stepping through the front door was a woman in her forties. About five feet six, her thick black hair was piled on her head in an intricate pattern. Matheson could see a mix of Asian and African heritage, but could only label her as exotic. Dressed in light blue scrubs and white nursing clogs, she slung her black shoulder bag to the table just inside the door before snapping the screen shut.

The hospital scrubs told Matheson more than he wanted to know. He grabbed the woman by the shoulders and shook her, as spittle sprayed her face. "What have you done with my grandparents?"

The woman thrust both hands between Matheson's, throwing him off guard and knocking his arms off her shoulders. She backed away, her feet shifting into a martial arts stance, her voice calm, clearly in command. "Keep your hands off me, and maybe I can help you." Fierce brown eyes blazed back at him.

Matheson took a large breath as he stepped backward, palms up in surrender. "I'm sorry. I'm running totally on adrenaline right now. Just tell me where they are."

"And you are?"

"Vernon Matheson, the grandson. And you are?"

"Kris Adia." She reached for her bag and pulled out a wallet. Matheson could see the blue-black glint and heavy rubber grip of a revolver in her bag. He focused again on the woman. "And before you ask for credentials, here they are."

Matheson glanced at the woman's driver's and health care licenses before he handed them back to her. "You're Kris. You're the nurse I'm supposed to talk to about my grandmother. Where is everyone?"

The woman motioned to a chair. "You might want to sit."

He resisted her sympathetic efforts. "I'll stand."

She cocked her head slightly and squinted her eyes at him, sizing him up. He felt like he was in front of his old drill sergeant at basic training. "Very well. Just as I arrived for our visit, your grandmother had a stroke."

Matheson felt his knees go out from under him. Kris caught him before he hit the floor. It was his grandfather who would have a heart attack or a stroke, not his grandmother.

Her voice was stern. Definitely a drill sergeant. "Next time, pay attention when I give you a suggestion." She dragged him to one of the living room upholstered chairs and forced him to sit. The unspoken '*Sir, Yes, Sir!*' hovered between them.

"What about my grandfather?"

"Out of an abundance of caution, he will stay overnight in the room with her, although not officially admitted by the hospital. He had a serious reaction to her stroke." She continued, her words clipped and precise with a lilt from somewhere he could not identify. "The monsignor and your grandmother's physician arranged a shared room, so they are together. However, I must say, I do not believe either of them wishes to be with the other. No matter, as the hospital will kick him out if it needs the bed. They are currently very crowded. Unfortunately, that is how it works in this country."

Matheson released the air from his lungs. He didn't know just how much more he could take. His mind bounced back to Katie. It didn't matter how he felt or what he thought he could take. She was still missing. He had trained for and lived through much worse than this. "I think my grandmother knows where my daughter is."

"If so, it may be some time before she can tell us, if she ever does."

"What do you mean?" His heart jumped with alarm.

"She is in a coma, Colonel Matheson. One from which her doctor is afraid she may never wake."

Matheson felt as if he had been slugged. His chest constricted, and he felt lightheaded. Before he could question Kris further, someone knocked at the door. Kris raised her eyebrows at him in question. Matheson shook his head. He was not expecting anyone. Kris opened the door to Detective Weaver standing on the porch.

"Do you know this man, Colonel?" She twisted to look at him over her shoulder.

"Do not let him in. He knows he's not supposed to be here, and definitely not to talk to me without my attorney."

"Thank you." She nodded. "I will take care of this." Kris turned back to Weaver. "Call the attorney as you have been instructed," she said to Weaver, shifting to close the front door.

"I'm here to talk to Mr. Matheson about his wife," Weaver said. "You need to let me inside, or send him out."

"You've been instructed to call his attorney," Kris replied, her voice showing her irritation. "You will not come into this home."

"Lady, you have no right—"

"I have every right. He cannot be questioned about anything until he receives medical treatment. He has just been through a shock, and I will not allow you to contribute to his condition."

Weaver reached for the screen door to open it and shove by her, but Kris slammed the wooden front door in his face and locked it.

"I am a police officer, lady," Weaver shouted through the door. "Open this door!"

"I will be calling attorney Danforth," Kris shouted through the door. "I suggest you leave before she arrives."

54

———

VERN

SUNDAY, 9:30 A.M.

rains of sand were pressed hard onto his tongue. The battle had been raging around him for hours. He tried to feel his feet, his fingers. Nothing. The smell of blood was thick, but he could not open his eyes, no matter how hard he tried. It was as if he were frozen. Biologicals immediately came to mind. Several factors may have contributed to these effects. What had they used? And how had the factions of ISIS they were chasing gotten hold of any biological weapons? His mind raced.

Matheson tried to swallow but couldn't. He opened his eyes and blinked, watching the ceiling fan's blades turn slowly counterclockwise. A bolt of pain the size of Montana shot through the back of his head as he attempted to sit.

"Don't try to get up." Matheson couldn't place the voice at first, then he remembered. His grandmother's nurse. Turning his head slightly caused another cannonball-sized jolt, and he gave up any thought of sitting. He looked sideways at her instead. She was sitting next to him on the floor.

"What happened?"

"You blacked out, seized for just a minute, but long enough to force you out of your chair. It was enough, however, to cause me concern given your pulse rate. You hit the corner of the table and have a gash on the back of your head. There is a bit of blood on the floor, but it has clotted on your head for now. You may need a stitch or two." She leaned over him to look at the back of his head while talking. "It appears you were having a flashback. Have you had these before?"

Matheson closed his eyes. She didn't have to tell him about his pulse rate; he could feel the cars rounding the corners of the racetrack in his chest. And he had no desire to tell her anything. He didn't know if he could trust her.

"What is happening with you?"

"Probably lack of sleep."

"Certainly. And from what side of the turnip truck did you think I fell this morning?" Her laughter floated up to the ceiling. "That detective did not help your condition one bit either."

Matheson cut his eyes and caught her sneer, even though it hurt. He quickly looked away, careful not to move his head this time.

"I will telephone 911 for the ambulance then," Kris continued. "Maybe someone at the Roper Hospital will get you to talk, or would you prefer the psychiatric ward at MUSC?"

He shot his arm to pull her hand away from her phone, wincing at the jolt that shot through his neck. "Don't do that. I can't find Katie if you do that."

"Why don't you let Lee do her job? She is good at it, you know."

Matheson did not answer.

"You have many of these episodes?"

"No." It wasn't exactly a lie, but he could see her roll her eyes at his response. They weren't episodes, just memories. He blacked out only when he was dead drunk. This was the first time he had dropped dead weight to the floor stone-cold sober, though. Maybe she had a point.

"They have people who can help down at the VA. I know you went through some nasty things overseas."

"Help with what? Lady, I'm just tired." Indignant, Matheson forced himself to power through the pain and sit up. He was angry at himself, but took it out on a nurse he didn't even know when she was trying to help him. He needed to chill. The vertigo hit him like the boom of a sailboat. He felt himself sway.

"Sir, you must lie still and let me please call the ambulance. You probably have a serious concussion and need to be where someone can keep you still for observation."

Matheson heaved himself to his feet, causing the vertigo to increase. Holding on to the wingback chair with both hands, he tamped down the rising nausea before he felt confident enough to answer. "Look. I'm sorry I'm taking it out on you. I've just been through a lot. It took me thirty-six hours to get home. I landed, found my wife and daughter missing, and no one gave a royal shit where they were. There was a dead lady on my bedroom floor, and the local detective, the man you just met, had a target on my back within minutes, even though there was no way I could've killed her. I then find out my wife's a junkie, a slut, and quite possibly has sold my daughter on the black market for drug money. Not to mention that my house burned down. So, I'm under a little stress and need to find my daughter." His voice rose with each word until he shouted at the end.

"Lee has told me all of this." The woman said quietly, refusing to get flustered. She stood, her hands on her hips.

He let go of the chair and stood with his feet shoulder-width apart, waiting for the vertigo to subside. "Then why are you giving me crap about a little bump on the head? I'm tired and angry for God's sake."

"Because I've seen the signs before. The people at MUSC worked wonders with my patients."

He stared a hole in Kris's forehead, refusing to meet her eyes.

"I can take care of myself right now. I'll visit the doctor later, and you should know that, since you're Dr. DeLeon's friend."

Kris snorted and turned her back, heading to the kitchen where she began to clear the table. "Yes," Kris replied. "Anything you say, Colonel. I am so sure that you do not need my help." Even with the accented syllables in different places, the sarcasm was unmistakable.

Matheson watched her shuffle back and forth from the table to the sink, afraid to take a step. He had no time for this dizziness. "What else can you tell me about my grandmother?"

Kris stopped what she was doing and leaned against the kitchen counter. "When I left the hospital, her doctor had called several specialists for their opinions. You may give him a call. Possibly, he can update you by this time."

"I have no clue who that is. I just got home from eighteen months away, remember?"

"Colonel, I'm doing my best to be patient with you. I have his number and I'll tell you whatever I can. But if you don't get that attitude in line, regardless of your rank or my friendship with Lee and Zola, I'm going to kick your behind back to Syria. And you should call your attorney about that useless piece of detective."

Matheson collapsed on the bottom step of the staircase. He pulled his phone from his pocket and hit Lee's number so hard on his phone that he thought he had cracked the screen.

"Danforth." Lee's voice, even abrupt like now, had become an automatic trigger, one of comfort and instant physical reactions deep into his soul. He wondered if his voice had the same response with her, then instantly doubted it.

"Thanks for the bodyguard for my grandparents. I thought she was supposed to be a nurse. Do you know she threatened to kick my butt back to Syria? And I think she could do it, too."

Lee chuckled under her breath. "I see you've met Kris."

"Nana is in a coma." His voice became serious. "And Weaver

tried to take me in for questioning, something about murder if Angela died. Kris wouldn't let him."

Seconds elapsed before Vern heard her exhale on the other end of the call. "I'll take care of Weaver. You have enough to deal with. I'm sorry about your grandmother. What happened?" Lee's voice was concerned.

He tried to keep his voice level, with no emotion. "I left them here with the Catholic priest for maybe an hour and a half, I guess. It must have happened right after I left, and I guess I was gone longer than I thought. Dishes were still on the table, food on the stove. Kris got them to the hospital, then came here to tell me." He looked at the health aide. "I should be grateful." His voice cracked with emotion as he continued. "Nana knows where Katie is, I'm sure of it. And now I'll never know."

"What do you think your grandmother did with Katie?"

"That's the problem. I have no idea."

He could hear a tapping sound over the line, probably her pen tapping on her desk. "Do you think it's possible she hid her somewhere?" Then her voice grew incredulous. "And forgot?"

"It's possible, but where?"

Something nagged at him. His grandmother had done something serious enough to cause her stroke. Why had she been repeatedly looking out the window? Matheson forced himself to keep going, pushing tiredness away as he closed his eyes and pulled up the memory.

"I need to go to the hospital," he told Lee. "Let me know what Weaver wants."

"I will. Actually, I'm surprised he's popped up. SLED is looking for him."

"Well, tell them he's still here harassing me."

"Will do. The storm is coming. I'll be getting the office ready."

Walking back into the kitchen, he went to the sink and looked out the window. The garage stood as it had. He saw nothing out of place. Where had Nana hidden Katie? Wiping his eyes, he knew the only place he would find answers would be at the hospital, either from his grandmother or his wife.

"Kris? What hospital did they take Nana to?"

55

VERN

SUNDAY, 11:00 A.M.

Hurricane Umberto continues north, increasing in size

Angela was in a room two floors above his grandmother at Roper Mount Pleasant Hospital, having been transferred by ambulance. He opened the door to her room, not bothering to knock. The painfully thin woman in bed, who looked nothing like his wife, smiled at him.

"Vern, you're home." Tears welled in her eyes, and she reached out to him. He ignored her tears and stayed away from her bed. Even though she was in a hospital gown and appeared reasonably clean, Matheson caught the unmistakable stench of body odor, greasy hair, and rotten breath. His first estimate of ninety pounds when he had brought her to the emergency room was wrong. She was only bones.

A flash of Katie in this same condition crossed his mind, and he almost knocked his wife to the floor and walked away. He should not be alone with her. Yet addiction was a demon that caused ordinary people to ruin their lives. He steeled himself and proceeded to her bedside. She stared at him as if he were a ghost.

"Are you really here?" she asked, "or am I seeing things?"

"I'm here, Angela."

Deep purple circles were embedded under her sunken eye sockets. Her pockmarked facial skin was so tight that her cheekbones protruded. As she reached for him again, he lightly grasped her wrist and turned her arm slightly, enough to see the needle tracks from her wrists up to her armpit. She was way past an addiction to pills. He couldn't decide whether she deserved his sympathy for being in this situation or his anger for allowing Katie out of her sight.

She slumped back into her pillow, her eyes closed. He let her arm rest on the bed. Her eyes shot open. "Vernon, you're home, baby."

"Yeah, you said that already."

Confusion crossed her face. "What?"

"Angela, where is Katie?"

"Katie?" Confusion wracked her face.

Vernon could barely resist the urge to rip his wife's head completely from her shoulders. "Our daughter, Katie. Remember?"

Angela smiled sweetly, her eyes closing once again. "Katie Bug."

He touched her shoulder, refusing to let her drift away. "What did you do with her?"

More confusion, then her confusion cleared. "I left her with your grandmother."

Vernon leaned down, his face inches from hers, trying to take advantage of the few moments of lucidity before she mentally left him again. "Nana is in the hospital in a coma. Katie is nowhere to be found." He had to stand upright again, the smell more than he could handle. "Where is she, Angela?"

"No, you're wrong. She never goes missing. She always stays where I leave her." Angela's eyes were still confused. She looked around the room. "Where am I?"

"The hospital. I found you at that apartment where you tried to get another fix."

"Oh. Merle's. I remember now." She nodded slightly before looking back at him.

"When is the last time you saw her?" Matheson stepped back as the body odor mingled with the distinct smell of urine. He would need to call the nurse, but not before she told him where his daughter was.

"Where is my purse? My phone?" Her eyes narrowed slightly, then went wide as she realized her arm was restrained.

"Why am I tied up like this?"

"I don't know Angela. You'll have to ask your doctor. Or maybe the police." He tried to return to the subject of their daughter. "When is the last time you saw Katie?"

"Damn it, Vernon Matheson, untie me." Her eyes clearing, she was coming around from either the drugs she had obtained from Merle or whatever the doctor had given her.

He shifted, his arms crossed over his chest. "Not until I get the complete story of where you dumped my daughter."

Hatred suddenly radiated from his wife like the flip of a light switch. "Yeah, big man who's gone years at a time finally realizes he has a daughter. Leaves us to fend for ourselves, with no money, and grandparents who are unwilling to help. It's been a real ride. But did you ever ask?"

Her words felt like a slap. Before he could stop himself, his arm came up. Angela's body curved inward, preparing for the slap, but he stopped just before his hand reached her face.

"Oh, go ahead," she said. "It's not like it hasn't been done before."

She hung her head, eyes fixed on the end of the bed, waiting for him to hit her. She was pitiful, but he could not find one ounce of empathy. And her statement about 'no money' was ludicrous. He could see where his paycheck had gone every month.

He wished he had paid more attention. Right now, he wished for a lot of things.

"Angela, I know about your ankle injury, the oxycontin, the doctor, the dealer at the bar, the one in the trailer with all the boxes, and now Merle. The whole world knows your sorry, sordid story. I honestly don't care about that right now. You're paying for whatever you've done. You can do what you want because I will be in court so fast for a divorce tomorrow that your head will explode. I want Katie. Did you sell her?"

Angela's lower jaw dropped in disbelief. "Sell her? Are you kidding me?"

"Angela, don't lie to me anymore. A woman, in our bedroom no less, was found dead four days ago, her head bashed in with a lamp. A trafficker, Angela!" His voice was cold, hard, and well past his control.

She stared at him then, and he could see that she remembered. He felt sick to his stomach. "I needed the money." The fingers on her right hand started to twitch. Tears welled in her eyes.

"Just tell me, Angela." He kept his voice soft, hoping she would remember. "Tell me where she is." He tried his best not to beg. He looked at the woman he had married, and even knowing the facts, still wondered how she had fallen this far. The laughing redhead he had thought was so special was gone, and in her place was this—thing.

"I don't know." The tears were falling fast now, snot dripping from her nose, but she refused to look at him. He had no idea if her confusion this time was hers or drug-induced.

"What is the name of the woman you sold her to?"

"I don't remember," she whispered. "Oh, Vernon, what have I done?" She dug her palms into her eyes as the sobs wracked her thin body.

"The woman who gave you the money was killed in our bedroom. Do you have any idea who could have done that?"

"No. I remember her stuffing the money in my hand, and then I left with someone." Her eyes grew wide as the memory took hold. "I didn't even kiss her goodbye. Oh my God, Katie."

A shiver of fear slid down his spine, and he wondered what his daughter must be going through. The thought made him want to lurch for the toilet.

The drugs had eliminated any concept Angela had of time or place. It was almost as bad as Nana being in a coma. The orthopedist had been clear that he saw her three days before with his grandmother, the evening when she tried to get more drugs from him, unless the doctor had lied, which was possible.

The neighbors had been sure that Katie had been with her just before he'd landed at their townhome, and he trusted them much more at this point than the orthopedist or his wife.

As he left her hospital room, he turned to look at her one last time. Angela's eyes were closed, and her body began to twitch. The drugs in her system had worn off, and with no muscle mass, the withdrawals would be torture. At least she was in the hospital rather than the nasty place he had found her across town. He hoped that Angela's need for the next fix would give her a larger dose of reality, and she would remember where he could find Katie.

They were halfway through day four. If Katie were held somewhere without food or water, she might not make it to day five, but Matheson had to put that thought out of his mind.

56

SHARPE

SUNDAY, NOON

Hurricane Umberto 250 miles offshore from Charleston, expected to turn inland.

The coming storm would soon steal the remaining daylight minutes like a thief, even though it was only noon, forcing him to finish the job despite the midday hour. Two hundred fifty miles offshore, Umberto's intensity had dropped to a Category 4 due to wind shear, but it was beginning to move closer to the coastline of South Carolina. The cloud bands were now closer together, and the spurts of harsh rain were more frequent.

The Mexican had taken too long, and then the surprise with the dealer in the apartment had caused him to leave them for hours in the back of his truck. Heading toward the gas station, he stopped once to ensure the tarp covering the two men in the back was tightly attached to the truck bed with no gaps. Wouldn't do for the cops to stop him now, here almost at the end.

As one car on Rhett Avenue ambled by him to make the turn three blocks down, he cut diagonally across the street into the parking lot. Traffic was light. From the news reports, he knew that most people had evacuated, but there were still people about. Overgrown bushes anchored the rear corners of the white concrete building, allowing him to pull around the northernmost corner and hide his truck in between them.

He whipped the tarp from the truck bed, catching the whiff of the dead mountain man who had already begun to bloat. Snatching his handkerchief from his back pocket, he tied it behind his head, covering his nose and mouth against the smell for what good it would do. A large gust slammed into the roof and rattled the little store, making the rusty swinging sign out front *scritch, scrap, scritch, scrap* back and forth.

Pulling one of the bodies by the feet, he stopped at the edge of the truck bed. This would not do. He had absolutely no desire, once he dropped the dead man to the ground, to heft the body back into the truck in its current state. The condition would be worse in a few more hours with the moist heat in the abandoned building. Another car passed in front of the station. He had no choice. He had to wait until darkness, or the storm, could hide what he was doing.

Taking a smaller tarp from his toolbox, he first wrapped and tied the body like a package. Because the tarp was too small, he had to leave the head free. He then rolled the body off the truck and onto the ground. Pulling with all his might, he dragged it into the back room of the abandoned building. The dead Mexican's eyes fluttered open. Then he blinked.

Sharpe jumped backwards, slamming into the doorframe behind him. The man had been smothered to death twenty-four hours earlier. There was no way he could be alive. But he was. The Mexican screamed under the duct tape while struggling to free himself from the tarp. Stuffed in the truck bed next to the dead man for the evening, Sharpe was suddenly petrified that someone had seen the man squirm in the back of his truck.

It was too late for that now.

Sharpe left the little room and retrieved the bat he kept under the front seat of his truck. Returning, he didn't hesitate, but swung the bat like a professional baseball player. The bat struck the Mexican across the face, crushing his cheekbone. Sharpe swung once more for good measure, causing the man's skull to collapse and brain matter to fly to the opposite wall. Checking for a pulse, he waited patiently, finally convinced this time there was none.

Repeating the procedure for the second man from the apartment as a precaution, he pulled that body from the truck bed and dropped it heavily to the ground on a second larger tarp. He wrapped the body and grabbed the feet, the head bouncing in the gravel from truck to door to its temporary resting spot next to the other.

He closed the door and placed a concrete block he found in the weeds against it. Checking his watch, he saw that he'd wasted thirty minutes. He had one last chore before the storm hit and needed to get going.

57

VERN

SUNDAY, NOON

Heavy gray clouds were rolling in from the Atlantic Ocean as Matheson exited the hospital's front door after seeing Angela. Gusts of wind buffeted him with large, sporadic splatters of rain. His phone buzzed in his pocket. The number was unfamiliar, but he answered anyway, too tired to care.

"Colonel Matheson, your grandmother is awake." It was Kris. "You should come now." The nurse did not wait for a response.

He turned back toward the automatic hospital doors as he called Lee. "I'm just outside the hospital. Where are you?"

"I'm in your grandmother's room. Her doctor came at 6:00 a.m., and there had been no change when he was here. She's awake now, talking a blue streak. They've paged the doctor, but he may no longer be at the hospital because it's Sunday. It might take him some time to get here."

"Does she know where Katie is?"

"She has no idea—and this is a direct quote—'what she did with Katie.'"

"What do you mean 'what she did with'?"

"I'm just quoting to you exactly what she said. Maybe you can calm her down. She doesn't know me well enough and is a bit distraught. Kris has stopped them from giving her a sedative until you talk with her."

"Thank you. I'm getting on the elevator."

When he reached her hospital room, Nana was laughing and whispering with two nurses as if she had no care in the world. He looked at Lee in confusion. She shrugged.

"Well, Vernon! I'm so glad you dropped by for a visit!" She called to him in a loud whisper, pointing to the curtain that separated the room in half, the bed filled by his grandfather. A loud snore came from behind the curtain, so Matheson didn't bother to check on the old man. He would talk with him after he woke up.

Happy that his grandmother at least knew who he was, Matheson was still surprised. Nana was not the least bit distressed. He tossed a quizzical look at Kris, who was dressed in freshly pressed scrubs and had her hair in another elaborate style.

"Zola was concerned that one of us should always be present should she wake," Kris said quietly, carefully watching his grandmother. "I came in at four this morning."

"Thank you, Kris. I really appreciate it," he told her, knowing it would not make up for his early attempt to give her as difficult a time as possible.

"Nana, how are you feeling?" Matheson turned to his grandmother, deciding to play along, keeping his voice in a happy whisper until the doctor arrived. "Has your doctor been by again?" The hospital nurse standing behind his grandmother shook her head.

"I don't believe so. I had such a good night's sleep," she said, her face scrunched with worry, "although I kept having bizarre dreams."

Lee touched his arm. "I'll let you two catch up." She left the room with Kris and the nurse, leaving the door open a few inches. He could see that she and Kris waited in the hallway, listening. He focused back on his grandmother.

"Tell me about those strange dreams." Matheson sat in the chair next to his grandmother's bed, pretending as if nothing in the world was amiss.

"I picked up Katie in a parking lot, but when I got home, she wasn't in the back seat where I left her."

"That's strange. Do you have any idea what that was about?" Matheson wondered if Zola or Kris had any way to retrieve the memory.

"No. I don't. And it's very upsetting."

"Why is that?"

"I think something has happened to Katie. Is she at home with you? Or has there been an accident, possibly with her and Angela?"

His grandmother was missing a chunk of time. He let go of the breath he had been holding and tried his best to play along, hoping that the more they talked, the more she would remember.

"I haven't seen Angela or Katie. I just got home, remember?"

"Oh, that's right. I forgot you just got here." She smiled at him, and Matheson swore she was instantly ten years younger than she had been yesterday.

A glimmer of hope sprouted. "I did. I was hoping you could tell me what my girls have been up to."

His grandmother brightened even more, her cheeks flushed. He looked at the monitor as the numbers for her blood pressure clicked higher. He would have to be cautious.

"Angela found Katie the cutest daycare. You will love it. And the teachers there—I guess they aren't teachers since Katie's only two—are so nice. I'm sure Angela can't wait to show you. She's been such a good mother, Vernon. You should be proud of her."

His grandmother looked toward the television mounted on the wall and intently focused on a game show playing silently in the background. It was as if he were no longer in the room. Her blood pressure began to stabilize, so he didn't interrupt her. He guessed it was her mind's way of protecting her body. He would have to discuss that with her doctor.

He ran his hands through his hair, confused and worried— three years, and—*poof*. Katie would have her sixth birthday in another month, having already spent a year in the five-year-old kindergarten in the Old Village. His plastered smile remained on his face. With his grandmother this way, it wouldn't help for him to fall apart, even though she was his last hope.

With his grandmother still focused on the television, he went out into the hall, leaving the door open. Kris's expression had changed from confusion to concern. This was the first time he had seen her other than in a strictly professional or calmly angry manner, as on the day before. She motioned to the curtain separating his grandmother's bed from the one next to the outer wall.

"Your grandfather isn't in the other bed," Kris said. "I just checked before you came. I warned you the hospital was crowded. They would never have put another male with your grandmother unless they were desperate for the bed."

Matheson returned to the room and straightened his shoulders before shifting the curtain. The man was not his grandfather. This man was much older and fast asleep, lightly snoring with the covers pulled to his chin. So where was his grandfather?

Kris stood at the end of Nana's bed, lightly massaging her feet through the covers. Nana had lain back on her pillow, her hair spread like a white halo, and her eyes closed.

His grandmother's voice was still a whisper. "Vernon, why don't you and Miss Attorney—I'm sorry, I forgot your name again —go get yourself some breakfast downstairs. I'm sure the doctor will be here soon. You can talk with him then. We'll call you when he comes."

Kris blinked her agreement. His grandmother's eyes still closed, he and Lee stepped outside the room.

"I'll meet you in the cafeteria," he told Lee. "Just get me coffee. I don't want anything else."

"You ok?" From the corner of his eye, he saw Darrell standing next to the elevator doors, tapping his foot.

"Come on, man. I'm not going to wait much longer." Darrell said.

"Yeah, sure." He looked back at Lee. "I just need a minute."

Once the elevator doors closed and Lee was out of sight, Matheson escaped like a squad of hornets was after him, bypassing his vision of Darrell and the elevators for the emergency staircase. He barely made it to the chapel on the first floor. It was empty, and he collapsed into the back corner, the sobs taking over as his heart cracked into pieces.

With his grandmother's mind missing three years of information, Katie was gone forever.

58

LEE

SUNDAY, 2:00 P.M.

Hurricane Umberto turns inland toward South Carolina

It was more than a minute before Vern found me in the cafeteria, and although I had concerns, I kept them to myself. Just before reaching Mrs. Moore's room with our coffees, her doctor stepped off the elevator. In his fifties with a paunch beginning to show, he wore a golf shirt and khaki trousers under his white coat. After talking with Vern's grandmother, the doctor motioned us to step out into the hallway with him.

"How long do you think she will have this lapse in memory?" Matheson asked the doctor.

"Right now, I cannot answer that question, Colonel. I will run tests, and we will evaluate her over the next several days. I think she is quite lucky to have her body fully functioning. Many stroke victims lose function on one side and often have trouble talking. To have some memory loss is not unusual at her age, even without the stroke. With the tests, I may be able to tell you more, as she is certainly a lot more mentally active than I would expect after being in a coma."

"You know about my daughter?"

"Yes, and I am very sorry. However, I can do nothing to force your grandmother to remember something that her mind does not wish to remember. It could trigger another stroke. You will have to be patient."

Vern said goodbye to his grandmother, with Kris confirming that another nurse from her service would check in for a few hours. He and I coordinated our next steps as we walked out to the parking lot. The weather was deteriorating by the minute.

"I need to check on my grandfather's house one last time," I said, "and make sure everything looks fine, and check the ocean height. He evacuated yesterday, heading for his cabin above Asheville, North Carolina. I need to try and get Clarice headed toward Philadelphia before the airport closes."

"He made it up without a problem?"

"Yes, there was heavy traffic, especially from Charleston to Columbia, but he has a driver. Tim is also a widower, so they decided to evacuate together. He listened to audiobooks the entire trip, and they were able to stop for a break in Greenville. He's fine." I heaved a sigh of relief.

"Why didn't you go with him?"

Standing in the parking lot, the wind was whipping around us, the gusts almost pulling my hair out by the roots. He stepped close to me to talk over the wind, then motioned for me to get in his truck. I opened the passenger door, surprised to find royal blue tooled leather seats and numerous new additions to such an older truck. It was a relief to be away from the noise of the wind.

"I can't leave you," I said. "Not until Katie is found." He grabbed my hand and squeezed it.

"I'll head over to my grandparents, but I doubt my grandfather is even home. I had a few hours before Angela was to show up last night, and I finished boarding up my grandparents' house. There are a few things I need to check there to make sure everything is secure."

"What about the farm in Awendaw?" I asked him.

"I never took the shutters down. It's already as tight as it's going to be. That old place made it through Hugo. I don't think this storm will do much worse, but we'll see."

"Would Katie have somehow gotten to the farm by herself?"

"I don't see that happening," Matheson responded. "She's a smart little girl, but it's thirty miles from here, and she's only five. The last time she was there, she was maybe two. I doubt she even remembers being there. Besides, it takes a credit card to grab an Uber. Surely Angela didn't give her one."

"It's something to think about. Who else knows about that farm other than me and Katie?"

"Well now Angus because I told him last night. My grandparents don't even know it exists. I still think Katie is somewhere close to their house, or within a ten-mile radius of the townhouse."

"A lot of places to hide in that ten-mile radius."

"Yeah, I know." He ran his fingers through his hair, giving him his hedgehog look again. "The thought of searching all of Mount Pleasant and the rest of Sullivan's Island, and maybe even IOP, is daunting." He craned his neck upward to look out the windshield.

I couldn't disagree with him. We were running this right down to the wire, and my gut said that without a miracle, we were not going to find that child.

Going our separate ways, I turned on Station 32 after Breach Inlet, finding my grandfather's house, Isles End, boarded up tight. The gas tank was off and strapped tightly. Nothing else was in the garage to be carried away if the breakaway walls were shoved by rushing water. The first floor of the house sat twenty feet above ground level, a testament to the change in building codes after Hugo, which brought a seventeen-foot storm surge.

The ocean was as angry as I'd ever seen it, and the waves crashed ten feet away from the heavy pilings holding up the house. I checked the tide chart, then opened the NOAA Hurricane app. The vast storm circled out at sea, a wide donut of clouds with a distinctive open center on the video, halfway between Savannah and Charleston. The edges of the outer circle were already coming ashore.

We were lucky, though. The anticipated time of landfall coincided with low tide, rather than high. It would keep the surge at 10 or 12 feet rather than 20. Or with a Category 5 storm or even a Category 4, I was deluding myself. The storm had slowed significantly for some reason, but it was still churning along in its deliberate path, scheduled to angle inland later this evening.

I called the number for the Police Chief of Sullivan's Island. His office already had a storm message up, so there was no way for me to check on any updates about Katie. The thought of that child alone and in a terrible storm was beyond frightening. It would cause her trauma for the rest of her life—if she survived. I didn't dare mention this to Vern. He was already on the verge of collapsing from fatigue and stress.

Finished on my end of Sullivan's, I headed to the other end and parked out in front of the Moores' house. As Matheson finished securing the home, I headed for the kitchen, made coffee, then searched his grandmother's refrigerator for something to eat. We could not keep running on caffeine. Making sandwiches for us, I wrapped several more in a to-go bag and put everything else that I could into Mrs. Moore's freezer in case the power went out.

Taking a long sip of my first cup, I felt the caffeine surge as Matheson walked into the kitchen. "As you can see, he's not here."

"Do you have any idea where your grandfather might be?" I asked.

"I've not been close enough with him over the past ten years to have a clue where he would go." Matheson picked up his phone, as if to call someone, then set it down again. "Darrell would have known, for sure."

Matheson's body language was tense, as if he was expecting something profound to happen as a result of this phone call. Or a bomb to explode. "It was always our strength that one of us could always see what the other could not."

"Good thing to have in a friend," I said. "What happened to him?"

His voice was solemn. "I can't believe I'm calling him my friend after what I did to him." My question went unanswered, which only increased my uneasiness. Something was bothering him about his friend's death.

"What do you mean?" I set down my coffee and waited. He looked out the front window, watching the ocean, his shoulders slumped in defeat. Whatever the problem was, it weighed heavily on him.

Finally, he looked over at me. "At first, he wore a prosthesis because of me. The IED blew a hole right through the Humvee, taking off his leg."

I held his gaze. "You can't tell me a war injury is your fault."

He sat back in his chair, his face resigned with guilt. "It is when I screw up the mission from the get-go."

"Why do I sense that is not all of the story?"

"Because it isn't. Darrell did come home. He went to the VA for physical therapy and outpatient treatment. He had the same things I do, flashbacks, seeing things, bombs, and guns constantly going off inside his head."

I waited, clear that this story would not end well.

"I can't talk about this today." Vern softly laid his head down on the table. "We have to find Katie," he continued, his voice muffled by the table.

"You're right," I replied, trying to make my voice more upbeat.

His smile, when he looked up, was weary, yet held a bit more energy. "I've been thinking that if we can just get Angela, or Nana, or even Da to talk, then someone would tell me where my daughter is. But that's obviously not going to happen."

"A miracle would be nice about now," I replied. "Who else could we have missed that might be a part of this mess?"

"No one. But I'm convinced Da is somehow involved in this. He has avoided almost every question I've asked."

"You've previously mentioned that tan SUV. Have you checked to see if your grandfather owns other vehicles?"

Matheson tapped his index finger on the table. "I never thought about him having other vehicles." He looked at me. "I'm assuming you can check vehicle ownership. That SUV tailed me to the doctor's office and again to the bar. I'm wondering if that is my grandfather, even though I've only seen his pickup."

I nodded, picked up my cell phone, and texted Nikki to search for everything Mr. Moore had registered with the Department of Motor Vehicles.

Matheson waited for me to finish texting before he continued. "His old truck has been missing for days. Only Nana's Olds has been parked in the driveway. The garage is empty."

My phone rang. On speakerphone, Nikki started talking. "Your subject is listed as the owner or co-owner of three vehicles. He is the co-owner of a 1989 Oldsmobile Delta 88, forest green, license plate NTW857. The other co-owner is Althea Moore. Individually, he owns a 2004 Chevrolet Silverado 1500, silver, plate XRP924, and a 2000 Ford Explorer, tan, plate PQM893. Is there anything else I can help with?"

"We're good for now, Nikki, thanks. I'll update you later and call if I need anything else. You and Angus should evacuate."

"No, Lee. We've all talked. If you're not going, then we're not going."

"Who talked? This storm is big, Nikki. You guys have to get out of here."

"Angus and me, Clarice and your grandfather. However, we

overrode your grandfather and insisted that he had to go to North Carolina. He can do whatever by phone or online."

"Well, thanks for that, but I don't need the rest of you guys to stay." I tried to be forceful with my reply without sounding ungrateful.

"Yes, Lee, you do. We all have safe places to ride this out, and we will be nearby if anything goes wrong. What do you want us to do first?"

The responsibility that my entire extended family was not leaving Charleston because of me weighed a ton on my shoulders. "Just try and figure out where someone could have hidden a five-year-old for days," I replied.

Stuffing one of the sandwiches in his mouth, Matheson abruptly stood and pushed his chair under the table. "I have to get going. This town isn't that big, and I bet I can spot him. I'll call you if I see him. Where do you want me to meet you in a few hours?"

"My office," I said. "It's built like a fortress."

59

SHARPE

SUNDAY, 2:00 P.M.

Rain bands begin, wind gusts of 35 mph and higher

Even though she was the last, she was the most important, the catalyst of it all. He'd given up on Weaver, not sure he could kill a police officer. Eyes wide over the duct tape, tremors convulsing her body, he left her that way, wanting her to contemplate thoroughly, for the remaining minutes left in her life, exactly what she had done to deserve this.

It had not been difficult to sneak her out of the hospital. He'd entered through the back door, swiped a set of scrubs and a rolling laundry cart from the basement laundry area, and headed upstairs. He wandered, anxious at first, until he realized no one paid him any mind. Then he found her name on one of the doors and waited down the hall until the nurse exited the room and returned to the central desk in the middle of the floor.

Angela's hands were tied to the bed, but only with cloth restraints, not handcuffs. Using his pocket knife, he cut them off, then lifted her off the bed and carelessly dumped her into the laundry cart. Even with his rough treatment, she never moved, and he assumed she had been given something to knock her out for the evening. If it had been cuffs, he would have been screwed.

The hallway was quiet, even in the middle of the day. He assumed there were fewer staff and visitors because of the hurricane. Typically, Sunday would be the busiest visitation day. Outside, the weather was angry. He looked up, gauging the thickness of the dark storm clouds rolling across the sky. He thought he still had time, but when he stopped to check the NOAA app on his phone, he saw maybe not. The donut-shaped storm was several hundred miles across. It had grown significantly since he last checked and was now hovering off the coast of South Carolina, in the middle of the Jet Stream, where it sucked up all the warm water from the Florida Keys and would gather speed to spin it ashore. He needed to hurry.

A yellow band flashed across the bottom of his screen. *Landfall is imminent within twelve to twenty-four hours. Evacuate immediately.* He looked up again. With the weather already this bad, he doubted he had even twelve hours before the front edge of the storm made his job impossible.

Struggling against the wind, he rolled the laundry cart through the parking deck to his truck. He had parked in the far corner, away from any openings and cameras in the darkest area. He laid her on the truck bed, then sat her upright, leaning her against the side. Taking a new roll of duct tape, he circled her hands, her mouth, and her ankles, then bound her legs in two more places and pinned her arms to her body. He talked over the sound of the wind.

"Thought you had me pegged, didn't you?" He kept his voice low as he ripped off the roll from his final loop around her upper arms. "Thought you could make fun of me, tempt me, say those things."

She mumbled under the duct tape, words he did not care to understand. Her head snapped right and left with her denial. Suddenly, her body shook in an epileptic-type seizure. He smiled at her when it finished, after her eyes refocused. She blinked at him, her body jerking with the shock of recognition, her nostrils flaring at her inability to scream her terror. A flash of lightning caught his attention. He slammed the tailgate and unfolded a tarp, tying the corners to the truck bed to hide the woman from passing vehicles.

He pulled out his phone and checked the freeway. The governor was supposed to order the freeways to be one-way heading out of town, but so far, the app showed nothing. Traffic as normal, light even, with only a few roadblocks and closures for the building rainwater.

Sheets of rain suddenly pounded the parking deck, blowing sideways into the large openings. The wind thrashed the palm trees, bending them one way, then flopping them back. Then the cloud was gone, shoved inland by the heavy wind, and the rain stopped. He started the truck and wasted no time heading for the dead gas station in North Charleston.

60

WEAVER

SUNDAY, 2:00 P.M.

Weaver had avoided several phone calls from Norcross, and his boss's messages were scathing. He had been assigned to desk duty after placing Matheson in the drunk tank, yet Weaver couldn't sit behind a desk while someone was killing his dealers. Putting Matheson on a 72-hour hold was the only way to be certain he wasn't the one dumping bodies at the marsh. Yet neither the Chief nor Norcross would hear of his reasons, especially after the crotchety old Judge got involved, and of course, now Matheson had been released.

He should have pushed his way into the house earlier that morning, taken Matheson into custody again, and shown Norcross who was really in charge. He was positive that Matheson was behind the disappearance of the three men and was the one dumping them into the marsh.

Then there was Harbin. The solicitor was all over him about losing Ellison, Rato, and a trailer full of pills. He'd made it very clear that if Angela Matheson implicated him in any way, he would hang everything possible on Weaver. That woman would have been dead if he'd only arrived fifteen minutes earlier at that scuzzy apartment. Now he had to deal with her here or else.

And the hurricane was not helping one bit.

Striding through the front door of Roper Hospital in north Mount Pleasant, he flashed his badge quickly at the receptionist. "I need to talk with a woman named Angela Matheson. I understand she was transferred here either yesterday or today from Trident."

"Yes, sir, one moment," the fiftyish-year-old woman replied, "and your name is?"

"Monroe. Harold Monroe." Weaver provided the name of his former partner from the Columbia police force. "Just need to ask her a few questions."

The woman scribbled the name on a pad and then looked at the computer monitor in front of her. "She's on the third floor, room 326. The elevator's down that hall." The receptionist pointed past him down one of the hospital wings, rather than asking him to show his identification to sign him in, which was the correct procedure. Maybe she was new. He didn't care. She had just saved him time.

On the third floor, Weaver began searching for room numbers, casually walking past room 326 and around the corner. He cautiously approached Angela's door just as a nurse headed his way. He retraced his steps and hid in a supply room, peeking through the crack between the door and the frame until the nurse left room 328.

The coast clear, he hurried down the hall and slowly opened the door to room 326. He'd downloaded a photo of Angela from social media to go with the photo from Mrs. Moore. He was only familiar with her from the stories told by Sean Carlton and Keith Ellison, but the sleeping woman strapped to the bed was so emaciated that Weaver thought he had the wrong room. He pulled up the photo on his phone and leaned closer.

This was her.

Angela Matheson would not last one more day. Connected to an IV on her wrist and an oxygen cannula for her to breathe, her breaths were raspy and shallow. He reached out and patted the hand that didn't have the IV.

"Mrs. Matheson, wake up. I need to ask you a few questions." The woman didn't move, so he patted her cheek. "Wake up, ma'am." The woman turned her head away from him, and he tried once more. "I'm from the Mount Pleasant Police Department. I need to talk to you about your husband."

The woman slowly opened her eyes, then turned and looked at him. "Who are you?"

"Detective Harold Monroe. I need to ask you a few questions."

"About what?" Her words came out slurred and soft. She closed her eyes.

"Your husband." He patted her hand to make her open her eyes again.

"Vernon isn't here. He's overseas." She turned her head away to go back to sleep. "Been gone a long time."

"No, ma'am." Weaver tried not to get irritated. "He's here in Charleston, and I think you know that. He's the one who brought you to the hospital."

"I don't know what you're talking about. Who are you again?" She squinted at him as if he were a long way away.

"Police." He needed to take a different direction. "Tell me where you got the drugs you took."

"From my doctor. I broke my ankle."

"What doctor is that?"

"Don't remember his name. Can't you leave me alone? Ask one of the nurses."

"Was it Dr. Carlton?"

Angela shook her head, then winced at the movement.

"Did your husband tell you anything about the men he killed? The ones who sold you the drugs. Know a guy by the name of Keith Ellison, maybe? What about a Mexican named Rato who lived in a trailer park?

"What? I'm gonna scream for the nurse if you don't get out of here. I don't know who you're talking about, and my husband's a soldier. If he's killed somebody, they were ISIS or whatever."

"Your husband is here. I've talked with him several times." This woman was making him more than irritated. He needed to be certain she would never be able to identify anyone in Harbin's network. So far, she hadn't, but he had to be sure.

"Vernon isn't home. He's in the Middle East somewhere. Syria, I think. Now leave me alone." She turned her head again, and Weaver finally gave up and let her sleep. It was useless trying to get anything out of her. He leaned back on his heels and studied her. Given her mental and physical condition, he had nothing to worry about here. He searched the room for her purse and phone, but found nothing. He needed that phone.

Leaving the room, he scanned the hallway, seeing a janitor in scrubs with a hospital logo rolling a laundry cart toward Angela's room. As a nurse entered the room, the janitor sauntered down the hall. Weaver turned his head away from the man, then quickly stepped into the supply closet. He waited until he heard the squeak of the cart's wheels coming back. Through the crack between the door and the frame, he watched as the old man went into Angela's room with the cart for only a minute, then came back out again. There was a noticeable bulge in the canvas cart.

Following the janitor to the elevator, Weaver took the stairs, scrambling down the three flights and out the back of the hospital onto the causeway that led to the parking deck. The old man reached his truck on the first floor. Weaver, hidden behind a panel van, watched as Angela Matheson was pulled from the laundry cart as if she weighed nothing and dumped onto the bed of the man's truck. He tied her hands and feet and placed gray duct tape across her mouth. Securing the truck bed with a green tarp, the old man slowly backed out of the parking space and headed for the exit to the garage.

Weaver didn't have to guess where he was headed. Sure enough, the old man took his time going from the hospital up

Highway 17 to the I-526 on-ramp toward North Charleston. The heavy rain bands and short heavy gusts were irritating, but at least most of the traffic was headed in the opposite direction. At the Rhett Avenue exit, Weaver slowly curved down the exit ramp, spotting the truck cross Rhett Avenue and disappear behind the abandoned station. Weaver considered his next move while sitting at the traffic light, relieved that everyone who had anything on him other than Harbin had been taken care of by the old man.

After the storm, SLED would eventually connect him to Rato. He would be on a witness stand, testifying against Harbin, which was a death sentence. It was time for him to evacuate to a non-extradition country. He put on his left blinker to turn left and get back on the freeway. But he couldn't do it. Instead, he turned right. Weaver again parked in the next block and followed the same path to the back of the gas station, only this time, he didn't hide in the bushes.

"What are you doing, old man?" Weaver stood before Sharpe, his service revolver out and pointed directly at the man. He didn't really need to use the gun. How much trouble could an eighty year old man be?

"This is none of your business." Wearing an old rain poncho, the old man was not surprised as he turned. "Either you turn around and leave, or you'll be her company."

Weaver took several steps toward the man while returning his gun to its holster. "I'm placing you under arrest for what you've done to Mrs. Matheson here, and what you did to the others." He walked toward the truck with handcuffs.

As the old man flicked his poncho to one side, and an ancient Colt Peacemaker was suddenly aimed at the detective's chest. The last thing Weaver remembered was the explosive sound of the single-action revolver and the pain as all six bullets entered his chest, one after the other.

61

SHARPE

SUNDAY, 2:45 P.M.

Once Sharpe finished moving Weaver into the back room with the others, he continued his monologue, his voice calm and patient. "Wish you had some of those pretty little pills about now, don't you?"

Angela opened her eyes and gave him a tiny nod, her eyes blinking with hope.

"Well, it's not going to happen. If there is one person on this earth who has no sympathy for you, it's me. You should know that, just from all the slutty things you tried with me behind my wife's back. Did you think I wanted to see your flat chest? And that skinny backside of yours in that floss underwear?" He shook his head slowly, looking like a Baptist preacher unable to fathom his congregation's sins.

He roughly turned her body and pushed her on her back, legs taped in an awkward seated position, arms pressed to her sides. Angela's head angled over the edge of the tailgate, her greasy hair swinging in clumps like strips of fly paper.

Another band of rain headed toward them in the distance. He opened the passenger door of the truck cab and reached for his rain jacket. The weather was catching up with him, but he still wasn't comfortable taking them over to the marsh while it was daylight, especially now that the number had increased. He wasn't a young man any longer. He had to wait until dark, even if it meant finishing this in the middle of a hurricane. Tired, he shuffled to his toolbox behind the truck cab and retrieved a long-handle ax, the one he used to chop the heads of snakes every summer. He raised it over her head so she could see it.

Angela's muffled screams began again in earnest. Tears ran down the side of her face, and alerted by the sudden smell, he saw the liquid drip from his truck where she had lost control of her bladder. He pinched her nostrils together with his free hand.

"Just calm down. I wanted you to experience what real fear feels like. Probably what your daughter's been going through now for months, not knowing if the man you're pokin' is gonna want her next, so little and not even understanding what it's about."

Angela struggled with the loss of oxygen until he released her nose.

"Don't think letting you live right now is how it will be. You'll be in there with those three until later." He pointed to the building where the bodies waited. "It's only a tiny part of what you deserve. After all you put that little girl through, I'm not gonna' give you one second of relief."

Angela tried to flip herself over, struggling to talk through the duct tape. The exertion caused another seizure, and her body shook violently, and this time she lost more than her bladder. Holding his breath at her smell, he pulled her from the truck and placed her on her hips, dragging her into the back room. The combined smells of filth, urine, feces, and death were explosive in the tiny room.

Angela moaned between shouts, tears streaming down her face. Snot bubbled from her nose, and he could no longer bear it. There was nothing she could say to him that he wanted to hear.

He closed the door firmly behind him, hoping a raccoon or something larger would not shove it open. But then again, it wouldn't matter if it did.

62

VERN

SUNDAY, 4:00 P.M.

Rainbands and gusts are increasing from Umberto.

Matheson stood on the front deck of his grandparents' house with a faraway look on his face. He had roamed around Charleston for an hour before realizing he was wasting time and would never randomly spot his grandfather. He returned to the island and spent the last two hours searching everywhere he could think of on this end of Sullivan's Island. He went to every one of his childhood haunts and hiding places. With the island practically empty, he had no trouble looking into garages, sheds, and other outbuildings. As each minute ticked by, and the weather got worse, he got more desperate.

He thought about walking down Middle Street and simply screaming her name, but the wind was already too loud. The gusts were more frequent now followed by groups of low-lying angry clouds and a thick haze out over the ocean. Rain bands were thrashing as they came ashore and then moved north. The clouds spun counter-clockwise, the erratic outer bands visible in the increasing intensity of the waves slamming the beach on the other side of the fort.

Matheson turned to lock up the house and make one final check before heading downtown to Lee's office. His grandmother was still in the hospital, and arrangements were being made for her to live in an assisted living facility off the Connector should she not be able to care for herself. Maybe if he had kept in closer touch with his grandmother, calling her regularly, she would not be in the hospital, and his daughter would be here beside him.

He smelled smoke. Highly sensitive to the smell, it was a trigger for his flashbacks. But this was not a flashback. This was real.

"Something's burning," he said aloud, interrupting the irritating voice reminding him of his failures. A lag in the gusts revealed a delicate tendril of smoke floating around the end of the house from the backyard. It headed toward the ocean before a gust of wind blew it in the opposite direction. Matheson leaped from the deck in one jump and rounded the corner of the house at a dead run.

He heard the faint *whoop-whoop* of a fire engine coming from Middle Street. Rounding the corner, his grandmother's old potting shed hidden behind the bushes was smoking heavily. He raced across the two yards to Middle Street to flag down the fire truck and saw that the next-door neighbor was already there, waving his arms to get their attention.

"Here!" he yelled to the neighbor. "Send them over here! The shed's on fire!"

Matheson ran to the corner of the house, grabbed the water hose, and headed for the shed. There was no reason for the dilapidated structure to be on fire. According to his grandmother, there was nothing inside, except for old pots, dirt, and other items she used in the garden. So why was it on fire? And why was it locked? Its shiny silver padlock taunted him, and he'd had no time to find a key.

"Locked up nice and safe."

The old man's words slapped at him from somewhere inside his head. What had his grandfather done? Smoke billowed out of the cracked window. Matheson heard scratching at the door, like a trapped dog. Or a raccoon.

Sounds of gunfire erupted around him, and to his left, an IED exploded. He felt his body floating in the air as the force of the bomb shoved the entire vehicle upward into the sky. He flipped through the air before he landed with a thud, the breath knocked out of him. Darrell! He could hear his friend screaming...

A child's frightened voice snapped him back. "Help! Please help me! Somebody!" The voice was Katie's. He would know it anywhere.

"Please," the voice called again, "Somebody! It's hot in here. Help me!" The sound of hacking coughs came through the crack in the window.

"Katie, get away from the door."

"Daddy! Help!"

"Katie, move back, I'm going to kick the door in," Matheson yelled. "Move out of the way, baby, so that it won't hit you!" Matheson shifted backward to apply the full force of his body for his lunge. He didn't wait for her to respond, but firmly planted his size fourteen boot just above the door handle. Rewarded with the splinter of the door, the glass shattered as it came off its hinges and hit the floor with a bang. Smoke roiled out of the doorway, and Matheson stepped forward to go inside just as someone behind him forcefully pulled him backwards.

"Let me go, damn it! My daughter is in there!" Matheson struggled to free himself from multiple arms that held him back. Another fireman grabbed him from behind, and the first man locked his gaze on Matheson. Only the man's eyes showed over the mask covering his face.

"Stay here," the fireman demanded. "I'll get her. Move back away from the smoke. You hesitate again in there, and it will kill you." The fireman flipped down his visor and turned toward the shed. Trying to resist the fireman holding him from behind, he fell backwards. Two more hands pulled him by his shoulders away from the shed, his boots dragging through the grass. Matheson struggled, fighting to get to his feet, desperate to get to Katie.

A fireman pleaded with him. "Let him get her. He'll bring her out. Calm down, and we'll let you go. But you can't go in there. It will collapse."

The shed was engulfed in smoke, and flames had popped up through the roof. This had to be a dream. His child could not die the horrible way he had seen so many others die. Matheson could hear himself screaming her name over and over as he finally sagged and dropped to his knees and covered his face with his hands as he sobbed.

A piercing scream shook him to the core. "Daddy!" Matheson was almost too scared to look up, terrified it was a scream of pain. Pain from fire was excruciating. He knew. He had watched that woman die, slowly burning to death as she screamed.

"Daddy!" A filthy child with bright red hair appeared in the fireman's arms outside the shed door. She violently squirmed out of the man's grasp, dropped to the ground, and then ran toward Matheson. He could not believe his eyes.

"Daddy, you rescued me!"

Matheson felt his heart nearly explode as his daughter's small body slammed into him with all her might. She hugged him so tightly that nothing could have pried her off him at that moment.

"Katie, oh my God, Katie." He could never remember feeling so happy.

63

VERN

SUNDAY, 3:30 P.M.

*Hurricane Umberto slowed by wind shear. High Category 3 predicted
at landfall.*

Inside the house and out of the rain, with some prodding from the firemen, Katie sheepishly explained how she had started the fire with an old, dusty matchbook and charcoal left under a long-since-rusted outdoor grill.

"It was hard to make that fire. It wasn't fast like you said." Her face screwed up into a scowl at the fireman. "But I kept trying. You said you only took two minutes to get anywhere on the island, so I knew you would come. I just knew it." She grinned at the perplexed firemen.

Katie kept up her precocious chatter. "I did the stop, drop, and roll, like you guys taught me last year. I was in kindergarten then, but now I'm big. This year, I start first grade."

As Katie chattered, the fire chief pulled Matheson aside. "What was she doing in there? We've all been hunting for her for days."

"Yes, I know," Matheson replied, needing to turn the conversation away from the possibility that one of his grandparents had locked her inside. "Once you guys leave, I'm going to talk with her and get all the details."

"Well, she looks like she's fine," the chief replied, concern etched on his face, "but I still have to interview her."

"I'll be happy for you to do that, but can we wait until after the storm? I need to make sure she's really ok and get her settled away from the storm." Matheson pointed to the boarded-up house. "I have to explain why everything is covered, then what happened to her grandmother…"

The chief patted his shoulder. "Sure. It's not like we all don't have our hands full. I'll check back with you in a day or so. I'll be sure Mount Pleasant PD also knows she's safe and there's no need to search. I'm sure someone from there will also be out here at some point."

Matheson nodded, although he doubted Weaver cared enough to call. Katie gave each of the firemen a hug and a kiss on the cheek after making them promise they would return to her first-grade class at Sullivan's Island Elementary to teach them again, but this time correctly. The fire chief made her promise she would never try to start a fire again, even if she were in trouble, calmly explaining that she might not be lucky next time. Solemnly, Katie promised, crossing her heart to the satisfaction of the Chief. As he watched the chief head back to the station in his vehicle, he looked skyward and thanked whoever was up there for the small town firemen.

Matheson wanted them all to go away so he could hold her and kiss every freckle scattered across her nose. His heart started to explode again, and he tried to hide the tears. He could have lost her. The firemen were gone, the garden shed was a ruined, soppy mess, and its new padlock no longer a mystery. Matheson had refused to let her go, even carrying Katie in his arms for them both to hug the neighbor who called the fire department until the paramedic demanded he hand her over for evaluation.

Matheson paced the dark living room until the paramedic

finally finished with Katie, suggesting she be admitted to the hospital overnight for observation. The medic relented after agreeing that while Katie was dirty and hungry, she was surprisingly unaffected by the smoke. Matheson promised to have her checked out as soon as possible after the storm so that the EMTs would leave. They waved to the paramedics and the rapidly evacuating neighbors and retreated into the house.

Katie's face screwed up with concern as she patted his cheek. "Daddy, I'm a big girl. Don't cry." Matheson touched the tears on his cheeks. Her head rested on his shoulder, and Matheson let loose with sobs as he clutched her.

"I'm so sorry, little one. You should never have been in there."

"But it was okay, Daddy. I slept for a long time. Dada visited every day and brought me lunch and a surprise, then I had another long nap. He said he had to hide me from that terrible lady who came to our house. But then I got bored. Dada gave me lots of water and chocolate bars. I wish I had a hamburger, though. Can we see Miss Cherie at Dunleavy's and eat now? Mama never lets me."

The rage began at his toes and rose steadily through his body, the familiar adrenaline rush as he prepared for battle. But there was no battle. He would find that old man—and God help him when he did. Holding Katie tightly, he was determined never to let his daughter out of his sight ever again.

"Katydid, let's get you cleaned up. Your Nana might worry if she saw you'd just come from a mud bath." Katie let out a giggle. He continued. "I bet there's something you'd like to change into after we get your bath. What do you think? Since there's a storm coming, we need to get packed up. We're going to a safe place. When we get back, we can go to Dunleavy's for that hamburger. Or better yet, I bet we could get Miss Cherie to deliver it here for you. You think?"

With a nod, the tiny girl grasped one large finger of her

father's hand, and they marched toward the guest bedroom. Matheson listened as drawers opened in the bedroom, and in the bathroom, he ran the bathwater with lots of bubbles.

"I can do this. I'm not little anymore." The cherub looked at him scornfully, her hands on her hips.

"Your hair and everything?"

"Of course. You can help me dry it. I'll show you how."

Closing the door, while leaving a crack so he could hear, he leaned against the wall while his daughter splashed in the bathtub. The old house creaked and shuddered with the wind gusts, yet he could hear soft singing as the water splashed in the tub. In a small bag he found in her closet, he packed several days of clothing and a few toys. They were just things. He could always replace things. His Katie was alive. Safe. Matheson collapsed in the hall, put his head between his knees, and sobbed.

He checked his phone. The eye of the storm was still a half day from landfall. Yet he had to get Katie to a safe location. He called the first person he thought of.

"I've found her. She's unharmed and I'm coming to you. Is there somewhere she can sleep?"

"Of course," Lee replied, "There is a full apartment upstairs and we are all here together."

Arriving at Archdale Street, after giving Lee the details, Nikki immediately took Katie's hand and he followed them upstairs. For two hours, Matheson slept the sleep of the dead, his arm wrapped around his daughter as they napped in the bedroom. When he woke, Katie was gone. With warning bells clanging in his head, his feet hit the floor and he skidded halfway down the stairs before her giggles registered. He found her sitting in Lee's conference room with a plate of toast sitting before her, and a blueberry jelly grin spread across her face. Zola DeLeon was sitting across the table.

"Daddy, come eat a snack with me. Miss Zola made my

favorite, see?" She held her hands up, her fingers purple with jelly.

Matheson kissed the top of her head, capturing the smell of baby shampoo in her sun-streaked carrot colored hair. Katie's chatter filled the room. The conference room was in the center of the building and had no windows. Lee's entire team was there, and they were watching the Weather Channel muted on a large television screen on one wall. The storm was massive, and seeing the growing eye heading toward Charleston made him realize that what he was about to do next would be dangerous.

Yet, it was amazing how much better he felt simply with two hours of sleep and Katie beside him. Zola motioned for him to step into the reception area. He grabbed a water from the refrigerator, kissed Katie's head again, and made sure the conference door was closed behind him.

"I wanted to see how you are holding up, particularly since you missed two of our appointments."

"I appreciate your help, but now that I have Katie, I can handle this myself." Matheson couldn't bring himself to look at the doctor.

Zola was incredulous. "Seriously? No, you cannot handle Complex PTSD by yourself. Not at this level. I have been through this same situation too many times. What is it with you veterans? Why do you think that you can escape the stress of war and its effects simply by being a he-man? It is ridiculous!"

"Zola, this really..."

"Yes, it is my concern. I am making it my concern. There are two elders and a child involved who need you. Finding Katie does not solve your problem. Either you get help with me or through the VA, or I will take action myself."

"What action?" Matheson took a step back.

"Involuntary commitment."

Electricity zagged through him like he had hit a downed wire.

"What?" The thought of being separated from Katie again made him breathless.

"You may not be a danger to others, but you are most definitely a danger to yourself. Lee is very concerned for you, particularly after finding Angela, who could not tell you where Katie was, and then having to sit in jail for no reason. Now that Katie is safe, you must focus on yourself."

Matheson abruptly sank into a chair in front of Clarice's desk. Zola was locking him in a cage, one he had been afraid of for a very long time.

"Vernon, look. Your child may have flashbacks of her own," Zola said. "She needs her father to support her. We do not yet know what she experienced. I will slowly and very casually attempt to bring this out of her, and you need to be certain you do the same. We will need to determine whether there is a trigger for them and how to avoid it in the future. But—she might be fortunate. She's a smart, resourceful girl, and that is why she's alive."

Matheson hated to admit it, but Zola was right. It was long past time for him to deal with himself. Now that Katie had been found, he could let Weaver figure out how all these people were missing. Or not. As for Angela, he never wanted to see her again. He needed to begin divorce proceedings and hope that no self-respecting judge would allow Angela near Katie, even though something niggled at him about the law always favoring the mother with small children.

He walked to the single window in the back door of Lee's office they had left temporarily un-boarded. The sky was filling with thicker clouds, and the wind was now a steady thirty miles per hour. The gusts were harsh, slapping at the large oak tree outside, flattening the flowers.

He finally spoke. "I promise you I will get help after the hurricane. You can't have me locked up now. Please."

Zola looked at him over the top of her reading glasses. "I have already contacted Dr. Harrison at MUSC. If you do not report to me the minute the storm is over, I will ensure you have no choice but to do so. He has a bed ready for you."

"Thank you, Zola." Matheson nodded his agreement. "I will call you when this is done. But right now, there's still something I have to do."

64

LEE

SUNDAY, 4:00 P.M.

Hurricane Umberto picks up speed toward Charleston

"Where is your grandfather?" I asked Vern. We were in my office with the lights on, since the wall of window panes had been boarded up for the hurricane, Angus placing the last one a few minutes earlier. I could hear the wind thrashing the oak tree outside, and my nervousness increased several notches. Riding out the hurricane alone was one thing, but the responsibility for my team and for Vern and his daughter was something else.

"Your guess is as good as mine," he responded. "I hunted for him earlier and gave up. I had double-checked the house and was about to lock up and go hunt for him again when I saw the smoke. I'm glad I was there. Had I left the house, the firemen would not have gotten to Katie in time."

"Will you wait to find him after the storm?" I asked him.

"Hell, no. I think I have a few hours before the worst part hits. And you know the backside of the storm will cause all the damage, and that is hours away. If I find him," he hesitated, "I'll let you know."

"Vern," I hesitated, realizing he would do what he wanted regardless of anything I could say. "Don't do anything you'll regret. Katie is safe now. Don't risk your life trying to find him."

"He's been on my ass my entire life." Vern's voice was just at the point of rage. I couldn't say I blamed him. "He locked my daughter in a potting shed, for God's sake. Whatever he gets from me is exactly what he deserves."

I followed him to the conference room where he kissed Katie, assured her he would be back in a few minutes, and left by the back door. I could hear his truck as it drove away, the roar of his screech louder than the wind.

Nikki stuck her head into my office doorway just as I sat. "I need to talk with you about something we just learned."

"What's up?" I asked, as Clarice triple-knocked on the door frame. I waved her into the room as I listened to Nikki.

"I think you need to hear the results of my investigation requested by Mac." Nikki pulled a sheet of paper from a stack of folders on the coffee table.

"That bad, huh?" I tried to joke, but the serious expression on her face had me concerned. I moved to the couch with my laptop, setting it on the coffee table, and Clarice sat next to me. Nikki looked at Clarice with a strange expression, then at me. "Mac and I thought it best that we investigate everyone involved in this matter."

"Ok, so what did you find?" I asked. Since this was my first case with Mac, I had no idea what was standard. She looked at the sheet of paper that looked like a checklist. "I checked them all. Matheson, both grandparents, Angela."

"What did you learn?"

"Mac got me Colonel Matheson's file from the military. A lot of it is redacted, but there is enough to tell me exactly what happened in Afghanistan, what happened later in Syria, and why he was forcefully retired. A copy of that paperwork is in the file for you. It isn't pretty. He was seeing things long before the bomb exploded on his friend. He needs real help, Lee."

I waited for her to continue.

"Mac and I ran a criminal check, credit report, and other background information. His credit is good, surprising given what I learned about Angela, and other than his military issues recently, there's nothing else."

"What about the others?"

"Nothing much on Mrs. Moore," Nikki replied. "She is an active member of the Stella Maris Catholic parish, but has never worked. Nothing else. No credit issues, no social media, and no criminal record. Angela, on the other hand, is a nightmare, which we already know. She obtained three mortgages against the Mount Pleasant townhouse that is jointly owned. I pulled the property records, and it appears she forged the Colonel's name on the mortgages. However, when I checked with the banks, the promissory notes are actually in her name only. All payments are behind and are in various stages of collection. None have shifted to foreclosure at this point, but are teetering close to the edge. You'll have to get involved in that."

"Nikki, if you'll send me that information, I'll get to work on the resolution of those for the Colonel," said Clarice. "Did you find any insurance on the home?"

"Yes," Nikki said, "the first mortgage required a policy, so you should be ok on that score. I didn't look for insurance on the others, as that isn't usually required."

Clarice nodded.

"What about Vern's grandfather?" I asked.

"Mr. Moore was a sharpshooter. He was a career enlisted soldier in the Army, joining in 1961 at the age of 20. He was sent to Vietnam when the U.S. sent in combat forces. He had the most verified kills of all shooters during the years he was on active duty. He was captured in 1969 and sent to the Hôa Lò prison."

I felt a little sick hearing that name. "You're talking about the Hanoi Hilton, where John McCain was tortured."

"Yes. Mr. Moore was also tortured, according to the information in his military file. He went through four years as a prisoner, and according to what I could learn, refused to talk about the entire experience to anyone, even his wife. Returning to the U.S., he ran a furniture store and was a respected member of the community."

"Was he trained just for sharp-shooting?"

"Not just that. The gamut. Hand-to-hand combat, knives, a bit of martial arts."

"So, he could be the one scorching the earth behind our client," said Clarice.

"He could," Nikki said quietly. "Or, honestly, it just as easily could be Colonel Matheson doing all this. You guys prepared his alibi list, but we all know that some of it is a stretch."

"Nikki, what makes you say that?" My stomach was suddenly in knots at how she was dragging this out. What was it that she didn't want to tell me?

"Darrell Jenkins," she started, reading from the page she held, "served in Afghanistan for twelve months as an Armor Reconnaissance Specialist, trained in intelligence procedures, and responsible for obtaining intelligence before any planned mission. He was legally separated from his wife for the duration of his entire last tour."

"He was injured six months ago," Nikki continued, "when an IED exploded on a mission led by Colonel Matheson. Returned from the hospital in Weisbaden, Germany, to Charleston, directly to the VA hospital rather than his home, Jenkins was under both mental and physical inpatient observation by the Veterans Administration for his injuries, then later outpatient care with significant physical therapy after a prosthesis was obtained."

"What mental treatment?" I ask. "Vern told me that Darrell

had the same issues he has. Who did he see at the VA? I need all the help I can get to convince Matheson to get help."

"For some reason that information is still confidential," Nikki replied. "I'll have to see if his wife will release it."

I wasn't sure how Nikki was able to obtain any of the medical information, but convincing a psychiatrist or psychologist to divulge information about a client wasn't possible without a court order, and possibly not even then. But from the look on Nikki's face, that wasn't the issue.

Clarice gripped my hand and shifted in her seat to be closer to me.

"Lee..." Nikki said, the pity in her voice giving me chills. "Once we told him the details, Mac got in a helicopter from Atlanta. He'll get as close as he can, then drive." Whatever it was, it had my investigator seriously concerned. She opened her mouth to speak, then closed it.

"Why? It's too dangerous for him to fly now. What is it, Nikki? Just spit it out."

"Darrell Jenkins committed suicide four months ago. He blew his brains out with his hunting shotgun while on the phone with Colonel Matheson, telling him goodbye. Hysterical, Colonel Matheson tried to take his own life in front of his team in Syria. The details are in his medical file. He was flown immediately from Syria to Weisbaden, Germany, and has been in an inpatient facility there for those four months. He was just released." Nikki looked at me with sympathy. "He holds himself responsible for his friend's death, and the medical reports indicate that, as for himself, he has a death wish."

And I'd just allowed him to leave in a hurricane to find his grandfather—and to do only God knew what to himself. I felt as if I'd been slammed in the stomach with a baseball bat. Even though I hadn't had an anxiety attack in months, my body violently revolted. Ripping my hand from Clarice's, I dashed to the bathroom, barely making it before everything in my stomach heaved upward into the toilet.

65

SHARPE

SUNDAY, 6:30 P.M.

Hurricane Umberto's eye 25 miles off the coast of Charleston, landfall
eminent

Umberto was twenty-five miles off the coast, slowly heading with its counterclockwise spiral over the coast of South Carolina. Wind shear had dropped the intensity from a Category 5 down to a Category 3, but it was steadily building again the closer the eye got to shore. The wind was now a constant fifty miles per hour, bending the palms almost sideways, with gusts of 100 miles per hour, some higher. NOAA was forecasting landfall between Charleston and Georgetown. He felt sure the storm would come ashore at McClellanville since that was where Charleston-bound hurricanes consistently landed, drawn to the long, flat marsh in that area that extended for miles toward the ocean.

Sharpe wondered if the roof on the old, dilapidated gas station would hold. As he stood outside, another band of rain began, the large droplets slapping the side of the concrete structure like a machine gun. The wind pushed him like he was a bobble toy on a dashboard.

The sounds brought back too many memories, ones he had to shove aside tonight. He had forgotten how distinctive the odor could be, how the smell of death invaded one's nostrils so violently. Even standing in the rain, with the wind thrashing the trees behind him, he could smell that horrible smell, the one he'd lived with for years in Vietnam. At least this time, he'd remembered the Vicks VapoRub.

Opening the door to the building, a horde of blowflies flew past him, and the buzzing inside was higher than the sound of cicadas in the summer. He flicked on the flashlight, and carefully stepped inside. The three dead men were blanketed with a layer of black buzzing. He ignored the woman.

Lightning jagged across the sky outside, and a sudden clap of thunder caused him to flinch. He could hear one corner of the tin roof on the building begin to flap in the wind. He needed to get going before the wind completely removed the roof. He could leave them here, he guessed, but that wasn't the point. Even though it would be physically difficult for him, they had to disappear. He wanted the other members of the drug network to live in fear.

He turned the flashlight toward the men propped in the corner and reached for the large burlap bags he had brought with him, then left them on the floor. In this storm nothing he did would keep them covered. He would have to chance being seen.

Glancing over, he saw the whites of Angela's terrified eyes. He ignored her. She deserved every second of this.

Wearing his old long-sleeved fishing shirt and rubber overall waders, he snapped gloves over his hands, one thin kind like the dentist girl's and another thick sort up to the elbow, that his wife wore when doing dishes. With an extra swipe of the VapoRub, he wrapped a paisley handkerchief over his face and got to work.

He shoved down the rise from his gullet. Shooing the flies, he picked up the feet of the dealer, the most decomposed body. Had he not known who it was, it would have been difficult given the level of decomposition in this heat. The man's face had swollen and turned dark, overlaid with a tinge of gray. He raised the body into the truck bed using the lift.

He looked around the corner of the building to see the level of traffic. Who was he kidding? In this weather, no one was looking for anything except shelter. Charleston was a ghost town. Given the approaching storm, he expected none, but it never hurt to be prepared. The people who had not evacuated were already boarded up and hunkered down.

He relaxed and retrieved the second body, pulling it by the feet as well. He relished leaving Angela alone in the dark, even for a few minutes.

The trees suddenly stopped thrashing, and the wind died as a rain band passed. The gap would only last a minute or two at most. He had lived through many hurricanes over the years, and it never ceased to amaze him how the circular bands of rain could create complete and terrifying havoc one minute and then disappear the next, leaving one to wait nervously for the next until the full brunt of the storm arrived.

After Weaver, he retrieved Angela, tossing her in the truck bed next to the others. Her muffled cries could barely be heard over the noise of the wind. Gusts continued to slam him against the truck, so he connected himself to the truck with a long bungee cord around his waist so he could tie the tarp down at the corners.

Leaving the back door of the gas station open, he knew nothing would dispel death's smell. It continued to cloak him, even all these years later.

66

VERN

SUNDAY, 6:30 P.M.

Front bands of Hurricane Umberto thrashing the coast of South Carolina

Matheson shifted the truck's gears as he headed down the steep Rhett Avenue cloverleaf, which dumped him on the road to Goose Creek. He had scouted every place in Mount Pleasant he thought the old man might go, including night spots and his old place of work, but found zip. Involuntarily headed toward Darrell's house, he stopped at the traffic light and hit his blinker, waiting through the long red light before he realized where he was headed.

A beat-up Silverado with a lift plate on the back crossed Rhett Avenue in front of him. *Damn.* He would know his grandfather's truck anywhere. No one was behind him, so he shifted to the right lane, preparing to follow. But there was no need to rush. The truck abruptly turned into the closed gas station on the other side of the road, its taillights disappearing as the vehicle pulled to the rear of the building. Taking a slow right turn, Matheson took his time up Rhett Avenue going in the opposite direction until he reached Park Circle.

He leaned forward and checked the weather. The storm clouds were thicker now, cutting much of the sunlight. Even though the rain was erratic, he knew from how the wind was rocking his truck that the storm was building strength. Some hurricanes came with significant rain, others with wind. With this one, the wind was a consistent fifty miles per hour and the gusts had pushed him sideways several times on the road.

He pulled into a closed business about a block from the gas station where he'd seen his grandfather and turned off his truck. Without thinking, he did what he always did when he was caught in a situation where he didn't know what to do. He called Darrell.

"Hello," a female voice answered.

"May I speak to Darrell?" Matheson's words tumbled out, his mind focused on his grandfather. "I need him quickly, please."

"Who is this?" the woman asked, her voice perturbed.

"Vern Matheson," he responded. "Can I just speak with Darrell?" He didn't have time to play twenty questions with this woman.

"Vern, this is Brenda, Darrell's wife."

He should have recognized her voice. "Brenda, hi. I told Darrell that we needed to get together when I got home."

"You told Darrell what?"

Matheson hesitated. Darrell's wife seemed confused. "I told him that we should go out to dinner one night. Is that a problem?"

"Where are you?"

"I just got to Charleston a few days ago. I'm staying with my grandparents at the moment."

"Vernon, you need to go to the hospital. Right now. There's something wrong with you. Unless you are crazy, you would never call here like this."

"Brenda, what are you talking about? I'm fine. I just need to talk to Darrell. I'm in the middle of something and I need his help." He did not want to give her the details of what his grandfather was doing at the moment.

There was silence on the other end of the phone for at least a minute.

"Brenda?" Matheson broke the silence.

"Vernon, Darrell committed suicide four months ago. You know this because you called me that day from your hospital bed, where you tried to do the same. He called you right before he blew his damn brains out. Yeah, he called you, not me. I'll never forgive you for that." The volume of her voice increased with each word. "If this is a joke, it isn't amusing. And given that you're the cause of his death, I think it's inappropriate that you're even calling in the first place. For God's sake, get some help, and don't ever call here ever again."

Matheson sat dumbfounded in his truck, his phone pressed against his ear, until he finally let his hand drop to his lap.

Darrell was dead.

That horrendous day flooded through his mind. Happiness in hearing from his best friend, then Darrell's confession of the lies, the end of his marriage, and his children no longer calling him dad, but giving that name to another man.

Then the decision to die.

Matheson remembered his begging, crying, pleading for his best friend not to kill himself.

The soft 'goodbye' and the shotgun blast through the phone.

His helplessness.

Even in his distress, he believed it was his responsibility to call Brenda, unable to put that duty on anyone else. Then he lost it. He doesn't remember much of what happened after that in Syria, only being trapped in a hospital bed later in Weisbaden.

But thinking Darrell was still alive now? This was the stuff of crazy town. He was losing his mind.

67

LEE

SUNDAY, 7:30 P.M.

Landfall targeted as McClellanville, South Carolina

"Where are you?" I answered sharply when his name appeared on my buzzing cell phone.

I hadn't heard from Vern for hours and expected him back at the office long before now. The front of the storm was upon us, and it was too late for any of us to evacuate to Orangeburg. I was concerned about his mental state, especially after hearing the information Nikki had uncovered regarding Darrell's death—and Vern's attempt to take his own life.

Then my discussion with Zola further ramped up my concern when she told me he had skipped two appointments, and that she had given him an ultimatum: either he sees her immediately after the storm, or she would have him involuntarily committed. Just the thought of what he must have been through to travel that far down such a desperate, dark tunnel made me shudder. It was time the man had some light at the end.

"Where are you?" I asked.

"I'm near the I-526 freeway at the Rhett Avenue exit." The wind noise coming through the phone was significant. "Coming from Charleston, exit at Rhett, then across the street there's an old gas station."

"What in the hell are you doing there?" I asked.

"Watching my grandfather pile dead bodies in the back of his truck," Matheson replied. "I think one of them might be Angela, but I can't get close enough."

The last time I'd seen her, Angela was in the hospital, chained to the bed. For a second, I couldn't speak. Had he finally mentally come undone? "This is a joke, right?"

"Lee, help me," his voice broke, sounding as if he were almost in tears. "We're running out of time. Could you call the police? I don't know what he'll do once I confront him. I'm pretty sure he has lost his mind. I've never seen something like this." He hesitated. "But I'm more worried about what I'll do to him if I do try to stop him. He locked my daughter in the damn potting shed, and..." His voice faded.

"Vern?" I waited, glancing at the phone's screen to be sure the call was still active, then heard another gust of wind blow from his end of the call.

"I'm close to losing it myself," he replied. "Darrell's dead. I tried to call him like he was still alive. Brenda says I'm crazy."

"I know about Darrell, and I'm really sorry." I didn't dare tell him I knew about his suicide attempt. "I don't think you should be in this storm, much less dealing with your grandfather."

"Help me," he said, his voice strained with emotion. "He can't get away with this...and I need to know."

"Know what?" I asked, caution flags popping up everywhere in my head.

"If it's real, or all in my head." The silence between us, even in the incoming storm, was deafening. I had to make a decision. There was no one else. And it wouldn't matter if there was. This man was important to me, to his daughter, to his grandmother.

"I'm coming. Can you stall your grandfather? The storm is here, and you know the first responders don't go out once it begins. It will just be you and me." And probably Angus, Nikki, and Clarice, as none of them would allow me to go out in this alone. Clarice's husband could never hear of this, or he'd force her to quit, and I'd lose my best friend.

"I'll do what I can to slow him down," Vern's voice was so soft I could barely hear him over the wind noise. "I don't want you to be here, but I need you."

"I'm coming, Vern. I'll try to help you make everything ok. Trust me."

As soon as the call ended, I punched in 911, then hung up. How was I to explain this to the emergency operator, even if they would send someone into a raging storm? Especially when this could be another one of Vern's hallucinations.

Would he hurt me? If all this was a hallucination about his grandfather, and he turned on me, could I defend myself? The thought of carrying my Glock made me want to throw up, but I grabbed it from the credenza and stuffed it in my raincoat pocket. At the back door to the office, I forced myself to stop and take a breath. I knew what PTSD did to a person. I had lived through it. The Timberline Farm case had thrust me into dangerous situations as well, and I'd lived through those.

Vernon Matheson cared for me as much as I cared for him. He was breaking apart because of his belief that he was responsible for the death of his best friend. He would not hurt me. He just needed my help.

I texted Angus and Nikki in the apartment upstairs to ask for their help since Angus drove a four-wheel drive truck, asked Clarice to please stay with Katie, then called Mac. The call went to voicemail, which was for the best. I had no time to have him try to talk me out of this. Providing him with all the details I knew, I asked him to use any influence he had to arrange for some police presence to meet me at the Rhett Avenue interchange once I confirmed what was happening. He would need to call me when he arrived, as I did not know exactly where we were all going.

Even though it was insane for them to be, I was glad my team was still here. Clarice came down the stairs.

"Katie is asleep," she said. "Thank goodness for this old concrete building. I got your text. Where are you going?"

"Vern found his grandfather, but he needs our help. You can track me through Find My, like you do normally. Angus and Nikki will help me, and I was hoping you could coordinate with Mac and the Judge while you stay with Katie. I need to get all the evidence I can against Mr. Moore before it's gone and he can deny it."

"Absolutely, even though I think you are crazy for doing this. But I know you well enough not to try to talk you out of it. Text me when you get to the location. I'll give you a status of what I know then about the possibility of someone coming to help."

Angus and Nikki came through the connecting door from the upstairs apartment. "What's happening?" Angus asked. I provided both of them with as much information as I had and emphasized the importance of capturing as much evidence as possible.

"It will be difficult in this weather, Lee," Nikki said.

I placed my hand on her shoulder. "You're not telling me anything I don't know. But I have to try. If he gets rid of all the bodies and no one can prove it, Matheson may forever be fighting Weaver's allegations that he killed them all." I turned to face them. "If you don't want to do this, then don't. Stay here. Just show me how to handle the camera and I'll do the best I can."

"Get on with yourself," Angus replied. "We'll take my Toyota. Leave your Audi here unless you want to drop it on high ground."

"We don't have time for that. This is all going down now."

He turned to Clarice. "I have an emergency beacon. Let me give you the app info that tracks it."

After Angus and Nikki packed their equipment and headed to the car, I let them discuss how to handle their equipment in this weather while I made a call to my grandfather in North

Carolina. As I turned up the sound to listen over the roar of the wind, I braced myself. He would be anxious to hear from me, then concerned when he learned I was still in Charleston.

"Lee, are you in Orangeburg?" he asked, his voice calm, but concerned. "I expected a text by now."

I almost lied to him, but I couldn't. Vern needed backup, and the Judge was my best source. Besides, I'd never lied to him before. Why start now?

"We're heading to somewhere near Park Circle." I increased the sound.

"The sound is terrible. What in blazes stopped you from leaving town? Have they completely closed the freeway? Take the back roads and get out of there." He was giving me a direct order. "The storm is almost on top of you."

"Judge, I can't. That's why I called. The case involving Matheson has all come to a head, and it's going to happen right in the middle of the storm. There is nothing I can do about it."

"What do you need?" True to form, he asked only how he could help. I sank into the back seat of Angus's SUV in relief.

"I left Mac a message, but we need backup. No law enforcement or anyone else will go out in this storm without a heavy push. You have to be that push for me. I'll confirm the details once I have them."

"I am ready, my dear. If it's keeping you in Charleston in the middle of a hurricane, it must be serious. Give me the general location to tell the police and fire and what is happening."

"Mr. Moore, Matheson's grandfather, is stacking dead bodies in the back of a pickup truck. We've got to catch the man before he gets away with it. He's the one who has to be behind all the fires and the missing people we've talked with."

The Judge didn't comment about how ludicrous this sounded. "You're in Park Circle, you said?"

"At the Rhett Avenue interchange on I-526. Locate me on Find

My on your iPhone. We'll be there in about twenty minutes I think, unless some of the roads are blocked."

"I will text you as I'm making calls and keep you updated. For God's sake, please keep yourself safe. I will also connect with MacCabe. And I will give him an earful about this as well."

"It isn't Mac's fault, Judge. I can't leave Vern like this. He needs help, and I'm the only one close enough to help. Angus and Nikki are with me."

"Please keep me abreast of the details so that I can relay to the officers."

"Will do. And Judge?"

"Yes, *mo ghràd*?

"I love you. Thank you for your help."

"Always, my dear."

Whatever was happening to Vernon Matheson, it needed to come to an end, one way or another. And I had to be there to help him through it. The cavalry was officially coming.

68

VERN

SUNDAY, 8:00 P.M.

Matheson looked through the windshield of his truck and wondered if what he was seeing was a hallucination. The old man was moving very slowly, pulling the second dead body from the back of the gas station after having rested for a long time after the first.

His windshield wipers were off in case his grandfather noticed the movement even from a distance. There was no way to check the license plate from this far away, but he knew it was his grandfather from the lift on the back of the truck. Da had installed it years ago when his back went out while building the garage.

Still, Matheson couldn't make himself get out of the truck and confront his grandfather. After his call to Brenda, there was a significant likelihood that this was one big hallucination. He continued to sit and watch, hoping Lee would arrive before the evidence was destroyed or his grandfather disappeared like a popped balloon, and he had to accept that he had gone completely mad. His phone rang.

"Ok, exactly where are you?" Lee's concerned voice snapped him back to the present. "The freeway is closed. Some of the streets are flooded, so we're going slowly. We've had to maneuver around some downed trees. Angus and Nikki are with me. Clarice is safe in the office with Katie. We have backup coming."

"At the old, dead gas station at the Rhett exit. Da crossed in front of me at the intersection. He turned in right there and parked behind the station as I waited for the light to change." He turned off the overhead light in his truck, donned his baseball hat, and got ready to get out of the truck.

"I can't tell you when we'll get there. Between the wind and the water, we are teasing our way through," Lee said. "What is he up to?"

"Lee," Matheson replied, "this is a mistake. I shouldn't have called you. Send somebody else. Get the police to come."

"It's too late, and there isn't anyone else. We are in the middle of a hurricane, remember? Everyone else has boarded themselves up and evacuated inland."

This was a disaster. He'd asked the one person who shouldn't be forced to help him to confront a killer. And she'd brought others? In a hurricane, no less. On top of that, he was prideful enough that he didn't want her to see him mentally lose it. She would never forgive him, and even if she did, he would never forgive himself.

"Are you still there? Where should we leave the vehicle once we get there, Vern?"

"Park at the hair salon on the south side of the freeway, a block past the gas station toward Park Circle. Like the others on that street, it's an old house that turned into a business. The house next to the gas station is a psychic. Just come in dark and slow. You'll see my truck. I'll meet you."

Minutes ticked slowly by. He watched his grandfather tediously move the second body from the back room of the gas station, the old man having difficulty pulling the weight of an obviously heavy body. Moore reached the back of the truck and sat on the lift gate, catching his breath.

Angus's Toyota Land Cruiser, its headlights off, crept in behind Matheson's truck. He got out of his vehicle, and the wind almost ripped the raincoat off his body. There was no need for stealth. It was practically dark from the heavy clouds, and the storm covered any sound he could make.

Lee stepped out of the car, followed by Angus and Nikki, and met him halfway. He couldn't help himself; he grabbed her and held her tightly as the storm raged around them. He silently checked the neighborhood quickly, then let her go. There were no lights, no movement. Matheson motioned for them to follow, and they moved behind the psychic's business to the hedge dividing the gas station and the hair salon.

Matheson pointed to the gas station and motioned for them all to lean closer so he could talk over the wind. "He should be back outside any minute. Just watch." He made hand motions to Angus and Nikki, instructing them to film what was about to happen.

"What is he doing?" Lee asked, her voice at his ear.

"I have no words for this. None. Watch."

The old Silverado was parked beside the bushes, the truck bed not too far from the building's back door. Moore was busy with something in the truck bed. Matheson realized he was wearing the same fishing clothes he wore every time they went flatboat fishing in the marsh during reds season. The old man lowered the lift at the end of the truck bed and stepped slowly toward the building, disappearing through the back door.

A gust blasted through the trees, and Matheson pulled Lee to him to avoid the slap of hard rain that followed. Even a half-block away, Matheson caught the distinctive overripe smell of death. Nikki pulled the scarf up over her nose as she held one camera to her face and Angus another. A dim light flickered inside the open gas station door. Stanley Moore, hunched over, backed out of the room, dragging something heavy. The wind drowned out the whir of the lift until it clanked to a halt at the bottom. The old man used his feet to slowly roll the bag onto the lift. He made one more trip inside, returning with something that looked like a small body in his arms.

"You saw this, right?" He looked at Lee, then at the two investigators.

"It's not a hallucination, Vern," Lee said. "It's real. Oh my God. And the smell is very real."

The old man walked jerkily around the side of the gas station, as if he were physically exhausted. They watched as he peeked out at Rhett Avenue, looking both ways, apparently checking for passing traffic. Vern watched as Lee took out her phone, adjusted the zoom camera, and began filming his grandfather.

"It won't hurt," she shouted over the wind, "to have one more copy in case theirs doesn't work for some reason. I need to get closer to see who is in the back of the truck."

"No." He grabbed her arm to stop her from moving, just as his grandfather turned and headed back to his truck.

Once more, the lift gate whirred. The old man arranged the bodies in the truck bed, getting blown over several times. Attaching himself to the truck's bed with bungee cords, the old man covered the bed with a tarp, tying the corners tightly. Unhooking himself from the truckbed, the old man got in and started the truck, heading for Rhett Avenue.

"I can't let him get away." Vern started to chase after his grandfather, but Lee grabbed his arm and held him back.

"He won't, Vern, I promise. We need to get all the evidence against him we can."

"Just as soon as he turns right," Lee said, we're going to hoof it behind the station, check that room to make sure no one else is in there."

But the truck did not turn right. It crossed the road, taking a two-lane rutted track that wound under the freeway. "What is he doing with them?" Nikki asked Matheson, fighting to be heard over the wind.

Matheson pointed to the marsh under the bridge. "Either snakes or alligators. Your guess is as good as mine."

Lee's eyes grew wide. "Oh, surely not. He's tossing them in the marsh? What if they're still alive?" She held the hood of her raincoat to keep it over her face.

"They won't be for long," Angus shouted as the rain slapped him in the face.

Matheson jogged toward the back of the station and waved for them to follow. "Film the back room," he shouted, "then we need to get down that marsh road." Lee nodded, but the investigators were already filming as much as possible without entering the room.

"Crime scene. Not going in," Angus yelled over the wind. "Got what we need. Let's go before the bodies are gone."

"I still can't believe no one's reported the smell," Nikki yelled at her. "Do the neighbors think that smell comes from the marsh?"

"You guys go ahead. I'll be right behind you," she shouted at them. "I need to check on the backup." Pulling out her phone, Lee covered it with her body and raincoat, texting Clarice, Mac, and the Judge her location and then, as best she could, that of the truck. Then Lee took off at a sprint, Matheson beside her. Catching up to Angus and Nikki, they waited until the truck turned behind the concrete pilings out of sight, then dashed across the road and followed the rutted track.

Halfway to the truck, the water was halfway up Lee's rainboots. "Vern," she spoke loudly over the wind and rain, holding on to his arm to keep her balance in the wind. "I have no desire to be alligator food. The water is rising."

"We're not," he shouted. "It's just rainwater. I've been here before with Darrell when we went fishing. It's all high ground, no gators." Yet he couldn't hide that the thought of alligators also made him nervous.

69

SHARPE

SUNDAY, 8:00 P.M.

Sharpe started his truck and carefully drove across the road, as visibility was almost zero. He followed the two-lane rutted track until it ended at a small clearing next to the marsh, hidden by the elevated freeway. While the two-lane track was flooded, it was not enough to stop his old truck. Soon, however, there would be a surge, the rolling wave of water that did not stop at the top of the active beach but rolled inland, rising in depth along the way. Depending on the tide and the storm's location, it could come before the storm, but usually after.

He still had time, and landfall was projected to be about forty-five miles north at any time now. The wind from the harbor swept through the pre-dawn marsh, flattening the grass, then instantly wrenching the stems upright and bending them in the opposite direction. Sharpe parked his truck behind the scrub trees. Grabbing his knee-high wading boots from behind the truck seat, he looked out over the small pool in the center of the marsh. The receding daylight gave faint definition around him, but he saw no eyes looking back at him. He hauled the first body through the muck and grass, and a wake formed in his path. There was no need to be quiet. The storm worked in his favor in this aspect, and he kept his stride, even though he was beyond tired, confident in his mission and the minutes he had left. All was on schedule.

Because of the storm, he needed to be sure the three dead bodies were handled quickly, and if the wind suddenly ramped up, they wouldn't be blown beyond the reach of his buddies. He pulled the first body through the march, pushing it hard at the end so it would float into the open pool. On his second trip, he was next to the massive freeway piling, looking to see if the first body was still there, when something large and heavy bumped his leg.

He jerked to a stop, a zap of fear running up his back.

The slowly rising current tugged hard at his boots, almost pulling him over. He held his breath and kept a tight grasp on the body. His exhaustion left him too tired to fight anything that might be lurking just beneath the surface. If it were to come for him, he needed it to come.

And get it over with.

The murky water sloshed right below his knees. Something circled his legs, slithering past, but not large enough to be a gator. He waited to see if there would be another pass, even though there was no time for a territorial disagreement. While he had no desire to tangle with a big snake, he was thankful the bump was too light for a gator.

Sweat trickled down his back. His long-sleeved shirt was plastered against his body, yet he ignored the muggy heat, the thickness created by the hurricane bearing down on him. He had been through much worse conditions in Hanoi after being captured. Here, he had waders that made life more than tolerable, even with the heat and humidity of the swamp. He'd not been so lucky over there. He shrugged off visions of the torture that tried to worm their way into his head. They might stop others, such as his grandson, but the memories would not control him.

The thrashing tips of the marsh grass and the increasing roar of the wind failed to silence the buzz from the flies that followed the burlap sack. He took a step and, with no resistance, continued toward the open pool. The cloying smell of death thrust scenes of combat zones at him again. Yet this time, the horrific odor was a result of his own actions, not a military order. The putrid smell of rotting human flesh was something the piece of filth had richly deserved. He was glad to clear the world of these men, ones that forced others less fortunate to do their unspeakable bidding with no cause save their own pockets.

Heavy rain began, and the wind picked up, the screaming sound causing chills down his back, and this time, both began to hold. Whatever was under the water circled his legs once more, oblivious to the weather. He ignored the rain, even when the wind blew his parka hood backward off his head and the rain thrashed his face.

He shuffled forward, expecting another pass from whatever it was under the water's murky surface that was now forming white caps. The wind increased, its scream growing louder. He could no longer wait. Umberto was here.

He shifted the heavy Mexican on his shoulder and headed into the wind, struggling against the current. Reaching the open pool, with his sinewy muscles straining, he heaved the man with a grunt, and the body slid into the shallow pool. Under the water for only a few seconds, the man's body broke the surface, torso face down, arms and legs extended as they bobbed.

When back on high ground, he turned, listening for the distinctive sounds. Loud splashing and popping noises echoed back across the water, even over the howling of the wind. Gaining no pleasure from the sound of the feeding, he wiped his hands on his thighs and went back to his truck.

Two more to go.

70

VERN

SUNDAY, 8:10 P.M.

Hurricane Umberto makes landfall at Bulls Bay, South Carolina

Matheson could see the old man's shape as he moved through the marsh, then the water's splash. He and Lee carefully shifted behind the bridge's concrete foundation to watch, the only hiding place other than under the marsh water. Even with the screaming wind and rain, being under the wide freeway bridges provided some protection. But only a little.

He had no idea where Angus and Nikki had hidden. He hoped it was close enough for them to record his grandfather and possibly identify the bodies. Lee used her phone to video what they could see, even in the gloom, even though they couldn't hear anything for the wind. The old man moved faster than Matheson thought possible as he scrambled for distance from the feeding alligators.

Matheson motioned for Lee to wait, pantomiming for her to continue recording. He edged around the freeway foundation and along the truck's opposite side. Matheson watched his grandfather continue with his activity, oblivious to his grandson holding on to the back of the Silverado in the hurricane-force wind.

Two bodies were in the back of the truck. Weaver and Angela. He leaned over and realized there was no way Weaver was alive. He counted a half-dozen bullet holes in his chest. Feeling Angela's neck, he felt no pulse. Even through his anger, his heart sank at the thought of his wife dying like this.

When Moore saw Matheson, the old man stopped dead in his tracks.

Matheson hoped others were coming, but he had to proceed as if they weren't. He tried to keep his voice level, but it took everything he had in him not to walk up and strangle his grandfather. Moore shuffled up to him, and Matheson wondered if he would have to fight the old codger. But there was nothing in his grandfather's rubber-gloved hands. He had clearly not expected anyone to interrupt his little alligator party. Even though Matheson was ready, Moore did not reach for a knife from a pocket or a pistol hidden behind his back, but stopped five feet away, his hands on his hips.

Vernon felt for the phone in his pocket and prayed it wasn't soaked with rain.

"What are you doing, old man?" he yelled at his grandfather as both of them held on to the truck, buffeted by the wind.

"I'm a doin' what you should have, young man," Moore yelled in return. "Cleaning up your wife's mess."

"You know they'll try to pin all these murders on me, don't you?" Matheson's shout did not hide his anger.

His grandfather snickered. "Not my problem, now, is it? Besides, your new girl will get that problem solved for you."

Matheson, for the first time in his life, didn't take the bait, but waited, the storm beginning to crash trees around him.

"I ain't standing out here in the rain while you yell at me," Moore yelled at him. "If you want to talk about this, we'll need to get into the truck. We're both running out of time."

Matheson hesitated, then nodded his head. He went to the passenger side of his truck, holding on to the door as the wind tried to wrench it off the truck when he opened it. Without turning his back on his grandfather, he took his phone out of his pocket and quickly tapped the last call in recents while holding down the volume so the ringing could not be heard. Then he tapped the record function in the corner. He prayed his call connected. His voice memo was already on and recording as a backup. He had no idea if they would work simultaneously.

"How many does this make?" Matheson motioned to the back of the truck. A gust of wind hit, causing them to rock inside the cab. The old man had been blunt his entire life, but Matheson thought he might try to lie this time.

"Well, let's see. The very confident doctor, the Mexican with all those boxes, and the skinny man from the bar. Then there was the creep from that God awful apartment where you found your wife. I would have left her there had it been me. I think that about does it. Oh yeah, that detective," His grandfather pointed this thumb to the truck bed. "And her. She's still alive."

Matheson glanced at the back of the truck. Angela was on her side, covered in duct tape, tied in a fetal position, rain thrashing her. He jumped out of the truck's cab, sprinting to the tailgate. He lifted Angela as best he could and began unwinding the duct tape, first from her face, then from her arms and legs. She was nothing but bones with a covering, her skin cold, lifeless, her hair like straw even when wet. When her head flopped to the side, he placed his fingers against her neck to check her pulse. There was not even a slight thread. Pressing his head to her chest, he listened hard, but the wind made it impossible for him to hear.

He shouted toward his pocket, the call, he hoped, still open to Lee. "Get an ambulance. I can't feel a pulse, but the old man says she's still alive."

But he knew he was too late. Even with all the times he had mentally wanted her death in the last few days...this is not how she should have died, tied up with rotting corpses in the back of an old gas station, then dumped in the back of a truck about to be thrown to alligators.

Yet he had no tears left for this woman.

So now what? Let his grandfather finish the job? Or let it play out however it would? He had more questions than answers, but those didn't matter. He laid the dead body of his wife flat on the truck bed. He looked toward the sky, letting the wind scream around him, and the pounding rain hit him in the face. He had seen repeated death, and he was sick of it.

Matheson climbed back inside the truck, where his grandfather waited. The heat from his anger had reached his diaphragm, making it difficult for him to breathe. "Anything else you took care of for me that I should know about?"

"Well, there's the blond bitch that started all this, trying to buy your child. You know your wife sold your damn child, don't you? You should thank me for saving her."

"You took Katie." The old man nodded slightly. Matheson's heart felt like it would explode at this admission of guilt. "You locked her in a damn potting shed, Da!" Matheson leaned forward, yelling in his grandfather's face. "You left her there with nothing to eat, and matches, for God's sake. She was almost burned to death. Did you care?"

"I had no place else to take her. Your grandmother hasn't been in her right mind for months, son."

"Don't call me son. I'm no relation to you." Lightning flashed, and right behind it, a loud crash of something tossed about by the wind that had crashed above them onto the freeway. A large oak slammed into the marsh, the top of the tree brushing the front edge of the truck.

"Oh yeah," the old man laughed, "and I also took care of the house for you. It was a nice place, honestly. Hope you at least had insurance on it. And the car."

"Why?"

"What, why? Why did I burn the house? Because I didn't want the evidence to be found. That's pretty obvious. My prints were all over your bedroom upstairs, including the lamp. And since I was in Vietnam, my prints are still stored in a system somewhere. Couldn't have that happen. Your grandmother just wouldn't be able to live through that gossip."

"That isn't what I'm referring to."

"Why did I do all this?" Moore grinned as if he were having the best time of his life. "Because of you, you bastard."

Matheson shifted in the truck's bench seat to cold cock his grandfather, then stopped himself. "What did any of this have to do with me?"

The spit from Moore's guffaw hit Matheson in the face.

"Do you think I wanted another brat moving in with us? I'd just gotten rid of that freeloading father of yours a few years earlier. If it hadn't been for your grandmother, boy, you would have grown up in an orphanage—where you should have." Moore's eyes took on a demented look as he continued to laugh, his face mocking Matheson in the slowly deepening gloom.

"You're repeating history, son." The man was shouting over the storm now, the windshield wipers useless as the rain whipped sideways into the truck. "Your father knocked up your mother with you, and you knocked up that bitch back there."

Matheson knew his parents' truth was worse than the repeating nightmare he now knew had to be a memory. He would not correct the angry words of a bitter old man. A lot of boxes were being ticked off: why he had been hated by his grandfather all of his life, why his grandmother had protected him so fiercely growing up, and why Moore had insisted he marry Angela. Yet he could think about all this after the hurricane.

"You forced me to marry Angela just to make me as miserable as you."

"Worked too, didn't it?" The old man snorted with another laugh.

"Not exactly. I have Katie. And she's worth everything you put me through."

Matheson could no longer tolerate being near the old man. He got out of the truck and slammed the door. A gust of wind bent the marsh grass completely flat, shoving at Matheson as he attempted to remain upright. Moore stepped outside, the wind and rain fiercely thrashing them as Moore pointed to the back of the truck.

"She's waiting for you," he yelled at Matheson. "Go ahead and take her with you. I didn't kill her. She was still alive an hour ago. I'll take care of that cop."

"She's dead." He looked over at Lee, now standing with Mac as they both held on to the truck, the storm shoving them back and forth like wind socks, as they waited for him to finish. Mac tilted his head toward approaching cars coming down the rutted track.

"She's yours, old man," Matheson shouted back at his grandfather as he pointed to the back of the truck. "You started it. I guess you'll have to finish it."

Lee tugged on his arm. They struggled to walk, leaning into the wind as they reached the first vehicle coming toward them. Matheson nodded to the cell phone in her hand. "Did you get all of that?" he asked.

"Yes," she said. "We'll let these guys take it from here."

Matheson stopped and turned, then watched, shocked, as his grandfather shuffled to the back of the pickup, barely able to stay upright in the wind. The old man gathered Angela's body and carried her to the swamp, the red and blue police lights strobing across the massive concrete supports. The triplet of cars pulled under the freeway, blocking his grandfather's truck. Before they could stop him, Moore tossed Angela's body in the water and turned. After the officers shouted commands, he raised his hands and dropped to his knees.

Matheson did not care to watch any further. Mac pulled him

forward, and they met Angus and Nikki coming from the high ground. Heads down, the party trudged through the shrieking wind and driving rain, heading toward their cars as they dodged debris being flung at them by an angry Umberto. Even though he had not heard or seen it, Matheson knew he would never forget the possibility of what the slap, roll, and crunch of the alligator sounded like, feeding on his wife.

71

———

LEE

ONE WEEK AFTER THE HURRICANE

D r. Zola DeLeon had saved Vern's life. Collapsing after finding his grandfather in the middle of the hurricane, Mac and I had rushed him to the hospital, where Zola had intervened with the hospital staff, explaining his condition, and making sure there were no physical issues other than the remainder of his mild concussion from blacking out, and exhaustion. He then had daily visits from the hospital psychiatrist, Dr. Harrison, and was placed on the correct medication. Zola also worked with him directly, helping him reach a point where he could function and begin the long-term plan to address the rest.

Because he was in the hospital, I handled the issues with the Moores and continued to manage the matters related to his townhouse and the economic disaster left by Angela. And at both doctors' request, Katie stayed with me. At first, I wasn't sure how I felt about her living with us, but Katie made it easy for me. She had been dropped off with so many different caregivers that, even though it hurt to think about it, we were just one more.

I was not allowed to see Vern for more than thirty minutes a week, and I visited when I dropped Katie off each week for her half-day visit. Both doctors believed that at this stage of his treatment, he needed to avoid triggers and trauma, fearing that he would have difficulty managing his emotions with me. He had a substantial negative perception of himself, and the doctors didn't want me to be a crutch, leaning on me to make himself feel better. He had to learn to be emotionally self-sufficient.

The doctors insisted that all couples—even though I insisted that we were not a "couple"—go through difficulties in relationships. If we fought, the trauma, trigger, and negative self-perception cycle would start all over again. Vern, of course, thought all this hogwash. Regardless of what either of us thought, he needed to heal. It could take months, according to the doctors, or even years.

Zola also took care of the most challenging part—telling Katie the truth about everything. I don't know what was said, and it took several sessions, but Katie seemed to understand everything that had happened, accepting that her father would stay in the hospital for more than a few days.

My emotions, at least from Dr. Harrison's point of view, were irrelevant.

I went my own rounds with Zola, still conflicted about how I felt about Vern. Yes, we were physically attracted to each other, but what was beyond that? I had isolated myself emotionally for over fifteen years. I needed to be certain before committing to a relationship that I could trust the person. Given Vern's precarious mental health, it would take a substantial period of time before I could be assured of that trust.

Jack left me all those years ago. After reading Vern's entire medical file with his approval, I had to consider the real possibility that Vern would leave me as well by killing himself. I knew it was selfish, but I had to protect myself.

Even though deep inside, it broke my heart.

. . .

"FLYING INTO A HURRICANE with a helicopter is a bit ridiculous, don't you think?" I asked Mac as we were sitting around the table after the debrief, which Mac requires after every assignment. We all agreed that, although we completed the job, there were several areas where we could have improved.

"You're calling me foolish," Mac responded, "standing in the middle of the storm with a killer? But you kept Vern out of trouble and got him the help he needed. I will never be able to repay you for what you did."

"I'm just glad it's over," I said. "Particularly given the surprise phone call I received this morning."

"From?" My grandfather asked over the speakerphone. He was still in his mountain cabin above Asheville, North Carolina, waiting for the all-clear from Charleston County before he returned home.

"Victoria Marshall has been captured on the island of Jamaica," I replied. "They will be holding her there for a few weeks, then she will be extradited to the county jail in North Charleston."

"That means her trial will be sometime later this year." The judge said. "Lee, you and I will need to discuss strategy when I return, and the rest of you will also need to be prepared. That woman may try anything, and we should be ready."

"Mac," I said, "I think it's safe to say that I should not be assigned any new cases until the Victoria Marshall matter is finished."

"I agree with that," he said. "Particularly since you're continuing to help."

"Doing what?" Clarice asked. She looked across the table at me, her forehead creased with concern.

"Zola and Dr. Harrison called me into their office yesterday afternoon," I said. "They let me know that Vern will not be released anytime soon. They are both still very concerned about his mental health and equally worried that Katie has a safe place to stay with people who care about her, so that he will be comfortable remaining in the hospital. I've enjoyed having Katie with me this week, and after talking with the Judge, we agree that Katie living with us will be the best thing for all of us."

Everyone sat in silence around the conference table, unsure of what to say. "Well, don't everyone talk at once," I said, curious as to their issue with this temporary solution.

"She's precious," said Nikki and winked at Angus. "Too bad our kids won't have red hair."

Angus put a clownish grimace on his face. "Hey, no talk of children yet." He looked to Mac for help, but the man shook his head.

"Personal matter, man."

"This is a big responsibility, Lee. And you've never had kids. Are you sure you're up for it?" Clarice asked.

"She is," the Judge replied over the phone. "We discussed this thoroughly last night. We're talking a few weeks to a few months. Lee never got a break after the Timberline Farm case, and she certainly needs one now to prepare for whatever Victoria will throw at us. So the timing is right, and I am available as well."

There was a soft knock at the door. "Come in," I said.

The door cracked, and Katie's freckled face appeared. "Can I come in? My movie ended, and my tummy's growling."

"Of course. Come sit with me." I grinned at her, and she hopped into the room and climbed onto my lap. "Miss Cherie is due any minute with your hamburger."

In the end, Mr. Stanley "Sharpe" Moore took care of his own loose end. Taken into custody early Sunday evening, he was resolute in jail, refusing to talk to anyone, even me, his lawyer for the moment, while waiting for his bail hearing and arraignment, which were tentatively scheduled for the first practical day after the hurricane had passed. Given the heinousness of his crimes, I doubted that bail would be granted, and my representation of Mr. Moore was limited to my appearing at the one combined hearing, allowing Vern and his grandmother sufficient time to hire proper counsel for the trial.

Regardless of bail, Vern was adamant that Katie never see the old man again.

The judge's blended ruling was unusual. I could tell from the mumbling in the courtroom of the other attorneys waiting for hearings that they were surprised. With no objection from the solicitor, the judge granted bail of one million dollars, but only required ten percent of that amount to be paid into the court. Moore had to report to the Medical University of South Carolina's Chester Correctional Hospital voluntarily within twenty-four hours. The judge granted him one day of freedom to settle his affairs and say his goodbyes, requiring Moore to appear at Chester on Tuesday morning. The judge went out of his way to ensure that Moore understood he would never be released from the correctional hospital.

Nana had prepared for the high bail, a shock to Matheson. I was used to clients coming through in a pinch, so I was not surprised. She had been saving meticulously for her last-ditch effort at reconciliation with her husband, a fiftieth-anniversary world cruise, used instead for bail.

Mrs. Moore found her husband on Tuesday morning, downstairs in the guest bedroom. She had not heard him leave their bedroom in the middle of the night, but was not surprised to find herself alone, she told me later. They had not been sleeping together much. Her husband could not tolerate anyone, and most definitely not her.

Tucked in properly in one of the twin guest beds, she shook him by the shoulder before she saw the empty bottles of pills on the bedside table. She sat on the bed next to his cold body, her husband having left her just like he did everything else—on his terms, without regard for others.

Once the death certificate was ready, I was able to have the bail percentage released by the court. After finding a realtor and listing the house, Mrs. Moore decided to take a trip before settling into her new assisted living home in the community of Franke at Seaside. Then, with a caregiver found for her by Kris Adia, she set out on her world cruise.

72

EPILOGUE

SIX MONTHS AFTER THE HURRICANE

Hurricane Umberto had officially come ashore at Bulls Bay, South Carolina, as a high Category 3 hurricane, fifteen miles from Vern's farmhouse. The first time he'd been allowed to leave the hospital, two weeks after the storm, he had expected there to be nothing left. The Francis Marion National Forest was a twisted mess. Trees were down everywhere, many blocking the road. The surge had reached a half mile inland, but because it hit at low tide, the damage was less than expected. Having to enter the farm on foot, he felt the minor damage to his house could wait until he was better and the roads were cleared.

Two months later, he was steady enough to return to work for a few hours. Local crews, he had learned from the owner of the Seewee Outpost, knowing he was in the hospital, had cleared his driveway with chainsaws. Vern was thankful he had purchased a four-wheel-drive truck, as the driveway was full of potholes and washed-out areas. The house looked the same as it always did on the outside. Inside, he found the roof had leaked in several places, but the structure was sound. With his doctor's approval, he was placed on outpatient visits, and he immediately went to work, ripping off the roof and replacing it down to the rafters. The physical exertion did him good, as did being outside in the middle of the forest, despite the damage from the storm.

Still, he saw Katie only once a week for a few hours. And Lee only for a few minutes. Yet it took months living on his own at the farm before the doctors felt he was able to take care of Katie on his own and deal with his possible relationship.

TODAY WAS THE DAY. Katie was coming home. They stopped at the Outpost to pick up groceries and anything else Katie might need, even though he'd fully stocked the house the day before from the big grocery store in Mount Pleasant. It was the first day in almost six months that he and Lee had been in each other's presence for more than just a few minutes. Glancing out the store window, he looked at Lee sitting in the passenger seat of his truck. She had agreed to come to the house to help settle Katie, but beyond that, she insisted on keeping her distance until his doctor gave the all-clear.

If it took the rest of his life to get her to love him, so be it. He wasn't going anywhere.

He saw the newspaper in the rack, with giant letters spread across the upper fold of the first page. A photo of Weaver was underneath the headline, accompanied by the headlines confirming his involvement with both drugs and trafficking. Matheson grabbed a copy and threw it on the counter, telling the clerk he would add it to the total when he finished shopping. Using a basket, he started down the far-right aisle in the small country store.

"Daddy, what are we doing?" Katie followed him every step of the way, attached to him like a magnet. Her incessant commentary on absolutely everything gave him a headache. But it was a welcome reminder that this was his living, breathing daughter.

"We're going to our new house, pumpkin, and this is where

we stop for quick gas and anything you might want to eat. This is our neighborhood store. Hurry now. We don't want to leave Ms. Lee by herself too long."

Katie followed behind him down each aisle, fluttering like a fairy, looking at things here and there, but never touching; her hands were always clasped behind her back. Matheson could see the strict manners of his grandmother in his child, and a wistfulness washed through him for a moment. His grandmother had done her best to give them both a good life. He was glad she was sailing around the world and finally enjoying her life, but was also thankful that someone Kris approved of was with her.

"We have a new house?" The lilt of happiness in her voice cleared his concern.

"Yep. It's a new house for you, an old farm out in the country. Right now, it doesn't look like much on the outside, but you can help me make it look better. I've done most of the inside."

She suddenly went quiet. "Are you glad Mama's not coming with us?" she asked, a hint of fear edging through the soft question.

Matheson stopped and turned, dropping to his knees. He kept his voice a whisper. "I don't know how I feel about your Mama, yet," he said, pulling the child to him in a hug. "Like Dr. Zola said, I think you and I will have to figure that out as we go."

Katie was abnormally silent then, pulling back from him while studying the scarred woodgrain in the heart pine floor. Matheson used his index finger to lift her head, his gaze gentle as he waited for her matching green eyes to meet his. "Katie?"

She met his gaze as he watched her resolve and square her shoulders. He was enthralled, seeing himself duplicated in her.

"She was mean. Sometimes very mean."

When her eyes shifted to one side, Matheson knew there were things he did not want to hear, but needed to know. Katie opened her mouth, then snapped it shut. He kept his voice soft. "Katie, you won't get in trouble with me for anything you ask, or anything you tell me. I keep secrets better than anyone I know. I won't get mad, I promise."

He made the cross-your-heart sign over his chest just like he had seen her do with the Fire Chief. She nodded her head but said nothing. She probably thought he was a big liar since she had lived without him most of her life. Matheson waited patiently, but there was no more discussion of Angela. He stood and grabbed his basket, making sure she followed as he turned the corner.

The lilt returned along with silliness. "Is Ms. Lee your girl-friend?" Katie's wide eyes were washed with sassy innocence, her red curls bouncing as she fidgeted. "I asked her, but she won't tell me."

"We're friends. She's helping me with a problem right now. That's what lawyers do. They help people." He knew that wasn't exactly true, but he had no way to explain all the complications to a five-year-old.

"Is she *my* friend?" She twisted the toe of her tennis shoe over one of the cracks in the wooden floor, a repetition he now knew that signaled she was serious.

He couldn't help but smile. "Absolutely. She's kept you safe while I've been in the hospital. She's probably one of the best friends you and I will ever have."

From Guerin's Bridge Road off north Highway 17, they took the unmarked driveway, a slow crawl necessary due to the washed-out ruts. Katie sat between the adults in the big blue truck, buckled in tightly. The child had protested until Lee assured her it was safe, but she still fussed constantly, complaining that she was too short to see anything and wanted her booster seat.

One more thing that Matheson needed to add to his ever-growing "Katie list."

"This is pretty," Lee said softly, "even with all the destruction. I can't remember the property lines. This part yours?" Her hand waved in a half circle toward the woods surrounding them, heavy with thick underbrush and fallen branches. In a drought, it would pose a fire hazard, but as wet as the past few years had been, much of the forest was now wetlands. He would clean up the forest around him as much as the government would allow. He had plenty of time now that he was retired.

Retired. If Mac had anything to do with it, his "retirement" wouldn't last long. Thanks to Zola, all the hoops had been jumped, and the medical paperwork had been filed with the Army. Because he had over 20 years of service, he received both VA and DOD payments, as well as TRICARE insurance. He could support himself and Katie on his retirement income, yet Mac wanted Vern to work with him, never letting up each time they talked. The big problem? Lee didn't know.

"Yes. That's the border with the Francis Marion National Forest. You know I wanted as remote a place as possible, and I got it." Lee nodded her head and continued to look out the window. He was nervous. "Don't freak when you see the house. I intentionally left it a little rough to stop people from breaking in when I wasn't here, and then, you know, the hurricane. Plus, the locals know about it, and because I allow them to hunt freely on my land, everything has always been left alone."

When he pulled up to the house, Katie unbuckled and scrambled over Lee, opening the door and hitting the ground running. Matheson instantly realized he would have a difficult time protecting her from the cuts and scrapes, as well as the local wildlife. He needed a plan for more than just the hurricane evacuations.

"Katie, whoa, stop!" he yelled as her bouncing red curls started to dash around the side of the house. "You can't run off. Until I clean up the place, you have to stick close to me." Matheson's voice brooked no argument, and a disappointed Katie stopped in her tracks and huffed while she waited for them to unload the truck. Feigning boredom, she walked over and sat cross-legged on the porch. The last load off the truck bed and onto the porch, Matheson took Lee's hand and pulled her into the farmhouse and around the corner out of Katie's sight.

"Vernon, seriously," Lee said, backing away from him as he leaned in for a kiss. When she flattened her palms against his chest to push him away, he felt the familiar energy pass between them.

"How long, Lee?" Vern knew he was pushing it, but he had to try. "Or am I wasting my time?"

"I don't know," she replied. "When the doctors say it's time. And when I say it's time. Let Katie get settled and yourself back to whatever normal will be for you."

He would let it go for now. "Thank you for taking care of my daughter." He reached out again, this time to softly caress her cheek. "I could not have survived in the hospital had you not kept her safe."

"It was a good experience for both of us, I think," Lee replied, leaning into his hand. "Katie taught me a lot."

Maybe he wouldn't have to wait too long after all.

A cough from Katie interrupted them. "You said she wasn't your girlfriend," she said, as she scowled at her father. "You won't let me play because you guys just wanted to kiss."

"We weren't kissing, Katie," Lee told her. "We just needed to have a grown-up talk, that's all."

Matheson followed his child to the front porch. He stopped before his daughter, a look of indignation on her face. "Katie, look at me." Katie looked up, and Matheson locked his gaze on hers. "That is not why I asked you to stay where I could see you. This is our new home, but it's old, and the yard and the forest are a mess because of the storm. The animals are still frightened because they lost their homes. You have to stay where we can see you at all times. One day, it will be a great place for you and your friends, but right now, it isn't. I need you to promise me you'll stay within my sight when we're here."

He could see her little mind whirling with possibilities of friends over for play dates. Red curls bobbing, she silently nodded her understanding, the left side of her mouth curling downward in disappointment—and something else he could not understand.

Matheson wondered exactly what his wife, or one of her 'friends,' had done to his child. Zola's reminder not to push slapped at his need to know. He would have to be strictly honest with his child from now on, and never hedge. Angela had lied to her too many times. He could not do the same, no matter how insignificant he thought it might be.

So how did he deal with this? She was only five. He did what he always did when faced with an upcoming battle and problems with his team. Lead. His daughter would follow his lead, just as his team did overseas.

"Pinkie swear, soldier."

Matheson stood ramrod straight and thrust his hand toward her, his smallest finger extended. Katie's eyes widened at her massive soldier-father standing at attention in front of her, muscles taut under the straining t-shirt, hand outstretched, waiting for her to respond. He cut his eyes toward Lee, standing in the doorway, and felt himself relax slightly at her wink.

Katie solemnly curled her small finger around his much bigger one, her voice soft, but precise. "Pinkie swear, I promise."

ACKNOWLEDGMENTS

While the location of this story is real, many of the details have been fictionalized, and real places have been modified for the narrative. Any errors are solely mine.

While writing may be a solitary endeavor, certain people always make the story better. This book would never have materialized without the Writers' Police Academy and its instructor, who discussed fire and answered all my questions. I appreciate your help.

Thank you to my editor, Barbara Burgess-Van Aken. Without her prompt assistance, this book would have fallen short. Thank you to Emily, the Magnificent Marketer, who, with her help and imagination, has brought the characters to life for you to see beyond my words. Thank you to Nick Castle, my cover designer, who understood even what I could not describe in words.

Thank you to my family, and especially my patient husband, who left me holed up in the office so I could finish this book.

ABOUT THE AUTHOR

R. S. Hampton is an attorney turned novelist, weaving suspenseful stories that unfold across various landscapes—bustling cities, quiet coastal towns, and places tucked just out of sight. With a legal career spanning three decades, her characters are often lawyers, their clients, and the people entangled in their search for truth—where morality is rarely black and white, and justice doesn't always follow the rules.

A lifelong traveler, she is drawn to places that spark curiosity, places with history, edge, and unexpected depth. Her stories are shaped by the settings in which they unfold, each becoming a character in its own right. Whether it's a courtroom in a city she once called home or a hidden alleyway in a country she's only just begun to understand, her novels reflect the intricacies of the worlds she explores.

She and her husband split their time between multiple countries, embracing a multicultural life that mirrors the layered complexities of her fiction. When she's not writing, she's usually on the move—seeking out the next place, the next story, and the next unanswered question.

For more books, updates, and contact information:
www.RSHamptonBooks.com

Help Indie Authors Succeed
Thank you for picking up this book! Whether you bought it, borrowed it, or stumbled upon it, I truly appreciate your time and

interest. As an independent author, sharing stories with readers like you is a dream come true—and you're already helping just by reading.

If you enjoyed this story, **here are a few simple ways you can make a difference:**

1. Share your thoughts

Whether it's a quick review online or a conversation with a friend, your words help other readers discover this book.

2. Tell your community

Mention the book to fellow readers, share it on social media, or recommend it to your local library or bookstore.

3. Show your support

Pre-ordering upcoming books or attending events when possible can help small authors reach new audiences.

4. Stay connected

Follow me on social media or subscribe to my newsletter for updates and behind-the-scenes glimpses into my writing journey.

Every little action makes a difference, and I couldn't do this without you. Thank you for being part of this adventure!

With Gratitude,

R. S. Hampton